CW00567329

Country Secrets

Fiona Walker

Country Secrets

HEAD of ZEUS

An Aria Book

First published in the UK in 2023 by Head of Zeus,
part of Bloomsbury Publishing Plc

9 7 5 3 1 2 4 6 8

A catalogue record for this book is available from the British Library.

ISBN (HB): 9781784977313
ISBN (E): 9781784977306

Cover design: HoZ / Nina Elstad

Typeset by Siliconchips Services Ltd UK

Printed and bound in Great Britain by
CPI Group (UK) Ltd, Croydon CR0 4YY

Head of Zeus
First Floor East
5–8 Hardwick Street
London EC1R 4RG

WWW.HEADOFZEUS.COM

For my dear Avalen inspirations,
Ruth and Christian, with love and thanks.
Here's to friendship, horse chestnuts,
apple orchards and limitless
happy endings.

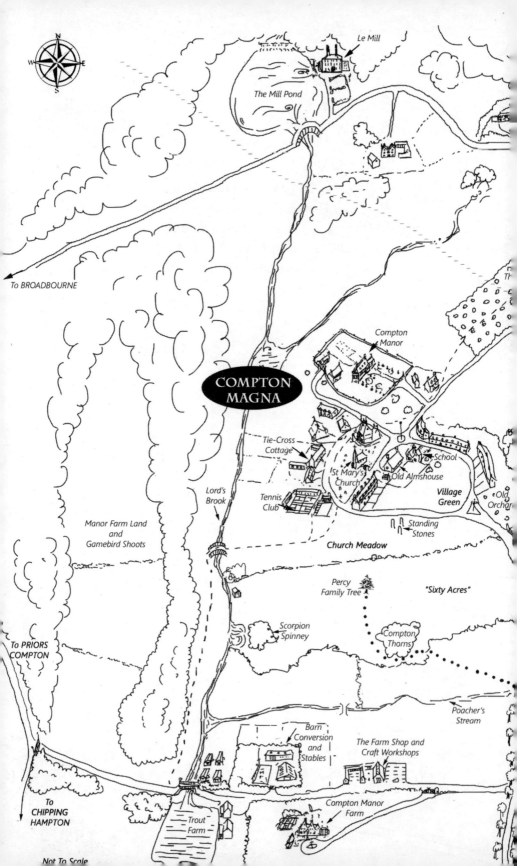

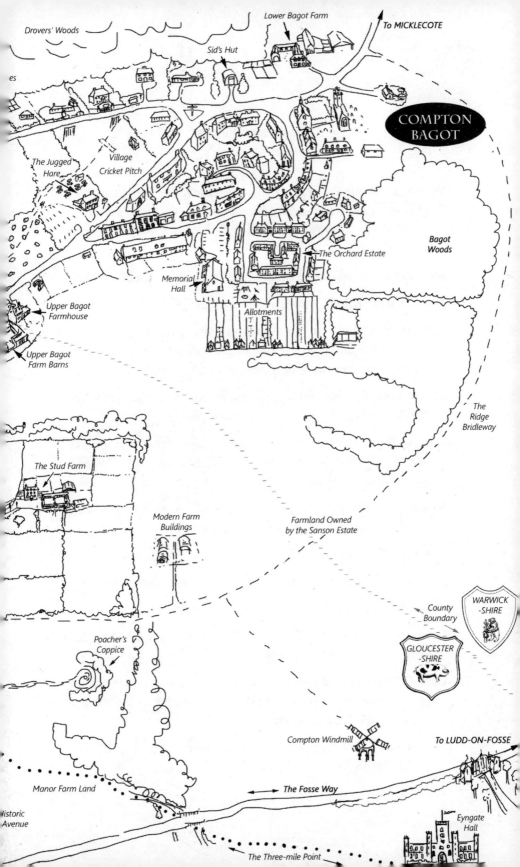

Veronica 'Ronnie Percy' Ledwell: chatelaine of Compton Magna Stud, a fast-riding blonde whose ill-fated marriage to handsome **Johnny Ledwell** ended with a swift exit in a lover's sports car.

Alice Petty: her estranged daughter, a bossy Pony Club stalwart.

Tim Ledwell: Ronnie's son, a debonair in South Africa.

Patricia 'Pax' Forsyth: their younger sister, the family peace-maker who has just left her battlefield of a marriage and returned to the stud where she grew up.

Mack Forsyth: her estranged husband, a tough property developer determined to come out tops.

Patricia 'Pax' Forsyth: their younger sister, the family peace-maker who has just left her battlefield of a marriage and returned to the stud where she grew up.

Mack Forsyth: her estranged husband, a tough property developer determined to come out tops.

Kes: their five-year-old son.

Muir and Mairi: Mack's parents, granite-faced Scottish puritans.

Lizzie: Pax's friend from junior eventing days.

Lester: the stud's tight-lipped stallion man, dedicated to his horses, his routine, and a quiet life.

Luca O'Brien: a globe-trotting rider and Irish charmer with a heart-breaking reputation, known throughout the equestrian world as the Horsemaker.

Blair Robertson: craggy Australian three-day-event rider known as 'Mr Sit Tight'.

Verity Verney: his wife, a reclusive Wiltshire landowner.

Carly Turner: animal-loving young mum, adjusting to village life and job juggling.

Ash Turner: her ex-soldier husband whose family rule the Orchard Estate.

Ellis, Sienna and baby Jackson: their three children.

Janine Turner: Ash's older sister, queen of cleaning and nail art empires.

'Social' Norm: the emphysemic Turner family patriarch, a settled Romany.

Nat Turner: Norm's oldest son, absent father to **Ash** and **Janine**, a legendary fighter and traveller still living on the road.

Nana Turner: Nat's long-abandoned, kind-hearted wife, devoted to children, Beswick horses and daytime TV.

Flynn the farrier: the Bon Jovi of the anvil.

Auriol Bullock: battle-axe headmistress of Compton Magna Primary School.

Helen Beadle: divorce lawyer and sharp-minded chairman of the school's PTA.

Bridget Mazur: Belfast-born member of the village's Saddle Bags, a hipster young mum married to volatile Polish builder, **Aleš**.

Petra Gunn: historical novelist and neglected wife, founder of the Saddle Bags whose gossipy hacks keep her sane while philandering husband **Charlie** drives her mad.

Gill Walcote: straight-talking member of the Saddle Bags who runs a local veterinary practice with Kiwi husband **Paul**.

Mo Dawkins: the jolliest of the Saddle Bags, a tirelessly hard-working farmer's daughter, married to cheery agricultural contractor **Barry**.

Grace: their pony-mad daughter.

Sid and Joan Stokes: Mo's aging smallholder parents, who live with adult daughter **Jan** and a lot of horse brasses.

Bay Austen: dashing agricultural entrepreneur, hunt thruster and serial flirt.

Monique Austen: his steely Dutch ex-wife.

Tilly and Bram: their high octane, free-range children.

Kenny Kay: stand-up comedian turned 'accidental' Hollywood star, a leathery roue with fond memories of the Comptons.

Santiago Kay: his son, a smooth golf pro.

Sir Peter Sanson: tax exile leisure tycoon who owns great tracts of the Bardswolds including Eyngate Hall.

ANIMALS

Beck: an explosive warmblood stallion, once Germany's hotly-tipped new star, as stunning as he is screwed up.

Cruisoe: the stud's foundation stallion whose winning progeny inherit his lion heart.

Spirit: a wall-eyed cold with a big man attitude and a bright future.

Lottie: a Compton-bred mare eager to take on the world and win.

The stud's broodmares: an opinionated bunch of matriarchs.

Magpie: Mo's trusty coloured cob who only has one gear.

Craic: Bridge's nervouscited Connemara pony.

The Redhead: Petra's rabble-rousing mare.

Coll: a brutish greedy Shetland and **Beck's** companion.

Lester's cob: as mannerly and well-turned-out as its rider.

Olive and Enid: Ronnie's sprightly little Lancashire Heelers, a squabbling mother and daughter.

Stubbs: Lester's unswervingly loyal fox terrier.

Knott: Pax's cautious deerhound puppy.

Laurence: a rescued fox cub.

PART ONE

1

R onnie loved flying into dusk, that sense of stealing across the sky to a faraway night-time galaxy, especially when horse-trading lay ahead. Descending through the clouds over Bremen, she admired the lights glittering below, imagining they were stars, jewelled curtains welcoming her on a stellar adventure.

And goodness, it was lovely to get away from home.

Fat snowflakes clustered against the plane's tiny window as they landed, obscuring her view of the airport's familiar glowing expanse. She'd travelled through here routinely once, dealing sports horses around Europe, occasionally hopping home to the UK, or to the US to see a client, her Mulberry weekender thrown open on the four-poster of a schloss one night, a horsebox bunk the next. That lifestyle had ended abruptly several years ago when she'd split from then-lover Henk, a globe-trotting Dutch bloodstock agent, resuming a more genteel English country life amid her old eventing crowd.

Her years of valet airport parking and flying business class might be behind her, but Ronnie relished being back in Germany during peak stallion show season, the buzz in her veins again. She didn't care that she was disembarking the cheapest flight she could find, or that her budget hire car felt doll-sized amongst the night-haulage traffic roaring south on Autobahn One as she drove through Lower Saxony. Her heart still soared when she reached the small city of Vechta, unofficial capital of warmblood breeding. This was where dynasties were formed.

February was the month the big German studs showed off their elite, some of the most beautiful sires in Europe on show. Tonight's was the hottest ticket of all, the Gestüt Fuchs Stallion Collection. Amongst the most valuable in Europe, Gestüt horses were the envy of the world.

But the most breathtaking Gestüt-bred horse was the one Ronnie had left behind at home in the Cotswolds: Bechstein, AKA Beck. Almost lost to the breeding world through a succession of bad deals, the former Olympic showjumper was standing at her family stud this season. His breeder, Paul Fuchs, wanted him back, and Ronnie was here to broker the deal. This evening she was a VIP guest at Fuchs' public show, followed by a personal backstage tour to meet its stars, then dinner afterwards with the great man himself.

If she played it right, the next few hours could turn around her family's fortunes completely.

It was snowing thickly by the time she arrived at her hotel a stone's throw from the Oldenburg Breed Centre, host to so many elite studs' showcases and sales that even the accommodation was horse-themed: the life-size sculptures of a mare and foal at its entrance bore icicle whiskers and snow rugs. The rooms here had been booked out weeks in advance, the stallion parades always drawing a big, knowledgeable crowd. Later tonight, the bar would thrum with chatter until the early hours. Right now, it was the *Marie Celeste* because everybody had already decamped across the road for the pre-parade buzz, cramming the marquee alongside the centre's big arena to talk horse over beer and Bratwurst. The Gestüt Fuchs' parade would begin at seven thirty.

It was already close to seven. Ronnie was cutting it ridiculously fine, but the money she'd saved getting a later flight paid for a lot of horse feed and arriving somewhere at full tilt suited her. When she'd ridden professionally, she'd been notorious for entering the start box at the last possible moment to keep her nerves at bay.

She hurried straight to her room, which was small, clean and functional with framed photos of German's greatest sports horses on its walls. One of Beck's famous grandsires was amongst them, which she took to be a good sign.

She cleaned her teeth while messaging home to let them know she'd arrived safely. Then, adding layers of cashmere and tweed above the workmanlike merino and jersey, she fired off a customary message to her lover, Blair, not expecting a reply.

He rang straight back, his deep Australian voice raised above background hubbub. 'What the fuck are you doing coming over here without me, Ron?' She could hear voices and music at his end, not the customary quiet of his Wiltshire farm kitchen. 'I just spotted your name on a chair.'

She was thrilled. Blair had a brilliant eye. 'What are *you* doing here?'

'Last minute thing. Thought you might be here. You're late. It's about to kick off.'

'I'll be there before it does.' She dug around in her case for her make-up bag. 'Are you sitting near me?'

'Nah, I've the best seat in the house, mate.' He laughed, blunt as a cudgel.

'Paul promised that to me!' Her mirrored reflection widened its blue eyes indignantly.

Friends for three decades, lovers on and off throughout and competitors in the same sport, theirs was a combative as well as comforting love affair. They'd met in the eighties when Blair was a rookie rider freshly landed from New South Wales, Ronnie the pin-up girl of British three-day-eventing, the engagement ring on her finger quashing the fierce attraction between them. Over the years, their fortunes had reversed, but never their mutual respect. The fact that they'd never been single at the same time might be a mutual cause for regret, but both acknowledged that it could also be why the chemistry still worked. Ronnie's marriage and riding career had peaked young, her subsequent adventures earning her a rolling stone reputation. Still at the top of his game in his fifties, veteran of multiple championships and hard knocks, Blair was a consistent legend in the sport, his nickname, Mr Sit Tight, well-earned both in the saddle and in wedlock. Although his marriage to a wealthy, older patron was sometimes viewed as one of convenience, his talent and drive were unrivalled.

His deep laugh rumbled. 'What hotel did his people get you a room in?'

'The horse one.' She found her mascara and spiked up her lashes.

'With the tourists?' He was offended on her behalf.

'It's perfect. I can catnap anywhere and it's going to be a late night.' Dabbing lipstick onto her cheeks before painting her mouth, Ronnie stifled a yawn. She'd been mucking out stables in Warwickshire at six thirty that morning. Reflected over her shoulder, the expanse of crisply made bed promised rare respite later.

'Come to mine afterwards.' Pulling rank, he named the town's smartest boutique hotel. 'I'll see you right, Ron.'

'I'm having dinner with Paul.' It did no harm to keep Blair on his toes, especially when he was being imperious. 'We need to agree the deal for Beck returning here in the summer.'

'He'll try and screw you.'

'And I'll tell him to Fuchs right off.' She laughed, smacking her painted lips together and rubbing the pink into her cheeks. 'Besides, I'm too old for him.'

'I'm talking about the money, Ron.' Blair had moved away from the background noise, voice hushed and urgent. 'We both know he's mean as cat's piss.'

Blair didn't approve of her plan to sell Beck back to Germany, which she put down to sentiment, a secret vice he'd unexpectedly developed in middle age. It was his wife who had spotted Beck

6

in a British auction ring, unpapered and catalogued under a stable name, but still entire. Back home in Wiltshire the stallion proved too hot to handle and when his microchip revealed he was warmblood royalty, Blair had traded him with Ronnie, not imagining she'd sell him straight on after standing him just one season. They argued about it often.

'This is how our business works, Blair.' She doused herself in perfume. 'You and I know it.'

'Yeah, well, Paul Fuchs doesn't deserve Beck to land back in his lap any more than he did Conch.' Blair's other vested sentiment was seventeen hands of turbo-boosted Teutonic talent named Big Conch that he'd taken from unbroken colt to medal winner more than a decade earlier, before ignominiously losing the ride. Recently retired, Conch had also relocated to stand at Gestüt Fuchs.

'Is he parading?' Ronnie asked vaguely, stepping into her warmest boots.

'I don't want to see you selling out to Fuchs like everyone else.' His gravelly voice was at its most boulder-blasting, touching even her hardened horse-dealing heart. 'I care about you, Ron, and that batshit crazy horse.'

'If you're here to try to stop me dealing, it won't work.'

'You know me better than that, Ron. But you wouldn't listen to me, so I figured actions speak louder than words.'

'I'm glad you're here.' She shrugged on her coat and grabbed her hairbrush. 'I'll kiss you in my head when I see you.'

'Me too. Tongues, teeth and all.' It was a well-worn sign-off, decades of passion and sentiment seamed into their public rock face, like gold through quartz. 'Watch out for yourself, Ron.'

Sweeping the brush through her short blonde hair, she smiled at her reflection, its blue eyes bright with anticipation, still seeing the same face she had from early womanhood and the thrill of cutting a deal. She was a big girl now. 'I'll be fine.'

★

Ronnie made it to her front row seat just in time, the arena lights already dimmed, Mozart blasting over the speakers and giant gold GF logos rotating on the big screens as Paul Fuchs strode out into the spotlights to welcome the capacity crowd, his audience jolly and pink-cheeked from the hospitality marquee. She couldn't see Blair anywhere, but she defied him to be any more ringside than this. All the seating tiers around the sand arena were jammed with eager faces. In front of them, on the big, golden rectangle of silica sand overhung with international flags and lit like a concert stage, Paul's figure glowed in criss-crossed spotlights, rounder and greyer than Ronnie remembered, but no less formidable and unsmiling. Dressed in a mandarin-collared shiny grey suit, flanked by two glamorous assistants in tight tailoring and black polo necks, he had a delightfully Bond-baddie air.

Ronnie's German was passable and she'd heard the sales spiel many times, so her eyes still hunted for Blair. As she searched, she spotted familiar faces: some leading British breeders, lots of the glitzy Euro-dressage crowd, her ex-partner Henk amongst a Dutch clutch. A few seats away from her sat Canadian legendary showjumping veteran, the Flying Maple Leaf, whose jutting jaw and fearsome reputation preceded him. There was no sign of Blair. Perhaps he'd been winding her up and was in his local pub in Wiltshire. It had been known.

The show began with young Fuchs' stallions, many unbroken and run up in hand or loose-schooled around a temporary oval track. Ronnie needed her wits about her if she was to secure one in part exchange for Becks at the end of this season, but of the three horses marked up in her catalogue as Paul's suggestions, none held a candle to Becks.

As Paul's small army of helpers in matching Gestüt Fuchs sweatshirts dismantled the white railings around the track, her attention wandered again, noticing the cameras panning along her row. The event was being streamed live on a specialist equestrian channel. Watching at home in the Cotswolds on his

8

iPad was her family's experienced stallion man, Lester, a recent convert to silver surfing while recovering from a broken hip. Remembering to check her phone, Ronnie found he'd messaged *none of those*. She sent a quick thumbs up emoji.

An hour of up-and-coming ridden stallions followed, dressage and jumping alternating every four or five horses to keep the audience alert and the sweatshirt-wearing work team busy.

Marking her catalogue, Ronnie assessed each of these top prospects, glossy as riverbed pebbles under the lights, springing along with balletic extravagance or catapulting stag-like over coloured poles, and she found it easy to imagine each one improving her stud's Thoroughbred and Irish bloodlines. An injection of big-moving spring was precisely why she'd bought Beck. But the trouble was, none of them *were* Beck.

Emboldened by the emoji, Lester messaged Ronnie throughout with his thoughts, but his dislike of warmbloods was too entrenched to entirely trust his judgement and his mastery of predictive text still too primitive. *Don't lick this one* he wrote of a power-trotting rising dressage star, adding *wife behind*, which made her turn round and check before realizing he meant 'wide behind', the horse's hindlegs moving too far apart.

Where was Blair? He had the real eye.

Ignoring her phone vibrating, Ronnie settled back to enjoy the spectacle as the big-hitting sires started to parade: international team horses, Nations Cup superstars, multi-million-euro horseflesh. Now *these* were Beck's class. Blair was probably right; she might be mad to let him out of Britain. He was just what their sport needed on home soil – but not based with her at Compton Magna Stud.

Ronnie still firmly believed that Gestüt Fuchs huge, state-of-the-art Saxony base, which had already bred a jaw-dropping, headline-making crop from Beck as a young stallion, was the place the horse had been happiest. Far better equipped for his mindset than her historic, old-school farm, it's temperature-controlled barns and AI facilities were precisely what suited highly-strung, anti-social Beck best.

Besides which, she was too cash strapped to hang onto him. When Blair had let her swap two talented young eventers for a six-figure horse and a lorry to transport him in, he'd known her dilemma.

The last half dozen horses on show from the Fuchs' elite were its most famous sporting descendants, legends in their own fields who had carried the stud's blood to highest victory, each one given an effusive introduction over the PA from Paul littered with *wunderbars* and *fantastischs*, and rapturous rounds of applause from the audience. The final horse of the evening, Paul told them with breathy excitement, was a special surprise not listed in the catalogue. An ambassador for the versatility of the stud's bloodline, he was standing at the stud to selected mares only, his appearance tonight a last-minute *glücklicher Zufall*. Born to a Fuchs-bred dam over twenty years earlier, he was the highest point-scoring event stallion in history, recently retired from competition and reunited here for the first time in six years with the man who had taken him from an unbroken youngster to two consecutive Olympics and two WEGs, stepping onto the podium every time...

Ronnie sat up. Now she knew why Blair said he had the best seat in the house.

The horse was quite simply a megastar, Paul went on, that had subsequently gone on to help Italy to individual Olympic and European glory, as well as its first Badminton and Kentucky victories.

The horse of Blair Robertson's lifetime was on show, Ronnie realized. The Australian had been devastated when the ride was sold out from under him just before their record-breaking third Olympics together, its owners making enough money to retire on. But that was all too often the nature of the sport, as was being reunited for a grand occasion, all the blood, sweat and tears forgotten. And who could blame him wanting to sit on his greatest campaigner one last time in front of a roaring crowd like this?

They were already clapping in time as a jazzed-up instrumental version of INXS's 'New Sensation' started blasting over the speakers.

And there was Blair, trotting up the centre line in his finest bib and tucker, lights sparkling off his helmet, his big craggy smile aimed straight at her, reunited at last in the greatest eventing partnership lost to profiteering.

Actions speak louder than words, he'd said. This was some gesture.

She smiled back, wishing the bastard didn't always have to be so sportsmanlike in his one-upmanship. God, but she loved him. If they ever said it out loud, they immediately retracted it, but Ronnie had no doubt he felt it just as deeply as she did.

They powered around the arena, the INXS medley melding into 'Need You Tonight', then 'Never Tear Us Apart', an ironic touch. Big Conch, now in his twenties, looked glorious, halting to take his standing ovation.

On her feet, Ronnie clapped hardest of all and, smiling as Blair raised his eyebrows at her, shook her head.

Nice try, but she hadn't come here to watch Blair trot round proving a point.

To her frustration, Ronnie found the VIP Tour around the GF stalls after the parade was a whistlestop group one, conducted by a Fuchs' lacky who repeated everything in three different languages with the aid of a tablet to accommodate the trio of nationalities following her: German, Spanish and English for Ronnie's benefit, along with that of the Flying Maple Leaf, six feet four of question-barking self-importance, equally irritated not to be getting a personal tour with Paul Fuchs himself. After a polite introduction in which she was careful to use her married name, Ronnie kept her distance from the Canadian legend, uncertain if he knew how close their connections were.

But then one of those connections stepped in beside them.

'Mind if I tag along? Good to see you, mate.' Blair lent forward to shake the Canadian's hand and that of his wife, then the rest of the group including Ronnie. 'Good evening, Mrs Ledwell.'

The group perked up now the star turn was with them.

Only Maple Leaf glowered at him. Their mutual animosity stretched back before even Ronnie's time, dating to the days Blair had competed internationally across two disciplines, his showjumping career bringing him into regular contact – and conflict – with the Flying Maple Leaf. As with many old rivalries, it came with a grudging admiration.

'Not a bad horse, that Big Conch,' Maple Leaf acknowledged gruffly.

'Yeah, I think so,' Blair replied even more gruffly, eyeing Ronnie.

She kept her focus on the tour. Closer inspection of the three stallions Paul had earmarked as potential trade-ins for Beck doubled down on her conviction that they weren't right for her stud, even with a generous balancing figure. Too young, unproven and heavy set.

'I need something more established,' she told Blair, 'and with more blood.'

Maple Leaf cut in. 'I might be able to help you there.'

'Oh, yes?' She looked up at the lantern jaw.

'Eventing's not my scene, lady, but we have a—'

His wife touched his arm. 'Honey, we're late to dine with Paul.'

'Then we can talk about it over dinner,' Ronnie realized, checking her watch. 'Although you're not late. We've half an hour yet.'

Maple Leaf was regarding her with amusement. 'You a rookie?'

'I need to borrow Mrs Ledwell for a moment,' Blair took her arm. 'Excuse me.'

'What d'you do that for?' she demanded when they were out of earshot.

'You're already trying to do a deal with one devil tonight, Ron, you don't want to do a second one. And everyone dines with Paul in ten-minute shifts, I thought you knew that?'

'Demystify me.' As a one-time part of the inner circle invited to share the Fuchs' legendary hospitality at home, she and Henk had never joined Paul after events like this, always too busy wooing clients of their own in luxury in central Vechta.

Blair took her to the bar, which was thick with cigarette smoke and horse-talk, old acquaintances hailing him from all sides. He bought them both a schnapps. At the opposite end of the marquee, Paul was holding court at his own high table, guests granted a brief audience over a beer and bratwurst.

'It's like speed dating or arm-wrestling,' Blair explained. 'Fuchs operates on a rigid timetable.' The German breeder liked to do business without pausing for breath, he told her, and take quick victories. 'You'll get told the deal, then you'll either shake hands or you'll walk away like Maple Leaf's about to.' They watched Paul and the Canadian black-slapping each other. 'He comes every year to lock horns. It's ritualistic. They're as bad as each other.'

'With a genius eye for horses.'

'Yeah.' Blair was still watching them. 'Maple Leaf flies over for the sales and stallion shows because his missus has family down in Munster, so it's a tax-deductible way for her to see her mother.'

'She looks nice.' She saw the pretty brunette with sad spaniel eyes glance across at them and smile. 'Is she the one he has a daughter with, the one he remarried?' She smiled back.

'How d'you know about that?'

'Someone told me they're the Burton and Taylor of Ontario,' she said vaguely, sensing his disquiet.

'Yeah, she's his first *and* fifth wife. He sows his wild oats on crop rotation.'

Ronnie laughed, then realized he wasn't joining in.

'He's a bully, Ron. He treats his family like staff. Ask your friend Luca O'Brien.'

Ronnie grimaced at the mention of her second – regrettably close – link with Maple Leaf. Luca O'Brien, the genius pro rider currently back at home bringing hot-headed Beck into work with infinite patience, was a recent ex-employee of the Canadian's. His departure had been very messy indeed. It was Luca who'd made the Burton–Taylor comparison, and Ronnie suspected he'd flirted with the daughter or wife – or both, knowing Luca. Thankfully, Maple Leaf didn't seem to have made the connection.

He was already back on his feet, making a big show of laughing and shaking his head at Paul, also on his feet, although a fraction of the big man's height. After a lot of extravagant forehead-slapping and upturned palms on both sides, the Canadian marched to the bar, pausing beside Ronnie to hand her a business card. 'Message me if you want info about that stallion. And remind that little Irish sack of shit you have working for you that I'll kill the bastard if he goes near my daughter again.'

She smiled defensively, tempted to point out that gorgeous, gentle Luca appeared far too captivated by her own daughter to spare his any thought, but he'd already moved away. A moment later, the card was plucked out of her hand. 'Oy!'

Blair ripped it into small pieces. 'You can't afford his horse. Go get what you want from Paul or walk away. Just treat Fuchs like he just did and you'll be fine.' He nodded towards the tall figure embracing friends at the bar.

'Take a maple leaf out of his books?' She couldn't resist it.

But Blair was still watching the Canadian, one arm round his wife, the other back-slapping and high-fiving.

'Ronnie Percy!' Paul was just as baby-faced, dirty-blond eager as she remembered despite the jowls and the silver wings above his ears, beckoning her to his table 'So punctual! So beautiful! You are my thirteenth dining companion. I have many, like your Mad Hatter, ya? *Bitte setzen Sie sich.* You like the horses I showed, yes? We can trade?'

Irritably aware that she was on a short timer, Ronnie settled in front of him and got straight down to business, outlining her plan again, and trying not to show how offended she was when he laughed uproariously and said *'nein'* nine times. 'You want me to pay big money for Bechstein *and* give you a proven stallion?'

'We agreed all this in principle.'

'And now we agree for real without principle.' Descended from a long line of cool-headed Saxony horse-dealers, Paul Fuchs was a notoriously smooth operator. 'Your price is too high'

Coming from similar Cotswolds lineage, Ronnie knew that selling Becks back to him risked undervaluing her biggest asset, but she wanted this deal. 'And your price?'

He named an offensively low figure.

'Your little stud is broke,' Paul said smoothly. 'And you have a very bad reputation personally and professionally, Ronnie. Gestüt Fuchs can help you if you help us.' Lowering his voice, he started outlining a plan that, even to Ronnie's untrained ear, involved importing horses illegally to avoid taxes and import costs. She was accustomed to some dirty horse-trading, but this was filthy. Blair's mistrust of Fuchs might be coloured by personal experience, but it was entirely justified.

She remembered too late to hold her hands up, press one to her forehead and laugh. 'Ha!'

'You have forgotten something?' he sneered. To either side, his lackies laughed.

'Now you mention it, yes, my moral compass.'

Ronnie felt the heart-kick of regret for not acknowledging just how much she needed Blair, her friend for more than half her lifetime, lover for much of that, wise counsel throughout.

He was right not to trust Paul Fuchs. She glanced over her shoulder. There was no sign of Blair, just another Fuchs client waiting to be invited to the table, diner fourteen queued and cued.

Ronnie determinedly pushed aside all second thoughts. There was no Plan B.

'You want Bechstein, you accept my original terms,' she told Paul, handing him her show catalogue. 'I've marked the stallions I'll consider in part exchange, with totals alongside. I'll need a 20 per cent cash deposit. You have until tomorrow morning to decide. Thank you for this evening.'

As she marched from the marquee, chin high, Blair fell in step with her. 'How d'it go?'

'I did jazz hands, stood up and sat down a bit and refused to negotiate. You were right about him. Has he got worse? Or have I got better?'

'I love you. I didn't say that.'

'Likewise. By the way, where *were* you?' she demanded.

'Getting this...' He held up a bottle of German sparkling wine. 'I thought you might fancy some mindless Sekt.'

'Your place or mine?'

'Mine's better.'

'Subjective. Mine's closer. Be a horse tourist.' She led the way. Outside the marquee it was sub-zero, a starry sky fighting against the orange gauze of light pollution. The snow had been cleared from all the walkways, but it creaked in the tree branches overhead and carpeted the verges ankle deep as they cut back towards her hotel by the quickest route.

The statue mare and foal were still wearing their white blankets; the bar was throbbing; the room was small, warm and basic – and everything they could want.

Overlooked by Beck's relatives, Ronnie didn't sleep a lot.

'I think I've lost my moral compass again,' she complained in the early hours, sweaty and sated.

'Let me see if I can find it...' Blair disappeared beneath the sheets.

'Ohmygod how do you always find it so *quickly?*' she laughed incredulously, shifting up the pillows.

'Neon signs.' Came the muffled reply.

Sex was almost always easy. It was sleeping together that was always the weirdest thing: the intimacy of their bodies, smooth and soft and hard and hairy and bony bits all slotted warmly together on these rarest of sleepover nights. It felt odd. Somehow right, but odd.

They couldn't do it for long, napping then loving, somehow aware that it was too precious to waste.

At three, she complained that they never went anywhere together as a couple. 'Just once, wouldn't it be great to be us, just us, doing something? Archery, zip-sliding, pottery, the cinema even?'

At four in the morning, returning from a clean-up-and-pee bathroom trip, she found Blair's face glowing in his phone screen light.

'I'm booking us a treat.'

When he showed her, she let out a whoop of delight.

Then she spotted the date. 'Really?'

'I'm not sentimental about it and the wife's certainly not. Would you rather I change it?'

'No, let's do it. I'd love that.'

Neither had the energy to make love again, but they kissed and stroked and loved all the smooth and soft and hard and hairy and bony bits fitting together.

At seven, her mobile rang.

'You can have any of the horses you marked,' Paul Fuchs told her. 'But half the cash.'

'That's not our deal.'

'It's my deal.'

'Then I'm afraid you'll be dealing with rejection.' She hung up on him and kissed Blair awake. 'It's contagious.'

'What?'

'Sentimentality.'

2

Pax had rules about crying in her car: never do it while driving, nor while parked in the driveway at home, avoid Waitrose car park in Broadbourne and garage forecourts, and *never* outside Kes's primary school or indeed anywhere in the village. If passengers were in the car, crying was strictly prohibited. Above all, do not cry in the paved courtyard in front of Baylis, Beadle and Bell Solicitors in Chipping Hampden because you are the one who wants this divorce, remember.

She'd broken all those rules except the last one in the past few months. Today that record was about to fall.

She'd could feel it building through her meeting with family solicitor Helen Beadle.

'The other party is being obstreperous with the financial disclosure,' Helen reported, by which she meant that Pax's ex, Mack, was being an arsehole about money again.

A mother, governor and PTA superpower at Compton Magna Primary School, Helen was the sort of woman Pax longed to be: immaculate, organized, forthright, not a hot mess with a drink problem who cried in cars.

She stared out of the window as Helen outlined her concerns that Mack was concealing assets. 'Matters are somewhat complicated by the fact you were in a business partnership until the marriage broke down...'

At first, it was the fight over son Kes that had obsessed him, almost destroying Pax in the process. That was still ongoing, but now his focus had shifted to the coffers. She longed to care more about it. Money was important, after all. Her mother was obsessed with it, and yet...

She could see the hills behind Chipping Hampden curving mistily beyond its rooftops, beyond the wooded crest of which was Compton Magna and the stud where she had grown up and once again lived, while the assets being discussed today were divided. Pax imagined galloping up those green miles to the little cottage she now shared with Kes, jumping hedges, racing through woods, bridging streams.

'... advising him to delay invoicing, spend any cash, delay paying himself any salary or bonus from the business,' Helen was saying, unaware her client had mentally left the building. On horseback.

Faster and faster, the wind in her face, her chest burning, up in her stirrups. Past the vale's famous folly tower and the huge Scots pines

'And the marital home is uninhabitable, am I right?' Helen had to ask it twice.

'Yes, sorry! We're renovating it, *were* renovating it.' A future self she would never be, chatelaine of an old village rectory, the Farrow and Ball Cotswolds daydream lifestyle destroyed by her unhappiness. Mack told her daily that she was ruining Kes's future too.

She fought the tears back down and stared out of the window to resume galloping home while Helen unpicked the Forsyths' complicated finances, their property development company's portfolio overinvested, the bank owning the lion's share of three unsold luxury barn conversions along with the Forsyths' part-renovated house – even the static caravan they'd been living in when Pax walked out after the most miserable and loveless Christmas she'd ever endured. Never again.

Kes was better off without his parents' toxic marriage, she

reminded herself. That Mack still claimed to want to save it astonished her, but her husband hated losing, and to him, this was still a competition with everything to play for. If till-death-us-do-part was a long game, decree absolute was about absolute power. Right now, that meant money.

'The other party's parents loaned a large cash sum to the business, I believe?' Helen was reading her notes.

'Not to my knowledge.'

The solicitor looked up. 'You're not aware that three weeks ago your husband repaid them a significant six-figure sum which is listed here as a family loan?'

'Six *figures*?' That sounded very odd. Her in-laws would split a restaurant bill down to the tap water, recycled wrapping paper and sat in near darkness to save electricity. 'Muir and Mairi sold up in Scotland last year to rent down here while they were looking to buy, so technically they had cash on deposit, I suppose, but I did all our company banking and never saw any payment from them. They're jolly careful with money, all that cliché Scottish parsimony.'

Helen gave a brief smile. 'This happens sometimes. At best it's a soft loan hidden from a spouse, at worst he's hiding your joint cash by pretending it was a parental advance and "paying it back" to them now to safeguard until you're divorced. But it doesn't alter the fact that, on paper, you have almost no marital assets at all, which I don't believe to be true.'

Pax was confused. 'None?'

'The other side is sparing with information.' Helen picked up her notes. 'Which again suggests they're hiding something. Not best practise but we all do it if that's what the client wants, I'm afraid. We can ask the court for a non-party disclosure to get sight of his bank account statements – he has several personal accounts in addition to the joint and business partnership ones, I believe.'

'Whatever you think's best.' Pax wanted it over, gone, behind her.

'I'll put in a polite request for more detail first, see where that gets us.' Helen made a note, and picked up a separate page. 'Also, the other side have queried the interest you have in Compton Magna Stud?'

'That's in a family trust, has nothing to do with the marriage. It was only set up last year, after Grumpa died.'

'Is it valuable?'

'I suppose so.'

'Ball park figure?'

A developer had offered several million for the farm recently, she told Helen. 'But it can't be sold so that's purely academic. My mother has a lifetime trust.' She didn't tell Helen that her siblings were both eager to use a loophole to boot Ronnie out and sell up. 'Mack can't possibly go after my share in that, can he?'

Helen sat back, pressing her hands to her cheeks. 'I don't usually like to tell clients this, but I think you have to prepare yourself for the worse, Pax.'

Pax gazed out of the widow again, her distant, mounted alter ego almost home, thundering across Austen land, onto the Three Mile Point and up the final ten-furlong sprint to the stud's boundary rails. She'd spent her entire marriage prepared for bad things to happen. That's what living with Mack was like. 'I already am.'

Outside in the cobbled courtyard, another client's car had blocked hers in. Her stupid little Noddy car looked tiny and silly, sandwiched between two big off-roaders and a hatchback.

That's all it took for the tears to overwhelm her.

There was nowhere to run. She sat in her car and wept. Not about the money or the deceit, or even the fact she missed her battered old Volkswagen and wished Mack had never bought her a car that people laughed at. She cried because divorce was all such a waste of love and hope.

A shadow fell across her passenger's door window and she cringed down in case they'd seen her, but it was just the driver of the neighbouring car returning to find he was also blocked in. Even with his back to her, she recognized him straight away – the broad shoulders, wide neck, short mop of walnut brown hair.

'Shit!' She slid as low as she could go.

It was Bay Austen. Why hadn't she recognized his Land Rover? He must have been meeting one of the other legal partners, she realized. He too was going through a divorce.

'Please don't see me,' she willed. Not much chance of avoiding her in this car. He'd tapped on the window more than once when she'd been parked up in village laybys shouting down the phone at Mack or crying about him. He'd smile, ask if she was all right, try and cheer her up with some outrageous flattery or teasing. And he would always say, 'This car is ridiculous.' Every time.

And every time her heart would lurch because she had loved him once. Bay. her first boyfriend. A pure, heady Romeo-and-Juliet love before all this bitter, wasted, married lovelessness.

Not now. Please.

She mopped her face and peered over the door sill.

Sitting in his own car, Bay had his head in his hands.

Pax observed him, fascinated. Bay who was an indefatigably happy Labrador of a man, friendly and bouncy, endlessly charming and a confirmed rogue, looked defeated. Dishy playboy Bay, who she'd loved with all her heart and soul at seventeen until he'd broken it, who was still an incorrigible flirt that half the women in the village swooned over, was utterly wretched. Entrepreneurial Bay, who had transformed his parents' farm to a money-making mecca for organic food and artisan craft devotees, seemed beaten.

He looked up and she ducked down again, braced, waiting. But he stayed in his car and when she peeked up once more, he'd slumped back in his seat, eyed closed.

Straightening up, gulping away the blocked nose sniffs,

she gazed at that perfect profile, with its toned jaw and short, straight nose, entranced by the misery etched in it.

Then, before she had time to duck again, she realized he'd turned his head and was looking straight at her.

For a few moments, it was a stare-off. Unsmiling, surprised, surreal. Then his window lowered. She lowered hers too. It was only polite.

His voice was devoid of its customary mirth. 'Looks like we're stuck here while another poor sod thrashes out who gets the Dualit.'

'Yes.'

'I don't suppose you want to go for a coffee?'

'Not really.' Helen's assistant had given her two so she already had the jitters.

'Ice cream?' Still he didn't smile. 'The parlour's open.' They'd gone there a lot once, joking they were more like fifties sweethearts than noughties adolescents.

'In February?'

'Good way to stop the blood boiling. That car's ridiculous by the way.'

Pax suddenly found herself craving ice cream, even though it wasn't yet lunchtime and spending time with Bay was a dangerous sport. But she needed him to look cheerful again so that she could stop feeling sorry for him and normal order was restored.

The ice-cream parlour on Chipping Hampton's historic High Street hadn't changed in Pax's lifetime, a golden Cotswold stone tourist trap even on the greyest winter day. They ordered the same as they'd always done fifteen years earlier – double waffle cone with salted caramel and Belgian choc for Bay, single blackcurrant for Pax – and instinctively settled at the back where they always had, occupying the small table half-hidden by a big upright beam.

'Hell, isn't it?' Bay ate his ice cream with the enviable speed of someone unfamiliar with fillings, dieting or neuralgia. 'Divorce.'

'Yup.' Now they were sitting here together, in a time warp, Pax realized the awkwardness of the situation. There'd barely had an amicable conversation since she'd screamed and wept at him for ruining her life at seventeen. There'd been some stiff-jawed small-talk at family occasions, when Bay usually flirted, and recent encounters in the village including the window-tapping car insults, where Bay had been flirty, and there had been one strange, shouty incident at the stud when he'd apologized for hurting her so much and she'd got upset and felt out of control. Had he flirted then?

'My solicitor wants me to lighten my cash load,' he confided now, not remotely flirty.

'Mack has been busy doing just that.' She was grateful to tell someone.

His blue eyes darkened. 'Buying himself expensive items like cars and yachts to offload it?'

'I wouldn't know.' She didn't mention that there was no cash left to spend, according to Mack's financial disclosure. Which at least kept it simple.

'Bloody dishonest thing to do. I told my solicitor to fuck right off.'

'I save that insult for Mack, occasionally adding and die.'

'That bad?'

She glanced up and wished she hadn't. Somebody had replaced roguish, garrulous Bay with a man whose eyes were hollow, who couldn't smile.

'Monique and I are still pretty civil thank God.' Bay's icily beautiful Dutch wife had been the one to walk out on the marriage after multiple infidelities on both sides. Local gossips had her living in a ménage à trois in a rented barn conversion near Broadbourne, although Pax suspected it might just be a barn with a manège. 'She knows I'll be fairhanded, although

I'm not letting her take any more horses. She's emptied half the yard. Don't worry, I've hung onto yours.'

'Sorry?'

'Your grandfather bred her. Monique persuaded me to buy her after Blair Robertson started her off and tipped her as a five-star prospect, but we're none of us event riders.'

'Yes, I remember now.'

'Needs a pro.' He ate more ice cream, his gaze moving restlessly round the little parlour. 'Maybe you can help?'

'I can ask round.' It had been years since she'd been actively involved in the sport and she suspected Bay had far better contacts than she did these days, but it felt lovely to be consulted, and her mother – who knew everybody who was anybody in eventing – would help.

The blue eyes were focussed on her again, 'No, I mean maybe *you* can ride her?'

Pax baulked, laughing. 'Have I just time-travelled back to seventeen or something?'

Bay's eyes lit up. 'God, yes, wouldn't that be fun? Let's do it!'

'Maybe we already have?' It was her turn to look round, unnerved by his enthusiasm. 'This place hasn't changed one bit since the noughties. It could be a portal.'

'You're on! If you're seventeen, I am—' He scrunched up his face.

'Twenty-one,' she filled in dryly, annoyed he didn't remember. 'Adult enough for Granny to accuse you of cradle-snatching.'

'I am very young for my age.'

'You can say that again. Totally immature.'

He had the grace to look abashed, fiddling with the same metal napkin dispenser that had undoubtedly been there the first time they'd shared the table, and glancing up at her every few seconds. She remembered that look. It made something deep inside her flip over.

Four years her senior, neighbouring farmer's son Bay had captured Pax's devotion from the day his skinny beanpole eleven-year-old-self gave her red-plaited seven-year-old self a lead through the water jump at Pony Club Camp. By twelve, she was swooning whenever the floppy-haired teenager came home from boarding school to shoot and hunt and drive tractors and tease her about how pretty she was going to be one day. By her seventeenth birthday, he was looking into her eyes wholly differently, taking her face in his hands and kissing her like he never wanted to stop. By the time she'd turned eighteen, he'd broken her heart.

'What I'd give to be back then.' His face was fast regaining its familiar amused warmth, blue eyes bright. 'You *live* to compete. I've never known anyone so focussed and funny and beautiful and addicted to Haribo sour cherries; I follow you round from event to event in that clapped-out Jeep.'

'Which usually breaks down on the way.'

'Because you go to places like France and Scotland on the Young Riders team. You are unbelievably good. You win everything.' The flatterer was back too.

'Hardly.'

'You must want to do it again now you're living back at the stud?'

She shrugged and bit into her ice cream, getting a stab of pain from cheekbone to eyebrow as reward. He was right. She thought about it obsessively. 'I thought we were being seventeen and twenty-one? Can't we talk about the Iraq War and Harry Potter?'

'You'd be such a good advert for the stud.'

'Which doesn't have the time or resources to compete a string this year.'

'Of course you do.' He made it sound so simple. 'You just need good owners.'

'Are you offering?'

'Speaking as a totally immature twenty-one-year-old, no.

But there's a thirty-six-year-old idiot I happen to know has been advised to reduce his cash in wasteful ways. He already has a horse. He can drop her off anytime.'

'Ha ha.'

He kept looking at her, a half-smile playing on his mouth, ice cream on his upper lip. 'I loved you so much at twenty-one. I didn't know what to do with it then, all that love.'

'Stop it!' She looked away. 'I demand you bring Bay back. The shitty one who knew exactly what to do with it and did it one afternoon in his parents' holiday cottage, and not with me.'

He pushed the napkin dispenser away. 'I could punch the bastard.'

There was a crack and she looked back to see his eyes watering, a red welt on his forehead that hadn't been there before.

'Did you seriously just hit yourself?'

'I don't recommend it.' His jaw quilted. His eyes were dark pools once more. 'Can we be kids again?'

Maybe peeling back the years wasn't so bad for a few minutes, Pax reflected, like ripping off a plaster. 'OK, so I'm seventeen and you're twenty-one. I'm horse obsessed and you have a rubbish car.'

He sat back, looking round, still on edge. 'What do we usually do after ice cream?'

Buy cider, walk up to the folly and kiss a lot, she remembered. Or head to Broadbourne's eccentric little cinema multiplex to watch a movie and kiss a lot. Or drive somewhere scenic to find a sunny spot to explore and kiss a lot, staying in the Jeep to kiss on cold days. Or go home, listen to music and kiss non-stop, and feel inside each other's clothes and sometimes take quite a lot of them off, and get oh-so-close before she said she wasn't ready and he said that was fine.

'I don't remember,' she shrugged, her heart hurting now.

'Come up to the folly. I'll jog your memory.'

'I must get back to the stud. Mummy's in Germany, so Luca's on his own at the yard.'

'It's the noughties.' Bay pushed his chair back. 'Luca's a spotty schoolboy in Ireland and Mummy's up t'north.' He got up, offering her his hand. 'It's just you and me, baby.'

She stood up too, not taking it. 'Let's check if our cars are free first.'

As they walked back along the High Street, Bay dived into the newsagents. 'Won't be a tick.'

She waited outside, tempted to bolt. The window had a Valentine's Day display ahead of next week, lots of bears hugging love hearts and cards the size of coffee table books. For years, she'd kept the one card Bay had sent her in the box file alongside old-fashioned letters to boarding school from her mother and grandparents, all crammed beneath postcards and press clippings, before finally purging the lot when Kes was born. Mack's dry, modern art Valentine's cards had always gone straight into recycling by the first of March.

Rejoining her, Bay had a bounce in his step as he walked with her to the offices of Baylis, Beadle and Bell.

The red SUV that had been blocking them in had gone. A silver Range Rover was now parked there to block them in instead.

'People who are divorcing should drive smaller cars,' Bay scoffed, ignoring the fact his huge old farmer Defender was the biggest of all. 'Let's walk to the folly.'

Pax asked herself why she was doing this a hundred times on the steep climb to Chipping Hampton's famous landmark. She had high-heeled boots on and it had started to drizzle. She'd forgotten how far it was. When they got there, the folly was closed and the clouds were so low, the view of the town below was barely visible.

But as they leant back against its sandstone side, Bay took her hand, squeezed it tightly and said in a breathless, broken voice, 'I'm so scared I'm going to lose my kids, Pax.'

She admitted that she felt the same way about Kes.

'Why would you lose him? You're his mother.'

'My mother lost me.'

Then they hugged so stupidly tightly, and for such a long time, it started to feel weird, yet impossible to let go until some walkers came along, complaining noisily about the drizzle and sheep droppings.

They broke apart and pretended to admire the view, even though there wasn't one.

'This isn't a thing,' she told Bay firmly, not looking at him. 'You and me.'

'Isn't it?' His gaze was fixed on her face.

She still couldn't meet his eyes. 'It hurt too much last time.'

'OK, so it can't be a thing.'

'You should have other things.'

She could almost feel the blue flame heat of his eyes on her. 'This is too big a thing.'

'It's *not* a thing.'

'I want you to know I'm here for you, Pax; I'll look out for you.'

'You don't need to.' She glanced at him then away, her face burning. His eyes were still dark pools, but laughter lines creased and the amused dimples deepened.

'And I want you to ride the mare for me.' He took her hand between his, as though to seal the deal. 'You need to compete again.'

'I'll suggest it to Mummy.'

'Just bloody well say yes.'

'Yes.' Where did that come from?

She felt her thumb trace its way up his palm, his hand broader and more calloused than the one she'd held at seventeen. It had touched many women since finding its way inside her clothes the first time she'd ever known love. Indeed, perhaps the last. Until now.

'On second thoughts, this is a bad idea,' she said, quickly removing her hand.

'Why? My grandmother used to own event horses. It's a family tradition.'

She crossed her arms, stepping back, groping for an armour and shield to protect herself. 'I've got close to Luca.'

'He's a spotty teenager in Ireland,' he reminded her softly.

'He's helping me through a very tough time. He's good for me.'

There was a long pause.

'Are you lovers?' he asked eventually.

'We've kissed.'

'So, it's a thing?'

'It's the edge of a thing.'

'I'm pleased for you.'

She glanced at him again. He was looking down and smiling, kicking a boot toe into the grass. 'You must still ride this mare.'

'I'm not sure that's wise, Bay.' Explaining how frightened she was that she would fall under his spell again sounded ridiculously teenage, besides which she couldn't speak anymore because she had a lump the size of a hoof in her throat.

'You'll be doing me a favour.' Stepping closer, he entreated, 'I won't interfere. I'll be a completely hands-off owner, I promise.' About to touch her arm, he stopped himself. 'See?'

Pax looked down at his hand, willing it to touch her arm, craving the reassurance of their long, silent hug. *I haven't competed in years*, she wanted to point out. *Of course I need my hand held.*

Instead, Bay started off back down the hill, expecting her to follow.

Pax didn't move, watching him striding away, the hoof kicking inside her throat now.

Her phone started ringing.

Ahead of her, Bay stopped to look back and she held it up in explanation, waving him on.

'Darling!' Ronnie was breathless, airport announcements behind her. 'Terrific trip! Everything OK with you?'

'Terrific!' she managed to parrot.

'Are you sure? You sound odd.'

'Terrific!' she managed again. She wouldn't tell her mother about Bay's offer yet. Ronnie would be set against it and it was bound to come to nothing. Only being able to say terrific was an added impediment. When Pax got back to Baylis, Beadle and Bell, the silver Range Rover and Bay's Defender were gone. There was a packet of Haribo cherry sours under the windscreen wiper of the Noddy car, along with a note. *From twenty-one-year-old me, with love. Horse to follow.*

PART TWO

3

'Keep up, Mo! You'll want to hear this...'
Too breathless to reply, Mo nudged her heels against the sides of her old cob who stoically ignored her, staying in a steady trot while the other riders cantered away, divots flying in their wake.

The Saddle Bags, out at first light, were blowing off steam before the school run and working days, which in February meant tacking up by frosty torchlight and wearing more high-vis than a motorway cone squad.

Familiar with the sight of her fellow riders' retreating backsides, Mo was accustomed to bringing up the rear.

First to disappear over the brow of the hill was speed merchant Bridge, a fluorescent streak of no-brakes daring on her dappled pony, pink and grey ponytails swinging, fluffy hat bobble wobbling as they careered off out of control. They were followed by competitive self-dramatist Petra, fantasizing herself fleeing Cromwell's army, her hot-headed chestnut mare in charge. But the only victor would be senior rider Gill, unofficial head girl of the group, eating up the ground on her rangy bay, swift as a Gold Cup winner closing down rivals in the final furlong.

Already far behind – her coloured cob Pie still stubbornly trotting with his great, mud-splatting four-wheel-drive hooves – Mo closed her eyes for a moment and enjoyed the dawn chorus rising above the others' distant voices. Even in canter, they kept up the chatter. She was far too puffed out.

It was Valentine's Day, and the four local riding friends (the self-titled 'Saddle Bags') were, thus far, all carefully avoiding mention of husbands, cards and flowers as they shared a drizzly daybreak hack along the ridgeway above the Comptons. The withered romance of their marriages was nothing to the hot gossip on all their lips, some of which Mo was now missing.

Not that Mo minded that much. She found their scandalmongering a bit much sometimes, this obsession with other people's private lives. She'd not wanted to come out – winter morning hacks were such a rush, tacking up in the dark never much fun, and even though hers was an early-bird farming family, there was always so much to do – but the others had been insistent, especially novelist Petra who was about to disappear into her 'plotting shed' to finish writing another book and needed scandalous inspiration.

Equine vet Gill had promised them all a big surprise, no doubt another juicy scoop picked up on her rounds. She was a font of local low-down, much of it involving the horse set, most recently starring erstwhile eventing pin-up and all-round galloping blonde Ronnie Percy.

Mo glanced down towards the Compton Magna Stud, once a feather in the cap of the Warwickshire's 'Bardswolds'. Like miniature football stadia, its two yards glowed under their tungsten working lights, a silhouetted figure moving around too distantly to identify. The old tractor was bouncing its way up to the Dutch barn, dogs distantly barking inside in the cab.

Having grown up on a smallholding just a few fields away, Mo viewed the stud as a place of absolute authority, much as she viewed the village school or church.

The horse-wise Percys had been ruling the Comptons with a crop of iron since the eighteenth century, and while the family name might have died out when old Captain Percy took his final tumble last year, it remained a headline act thanks to his only daughter and wayward heir, Veronica 'Ronnie' Ledwell. Village lifers like Gill and Mo still called her Ronnie Percy, although she'd been a Ledwell by marriage for years.

Now at the stud's helm, Ronnie had kept the local rumour mill grinding since the previous autumn: her controversial new stallion bellowing; her married lover coming and going; her dashing Irish work rider setting the Bags' hearts racing, then tongues wagging when he cosied up with Ronnie's newly separated daughter, Pax.

Rumours had been circulating since the Captain's death that the place might be sold, but Mo hoped not. She'd seen too many farming neighbours sell up, land stripped, barns converted, locals priced out. Wealthy city folk bought into the country idyll with no heed for the working rural community, that dying breed like her parents, still tending their ramshackle village farm. The Captain had overseen his beautiful rolling acres to his last breath.

Cresting the hill at last, Mo spotted the trio ahead, back in walk, Gill still holding court as she explained in her WI lecture voice, 'In the eighties, every other ex-footballer or retail tycoon owned a showjumper.'

'What have I missed?' Mo panted as she slowed Pie to a walk beside Bridge's grey pony, Craic.

'Usual old bollocks about the stud,' Bridge said, shrugging as she pulled out her phone to check messages while they were high up enough to get 4G. 'Back when Gill's dad was the Compton's answer to Siegfried Farnon.'

'Shh!' Petra was trying to listen.

'The place attracted some jolly big names once,' Gill gathered her audience, 'you must remember, Mo?'

Mo glanced down to the stud where the tractor was turning into the Dutch barn, its lights bouncing off a wall of plastic-wrapped haylage bales, like giant green spearmints. She thought back to her childhood when it was famous horses, not celebrities, that had been her pin-ups. 'Like Mr Tiger and Warm-Up Man, you mean?'

'Both owned by one Kenny Kay.'

'Of course!' Mo gasped.

'Big British TV star at the time,' Petra told Bridge, who was looking shocked.

'I know who he fecking is,' Bridge scoffed. 'He's been in Tarantino stuff.'

'In the eighties he was a stand-up comedian with a terrible reputation,' Gill reminded her, the expression on her long, disapproving face matching her big bay's as she left a dramatic pause before announcing. 'And this year, Kenny Kay is the new owner of Compton Manor.'

Mo let out a squeak of delight. 'You are *kidding*? My Barry loves him.'

'There goes the neighbourhood,' muttered Bridge.

'I jabbed the conveyancing solicitor's hunter yesterday,' Gill told them, 'and she tells me Kenny's cheeky cash offer's been on the table for months, but the owners were holding out for more. Now they've caved and the sale completed this week.'

Mo squealed again. 'Wait till I tell this at home! Dad still talks about him drinking in the pub.'

She was too young to remember Kenny Kay being part of the stud's heyday, but Dad had long regaled them with tales of the comedian holding court at Jugged Hare lock-ins, all cigar smoke, dirty laugh and dolly birds back then. Barry loved hearing all that.

'Why can't the Comptons get some cool Londonshire neighbours?' Bridge was complaining. 'A party-girl actress with a load of Soho Farmhouse mates? Not a fecking prime-time dinosaur who got lucky playing dirty old men in movies.'

'He's a national treasure, Bridget,' Mo corrected.

'Same difference.'

'I thought he lived in America?' queried Petra.

'Florida Keys.' Mo had bought Kenny's latest autobiography

for husband Barry for Christmas. He'd grown up idolising Kenny on Saturday night TV, all cheeky Brummy banter and on-point impersonations, that toothy grin never slipping. Later reinvented as a character actor – he'd even won a BAFTA – he was now semi-retired, with a golden-skinned American wife and a big golf habit.

'Another bloody weekender, then,' Bridge scrolled her phone notifications.

'With seigniory rights,' Gill reminded them. 'Ownership of Compton Manor comes with the title Lord of the Manor of Compton Magna.'

'Maybe he's bought it because he's never made the Honours List?' Petra suggested.

'Fecking hell, the man has a star on Hollywood's Walk of Fame,' said Bridge who was Googling him now. 'He's no need of a Lordship.'

'I bet Kenny remembers the village fondly,' said Mo who could just imagine the look on Barry's face when he heard who their new Lord of Compton Magna Manor was.

'He and the Captain had a dreadful falling out,' Gill told them.

'What about?' Petra asked.

'Nobody seems to know exactly, but there was awfully bad blood between them.'

Mo had heard that too; it had been village tittle-tattle for years afterwards.

'Literal bloodshed.' Gill was beckoning then onward again. 'Someone got shot.'

'Ohmygod!' Mo covered her mouth in recognition. 'The shooting over at Eyngate Hall. That was Kenny?'

'Now he's back for revenge.' Bridge perked up at the prospect of drama. 'I hope Ronnie's got a bulletproof vest handy.'

Ronnie speared a haylage bale with the tractor's front spike, pushing down the lever to hoist it aloft before reversing from the Dutch barn. Climbing down from the cab to close the gate, she spotted the silhouetted heads of early morning riders moving along the ridge, a scarlet and salmon daybreak glowing behind them.

Despite the old shepherds' warning, she was in celebratory mood. Her bank account might be as red as today's dawn, but Compton Magna stud's brilliant new stallion sire, Bechstein, was passed fit – and sane enough – to stand here this season, had just been approved by the Anglo-European stud book and was starring in *Horse & Hound*'s sports horse breeding feature this week, which described Beck as 'the best-kept elite secret in Britain'. No surprise Paul Fuchs had sent a grovelling email asking to reopen negotiations. Now she just needed more bookings to breed future superstars.

Despite the early hour, her phone burst into life, which felt like a sign.

The stud's phones had been ringing a lot this week, dawn to dusk, the landline's outdoor klaxon cawing along with Ronnie's familiar jangling mobile ringtone, in regular use now that she'd learnt all the signal sweet spots in this patchy backwater. Up here by the Dutch barn was one. All phone calls were intercepted with a brisk: 'Compton Magna Stud, Ronnie speaking.'

Each time she prayed it was a mare owner, February being the traditional month the coming season's bookings started picking up. They must have seen one of the many listings she'd forked out on or heard on the grapevine about Beck's gold standard progeny emerging on the Continent.

But they all wanted to know the same thing.

'Lester back on his feet yet?' barked a proprietorial voice, and she recognized the outdated haw of neighbouring landowner, Sandy Austen.

Since breaking his hip out hunting some weeks earlier, stallion man Lester's recovery had become a hub of local interest, not least the shooting-vested interests of the Austen family, fellow country sports devotees with whom he was in close cahoots.

'He's not on his feet at this precise moment. At least, I hope not.' Ronnie glanced at her watch. It wasn't yet eight, midway through a busy morning in countryman time. Before his accident, Lester would have been found taking breakfast in his cottage at this hour after feeding and mucking out. Instead, he was in his temporary 'recovery suite' in the dining room of the main house, waiting impatiently for someone to bring him his first cup of tea, banished from making his own after a tumble down the steps into the kitchen corridor had set his recovery back.

'Viv's done him some homebaking,' Sandy said. 'Know what a sweet tooth the old boy's got – and there's a letter for you about this church roof committee. Bay will drop them in with you this morning.'

'Must he?' She looked heavenward. 'We're jolly busy.'

'Says he's got a little something for Pax.' He cleared his throat for emphasis. 'Insists on delivering it personally. I take it you know what's going on? He's awfully keen.'

Sandy was far too gallant to say it out loud. His newly single serial philanderer of a son was making a play for Ronnie's youngest and wildest daughter. Again.

Ronnie had grave reservations. Pax had been sheltering at the stud for barely two months since fleeing a toxic marriage, and was still extremely vulnerable, especially when it came to Bay's boundless charm.

'Thing is, Ronnie,' Sandy cleared his throat again, 'I'm calling to ask you not to encourage Bay to buy any more horses.'

'Does he want to buy more?' She pricked up her ears.

The Austens – who loved the owner's enclosure and sponsor's lunch – kept a yard full of show hunters and point-to-pointers, many of them bought from the Percys. There was always room for another, especially now Bay's Dutch wife had danced off with her dressage string, leaving plenty of empty stalls.

'The boy is all over the place, not thinking straight. Lester's been messaging him.'

'Oh yes, Lester's rather a whizz at that now.' She smiled to herself. Lester was rarely off his iPad, his Facebook friends a veritable *Who's Who* of the horse world. By contrast, Ronnie found most technology invasive, like the persistent pinging in her ear now telling her she had another call waiting.

'Bay's got a bee in his bonnet because Monique's taken the family trophy winners away,' Sandy went on, 'but with a costly divorce on the horizon, now's not the right time to fund competitive pastimes. He has some fanciful idea about owning a string of eventers and I won't see him throwing good money after bad.'

'No money is bad when you're in my position, Sandy,' Ronnie said brightly. 'And no Percy horse is bad either.'

She had no truck with men like Sandy pleading poverty, his diversified farming empire copper-bottomed and gold-plated – a far cry from the stud's tarnished reputation and rattling petty cash tin. She'd calculated they had enough money to last two months, tops, without some serious horse trading. If Bay wanted to buy her home-bred winners, she had no problem with that.

'Bay's grown up enough to make his own decisions,' she told him. 'Now, if you'll excuse me, I have another call waiting.'

She looked at her phone's screen, swiping away Sandy's name. Blair's craggy smile beaming from the thumbnail photo cheered her no end.

They'd been speaking several times a day since their night together in Vechta, their recent intense run of togetherness dangerously committed for a pair of lone wolves.

This evening was the special treat he'd booked from their hotel bed after too much sex and Sekt, another rare night together in store, and yet more reason for her early morning cheer.

His familiar gravelly voice was waiting like a comforting

hug, 'I can't talk long, Ron but—' the receiver was abruptly covered, a muffled conversation beyond.

As she waited, Ronnie wondered which of the current youngstock she could sell Blair Austen. Last year's crop was a mixed bunch, but one or two of the yearlings had exceptional class, like her favourite buckskin colt. That one wasn't for sale at any price, especially not to a player like Bay who undoubtedly just wanted to buy his way into Pax's knickers.

Ronnie watched a pair of buzzards circling noisily, knowing she was no one to play the hypocrite. Here she was on the phone to a man who had bought her favours when she'd needed them most – last year's purchase of half a dozen Compton stud youngsters was the reason they were still trading – and who continued to be the gravity around which she orbited.

He came back on the line. 'Don't go anywhere, I'll ring you right back. Lot going on here.'

Dropped calls were their leitmotif, the snatched conversations of adulterers.

She studied the red morning horizon, brighter orange now, young trees silhouetted like foot soldiers' pikes. Now she understood its warning.

Blair was going to cry off. She always knew.

She looked down at his photograph on screen again, that tiny badge she waited to light up all too often.

She couldn't afford to hang around for disappointment. There were horses to feed, Lester to tend to and Pax to check on.

Rejoining her dogs in the tractor cab, she roared down the track, far away from the phone signal.

'What d'you want to buy a place here for, Papi?'

'Are we nearly there?'

'Sat nav says two minutes.' Santiago Kay – known to all as Iago – was driving his father into the Cotswold village of

Compton Magna. With the Tesla headlights on full beam, they emerged from the tree canopy into a damp, grey dawn, pheasants scattering on the lane ahead. 'Where's the golf course?'

'There's a good one not far away, son. You like it round here? Pretty as a choc box, yeah? Tell me it still is?'

'It still is, Dad,' Iago reassured him, silently adding if you like ye olde worlde overload.

'Describe it!'

They were passing a long expanse of park railing guarded by a row of horse chestnuts, beyond which lay neat squares of grazing paddocks between hedges and drystone walls, chequerboarding up to a distant, grand house.

'I can see a lot of grass... and trees,' Iago ventured.

A lifelong wearer of dark glasses who regularly walked into the furniture when drunk, his father still made out to fans that he had twenty-twenty vision. Only his closest family, staff and colleagues knew that macular degeneration had reduced Kenny Kay's eyesight to a blurry kaleidoscope.

'Bet it hasn't changed a bit.'

'Yeah, it's out of the dark ages all right!' Like his Colombian mother, Iago preferred his homes – and clothes, cars and consorts – bespoke. 'Where are the serfs and oxen?'

'I'll buy a matching set of each when I move in,' Kenny chuckled, buzzing down the window to breathe in the scent of wet turf and old money.

Oak-skinned from overwintering in Key West, he'd been so excited about his new purchase that they'd driven straight here from Birmingham airport where Iago had met his father off an overnight flight. Unusually, he'd flown in alone, his American wife staying behind along with the couple's trusty PA. Apparently this was to nurse an elderly French bulldog who was at death's door, but Iago smelled trouble.

Kenny had been bragging non-stop about buying the house since shaking on the deal, phoning old friends he'd barely spoken to for years. Iago's mum insisted the silly old fool was trying to buy back the past.

'You know your godfather's coming over today? Just like that!' Kenny clicked his fingers, arthritic joints and heavy silver rings cracking. 'One call's all it took.'

'You told me.'

He smiled, smacking his lips. 'Only right.'

Iago barely knew his godfather, a shadowy character who had faded away after a childhood of birthday and Christmas cheques and a surprisingly generous severance payment at eighteen. He belonged to a past Papi had carefully rewritten in multiple interviews and two ghosted autobiographies.

'So why *do* you wanna live here, Papi?' he asked as they passed the entrance gates to the big house on the hill, poplars playing sentry either side of a long straight drive.

'I spent a lot of time here with Tina before I met your mother. Happy memories, son.'

Irritated, Iago said nothing, glancing at the sat nav as they closed in on the red flag. His mother had been Papi's second wife, as hot and bubbly as he was bone dry, their arguments legendary. In his memoirs, Kenny had credited the former beauty queen as the reason his career lasted so long 'to pay for the divorce'.

But it was the first Mrs Kay he eulogized as saint to his sinner. Tina Kay, who grew up in care with Kenny in the sixties, belonged to the same short opening chapters as Iago's shady godfather. Papi's rose-tinted memories of Tina – a childhood sweetheart he'd treated contemptibly when he'd ditched her after finding fame – were sacrosanct, their long estrangement adding yet more height to her pedestal. When Kenny had received news of her death, it had sparked a wave of lavish sentimentality, of which Iago suspected this property purchase was a typical nostalgic gesture. Kenny had not even viewed the place before making an offer.

'Prettiest house in the village, Compton Magna Manor,' he sighed. 'I used to go nought to sixty up its drive in my first

Ferrari. Drove the Captain nuts. He had beautiful horses. Tina loved horses.'

They were driving alongside a picture-postcard village green with thatched cottages prettily grouped to one side, a Victorian school with a belltower the other, a silver brooch of a duck-pond between.

'This is it,' Iago slowed as they rounded the corner to find the high walls in front of another grand-looking house, much like the one on the hill, engraved plaques on its limestone gateposts announcing The Manor.

Pulling up in front of its wrought-iron gates, he admired the big Georgian-paned windows. 'Sweet.'

Kenny lowered the car window further, gulping in air now. 'Tell me what you see! Proper doll's house, yes?'

'Yeah, it's certainly that.' Iago couldn't deny its kerb appeal. 'It got a back drive. Then? No way you'd get up to sixty on that gravel carriage circle.'

'What d'you mean?' Kenny was out of the car in a flash, fumbling his way to the gates to peer blurrily through them, hands gripping the bars.

Iago stepped out to join him 'You going to show me round, then?'

Kenny said nothing, face like thunder.

'It's a great-looking crib, Papi.'

The pause stretched on a long time before Kenny said, 'I heard the old bastard had died, heard there were money troubles. I thought the stud *was* the village bloody manor!'

Iago took a moment to twig. 'You saying you bought the wrong house?'

'Drive me home, son. I need some bloody kip.' His father turned wearily back to the car. 'This day can't get any worse.'

'You're meeting Pete, remember,' Iago reminded his father gently. His godfather was flying into the UK especially.

'*Now* it's got worse.'

★

The Bags and their horses were ambling slowly along the highest stretch of the ridge, a pink sun glowing alongside them now. Mo was eager for a change of pace and subject, but the others were still quizzing Gill about the time Kenny Kay had scandalized the village and the disastrous pheasant shoot that had ended in bloodshed. 'One of the beaters took a peppering, I believe.'

'Did he *die?*' Bridge looked up from her phone, starting to take an interest.

'I don't think anyone died,' Mo insisted, although she couldn't remember what her father has told her about it. It was so long ago. 'Is anybody doing anything nice tonight?'

'I'm sure I heard it was linked to underground crime,' Gill murmured.

'Gosh, how thrilling!' Petra's dark eyes stretched. 'And nobody knows what they were arguing about?'

'Money, probably.' Gill turned to look over her shoulder at the sound of an approaching helicopter.

'Or a woman?' Bridge suggested, turning too, the noise making her pony flatten its ears and bunch its back.

'All I know is Kenny took his stallions away from the stud the next day.' Gill had to raise her voice as the helicopter drew closer. 'My God, this chopper's low!'

'Traffic police I 'spect,' Mo looked up to find it was alongside them, blasting past in a downdraft that sent the horses spinning, its side emblazoned with a corporate logo shaped like a ribboned S.

There was a squeal up ahead. 'You OK, Bridge?'

'Hanging on!' The grey pony sprang in and out of a ditch, almost sitting down in shock.

'Too low!' Gill waggled her crop disapprovingly as the helicopter swept on. 'That's not traffic police, Mo!'

Petra stood up in her stirrups to look. 'It's heading for Eyngate Hall.'

'Not the only one!' wailed Bridge as her pony charged off.

'Turn him, Bridge! Pull the rein!' Gill boomed, giving chase, Petra on her heels.

By the time Mo caught them all up, Bridge had pulled up in a gateway, examining a crack on her phone screen. 'Feck. I only got this last month.'

'You really shouldn't use it while you're riding, love,' Mo chided breathlessly.

'At least I got a picture of that bastard thing flying past.' She held up a glowing, crazy paved rectangle. 'I'm going to share it to the village Facebook group.'

'Might stop them obsessing about the Travel Lodge Adulterer for five minutes,' sighed Petra, still watching the helicopter.

'Petra, we *agreed* not to mention that,' Gill muttered tightly, glancing at Mo and adding over-casually, 'because it's all total rubbish.'

'Course it is,' Mo said supportively.

The Comptons Facebook group had got increasingly out of hand of late, infiltrated by several suspiciously fake-sounding accounts that were spreading rumours based on spurious evidence, such as 'the married villager's car spotted regularly outside Evesham Travel Lodge'. Efforts to identify him were bordering on the defamatory. Petra's husband's name had cropped up more than once, outraging the loyal Bags, especially Mo, who didn't have much truck with social media.

'I'll also post the news about Kenny buying the manor, shall I?' Bridge suggested, thumb tapping on the screen. 'That'll move the conversation on for sure.'

Gill again glanced at Mo before giving gave a quick nod, 'Just don't attribute it.'

'Look – told you!' Petra was pointing a gloved hand as the helicopter came down to land across the valley at vast Regency pile Eyngate Hall. 'Surely it's not Peter Sanson himself?'

'*Sir* Peter,' Gill corrected.

'Another chuffing weekender.' Bridge was thumb-typing frantically.

'Peter Sanson never visits these days,' Mo pointed out. 'You must be mistaken.'

The Eyngate Estate had been owned by tax-exile leisure tycoon Peter Sanson for decades. Run as a visitor attraction and corporate events venue, he was rarely ever in situ, and then only for a few days' sport with clients. With the shooting season over and the house closed this winter to repair its storm-damaged roof, it seemed an unlikely choice for a Valentine's minibreak.

'I'm sure it's him!' Petra breathed. 'You saw the logo on the helicopter.' She had a fetish for cruel, land-owning squires, which Mo put down to writing racy bodice-rippers. That, and having a shabby husband.

She made a mental note to defrost Barry's favourite cottage pie for Valentine's supper, grateful for her husband's DIY-obsessed docility, even if she sometimes longed for a bit more passion. Or even a finished bathroom. Being swept off her feet into a beautiful fairy-tale house like Eyngate was best kept for fiction, she felt. Then she remembered something from the celebrity memoir she'd given Barry. 'Isn't Sir Peter an old friend of Kenny Kay's?'

Gill was already kicking her big bay back into canter. 'I predicted the suitors would start queuing up once Ronnie came back, didn't I?' she called over her shoulder triumphantly. 'Let's go down there and take a closer look!'

'What do you mean "*suitors*?"' Petra demanded, right behind her friend, divots splatting back at Mo.

'I must get home before Grace goes to school!' Mo pleaded, wiping them off. She'd had more than enough of the Bags' obsession with the lives of the Cotswolds elite for today.

'Come on, Mo!' Gill shouted back. 'It's only a tiny diversion if we go through Poacher's Coppice to the Three Mile Point!'

'It'll take ages!' she complained. 'I'm goi—'

'Stop, Craic, argh!' Bridge's pony charged in their wake, sending her phone flying. It landed neatly in the cleavage of Mo's padded gilet and started playing Dua Lipa.

'—home.' Plucking the phone out, Mo let Pie help himself the sparse grass growing in the centre of the track and tried to work out how to silence it.

Bridge had left Facebook open.

Beneath a pinned post on the village group about refuse collection was now an eighties photo of a big-quiffed Kenny Kay alongside a vintage one of Ronnie holding up an eventing trophy, captioned: OUR NEW LORD OF THE MANOR? TELL ME ABOUT IT, STUD.

'Bridge, you must take this down at once! It's libellous!' Trotting after them, she was already too far behind to be in earshot, Dua Lipa singing not to show up or go out. 'And how do I stop your phone playing music?'

4

Brrrrrrrrrrrrm, grrrrrrrrrrrrrrrrrrm, CLANK, CLUNK. Dogs barking. 'Fuck it!'

Pax wished her mother wouldn't always drive the tractor as though she was taking part in a demolition derby, especially around nervy, greedy youngstock.

Swallowing yawns, she spread her arms wide, keeping the stud's adolescent bachelor pack safely back in the covered barn while a new bale was lowered in their big feeder. Over winter, this lot were sectioned away from other herd members in one of the farm's modern broad-span buildings, a rumbustious gang of unbroken delinquents led by a wall-eyed buckskin colt already marked out by Ronnie as a future Olympian. A blingy dandy with his white face and legs, gold coat and black points, he was studying Pax with one clever blue eye, working out what fun was to be had.

She was half-watching Luca trying to guide Ronnie's increasingly wild attempts to drop the round bale on target, the swinging front loader threatening to decapitate him with each wrong approach.

'Almost there, Ronnie, my darling! Getting better!'

How could he be so *positive*?

When he'd arrived from Canada six weeks earlier, Luca O'Brien had been so Viking-like with his curling blond beard and mane, eyes green as water dragons and glacier white teeth that Pax had taken him to be an invading berserker. But he was far more urbane and polished than that. Now clean-shaven and close-cropped, he was such a multi-skilled lieutenant of modern yard management, even her punctilious military grandfather Captain Percy would have approved.

Watching the big bale swing round again, Pax wished he'd just jump in the cab and take over from her mother, his tractor skills far superior to Ronnie's clutch-crunching gung-ho.

The stud's visiting Irish pro did most things effortlessly, which was both deeply attractive and mildly infuriating. From breaking and riding the sharpest horses, to handling dangerous equipment and difficult clients, to coaxing Pax out of the blackest mindset, Luca O'Brian was God's ever-generous gift. As if it wasn't enough that he cooked like a dream and spoke several languages – all with a pronounced Irish accent – he played the fiddle on top. He undoubtedly matched up in bed, but Pax couldn't let herself go there in mind or body yet. Well, not in body at least.

They'd take it slowly, they agreed. He had another job to go to in summer. He was a rolling stone; she was her family's cornerstone. One day at a time.

But it was a hard ask. Harder still when she'd been amongst the very few to glimpse the wild beneath.

Like her, his calm perfectionism masked a far messier, more addictive psyche. Luca, the nomadic horseman, might travel light, but there was *a lot* of baggage in storage. They'd only unpacked a little so far. Enough to sense a dangerous synergy.

He'd left his heart on the floor in Canada; she was picking up the pieces of hers here. They both had addiction issues.

It had almost come as a relief to be warned off entering any serious new relationship by her divorce lawyer, Helen. 'I'd urge caution, given the other party intends to seek primary custody should the marriage not be reconciled, and that he intends to use your history of unsuitable relationships and alcohol dependence to support this.' Mack, who viewed her drinking as cause, not symptom, of the split, was already gunning for Luca, and in Helen's words, 'Your domestic situation with Mr O'Brien is open to interpretation.'

Yet Pax needed that rare understanding of a fellow addict, the support Luca brought. They'd vowed to quit drinking together, an honourable pact she was shakily upholding, determined to prove she could do it, not return to the dead water in which she'd tried to drown her pain, in the same way he'd washed up here on a tide of scuppered dreams. Luca was an exemplary lifeguard: kind, conscientious, eager to save lives.

'Careful!' he laughed, jumping back to save his own from a ton of fast-moving fodder bale. 'Left hand down, Ronnie, angel! Outta the way, Knott! Go to your mistress!'

Even Pax's young deerhound doted on him, bounding around him now, a streak of wiry grey adulation, heedless of the tractor.

She whistled Knott back and Luca glanced over his shoulder.

He also possessed the biggest, widest, warmest smile she'd ever encountered, a bright new dawn of a smile.

It blinded her sometimes. She watched the youngstock again, their presence soothing her. New beginnings amid familiar old souls.

Perhaps it was a deliberate contrariness that had led Pax to marry a man with no interest in horses. She'd run away from all this before meeting him, moving to London in her late teens, triggering her first uncontrolled downward spiral of dependence. At the time she'd believed it was Mack who had saved her, not spotting the downward spiral simply changing direction.

Estranged husband Mack disliked horses, the lifeblood that had fuelled her youth. The cure to her unhappiness, as it turned out.

Throughout her marriage, she'd missed being around horses so much it hurt. Yet whenever she'd tried to reach back to them, she'd been told, 'you canna risk hurting yourself, wee bird'; or 'it's too expensive'; or 'you're a mother now'. Or simply, 'You'll look like a fool, Tishy'.

Mack always called her Tishy, his pet foreshortening of Patricia. She hated it. Pax had been her name since infancy, the Percy family peacekeeper. Tishy was the wimp who did as she was told, who denied herself passion, who craved the scaffolding of his rigid rules, that protective cage to calm the wildness within, only to find herself drowning in vodka, ennui and self-loathing. Tishy was long gone. On horseback.

Luca called her 'Pax' or 'Pax, my angel' or 'Pax, *mo cuishle*' or 'Pax, *Tesoro*' or he just had to look at her and she knew he was thinking her name. He loved watching her ride. 'Pax, you superstar!'

The tractor slammed against the feeder as Ronnie misjudged her approach, making the youngstock around Pax spiral away in a cloud of flying straw.

'Almost!' Luca laughed good-humouredly.

How could he be so *patient*?

The little buckskin high-stepped back first, tail aloft.

Familiar butterflies took off in her belly, wings rapidly growing to a flock of birds.

Since the monstrous realization that her marriage was over, Pax had been pinging off the walls in need of something solid to rebound off. Somewhere to focus all this newfound energy and passion.

Now, from nowhere, she'd been ambushed by it.

The greatest surprise Pax had found from her marriage ending was the speed with which she'd plunged headlong in love again. During one of the most tumultuous periods in her life, she'd fallen just as deeply and wholeheartedly as the first time. She knew the dangers involved but couldn't help herself; it was high-grade addiction and appallingly ill-timed.

She understood from talking to divorced friends that the exhilarating liberation she felt since the separation was normal, the giddy life-saving joy along with its flipside of overpowering guilt, the bleak exhaustion of grief. But this insane, unstoppable love was a curveball.

Standing in the barn now, she closed her eyes and breathed in deeply: the earthy sweet smell of her happiest years. Of her greatest love, renewed.

Pax had fallen back in love with horses.

A warm breath at her ear made her turn; the dun colt was up close, eager to barge past to be first in line for the new bale. She picked up the hose that was filling the big drinking trough and he backed off, wall-eye playful, the stud's golden boy. He knew it, constantly pushing boundaries to test his brilliance. Like Luca, he was almost too good to trust. They both enchanted everyone, her included. But it was horses that had won her heart back first.

Pax was playing it down, determined to protect Kes, although mother and son now shared the same passion. Her son's was as shiny and new-formed as hers was an excavated, long-buried, jewel. Kes brandished his to everyone flamboyantly, whereas she only took hers out when alone. Watching them gave her goosebumps.

Bay had been right about her need for horses.

Pax was suddenly as besotted by them as she'd been at Kes's age. She could think of little else, talk of nothing else, dream of nothing else, this love she'd already won and lost and hadn't expected to ever welcome again. Yet it fought off all comers like a forcefield: her husband, who wanted to win her back; her first love who longed to woo her back; her new soulmate who had her back. This great, rekindled burning love overwhelming her wasn't for any of them.

The colt took advantage of her distraction to plunge towards her, eager to play rough with a quick attention-grabbing nip. Before he knew it, the sharp splash of cold water from a thumb-covered hosepipe hit him on the nose making him rear back, his expression indignant. They'd played this game before.

She squirted his hoof and he danced away, coiling and

spinning, showing her his hind feet as droplets arced after him.

Pax laughed.

She wanted to sing it at the top of her voice like Donna Summer, 'I Feel Love!'

There was a shout behind her. The tractor was wide of the mark again, a rev of the engine and more muffled expletives revealing Ronnie's frustration.

'*You* bloody well do it, Luca!' She clambered out of the cab.

At last.

Pax sensed that the boundless Ronnie Percy humour was stretched ever thinner these days, her mother on a constant hair-trigger. Theirs was not an easy relationship, mutual distrust shielded behind brittle British manners, the family's competitive streak running as close to their hearts as a pulmonary vein.

Ronnie was already stalking across, wearing her chin-up smile. 'How's my superstar doing?'

About to admit she'd felt better, Pax realized her mother was addressing the buckskin colt.

Then Ronnie bent down to greet Knott. 'Hello, beautiful!' Finally, she looked up at Pax, blue eyes expectant. 'Aren't you riding this morning? You should get going!' She glanced at her watch. 'I'd offer to join you but I've a mountain to do. Why not give Lester's chap a decent pipe-opener? Take as long as you like.'

Pax's mood lifted, surprised by her mother's largesse. Returning to the saddle was a pure oxytocin rush. She couldn't get enough of it, a natural high she'd forfeited for years.

She knew this wasn't entirely unexpected. The Cotswolds were full of unhappy wives reverting to the pony-mad girls they'd been before the opposite sex came along to break their hearts. Many women turned to horses when their relationships soured. Horses didn't know how to lie or be deceitful; they offered a safe salvation. They also gifted a cavalry of allied outriders; Pax's new friend Bridge kept trying to persuade her to join a group of local women she hacked out with, and

Ronnie was constantly entreating her to 'blow off the cobwebs' with her out on the nearby gallops.

But Pax had no desire to amble around the byways, bellyaching about her marriage. This renewed, all-encompassing love ignited the warrior in her, the girl who had survived the aftermath of her own parents' catastrophic marriage by becoming invincibly, unbeatably competitive. She preferred riding alone, the sound of thudding hooves a drumbeat that now ruled her heart.

With a rattle that made her jump, the bale landed on target, Luca swiftly reversing to release it before jumping out to unfold a knife and slice away its wrapping. She watched him, transfixed by how deft and practical he was, this fallen angel.

'He's good for you.' Ronnie was watching too. 'Just what you need. Safe and steady.'

Pax said nothing, not wanting her mother's opinion, although both knew that Luca had arrived with quite the opposite reputation.

'Have a bit of fun with him, I say. Won't dump you and run, that one.'

'He's hardly staying long!'

'Don't be silly, Lester will never part with him. And a smart little cob is perfect if you've really lost your nerve.'

Realizing a beat too late that her mother was still talking about Lester's trusty hunting companion, Pax muttered. 'I have *not* lost my nerve.'

'There's no shame in it. Plenty do.'

Luca was back in the tractor and driving it out into the yard, beckoning over his shoulder for them to follow, easy smile in place.

'He's good for you too,' Ronnie winked before striding out of the barn behind the tractor, her two little black-and-tan-heelers racing to catch her up, Knott disloyally loping after them in search of Luca.

Pax didn't move, letting the tractor engine fade away.

In the silence that followed, the colt stepped closer again, blue eye gleaming, respectful of her now, but no less eager to be first to the new bale.

'I wish you were older,' she told him.

I do too the blue eyes agreed. Then his black ear tips pricked sharply together.

For a moment she let her thoughts drift to Bay, who alone had read her mind and offered help. But that way lay danger.

Luca was calling her name from the main yard.

She stayed still and silent a moment longer, breathing in horse and love, revelling in its secrecy. Not even Luca knew what was in her head night and day, this all-consuming desire to prove herself, to find her lost soul and to be a winner again. He'd laughed when she'd told him about Bay's offer, telling her she must surely see right through it, as though she hadn't already, as though she didn't keep looking and finding herself back at seventeen, wondering what she might have become.

The colt stamped, losing patience, eyeing up which bit of her to bite first. Fight, flight and greed ruled him.

Waving him past with an indulgent smile, Pax waded out of the straw, letting the young herd charge, kicking and nipping, to the new bale, headstrong and impulsive.

Horses were the only things that made sense to her right now. The only thing she trusted.

Lester rang his bell. No answer. He rang it once more. Nothing.

The old service door from the dining room was open, its facing baize threadbare, the scrubbed steps beyond it leading down to corridors through which a small team of soft-soled staff would once have hurried. He'd heard Ronnie clomp back into the house several minutes ago, heavy footed in yard boots – the old Captain would have had a fit at them not being taken off in the boot room – then the dogs being fed, the kettle going on, the *Today* programme on Radio 4.

He rang the bell again, and again heard no response.

The confounded thing had been her idea in the first place, mimicking the bells that had last rung from upstairs to downstairs in the bygone era of house parties and hunting between the wars.

'I'm here!' She appeared, bearing a mug of tea, her small dogs and Pax's gangly young hound scrapping underfoot, his own fox terrier Stubbs growling territorially from beside his master's bed.

'At last,' Lester growled too.

'You rang?'

Even in her fifties, Ronnie possessed the same whipcrack energy of the girl he'd taught to ride as a tot. Fearless and indefatigable, she marched everywhere at a forward tilt. An outdoors life full of laughter had cross-hatched her pretty face with lines, but her eyes remained the same fierce blue as the Spode her mother had once hurled at walls after disagreeable dinner party guests had finally departed.

Although Ronnie had made it clear she preferred it if Lester stayed put, he felt ridiculous lying here in a loaned hospital bed like a wounded warrior. He could get up and dress himself adequately enough, and even perform his physio exercises – albeit slowly and with discomfort – and there was a downstairs lavatory within a short, crutch-swinging walk that mercifully didn't require navigating stairs. But some things were beyond his control.

'The signal box has stopped working.' He pointed at it.

'It's called a Wi-Fi router, Lester. And not again!'

Lester regarded her boots with disapproval as she marched across to it. The tablet Pax had given him to keep him occupied had stopped responding midway through the *Express*'s online quick crossword, its screen frozen on eight down: *Harbinger of change, upstirred (anag)*, to which he'd been typing STIRRUPED.

At Pax's insistence, the Internet had finally arrived at the stud earlier that month, dragging the last village outpost out of the dark ages. Its box of tricks had been installed right here in the dining room in Lester's honour, a small black plastic 'router'. Wary at first of technology, he would have preferred it out of sight, but it seemed that the contraption was designed for more modest properties and could broadcast its magic signal no further than the four thick, wood-panelled walls of this room. It also regularly cut out completely, its arc of green light turning red, as now.

Ronnie regarded it with suspicion. 'Can it wait? Pax should be in soon.'

'She powered it off and on last time, I believe.'

'Very well.'

Lester had been introduced to the world wide web in hospital by a neighbouring patient who, identifying his tipster potential, had taught him to navigate BetFred.com on an iPad. To Lester's surprise he was something of a natural techie, swiftly mastering *Horse & Hound* online, stud book registers and something marvellous called Facebook, on which he kept abreast of the goings on in the village and hunt. Now home and confined to barracks, Lester's newfound world was a revelation. Until the magic box's green lights turned red.

Ronnie switched the socket on and off at the wall, and they both watched as the router's lights gave them a brief disco show of purple, blue and orange. Then the tablet started pinging with notifications and STIRRUPED was rejected.

Ronnie headed towards the door. 'Two rounds of toast and coarse-cut marmalade, yes?'

'Not burnt this time.' He swiped down to read his incoming messages, not realizing that she'd turned back to study him.

'Lester, are you trying to sell Bay one of our horses?'

'Not as such.' He didn't look up.

'Then I don't think you should be encouraging him to interfere here.'

His eyes stayed fixed on his screen. It wasn't his place to point out that Bay Austen was a horseman, countryman and superb businessman who had revived his own parents flagging farm's fortunes, making him a good man to have on side.

Ronnie wasn't unusually a sentimentalist; practical and fiery tempered like her father, she was a doer not a thinker. Then again, Percys were unforgiving sorts with long memories.

'Pax needs time to settle,' she went on, making her sound like a mare, not a daughter.

Lester privately thought Ronnie far more likely to bolt off again than Pax. Pax might share her mother's hot head – Lester considered her romantic dalliance with the new Irish yard manager Luca over-hasty for a start – but she also had an organized mind, her father Johnny's instinct for breeding and the Percy genius for competing.

'She needs to ride,' he told Ronnie.

'She *is* riding. She's about to take your cob out for a spin.'

'Out campaigning again, I mean. Crying shame she stopped so long, if you ask me.' He'd never forget the sight of Pax blazing across country at full pelt as a teenager, unbeatable in the saddle. Less of a showboater than Ronnie, she'd been capped as a Junior by fifteen, representing Team GB all over Europe in coming years, taking bronze in the Europeans as part of the Young Riders squad. Had she stuck with it, Lester had no doubt she'd have gained the stud its first Olympic ticket. She still might, if he had his way.

'And we know who put her off her stride last time.' Ronnie was saying. 'Bay Austen is trouble.'

He waited. He knew she'd ask.

'What sort of horse is he looking to buy?' Oh so casual, but she couldn't stop herself, so like her dad.

'Established eventer, I believe. Fit and ready to run. Must be top class.'

'We don't *have* one of those!'

'I thought Mr Robertson might be able to help?'

'You've taken leave of your senses, Lester!' She was already a Percy firework. 'Bay's playing with you. You're no horse broker.'

Lester might view Bay Austen as more ally than enemy – and

the stud needed as many of those as it could get right now – but he knew better than to take on Ronnie in this mood. 'If you say so.'

'I do say so.'

He eyed his screen mutinously, switching tabs from crossword to Facebook and starting in recognition. 'What was the name of that fellow who stood showjumpers here back in the seventies? Had a couple of big international sires.'

'Plenty of top horses stood here then, Lester.'

Lester peered at the tableau, in very poor taste, which some joker had posted on the village page.

'This one owned more than most. Young gentleman from Birmingham. Presented popular quiz shows on the television and did a bit of vaudeville. Took quite a shine to you, as I recall.' More than that. The man had hung off her every smile, Lester recalled. They all did, then.

She looked surprised, this skeleton not one she'd been expecting. 'Ghastly bubble perm and Page Three wife? Lenny something? He and Daddy fell out terribly badly over money.'

'Could it be Kenny Kay?'

'That's it! Goodness, I haven't thought of him for years. Is he still alive?'

'He's something of a film actor now.' Lester reread the Facebook notification twice more. 'It seems he's moving into the village.'

'What luck!' Her smile was too bright, fireworks still blazing in them. 'Then we must invite him for a drink.'

'Your father took against him, you'll recall.'

'And the rest,' she dismissed this with an amused huff.

He looked up sharply. She remembered more than she was letting on. They both did.

'I'll make your toast,' she said defiantly, turning on her heel to march back out before he could remind her that whenever Kenny had visited Compton Magna in the past, Peter Sanson was seldom far behind.

Swiping the message away to return to his crossword, he unscrambled the word in front of him: *Harbinger of change*, DISRUPTER.

Peter Sanson, a lifelong science fiction fan, liked to envisage himself a captain at the helm of a great spaceship orbiting ever wider, leaving stations and satellites behind as monitors and markers, his business interests now a multi-faceted global empire. While his world now revolved at a far greater distance and speed to that of the sleepy villages which dotted the northernmost crease of the Cotswolds, his UK team was briefed to keep close tabs on all his assets there. Sanson Holdings owned great swathes of the profitable agricultural land surrounding the Comptons, along with their one-time feudal bastion, Eyngate Hall. That team was supremely efficient, as he'd just discovered. They even watched the local Facebook group.

Standing in front of his Palladian showstopper with the snazzy folding tablet his assistant had just passed him, his face gave nothing away as he read the page text, but his mood lifted as though the eighteenth-century limestone steps sweeping up in front of him were an escalator. Handing it back, he stooped to pick up the large jar at his feet before climbing them two at a time.

'Always said he was half-soaked,' he told it, using an affectionate Brummie term for slow-witted they'd shared at kids.

The Eyngate Hall Estate was one of the worst investments Peter had ever made, yet he still held a grudging affection for the place and the lessons it had taught him. He'd only ever bought it for a bet, after all.

The wager was one that still stood forty years later, which was why he was waiting here under the portico, afforded the best view of its long parkland drive, waving away offers of coffee or a warm seat inside the house.

The house had always bothered him. He disliked seeing

such a magnificent place reduced to a passing stop-off for the tea and wee brigade, its green Exit signs glowing alien amid the splendour. He still remembered the power he'd felt buying it, the sheer indulgence of having his own country estate. Its ownership had transferred overnight from the aristocratic family it had belonged to for over three hundred years to his, Pete Sanson, the boy from Brum.

For a bet.

He'd reclaimed the 'r' in Peter after that. It felt grander, more in keeping.

They'd met as kids, Pete, Kenny and Tina. They went to the same schools and lived in the same children's home between foster placements. Having grown up uncertain whether the roof over their heads would last until their next birthdays, the three friends had formed childhood attachments to the houses in the battered Ladybird fairy-tale books Tina loved. No wonder she'd fallen for the picture-postcard stud at Compton Magna the moment she'd set eyes on it, like a child with a doll's house. All those windows! All those acres! The beautiful horses! She'd wept for wanting it.

When nearby stately pile Eyngate had come up for sale with even more windows and more acres, Kenny had dared Peter to make an offer.

'Now *that's* a real dream house!' Kenny had told him. 'I haven't got the readies, but you do. Proper princess palace that. Can't you just see our Tina running down them stairs like Scarlett O'Hara?'

Theirs had remained the closest of trios even after Kenny and Tina wed. They were Peter's unofficial family: his brother and sister, his parents, his children. He shared Tina's birthday which she said made them 'astral twins'. Moneymaking came easy to Peter – from teenage protection rackets to running boxing gyms, opening sports centres then hotels – but making friends confounded him. It was always just Peter, Kenny and Tina, like a sixties singing trio. He'd been best man at their wedding, had chauffeured for Kenny through his early gigs, held Tina's hands through each nail-biting round of *Opportunity Knocks*, provided Kenny with alibis for the sleazy affairs after fame went to his head. He could deny them nothing. He even invested in a princess palace to make Tina happy because Kenny suggested it and she deserved it. And because he liked spending money. Also showing off.

And because he secretly thought it might make her love him more than Kenny.

But when Peter had bought Eyngate – three thousand acres of prime Cotswolds that had once belonged to the wealthiest arm of the Percy family, with a slab of Grade I listed stately pomp in the middle – Tina hadn't loved it as much as expected. It was bigger and far fancier than the stud, more like the mansions in those Ladybird fairy tales, and yet...

'It's just all so very *grand*,' she'd explained. Its imperious ghosts made her anxious – links to slavery, patrician rule of an entire village, lavish Edwardian decadence and even rumours of wartime sympathy for Hitler. 'They weren't nice Percys like the Captain and his missus, although the park's pretty.' She'd loved Eyngate's wildlife, especially its lake where rare wildfowl flocked, but the house's high, gilded ceilings and sprung ballroom floor intimidated her. 'Reminds me of them fancy hotels Kenny likes, all long corridors and velvet bell pulls.' Secretly, Peter felt the same, disliking its rococo excess and endless stairs, remembering too late that Scarlett O'Hara had fallen down the ones at Tara and lost her baby. Tina's childlessness was something they never spoke about, although he sensed her sadness.

Kenny might have married Tina, but it was Peter who felt her pain most acutely, like a twin. An astral twin.

Not that either man had understood what made Tina happy back then. They'd been too obsessed by glittering trophies, ignoring the precious human one under their own noses. Kenny had bought her horses as child substitutes and played pranks to cheer her up.

By snapping up the nearby estate from impoverished aristos, Peter had become the fall guy for one such practical joke. How Kenny had laughed, unaware that he'd just sown the seed of an idea that would one day take his friend's business to whole new heights. Peter had subsequently become a master at stately home reinvention, creating luxury golf spa hotels worldwide. Eyngate alone remained a commercial flop, a memorial to an unsettled wager.

He was legally limited on making changes to Eyngate, even if he wanted to. Until today.

'It's all about faking it, isn't it?' he told the urn in his arms. 'Having the last laugh?'

A car was making its way along the drive, unexpectedly modest and white. Nothing like the roaring penthouses on wheels they'd driven back then.

A drunken day of celebration had followed his purchase of Eyngate. Peter had driven his custom Range Rover up to Compton Magna to drink in the pub with his trio, his brother-in-arms Kenny, wise-cracking artful dodger to his hard-nut straight man, and gentle, astral twin Tina who knew what a soft touch he was under the glower.

From an early age, Peter's quiet watchfulness had been mistaken for thuggery, and he'd done nothing to dispel that myth then or now. A surly reputation matched his unblinking Brando snarl better than lifelong social awkwardness. A poker face and a quick mind had its advantages. It was only when drunk that he metamorphosized into a hellraiser, although that was nothing to Kenny's gregarious party animal, especially in the eighties when fame and money had brought a lawless sense of entitlement.

'This is your new overlord!' Kenny had introduced Peter to the unimpressed lunchtime drinkers at The Jugged Hare that day, who had perked up when he announced: 'The drinks are on us!'

They'd liked having him around back then, before it all went wrong. Before shotguns and curses and local posh totty, and the rift that meant he and Kenny had barely spoken in decades.

He watched the white car sweep into the carriage circle, now recognizing it as a Tesla X, no doubt fully loaded. Typical of Kenny to go space-age eco-tech. He'd been the first man Peter knew to own an Italian supercar; Peter had been the second.

He'd all too often been second to Kenny.

But he was one step ahead of him today.

He glanced at the waiting helicopter, then back to the carriage sweep where the car had stopped at a distance from the steps, idling there, the music booming inside faintly discernible – an old two-tone track if he wasn't mistaken. Peter sensed gameplay, but he'd already planned for it. Today had been a long time coming.

Surprised by the hammering pulse in his neck, he pulled his scarf tighter, clutching the big metal jar to his chest and made his descent with a brief nod of acknowledgement in the Tesla's direction before crossing straight onto the parkland that swept down to the lake. Behind him, his PA hurried to the car to welcome Kenny and brief him to follow.

It was twelve years since they'd last met. The boys who had been inseparable growing up now communicated through assistants, and then only rarely. All attempts at rapprochement had failed. Even this much-postponed duty was born more of rivalry and brinkmanship than honour.

Which made it unfortunate that, at the precise moment they faced one another for the first time in over a decade, wind ruffling the lake's surface, a whiff of Spaghetti Western in the cold February air, four riders came thundering out of a nearby woodland track at full pelt.

'Morning!' they called and charged on by, turned a ragged loop by the boathouse and then charged back.

The lead rider on the biggest, darkest horse – a tall figure with a furry bobble on her helmet silk like a tethered chinchilla – seemed inclined to stop and say hello, only realizing at the last minute what he was holding, her face tightening into an apologetic grimace as she ushered her outriders onwards, passing him by with a polite nod of the head.

Peter nodded back.

They thundered away, the rider at the rear – a small, dumpy woman on something hairy that looked as if it should pull a gypsy caravan – playing loud pop music from a coat pocket.

The encounter put Peter off his stroke. He wasn't superstitious, but Tina was, and this felt oddly like her idea of a joke. He patted the urn lid to reassure himself all was good. They were all playing tricks today.

Standing beside him, Kenny cocked his head, saying nothing. He'd been helped across the grass by his son with funereal steadiness. Wearing very dark glasses and a leather jacket, his teeth chattering, he looked out of place and faintly ridiculous amid a sweeping landscape once designed for Regency bucks to take the air. Not that Peter's cashmere coat and business suit was much better, his trousers hems sucking up the wet grass like mop ends. They'd never fitted in around here, either of them.

But they had both loved Tina. And Tina had loved it out here by the lake, surrounded by wildlife, her back to the house she found too big. What had once divided them now united them.

'You ready?' he asked.

'As I'll ever be, eh, Iago?'

Kenny's beefcake son had his arm around his dad's shoulders. Peter resented his presence, but knew it wasn't the occasion to say so.

'Let's get this over with.' He led the way onto a fishing pontoon on the edge of the lake. 'We'll see her off in style.'

Kenny followed, helped by his son.

Peter levered the lid off the urn. He wasn't sure what the protocol was, having never scattered ashes before, nor was he sure how many ashes 'made up' a human. He peered inside hoping it was about right, then held it out to Kenny like a jar of roasted peanuts.

Kenny ignored him.

Two swans came gliding over to investigate in case they were about to throw food.

'Take some, then,' Peter urged, still holding out the urn.

'The ashes, Dad.' Iago nudged his father who bent down and peered very closely at the container before feeling his way to a handful. Peter took one afterwards and threw them across the water like a puff of cigar smoke.

'Bye, Tina love,' he said gruffly, wishing he'd got his team to find a poem to read out, a bit of Shakespeare or the Romantics. A song lyric, even. Her favourite had been 'Leaving on a Jet Plane' by Peter, Paul and Mary, but it didn't seem quite fitting

'Goodbye, my darling girl,' Kenny's voice choked up as he threw a handful, big rings glittering. 'Now at least we know the kettle's always on in Heaven.'

The beefcake son chuckled, then shut up as he took in his father's pinched face, grief bleaching the Florida tan.

Kenny cleared his throat, magnanimous in mourning. 'It's good of you to look after her all these years, Pete.'

Peter gave a grunt of acknowledgement.

'Bet she loved living in your villa in the South of France. Were you there much?'

'Not much. She had her cats.'

'The allergy cleared up then?'

He gave another grunt.

'She didn't suffer, you say?'

'Very peaceful, mate. She just slipped away.' It wasn't entirely a lie.

'You were like a brother to her, Peter.'

'Astral twin,' he reminded Kenny.

'Yeah, and I was her husband.' The rejoinder was less noble.

'Even though she never wanted to talk to you again after the divorce.'

'Give us that urn again,' Kenny snapped, bending over and feeling for it.

'You have trouble seeing, Ken?'

'I could always see straight through you.'

Swallowing, Peter said nothing as they both took another handful of ashes each.

'Can't believe she's gone,' Kenny muttered, cupping his between his hands. 'She don't feel dead, somehow.'

Peter tensed, hoping he wasn't going to ask any more awkward questions or make a scene.

Kenny raised his clenched hands close to his mouth, addressing the ashes as though cupping a small bird. 'You said you'd always love me, no matter how mean I was to you. And I *was* mean. But I always loved you too, bab. You were my wench.'

When he released them, as though letting the bird take flight, the ashes mostly fell on him, and he chuckled, brushing them from his hair, shoulders and chest. 'Now she really is getting on my tits.'

Again, the son laughed, again he was silenced as Kenny repeated, 'She don't feel dead. It's like she's still here.' He banged his fist against his chest. 'Give us that urn, Pete.'

Gritting his teeth, Peter handed it across, saying nothing. He worried Kenny might say something about the lack of ashes – just his style to crack a joke about his first wife never putting on an ounce of weight – but he did something far more unexpected. Handing the urn to his son for safekeeping, he took a plastic ziplock bag from his pocket, the sort used on flights. Thrusting his other hand deep back into the urn, he extracted a fistful of ashes which he deposited into it and sealed inside.

'We both know where her heart belongs so I'll keep this safe,' he said gruffly, pocketing the bag and handing the urn back to his son, then patting his hands together to remove the dust before turning away ungraciously.

'She wanted you and me to put the past behind us, Ken,' Peter hissed.

'Too late for that. Iago!' He set off unsteadily across the grass, the hulking son thrusting the urn back to Peter like a ticking bomb before hurrying after him.

Peter wondered if that that rhino hide was finally cracking, but when he looked over his shoulder, Kenny had his mobile phone pressed to his ear, barking into it, hulk at his side.

He took his time emptying the remaining ashes from the urn, watching his debt to her flutter away over the water like a thousand tiny insects. *At last.*

Now he could finally do what he wanted with Eyngate, the house he'd bought in error. Perhaps he wasn't the only one to do so.

When he turned again, Kenny and Iago had almost reached the high-tech car, its back doors lifting like bizarre bird wings. For a moment, Peter imagined it undocking from the space station to fly to another galaxy.

He marched back towards the house after them, calling, 'Your message said you'd bought the stud, not the manor!'

Kenny stopped, chin lifting, 'I bought the best-looking house in the village.'

Peter closed in on them, trouser hems so heavy with dew he was walking like John Wayne. 'You're really moving here?'

'Comes with its own title, does the manor.' Decades of smoking and carousing had given Kenny's trademark chuckle a death rattle. 'Cost less than your gong and no Tory decorated his flat with my hard-earned money.'

Peter bristled, resenting the implication that his knighthood had been bestowed for being a big Tory party donor, even though it had.

'You didn't say you were getting a title, Papi?' The son was back-slapping Kenny, almost knocking him straight into the car.

'They have long memories round here, Ken,' Peter warned. 'They won't welcome you back.' He thought about the

Facebook page he'd just seen. 'You were warned to stay away, remember?'

'Take more than some phony gypsy curse to scare me. And that old bastard at the stud got what he wanted. *Over my dead body* was what Captain Percy said.' Kenny climbed in the back of the Tesla with some difficulty. 'Guess what? He's dead.'

'Tina believed all that curse stuff, you know.' Peter laid it on thick.

'Yeah, well she's dead too. Comes to us all soon enough.' He patted the pocket with the ziplock bag in it, but his face was even whiter.

'What curse, Papi?' The beefcake turned round in the car.

'Don't get me started!' Kenny's short fuse had already burnt out, his breathless fragility exposed as he slumped, grey-faced, against the leather upholstery. 'Your mama was bad enough with her Holy Water and keepsakes. Well, Tina was worse.'

'Like a witch's curse?'

'Got on the wrong side of the locals, your godfather and me. Long time ago, son,' Kenny huffed, looking out at Peter who crossed his arms and huffed back, wondering which version of the truth they were up to now.

'A serious curse?' Iago demanded again.

'Stuff and nonsense,' Kenny chuckled disparagingly. He pulled off his gloves, exposing the middle finger on his left hand, which was foreshortened at the first knuckle, emphasised by a chunky gold ring. He held it up to Peter. 'They've already got their piece of me, so I'm not bothered by all that hocus-pocus. The Manor will be my Taj Mahal for Tina. I promised I'd buy her a beautiful gaff here one day and now I have.'

'Gaffe being the operative word,' sneered Peter, 'seeing as you've got the wrong house.'

'Touché.' Kenny laughed gruffly. 'And you bought this castle in the sky, remember?'

Peter glanced up at Eyngate's big Regency face. 'Well, you kicked the ladder away.'

'I'm glad you never turned this place into a jumped-up leisure resort like the others,' Kenny sneered, 'especially now I'm a local. Lowers the tone.'

The son looked startled, 'But you practically live at the Ocean Reef Club, Dad.'

'I'm a country squire now, son,' Kenny told him. 'I've hung up my nine iron. And Florida's too bloody hot and sticky. Your old dad's always fancied retiring round these parts. I was always happy coming here.' He waved a hand vaguely, and again Peter sensed his vulnerability, the shadow of old age darkening.

He stooped down until his eyes were level with Kenny's sunglasses. 'You're making a mistake, Ken. She's gone. We just scattered her on the lake. Find your happy place somewhere else, you old fool.'

'Don't talk to my dad like that!' Iago demanded from the front.

'Ignore him, son.' Kenny's dark glasses had slipped down his nose and just for a moment, before he pushed them back up, Peter caught sight of his eyes, their denim blue now faded to palest stonewash, watery and unfocused. 'Close the doors. I have her heart, Pete, don't forget. Always did.'

The Tesla's wings folded down.

Harrumphing and turning away, Peter heard the window lower behind him with a high-tech purr.

'I take it the bet's still on?' Kenny called.

'It was never off.' Peter smiled to himself. He kept walking, beckoning for his assistant.

'Change of plan,' he told her as he strode back to the helicopter, wet hems spraying, 'we're going to London. Call ahead and tell them to get my suite ready.'

'How long shall I tell them you're staying, Sir Peter?'

He glanced to the silent white car snaking away along the drive. He'd give Kenny a curse to think about. 'As long as it takes to get permission to transform this place into the biggest golf and spa resort in Europe.'

5

Pax notched up the girth buckles, avoiding Luca's direct gaze as he asked if she'd slept at all last night.

'I'm fine.' She led Lester's cob from his stable, looking up as a helicopter rattled into view, climbing out of the next valley and sweeping past alarmingly low before racing away to the south-east.

He followed her to the mounting block. 'You look done in.'

'Flatterer.' She pulled down the stirrups, her nerve ends popping, in need of clear air and speed. Luca, all warmth and touch, earthed her wildness in something far too tempting and carnal for early mornings.

'Even done in, you're beautiful, my fire-haired harpy.' He reached out to tuck an escaped corkscrew of it under her helmet harness and Pax ducked her head away so fast she cricked her neck.

She had issues around having her hair touched. When she and Mack had first married – in the brief glow before he'd set about destroying her self-esteem, his hapless child-wife – he'd been fond of tucking her curls behind her ears with fatherly care. Now the gesture was like an electric shock.

'It needs washing,' she said, covering up.

'At least let me come along too. I can be on Beck in five minutes. He could use the work.'

'I'm good.' She wished he'd grasp that, unlike his, her addictions were solitary ones.

'Staying focussed on your international comeback?' he teased.

'Gold medals and grand slams, here we come!' She played along.

It was easy to joke about Lester's masterplan, although Luca seemed to find it much funnier than she did. 'I'll come and screw your studs in at Badminton.'

'You'll be halfway across the world, sitting on million-Euro horses again by then.'

'I might sell you one now you've found a rich backer.' He was teasing her about Bay Austen again.

She'd told Luca that all Bay's idle talk of sponsoring her comeback on his home-bred mare was just hot air, but it was hot air that nonetheless made her flush when he ribbed her about it. It didn't help that the stud farm's old stallion man was so caught up by the notion of her competing again, he was already planning her campaign.

'Lester is getting a syndicate together,' she told him, before admitting, 'which so far is just Bay trying to get his hands on this farm. Or on me,' she added, to stop him smiling so affably.

It didn't work. His green eyes sparkled on. 'Sure, it takes rich dreamers to back horses.'

'You don't mind?'

'That Bay's rich? As long as the horses get fed, I don't care who's paying the bills.'

Pax sensed the Horsemaker had said it often in his career, just as he'd made women feel beautiful just by smiling at them.

'That he's trying to buy my affection?' She played his flirtatious tone back, his lack of jealousy a novelty after years of Mack's possessiveness.

'You're way out of his price range, angel.' He tilted his head to admire her climb up onto the mounting block. 'And not very affectionate.'

'I *am* affectionate! Come here!' She put her arms round him, the height advantage from standing on a mounting block turning her into the BFG.

'I was hoping for something more sensual,' he complained into her coat pocket.

'I've been legally advised against conducting romantic relationships, remember?' She'd told him her solicitor's advice. 'No ships allowed apart from championships.'

'Sure.' He grinned up at her, eyes no less lively. 'It's Lester who scares me. He'll stop at nothing to have you back here for good, winning pots, so he will.'

'Don't laugh at him.' Or at me. 'I know it's a pipe dream but he needs to think happy thoughts right now.'

'Hey, I'm smoking that pipe too. We all are, even Kes.' He cast her a joshing look as he walked to the cob's offside to hold the stirrup, and she felt grateful that Luca – who was so good at everything, from flirting to sleep – was so adept at lifting her mood.

'Kes is five,' she reminded him, 'so no pipe-smoking.'

'Not even a bubble pipe?'

'Isn't that a crack cocaine thing?'

'It's a popular children's toy, Pax.'

Her smile turned into a yawn and his playful look turned into a wise one. He knew that Pax's determination to put Kes first was making her conflicted about competing again. He also knew she suffered crippling insomnia on the nights Kes stayed with his father, leaving her brittle with tiredness on mornings like this. It was always Luca who sensed the razor blades scratching her skin.

'Bad dreams again?'

'No, honestly, none!' The truth was she hadn't been asleep long enough.

It wasn't that she thought Mack would do anything foolish anymore. The threats to take their son home to Scotland with or without her permission had now stopped thanks to the calm, firm intervention of Helen Beadle. Having grudgingly accepted that she was six weeks sober and counting, Mack had dropped the hard line that she was an unfit mother, saying he wanted what was best for Kes too.

The powerplay over money and assets didn't frighten her either. Her recent meeting with Helen had just left her more single-minded than ever that Mack wouldn't intimidate her anymore, news of his dirty tricks barely quickening her heartbeat, certainly not compared to her one-twenty-beats-per-minute encounter with Bay afterwards.

Yet her eyes stayed pinned open in the early hours by the runaway conviction that she alone had torn their child's life in two, a worry bead she played back and forth like a tumorous lump until dawn. To cope, she did what she'd done since childhood. She forced those eyes to close tight and she galloped in her mind. Galloped and galloped and galloped.

But it was only when she did it for real that she could truly shake off the demons.

Luca watched her swing into the saddle.

While her demons still clung to her back, he'd outraced his. He had left a dark part of his heart behind in Canada, where his relationship with married Meredith had been secret and destructive, a stop–start deception lasting years. Their daughter Dizzy, not much older than Kes, had no idea who her real father was. To cope, Luca threw himself into his job, big-hearted and industrious. And devoted his kindness and attention to Pax.

He fell in step beside her as she rode towards farm track. 'I'll make breakfast for when you get back. Need you competition fit.' He reached up a hand up to give the cob's neck a pat.

Luca was big on breakfast. Her stomach grumbled at the prospect of warm soda bread piled high with roasted cherry tomatoes.

He let his hand trail back to her leg and kept it there, warm and reassuring.

Luca was also big on touch.

'Loosen your knee when you gallop,' he suggested, giving her leg a shake to demonstrate. 'Your lower leg keeps slipping back.'

He was big on wise advice.

Bending down until her eyes were level with his, she drank in their greenness. 'You're too good to me.'

'I know.' He took her red ponytail in his hand, tugging it gently, eyes smiling into hers. 'Get some wind in this.'

Pax determinedly didn't react. So, people always treated her hair like a lapdog. There was a lot of it, Cavalier spaniel red. If Luca had hair like this, she'd touch it. It was harmless, just like kissing him was no more than a friendly peck, especially from horseback.

The belly flip of it was still a novelty that took her by surprise each time. Then he kissed her back and it revolved like a wind spinner.

'No ships,' she reminded him, sitting up guiltily, annoyed at herself.

'Sure, there's not even a dinghy going on here.'

'Nor a kayak.'

'Not even a pedalo.'

'Paddleboard?'

'No. So put that in your bubble pipe and smoke it.'

Oh, that smile! That smile was a thousand ships...

Pax's friends told her Luca O'Brien was just what she needed – a breezy, refreshing romantic detox with little risk of long-term complications. Ride the wave, they said. Love doesn't have to be long-term.

But they knew nothing of those dark demons the two of them shared, or that she often felt as though she was braced on a clifftop, staring out to sea, the future a storm. Nor did they know that her first love was still washing in and out like the tide, foghorn sounding, lighthouse flashing and Land Rover roaring.

They could hear the car engine on the stud's drive beyond

the barns, a deep, throaty diesel familiar from the village lanes – Bay.

'Here comes the affections shopper.' Luca's gaze held hers. His face, all clean-cut angles and laughter, showed no flicker of concern.

She badly needed to gallop, her insides churning. 'Do you mind if I don't hang around?'

'Sure.' Still he smiled. 'I'll sell him my affection instead.'

Pax felt a sting of resentment that he was so dismissive of Bay, who often haunted what dreams she had.

'Thank you. I'd do the same for you if it was Meredith.'

His green eyes blackened at once.

Pax found she had to test it sometimes, like a safety catch. His ex's name was the only thing guaranteed to stop that smile in its tracks.

The cob was already jogging, accustomed to their routine. She barely had to touch his sides before they bounded away across the empty top field towards the hunt jump that led into the woods and on towards the three-mile point.

And one by one they all fell away: the terrors, the self-hatred, the neediness, the disappointment, the grief, until all that was left was hooves and rushing air and speed and freedom, the closest thing to flying she knew.

It wasn't just her own past she was galloping from.

The Bags were storming towards home, eagerly speculating whose ashes might have been in the urn to bring Peter Sanson and Kenny Kay together.

'It looked *very* cloak-and-dagger,' Petra was already rewriting the scene for spin. 'I'm sure I read somewhere that Sanson met Kenny in Borstal.'

'It's *got* to be gangland!' Bridge loved a conspiracy theory.

'A mutual friend, maybe?' Mo called across. Beneath her, Pie was at top speed and rolling like a ferry in rough water.

In her puffa pocket, Bridge's phone was still pumping out her workout playlist: M.I.A's 'Bad Girls'. Mo couldn't figure out how to silence it, but every time she tried to hand it back, Bridge's pony shied away in fright.

'Mark my words, this is connected to what went on in the eighties!' Gill cried over the drumming hooves.

'The shooting?' Petra gasped.

Taking a lot of fresh divots in the face as she pummelled Pie's sides to keep up, Mo suspected the trio had watched too much *Peaky Blinders*.

'I was in my teens,' Gill shouted as she thundered ahead, 'but I remember that those two chancers were always flashing their cash to try to catch Ronnie Percy's eye.'

'Perhaps *they're* the real reason she bolted?' cried Bridge.

'Johnny Ledwell was a jolly dark horse,' Gill called back.

'Could he have been involved in shady dealings?' Bridge was sounding very *Line of Duty*.

'Drug running or the illegal gun trade, maybe?' Petra suggested, no doubt plotting it into a book idea.

Mo was far too puffed out to point out how disrespectful this talk of shotguns and vice was. In her pocket, a Skepta track was now referencing both. Up ahead, the others were still cantering and shouting.

Her mum, Joan, still had a framed photograph of Mo as a pudgy-wristed toddler throwing rice at the society wedding of Ronnie and handsome huntsman Johnny Ledwell outside St Mary's Church, a horseshoe-shaped balloon tied to her big sister Jan's wheelchair. It was true that by the time Mo turned ten, Ronnie had fled, leaving her three small children behind – the legend of 'The Bardswold Bolter' was still talked about amongst the old country set – but that had involved a handsome jump jockey with a sports car. Nobody had called in the vice squad.

'I wonder if Ronnie misses her temptress days?' cried Petra.

'Those days are still going strong!' laughed Gill, looking

back over her shoulder as she led the way. 'But Blair Robertson keeps a very possessive eye, I sense.'

'Doesn't his wife mind?' called Bridge.

'Has dementia, poor thing.' Gill tutted. 'Lady Verity Hallam as was, child bridesmaid to Princess Margaret, later married Earl Verney. She's almost twenty years older than Sit Tight!'

'So, Mr Sit Tight was a gigolo to the gentry?' Bridge whistled.

'She bought him a *lot* of horses!' Petra shouted.

Trailing behind, Mo's strangled 'mind your tongues!' was drowned out by Pie's hooves and pocket hip-hop.

'Pretty fecking tragic, a toy boy playing away just as his elderly wife reaches second childhood!'

'Aristos have different rules on infidelity,' Petra said airily as the riders pulled up, ready to pass through a gate from Sanson to Austen land, horses blowing.

Gill reached down for the hunting latch. 'Blair and Ronnie go back a long way, long before he married Verity, certainly. They just never got the timing right.'

'Oh God, that's sexy!' Petra closed her eyes with a shudder. 'Still sizzling like a forest fire that never quite went out.'

'Well, me and Aleš are a fecking inferno!' boasted Bridge. 'Ladies?'

'Damp log!' groaned Gill.

'Toast!' wailed Petra.

'Rayburn,' Mo wheezed fondly as she finally caught up, making a mental note to dig out her party dress and some nice undies to go with Barry's Valentine's treat cottage pie supper later. Grace had a sleepover that night; it would be a shame not to take advantage. While they might not have Ronnie and Blair's white-hot, on-off passion, they loved a snuggle. It had been a while.

Riding through the gate after the others, she checked her watch and let out a cry of horror. It was past eight. The Bags were never normally out this long on a weekday.

'We must get back!' she panted as the gate slammed shut.

'Is everything OK, Mo?' Petra asked kindly.

'There's a lot going on at home. My Barry was out most of last night,' she explained. He was helping the Austens with lambing and was lying in this morning, which left her with twice as much to do. Although Mum and Dad usually gave Grace her breakfast before she set off to school with her friends from the village, Mo couldn't afford to dawdle.

The other three were gaping at her again, she realized. Given she was now mud-covered, oxygen-starved and in a rare bad temper, she wasn't surprised. In her pocket, the rap switched to 'Mr Brightside'.

'How do I turn this thing off, Bridge?' She pulled the phone out again.

'Button on the side – give it here.' Before Bridge could reach for it, her pony backed sharply into Petra's mare and kicked her, the pair squealing furiously.

After both were declared none the worse for it, the Bags set back off in a sedate musical walk.

'Let's have some girl talk!' Petra entreated.

'Sure, we're in no hurry!' Bridge said.

They rode to either side of Mo and Pie like mounted police seeing home a Cheltenham winner.

'Actually, *I* am!' Mo tried again to hand back the noisy phone.

Boggling at The Killers' betrayal anthem, Bridge's pony swerved sideways, making his rider laugh. 'Aleš is off today and I'm not in till eleven.'

'Well. I have my Girl Friday in this morning,' Petra pointed out, 'plus Charlie's working from home today, so maybe I should get back for her sake...'

'Nonsense. My first appointment's not till ten,' Gill said, filling Bridge's vacated flank. 'Plenty of time to enjoy a lovely morning!'

Mo looked at her askance. The damp chill was bone deep, rain clouds lowering around them. Her bad mood solidified.

Gallivanting around scandalmongering was a pastime she could ill-afford, unlike the others.

Bridge and Craic jogged back alongside. 'What's said in the saddle stays in the saddle, remember Mo.'

It was The Bags' unofficial catchphrase.

Which was when it dawned on Mo that all this gossip, this wild detour, must be a smokescreen. 'All right, ladies,' she sighed impatiently, 'is there something going here on I've missed?'

'You tell us.'

'Tell you what?'

'You really don't know?' Petra was wide-eyed.

'Queen, *every*one knows.' Bridge whistled.

'Well, I don't care for tittle-tattle,' she reminded them sternly.

'Quite right, Mo.' Gill beckoned them forward, glowering at the other two. 'You heard Mo, ladies. It's just tittle-tattle! Let's trot on!'

Soon trailing behind again, aware of an argument taking place up ahead – Bridge's phone now belting out Shaggy's 'It Wasn't Me' – Mo wondered if this was still about Ronnie Percy. Much as she couldn't abide loose lips, some of the well-worn legends about Ronnie were hard to forget, like her riding round Badminton when she was six months pregnant or running off with her jump jockey lover in just her nightie. Then there was the rumour still circulating about her seducing Pax's first boyfriend right under her nose. Some said if it weren't for Ronnie, they'd be married now.

In the stud's thick-walled, cavernous kitchen, Ronnie had burnt several rounds of toast to charcoal while totting up figures on the back of an envelope, grateful that the ancient smoke alarm's battery had long ago packed up because it was coming out of her ears as well as the Aga hotplate. She was equally relieved to be insulated from a mobile signal on which Blair could call back to cancel tonight. But there was no escaping the other sirens playing out all around her.

Briiiiiiing! The landline started up again, no doubt another of Lester's countryman army inquiring after his recovery.

Ding-a-ling! Came the bell from the dining room.

Beep! A car horn signalled Bay's arrival outside.

Steeling for a fight, she chose the greatest of three evils, marching along the flagstoned service corridor to the rear vestibule, still lined with generations of fossilised Percy hunting boots, hats and wax coats, dogs bustling around her as they anticipated a walk.

Ronnie ignored the distant *Ding-a-ling!* from the dining room, closing the door behind her and striding across the cobbles to the courtyard gate, dogs yapping at her heels.

The patchy morning drizzle was hardening into rain, all colour wiped from the sky. Bay Austen's Land Rover purred in the arrival's yard – an increasingly familiar sight – lights white-blue, wipers swishing sporadically, gun dogs barking from the boot.

This time, he was towing a horse trailer.

He *was* keen. Ronnie didn't care what Sandy said – if he wanted to buy a Compton Magna horse, she'd sell him one. She hadn't paid Luca or Carly the Saturday girl in a fortnight.

'Morning!' Bay buzzed down the driver's window. A once-ravishing blue-eyed boy who hadn't dropped a percentage point in long-lashed, dimpled chin adulthood, he didn't look quite so hot this morning, those blue eyes baggy, hair unkempt and chin stubbled. But Bay's bad days were still most men's brooding best. 'Pax around?'

'Out.' She fixed a no-go smile.

He flashed back a brighter one, glitchy as a failing neon sign, glancing in his rear mirror at the trailer. Inside it, an impatient hoof slammed a partition. 'Just dropping off her token gift-horse. I take it you know about this?'

Ronnie thought fast, remembering Sandy saying the same thing. It turned out she didn't know as much as she thought, certainly not about her daughter. What was Pax up to?

She didn't betray her surprise. 'I was rather under the impression you want to *buy* one?'

'Tempted to.' He jumped out, towering over her. Behind them, the trailer swayed. 'Lester certainly thinks I should – an experienced running mate for this one. Best mare your pa bred this side of the millennium, according to your Aussie mate, but she has no mileage.'

Ronnie's smile thinned, cogs starting to turn. Having bought the cream of the crop last year, Blair had tripled his money when the Austens came looking for a new acquisition.

'This is the Compton youngster that Blair sold you?'

A hoof hammered the trailer wall again.

'Yep.'

Ronnie's brows lowered as she watched him shrug on his padded jacket. 'And you want to put her in foal?'

'Christ, no. Breeding's a mug's game. She needs to be out there campaigning. Burghley Young Horse classes and all that. Just Pax's type.' He sauntered round to the rocking trailer. 'We keep telling her, it's a perfect advert for the stud.'

It took a moment to realize what he was saying. 'You expect Pax to *compete* her?'

'Absolutely. Hasn't she told you? Put this place's name back on the map.' He released the ramp catches. 'Travesty she ever stopped.'

Ronnie had heard it said already today. Oh, Lester! *Now* she knew what he was up to. To learn that Pax was in on it felt doubly devious.

'This is ridiculous!' She marched after him, indignation mounting. 'She's in no position to take this on.'

'Why not? Just what she needs if you ask me, picking up where she let off.'

'We both know perfectly well why Pax stopped competing.'

'Time to make amends, don't you think?' He lowered the ramp.

'Those days are long gone, Bay.'

'Rubbish.' Bay looked at her over his shoulder, eyes bright as gas burners. 'You of all people know how much she needs this right now.'

In the trailer, the mare looked round too. Ronnie didn't remember her at all, a limpid-eyed bay with ridiculously big, black-tipped ears and a white star shaped like a V.

Her Percy family nose for a horse smelled the coffee already. Blair had been right. This was the complete Percy package

And with a stab of jealousy that took her by surprise, Ronnie realized she knew exactly how much her daughter needed this.

'It was Lester who originally sowed the idea.' Bay was clambering in through the empty partition. 'And when I bumped into Pax the other day, I thought why not?'

'Lester might break another hip skating on all this thin ice,' she growled under her breath, turning away, relieved to spot a figure crossing the arrival's yard with his loose-hipped saunter. 'Luca, come and look at this!'

Luca was all smiles, raking a hand back over his short, tufted blond curls, the young deerhound at his heels. His cheeriness always reassured her, that indefatigable horse sense. Beneath the quiet charm, Ronnie had always suspected he was also tough as a marine, and potentially as ruthless.

'Where's Pax?' she muttered as soon as he was alongside, both watching as Bay backed the mare out.

'Off for a blast as you suggested.' He looked at the mare skittering onto the tarmac and whistled, head tilting. 'Heard she was smart.'

'You *know* about this?' Ronnie was even more shocked.

'Nothing gets past me.' His smile widened as Bay pulled off the tatty wicking rug the mare had travelled in to reveal an equine supermodel, nostrils flaming wide as she fanfared an 'I'm home!' whinny.

With the see-all expression of the brightest girl at school coming back after her first term, the mare was a polished diamond Ronnie had barely registered in the rough. One of the five-year-old crop her father had been too ill and intractable to sell when he should have, she'd been a gangly, overgrown mud-monster six months ago. Blair had hot-housed her, breaking her straight in, followed by a clipping and trimming makeover, some baby competitions and a few days' hunting before swiftly adding a zero to her price and selling her on, ready to affiliate. It was his favourite alchemy. And the Austens knew how to spot a winner.

'Don't pretend you don't like her.' Bay stood back admiringly.

'Yes, but we're not competing anything right now,' she told him ungratefully.

'I'm picking up all her costs, Ronnie darling, you just have to pick up the pace.' He fished an equine passport from his poacher's pocket.

Reluctantly taking it, Ronnie watched Luca pulling off the padded travel boots, revealing strong, clean legs with short cannons and hocks good enough to make a Windsor judge whoop. The mare was still calling loudly, stallion Beck bellowing back that he was the one in charge these days.

Luca's smile was wide as a paper boat as he looked over the new arrival again. 'I'll find her a stable. What's her name?' he asked Bay

'Must be in her passport. We just call her Lottie because she cost a lot. That Aussie chap of yours drives a hard bargain, Ron.'

Indignation bubbling, Ronnie felt another spike of fury at Blair and his horse-trading. She longed to insist Bay take her back home, but they badly needed the money – any money – and who was she to deny Pax this opportunity?

Luca was already leading the horse away, a bounce in his step, delighted by the new arrival. Nothing fazed him. It was why she'd hired him. His was a rare soul, not unlike Blair, optimistic opportunists who made every horse they sat on look like a winner and took everything in their stride.

She turned wearily to Bay, who was hauling up the ramp. 'You won't win Pax back this way, you realize.'

'She's the one we want to do the winning.' He regarded her briefly before clicking in the catches, his face unusually serious, big blue eyes earnest. 'She just needs the horses.'

'Come inside to talk money. I'll need cash up front.'

'In a rush, I'm afraid – email an invoice with the contract.' He was climbing back in the car. 'Pass on my best to Lester. Tell him to message me if finds an experienced stablemate for her, even if it's just a leg. Oh, I nearly forgot!' He reached for a flowered biscuit tin on the passenger seat. 'These are from Ma. I hope he has dental insurance. There's a letter for you in there about next week's church roof committee meeting. She said to remind you that they desperately need you and can you call her?'

'Of course.' Taking the tin, she made a mental note not to. The klaxon started honking out again, another call that might turn luck her way. 'I'll email you that invoice ASAP.'

'No hurry!' His car roared away, empty trailer rattling and dogs barking, her younger heeler chasing it halfway down the drive.

Luca had cross-tied the mare in the unoccupied open stalls so that he could put down a bed of shavings in the more luxurious, des res quarantine stable nearby.

It was obvious she didn't like to be kept waiting. She was matching the yard klaxon ring for ring with her shrill whinny, deep ribcage shaking.

About to go in search of a rug, Luca paused to admire her. Who knew a stalking horse could be so beautiful?

'Welcome back, Lottie. I know what your owner is up to and it stinks, but you have a beautiful face, so I'll forgive you.'

Her eyes blazed like a silent movie star tied to railway lines, her V-sign of a white star bobbing up and down. Luca had encountered plenty of quick-minded mares with separation issues in his career, and enough jaw-dropping equine athletes to recognize her class straight away, but he'd only known one other horse with a face marking like this.

His old boss in Canada had bought that in as a three-year-old, a colt christened Harvey Smith after the vintage showjumper who'd famously flicked a V-sign live on air. Belligerent as his namesake, yet with unparalleled raw talent, he'd caught the eye of the boss's daughter Meredith when Luca was breaking him in. As had Luca

Their on-off affair, lasting many years, had almost destroyed them both.

Late last night in Ontario, four in the morning here, Meredith had sent a message: *Where are you, I wonder? Do you care enough to reply?*

It wasn't the first time she'd tried to make contact since he'd come to Britain. He had yet to respond, but his blood ran hotter each time he read it. And Bay's gift horse had made him think about it differently.

Lottie whinnied again, nostrils flaring red, straining towards Beck's loud reply from the neighbouring yard.

Staying to soothe her, he pulled out his phone and took a photograph of that distinctive white V before clicking the share icon, then hesitating. He studied the photo, his own big V-sign. There was no signal here, so it might never reach its destination.

A breath warmed his face as Lottie strained towards him, nickering, eager for reassurance.

He ran his fingers distractedly from the whorl in that V star up to her forelock, letting a quiet warmth transfer through them, second nature to him. The O'Brien family touch was well known, Luca's gift for calming horses no less instinctive than his horse-dealer father and brothers. The family motto was that a horse's trust was a gift beyond all others.

He pressed his forehead against hers, drawing strength, sensing her relax.

Under no illusion about how shabby Bay's motives were, Luca was equally aware that this place needed patrons, and he was a bird in the hand right now. It was why Lester pressed advantage with the Austens, why Pax quietly complied and why Ronnie remained stiffly civil with Bay to survive. Owners called the tune in the horse business and paid the piper. Luca was part of the house band now, fiddling while Rome burned.

It doesn't matter who pays so long as the horses get fed, he'd told Pax, something he'd been taught alongside his prayers, first by his dealer dad and then by countless bosses. But the older he got, the more Luca realized it *did* matter.

The mare bobbed her V-sign head, on her third owner in a year, no doubt destined for many more if her value rose.

He looked down at his phone screen again, the share button waiting to be pressed. It was Bay Austen he wanted to flick a V at, not Meredith. Arrogant, wealthy, unscrupulous Bay, entitlement rising like sauna steam from his skin. The horse world was full of Bays. Luca had lost Meredith to one and knew how miserable her marriage made her.

He reread her message. *Do you care enough to reply?*

They both knew he did. Compulsive love like theirs permeated everything, led to other addictions. They'd always cared too much.

Pax was the same; it's what made her burn so bright, why he'd been so immediately hooked, like a thorn dragging him to the sweetest tea rose. And it was how he know what a struggle she had, kicking her own engrained habits. Habits like Bay, who now had a reason to call round even more often, to message every day. For all Pax treated it as a joke, Luca sensed danger. He'd been there before. A part of him was still there.

Remind you of someone? he typed beneath the picture of the mare, slamming his thumb down on the green SEND arrow.

The moment he did, he regretted it.

*

The landline rang on and on, accompanied inside the house by Lester's bell still *ding-a-linging* from the dining room.

Tripping over dogs and boots as she dashed the length of the glass-sided vestibule, through the back service corridor and into the kitchen to grab the phone from its wall bracket, Ronnie cursed her father for not having more handsets.

'Compton Magna Stud!' *Please let it be a client.*

'Gotta cry off tonight, Ron.' Blair's deep rasp of a voice was full of regret.

She pressed her forehead to the cool tiles beside the phone cradle. Not the turn of luck she'd been hoping for.

'I guessed as much,' she said eventually.

Ding-a-ling! still chimed from the dining room.

Spotting the toast she'd made for Lester half an hour earlier still in the tennis racket griddle on the Aga lid, Ronnie cupped the receiver to her cheek with her shoulder as she scraped marmalade on its least burnt upper side.

'Been trying to call you all morning,' Blair muttered.

She should have guessed he'd eventually track her down on the kitchen walkabout phone, the old-fashioned landline still their most reliable source of communication in this Bardswold not-spot. She could hear a coffee machine at his end, picturing him in his own cluttered – if far higher tech – kitchen, surrounded by dogs, paper piles and horse paraphernalia just as she was.

'Vee's had a bad night,' he said, his voice tightened with tension. 'The doctor's with her now; I'm pretty sure it's another stroke.'

'Oh God, that bad?'

Ding-a-ling! The little bell rang furiously from the dining room. Ronnie ignored it.

'She doesn't know what way's up, poor darling. I can't leave her.' His voice cracked with exhaustion.

'Of course not.' Compassion flooded through her, chased by guilt. They'd been selfish planning this – never meet up on Valentine's night, said the mistresses' code. But the significance of the date had seemed a silly irrelevance when Blair had scrolled ticketswap.com and spotted two stalls seats for the musical Ronnie was dying to see. Currently on the last leg of a sell-out tour before moving to the West End, playing close enough to the Comptons for a night together here at home afterwards, it had seemed too good to be true. They might have guessed it was fated to failure.

'You must still go,' Blair urged. 'I'll email the tickets. Take a mate. Lester, maybe.'

Ronnie laughed dryly. 'I'll go alone just to get away from him.'

Ding-a-ling.

'Still trying to run the place?' he asked distractedly.

'He thinks he's setting up an event team here.'

'No shit.'

'I'm surprised he hasn't messaged you about it.'

'He has.' Even this wrung out, Blair wasn't too preoccupied to pep talk. 'And he's bloody well right – you *should* be out there running the stud colours.'

Tempted to let rip about the homebred mare he'd sold on to the Austens landing back here, she stopped herself. Blair didn't need that right now, however aggrieved she was by his part in it.

Ding-a-ling.

'That him?'

'Overdid his physio yesterday, silly bugger,' she reported instead. 'He's determined to get back on a horse before the hunting season's over. Claims seventy's no age, which is true, but he's at least eighty by my calculation. Not that age is an impediment.'

The ensuing silence, even longer this time, told her that was no less thoughtless a thing to say. Verity would never get back on one of her beloved horses again, her diseased mind stealing away all memory of it, a succession of TIAs rendering her barely mobile.

At last, he spoke, voice deep with regret, 'Ron, we've got to cool it.'

There was another long pause for thought. They both hurt. 'She's too ill.'

This had happened before, more than once. She just had to stay calm. Not sulk. Probably for the best. She had a lot to get on with. 'You're quite right.'

'You're mad at me.' He sounded surprised, offended.

He knew her too well to deny it, so she stayed silent. Not mad about this, not about Verity, she wanted to say. But then she'd have to explain why.

Their longest silence yet followed.

In front of her, the mare's passport was now covered with butter that she wiped off, studying the registered name through the little letterbox in the plastic cover, typed after the usual Compton Magna prefix was: *The Butterfly Effect.*

Wasn't that something to do with chaos theory? She vaguely recalled a radio discussion about it. Apparently small, insignificant things that can cause momentous change later. Her father had grown increasingly eccentric when registering foals in old age, plucking them at random from things he read in the *Telegraph.*

Ding-a-ling!

Ronnie pulled her lips tightly beneath her teeth, angry at Blair for spotting the mare's class when she hadn't, at Bay for his luck and largesse, furious at Lester for collaborating behind her back, and at Pax for her secret ambition. More than that, Ronnie was mad at Blair for three decades of almost-but-not-quite, and for being married to somebody so lovely and so devastatingly ill. Too right she was mad at him. Another day she'd round on him for putting her in this predicament. For his glib, easy-come, easy-go, 'let's cool it, Ron' assumption that she would sit pretty while Mr Sit Tight rode this through. Again.

For his heartbreaking butterfly effect.

'I want you to promise me something...' He broke the silence urgently, voice rift deep.

'Of course.'

Ding-a-ling!

'Go out there and have some fun.'

'I'll paint the town red for us both tonight,' she promised hollowly. As red as today's bloody dawn.

'I don't just mean tonight.'

Ding-a-ling. Ding-a-ling.

'Time to kick on, Ron. Talk soon.' He rang off.

There were few prevarications between Ronnie and Blair, their shorthand born of long acquaintance, two hopeless romantics in deep cover. This, Ronnie knew, would be the last she'd hear from him for the foreseeable future. He was granting her a free pass.

It felt like a bone cracking in her chest. Please God, not long.

6

The Saddle Bags were on the final stretch of the Three Mile Point, back to a steady trot to accommodate Mo and Pie's low gear, although Mo was kicking Pie along as fast as she could. She had another stitch, increasingly fed up that the usual forty-minute circuit had turned into such a Hidalgo-length marathon. In her pocket, Bridge's phone had at least fallen silent, no longer picking up enough signal to stream music.

The others were now gossiping about Pax Forsyth's broken marriage.

'Men are always quick off the draw round here when a pretty wife is back on the market!' Gill called from the front.

'Gives us hope, hey, Mo?' Petra looked over her shoulder at Mo, who – lungs bursting too much to speak – decided to take this as a compliment.

'Then again, Pax *is* very beautiful,' Gill pointed out.

'Stand-offish,' Petra said, wrinkling her nose.

'She's great when you get to know her,' said Bridge.

'Gets all that marvellous red hair from a mad grandmother, I believe!' Gill enthused.

'Along with the madness,' Petra observed.

'Redheads *do* have a bit of a reputation,' Gill pointed out.

'Yeah, all the fellas fecking love them!' Bridge let out a

whoop as Craic shot forwards, shying at something behind them.

'If you ask me, redheads, like chestnuts, get a disproportionate amount of bad press and sensationalised attention.' Petra patted the neck of her much-maligned chestnut mare. 'Men lust after titian-maned woman in the mistaken belief they're hot and wild whereas most are descended from doughty, practical Highlanders and *very* quick to switch off the central heating.'

'She's... looking... ever... so... thin... these... days,' Mo panted worriedly.

'My sister lost two stone when her marriage broke up.' Gill gestured at them to keep trotting. 'Or twenty, if you count her ex.'

'*Now* you're tempting me.' Petra trotted upsides their leader to pick up the pace again as they rode onto a headland track, two abreast.

'Easier that cutting carbs, eh, Mo?' Bridge slotted in beside Mo who smiled encouragingly, too puffed out to add anything more.

Up ahead, Petra was romanticising... 'Pax probably needs lots of delicious sex to cheer her up! No wonder lovely Luca's smitten. I swear he's part-man, part-Centaur, ladies.' She'd wasted no time casting the stud's new Irish manager as a sexy seventeenth-century cavalier in her latest bodice-ripper. 'The sight of him on that big grey stallion gets me every time.'

'That horse is an utter menace.' Gill frowned down at her. 'And Luca will be globe-trotting off to another job soon. It's his living. Pax should be careful. She's barely out of the marital door.'

'But who needs tomorrow when you have a man like Luca to cuddle tonight?' she breathed in her northern Brontë voice, dark eyes wide.

Alongside Mo, Bridge clicked her tongue teasingly. 'He is fire.'

'Imagine him in bed,' sighed Petra. 'I bet he has amazing hands.'

'And those rock-hard legs,' Bridge agreed.

'Ladies!' Gill chided.

'Buttocks like marble...' Petra ignored her.

'But so sensitive and unhurried,' Bridge mm-mmed, 'and always ready to roll in the hay at the slightest signal. He has that look, y'know?'

The Bags fell momentarily silent to acknowledge that they knew.

The headland widened and they trotted four abreast, Bridge's pony napping and spooking, ears flicking back continually.

Now so puffed out her heartbeat was drowning out the conversation round her, Mo half-listened to Gill complaining good-naturedly that her husband, a partner at the equine clinic, had developed a suspicious new interest in stud work. 'He keeps volunteering for routine visits now Pax and Ronnie are there.'

'There's no way I'm letting Aleš round there with his toolkit, ladies, I tell you.' Bridge cocked her chin. 'One minute it's "poor Pax has a broken washing machine", the next, they're on speed dial.'

'I'm only grateful Charlie's rubbish at plumbing,' said Petra. 'Helping a maiden in distress would totally float his ballcock.'

Bridge's pony was still on springs. 'Your Barry is always helping out neighbours, isn't he, Mo?'

'He is... ever... so... kind,' she panted, realizing all three Bags were looking at her intently now as they thudded along the wide track.

Having long endured soft-hearted husband Barry being 'borrowed' for handyman jobs by single mums on the Orchard estate – and usually bellyaching about it afterwards – Mo admitted breathlessly, 'I get a bit miffed if I'm honest, him being taking advantage of.'

'Barry is such a generous soul.' Petra pressed the point. 'Might he find it hard to say "no"? In theory, say?'

'What exactly are you talking about here?'

'All Pax's admirers queuing up at the stud!' Gill said over-brightly as Bridge's pony started crabbing sideways, still spooked by something imaginary behind them.

'Like Bay scent-marking it every opportunity he gets,' Petra lamented, her long-standing crush on their village landowner under threat.

Annoyed to find Barry dragged into their soap opera, Mo felt obliged to point out, 'Pax *did* walk out on her marriage, and her little boy's not yet six. Someone should tell her the grass isn't always greener, no matter how many men she has lusting after her skinny backside.'

'Grass *is* greener in the emerald isle where Luca comes from,' Gill pointed out over-cheerily. 'And Bay Austen has a lot of grazing pasture.'

'A player like Bay won't let the grass grow, now his wife's gone,' Petra sighed again.

'Maybe Pax doesn't want some new fella hanging around to mow the fecking lawn?' Bridge jogged beside them, her pony on springs, eyes boggling. 'Not her fault men can't resist her, is it?'

Having never been the irresistible type, Mo wondered wistfully what that must feel like.

'She and Bay always seemed a jolly good match, I thought,' Gill mused.

'Oh, she'll never have Bay back,' Petra predicted confidently.

'Whyever not?' argued Gill. 'He's divorcing too. The two of them adored one another as teenagers.'

'Until he slept with her mother behind her back,' Petra said matter-of-factly.

'That was *Bay*?' Mo gasped. 'Bay slept with Ronnie?'

When the other Bags oohed, Petra batted her big, dark eyes in surprise. 'I thought everyone knew that? Or was that one of the things I promised not to repeat?'

'One more canter?' A red-faced Gill was already bounding

rhythmically away as though heading down the centre line in a dressage test.

The final few furlongs of field lay ahead, leading up to the village lane, a vast track of Austen set aside.

Mo had no breath left after trotting so long, not bothering to try to kick Pie on this time as the others surged ahead. The hairy cob, also completely puffed out, slowed gratefully to a walk, leaving Mo once again trailing behind to catch her breath. In Mo's pocket, Bridge's phone picked a data signal again and sprung not life with the last few bars of the Pussycat Dolls' 'Don't Cha'.

'You lot have plenty to talk about,' said a voice just behind her.

She almost fell off to find Pax Forsyth there. Ponytail the same deep copper red as her mount's, she was riding a familiar-looking cob, its nostrils flared and coat steaming from a recent burst of speed.

'Oh, we were just… you know… passing the time…'

'I heard.'

Burning with shame, a blush stealing up her cheeks, Mo wondered how long Pax had been there.

'I've always found it a bit of a curse.' She rode alongside and regarded her levelly. 'Red hair.'

'Oh yes?'

Quite a while then.

'People can't always see past it. The Demelza Poldark schtick is such a cliché. I've spent a lifetime dispelling the hot-headed myth by staying calm when people expect me to be angry. Like now.'

Mo glanced at her beautiful face. Like her soft, deep voice, it gave nothing away.

In her pocket, Ava Max had started singing 'Sweet but Psycho'.

'Do you usually listen to music when you ride out?' Pax asked.

'No usually, truth be told.' She was tempted to sling it in a hedge. 'This isn't my playlist. I'm more of an Elton John fan.'

'I might try it. I rather like the idea of a mini-festival on horseback.' She didn't smile. 'He didn't know it was her, by the way.'

'Beg pardon?'

'Bay didn't know it was Mummy. They didn't recognize each other. I like your cob. Your friends are total bitches.'

She set off at full pelt, closing down the other Bags in seconds and flying past them, red ponytail whipping, the Demelza myth firmly intact.

Ronnie carried another cup of tea through to the dining room.

Interrogating Lester was not going well. He was still sulking for leaving him starved of breakfast and stranded so long, his crutches having fallen out of reach when he'd sat down in to put on his socks. Cold and undignified in his dressing gown and underpants, he'd been clicking his fingers at her ever since, evading awkward questions. Several cups of tea and an extra round of toast later, he was still holding onto the upper ground.

'What were you *thinking* of Lester?' Shutting the door behind her, she launched back in, '*Bay*, of all people!'

His face gave nothing away, lids creased over his eyes, finger drumming on Viv Austen's flowered metal biscuit tin resting unopened on his lap. 'Your father held onto that mare for a very good reason.'

'He's no longer here to corroborate. And he hated the Austens, if you'll recall, especially Bay.'

'He wasn't acquainted with the full story of that betrayal.'

She stiffened.

Thankfully, at that moment Lester's tablet pinged with a notification and he was soon distracted by it, letting out an 'aha!' followed by a 'well I never', then glancing up at Ronnie with an 'of course I won't' before resuming reading.

Ronnie thought about Pax, their Helen of Troy. Bay had broken her heart so catastrophically once it had changed the entire direction of her life. Perhaps he really did simply want to make amends as he said. Could he be rewriting history, supplying the army to fight at her side, not the destroying force? Maybe it was Ronnie who should be prepared to fall on her sword. She was equally responsible.

'How do you like the sound of this?' Lester was still glued to his screen. 'American-bred stallion by Master Imp, still only nine and already scooping up double clears at four-stars in between servicing his mares.'

'Who wouldn't love the sound of it in our business? Is there a point to this?'

'We've just been offered first refusal.' He looked up victoriously, resting his iPad on the biscuit tin lid. 'Perfect for a syndicate. Mr Austen's looking for a share.'

'Put that away, Lester! You must *stop* this. We're not competing, and we already have a new stallion standing this season. Beck's pedigree is second to none; his first foals are superstars in Germany.'

'Not exactly flavour of the month.' The fingers rattled on the tin lid.

'This stud has been out of flavour – favour – for years. The bookings will come eventually.' He'd got far too impertinent since moving into the house to convalesce, she felt.

Now in range of the router, Ronnie's phone was having a lively time in her pocket as emails and messages landed. She pulled it out and held it up like a duelling pistol to match his.

Blair's name leapt out, making her neck muscles tighten again. Please let him have changed his mind.

But it just was the e-tickets for the musical, its accompanying message simply: *Kick on...*

Ronnie certainly wanted to kick something. Right now, she wanted to kick Blair for selling that horse to the Austens, and for deserting her when she had so few allies. She had no desire to go out on the town. She needed to save her stud. To do that, she needed to make money. And send away Trojan horses.

'I'm going to tell Bay to take the mare back,' she told Lester.

'If you say so.' He regarded her over his tablet. His catch-all catchphrase seldom indicated agreement.

'I say so!' She glared at him over her phone.

It was a long stand-off.

He lowered his weapon first, setting the tablet aside, fingers drumming the tin lid. 'This little American Thoroughbred already has over thirty bookings for the season. What's more, he's fit and ready to compete.' He raised an eyebrow, and she realized her mistake. This was an ambush.

'Where on earth did you find a horse like that?' Ronnie regarded him incredulously.

'I'm not yet at liberty to say.' Lester raised the other eyebrow and revealed that the stallion was already qualified for Maumesby Park, the first top international competition of the British season, a flag-waving fanfare that got that year's big hitters noticed.

'Maumesby's *way* too soon for Pax.' She held her ground, but her whiskers were well and truly twitching.

'Plenty will take the scratch ride. Or deputise yourself?'

'Don't be ridiculous, Lester.' *Oh, clever bait!*

'I'm assured the horse is easy as they come.' He lifted the tablet to peer at it. 'I'm downloading the videos now.'

'There's a video?' Ronnie could never resist a stallion showcase, especially an eventing stallion.

Sensing her resolve weaken, Lester's old face transformed, creases unfolding into a rare smile. 'If I may be so bold, he's perfect for someone coming back to the top level.'

If they were going to take in one Trojan horse, she reasoned, why not a running mate? 'Show me the video.'

Pax heard the new arrival long before she saw her, a shrill fanfare welcoming her on the drive.

Walking out from beneath archway to greet her, Luca wore his smile as easily as ever. 'Get ready to live the pipe dream, angel—' Stallions Beck and Cruisoe drowned out the rest with duet of competitive bellows. The shrill whinny blasted back. 'Bay just dropped off a horse for you.'

Her jaw fell. 'He brought the mare *here*? I thought it was all talk. I haven't even run the idea past Mummy.'

'That'll explain her surprise.' He took the cob's reins. 'I'll wash this one off while you two get acquainted.'

Beyond the arch, the trio were now whinnying so loudly they might have been performing *Don Giovanni*.

'What did Mummy say?' she asked breathlessly, jumping off.

'It was all very polite.' Luca's gaze stayed on the cob. She could sense tension, but he held up his shield of a smile. 'She's something else. Go and see.' He waved her away, adding lightly, 'Tread softly because you tread on all our pipe dreams.'

'Come too?' she entreated.

He shook his head. 'I'll look after this fella.'

Pax was too excited to dwell on his diffidence. She'd never imagined Bay would actually bring the horse, seemingly as casually as dropping off a book for her to read.

She hurried through the main yard, in which the stallions were bellyaching from opposite corners, then on beneath the clocktower arch to the second, smaller yard where the isolation stable between the old machinery and grain stores was now occupied, a head over the door with a big tick of a white star bobbing.

Approaching, Pax felt a wave of déjà vu rising through her like a tsunami, part elation, part nausea. It stopped her in her tracks.

She wasn't sure how long she stood there, just staring, from several metres away. She was vaguely aware of Luca whistling in the other yard, of the hose running, a door banging, hooves crossing cobbles. All the time the stallions shouted and the mare in front of her replied, her dark eyes blazing. Every so often she stopped to look at Pax, gazes locking.

I know you, she seemed to say.

And Pax knew her too.

This was the horse on which she galloped through every sleepless night.

The thoroughbred stallion's video showreel was as glossy as a perfume ad, but Ronnie barely noticed the 4K definition, snazzy cross-fades and booming backing track.

She peered at the competition captions. 'Lester, this horse is on the other side of the Atlantic! When you said he was American, I didn't realize you meant he was still out there.'

'Flying over here as soon as his paperwork's signed off.'

'He certainly can fly,' she said, admiring him streaking over huge pieces of timber with a curious sense of déjà vu. She could almost be watching an old home movie. This horse was the sort of stamp she'd loved in her own international days, wiry full-blood lionhearts that toughed out the old-fashioned blood-and-guts endurance tests of yesteryear, before everyone got scared. No wonder Lester was misty-eyed.

'He's too small for Pax,' she said repeatedly.

'Keep watching,' Lester replied each time.

The same rich bay as polished oxblood brogues, the stallion was barely more than a polo pony, so compact, fast and scopey it quickened Ronnie's blood. She'd have ridden it like a shot back then.

This was now, she reminded herself. The sport had changed beyond all recognition. It was more technical, trappier and prettier, full of powerhouse geometry specialists that could float through a dressage test then jump a skinny on a curving line without breaking stride. Horses like Bay's big-moving mare. Horses bred from big-moving kingmakers like Beck, surely?

This little American missile was pure Exocet. It needed a

breeder brave enough to swim against the tide. And it needed a jockey who knew no fear. Pax dived for cover whenever the kettle whistled.

'He's too bold,' she also said repeatedly. 'Too opinionated.'

'Keep watching,' Lester replied each time.

Doing so, Ronnie's thoughts drifted to Blair, wishing she could ask his opinion. This horse would be catmint to him. It was like the tough little Aussie stock horses Blair had brought over decades ago to scoop every trophy in sight: Badminton, Burghley, Blenheim, gold after gold, outwitting all the big-boned British hunter chasers. But none of those had been stallions. They'd joked then that if they were, they could have hatched a dynasty. Indefatigable, intrepid and unbeatable.

'We don't have the capacity to stand another stallion this season,' she also said repeatedly.

'Keep watching,' Lester replied each time.

Blair would understand how much seeing a horse like this conflicted her. How it took her back, tempted her. He'd been there too.

Kick on...

His call had coloured everything today. She was lamed by it, hobbled by the prospect of enforced separation. It hit her afresh every few minutes, her patience shortening. Bloody Blair. Bloody Bay. Bloody Lester.

'I think you might be right, Mrs Ledwell,' he said regretfully when the videos finally came to an end.

'Too small, bold, sharp for Pax,' she nodded, surprised by her disappointment.

'Far more your type than hers.'

They had another long standoff, his creased eyes on her. He seemed to be waiting for something.

'How much did you say they want for it?' she asked to fill the silence.

He smiled toothily. When he told her, she laughed in disbelief. 'What madness!' Then, humouring him, 'And d'you think we can get it? A syndicate, you say?' And she was the original sinner for considering it, especially if Bay Austen was involved.

'Leave it with me.' This new, assertive Lester astonished her. He sounded like her father.

She snatched up his mug. 'More tea?'

She could tell Lester was smirking as he watched her go.

Still mortified after her encounter with Pax, Mo had hacked back up to the village with the others in seething silence, ignoring the idle chatter. It was only when Petra and Bridge sandwiched her between their horses by the Church Meadow to ask what was wrong that she could bring herself to speak.

'I've had just about enough of your loose talk,' she told them. '"*Don't spread with your mouth what your eyes don't see*", Mum says. People get hurt by gossip. It's cruel.'

Her three companions all glanced at each other like naughty schoolgirls.

Mo was tempted to resign from the Saddle Bags here and now. Enough was enough. But Gill was already speaking up for her.

'Mo's quite right, we cannot believe *unsubstantiated rumours*, ladies.' She glared at the other two, which Mo thought was a bit ripe given she was just as bad at spreading them. Mo would never be able to look Pax in the eye again.

Petra looked discomforted, demanding, 'What if the *unsubstantiated rumours* affect one of us?'

'Let's hope the *unsubstantiated rumour* didn't fecking happen,' Bridge muttered.

'Whatever it is, I don't want to know,' Mo said firmly, glancing at her watch. 'I've had enough talk for one day, thank you.'

'Yeah, we've been out long enough for several *unsubstantiated rumours* to come and go in this fecking village.'

'Fair enough,' Petra said quickly.

'Onward!' Gill led off again. 'Time to spy over garden hedges, ladies.'

Mo tried not to feel hypocritical as the Bags enjoyed their customary peer into the well-lit kitchens of breakfasting villagers, rewarded with the sight of Brian and Chris Hicks eating All Bran at their pine table, reading His and Hers Valentine's cards, and the new couple in Rose Cottage embracing, semi-naked, against a granite-topped island.

A florist's van passing by made them all sigh.

'God, what I'd do for some passion on Valentine's Day,' Petra groaned. 'Charlie's working from home this week, but he's utterly unromantic. *Please* tell me you got more than a hairy back in front of the bathroom basin this morning, Bridge?'

Bridge smirked the smirk of the breakfasted-in-bed centre of her husband universe.

'Paul and I agree it's all far too commercial to bother with,' Gill said stridently.

'My Barry always clean forgets, bless him,' Mo confessed, eager to make them feel better after her grumpy moment.

Again, she found all three Bags swinging round in their saddles to look at her.

'Nothing particularly unusual about today, then?' Petra eyed her closely.

Mo hadn't been going to say anything but seeing as they'd asked... 'Truth be told, I have witnessed a bit of furtive husbandly behaviour this week that I'm hopeful might manifest in romance,' she revealed excitedly, having noted extra grooming and some secretive phone fiddling suggestive of an Amazon purchase. 'So I've decided I'm going to make an extra effort too: best frock, cottage pie, bottle of wine.'

'Good for you!' Gill gave an enthusiastic head-girl cheer. 'Isn't it, ladies?'

Petra and Bridge agreed obediently.

Mo beamed at them all. Barry might not be the handsomest

man in the village, but his brand of solid, dependable kindness was rare round these parts.

'Oy, oy!' Bridge was up in her stirrups looking over her shoulder as the florist's van turned into the stud's entrance. 'That'll be a dozen red ones for Ronnie from Sit Tight, I reckon. Bound to be old school.'

'Now, ladies,' Mo chided. 'No unsubordinated rumours, remember?'

The others looked suitably shamefaced.

'We love you, Mo,' Petra blurted. 'Never forget it.'

Perked by this, she decided to forgive them for making her trot so much and go so far that she'd missed breakfast with Grace.

Ahead of them the lane forked to either side of the village green which was rammed with eco-cars belonging to the Cotswold mummies dropping children at the primary school, head teacher Auriol Bishop manning the gates with a long-suffering TA who was wearing love heart antennae. Both exchanged a wave with Bridge, the school's part-time secretary and unofficial Svengali.

'Pax's ex is parking up at ten o'clock,' she now hissed through a ventriloquist's smile.

The Bags' heads turned like guardsmen's to watch Mack Forsyth leap from his big shiny Mercedes and open a rear door, far better looking than they remembered, a well-manicured, yoke-shouldered, salt-and-pepper bull of a man. Dark-haired little Kes scrambled from his booster seat to charge across the Green and join his best friend, Ellis, whose mother was Petra's home help – as well as an occasional groom at the stud – and a great source of insider info.

'Mack's had to come off Tinder on the advice of his lawyer,' Petra whispered, ignoring Gill's tutting, 'it's a *substantiated fact*.'

'And *that's* Pax's divorce lawyer,' Bridge breathed, pointing out a bobbed blonde in a business suit dropping off two little blondes. 'Helen Beadle. She's shit-hot, ladies, if one of yous ever need her. *Also fact.*'

'Goodness, it's all a bit close-knit, isn't it?' Gill baulked.

'Fecking handy, though,' she pointed out.

Finding Bridge was looking intently at her, Mo remembered to dig in her pocket for her friend's phone which now had a dead battery. As she did so, she spotted her daughter across the Green.

'Grace love!' Thrusting the phone at Bridge without looking at it, she inadvertently sent little Craic into a tizzy as she whooped and waved at Grace queueing by the gates with the big gang from Compton Bagot that walked to school together. Mostly Turners, their dark, wolf-eyed wildness contrasted with her round, pink-cheeked face and mop of mousey curls, all now watching the grey pony pogoing on the spot.

Grace came racing over, trailing her book bag. 'Mum! Where've you *been*? Some woman came round to Nan and Grandad's looking for you!'

Before Mo could reply, Petra and Bridge demanded 'What woman?' at the same time, like Daphne and Velma.

'She didn't say.' Pony-mad Grace dropped her bag to make a fuss of the horses.

'Did she have flowers?' Gill asked hopefully.

'Don't think so. Nan thought she was Jehovah's. She was well weird.'

'In what way weird?' Petra and Bridge duetted again before Mo could say it.

'She wouldn't leave. Said Mum must be expecting her. Gran called Dad to come round and sort it in the end.'

'Poor Barry,' Mo fretted as Grace gambolled away to go into school. He'd not got in until past three having been up half the night helping with the lambing at the Austen's farm. 'Bound to be someone about DIY livery,' she told the others. 'Horsey women can be funny types.' She was tempted to add that she was with three of them right now, all gaping at her as though she'd grown horns.

Dark eyes flooded with emotion, Petra opened her mouth to say something.

'*Unsubstantiated!*' Gill's growl closed it just as Auriol Bullock came thundering across the Green, a Boudicca in Boden tweed.

'I must ask you horse riders to move on! This presents a substantial Health and Safety risk to my pupils! I'm surprised at you, Mrs Mazur.' She chastised Bridge before spotting Mack Forsyth about to climb back into his sinister Mercedes. 'Oh, Mr Forsyth! Coooee! Don't run away before I have a word about my opera group.' She sprinted off to intercept him.

'Did I imagine white-hot sexual energy just then?' Petra whispered.

'Well spotted,' Bridge whispered. 'She's got one hell of a crush on him and she's—'

'*Stop* it!' Mo growled.

'But she's been trying to get him to—'

'I said stop!'

They stopped.

Still trapped with Lester and his iPad – now up to the tenth generation of the thoroughbred stallion's pedigree on his American dam-side – Ronnie leapt up gratefully when the stud's ancient doorbell pulley clanked into action, racing after the barking dogs to the little-used main door.

Lester called after her grandly, 'If it's for me, I don't want any more fruit baskets!'

Standing on the doorstep was a giant bouquet of flowers with two booted legs beneath.

'This is the biggest one I'm delivering today by far!' the legs confided.

Despite herself, Ronnie felt a thrill. Doggedly old-fashioned and generous, Blair was fond of big gestures, especially in extremis.

Taking them in her arms, she examined the name of the envelope.

They were for Pax.

Luca was in the kitchen doing something modern and vegan with pumpkin seeds and jackfruit when she stomped in to put them in the sink.

'Someone loves you,' he grinned over his shoulder.

'Not for me.' They were far too ostentatious, spilling out over the draining board and splashbacks. 'Or from you, I take it?'

He wiped his hands on a tea towel and came to look. 'I prefer my plants living. Besides, you've not paid me, so I'm broke.'

This irked Ronnie. 'No girl likes a man who whinges about money, Luca. Show a bit of old-fashioned passion! Any fool can buy flowers. Or a horse for that matter,' she dismissed vaguely.

'Sure.' The good-natured laughter was back.

'I can offer you two theatre tickets for tonight? I'll babysit Kes.'

'We've plans, thanks.' He headed back to his chopping board. 'Want some breakfast?'

'Not for me.' She rolled her head to loosen tense neck muscles. 'Pax not back yet, I take it?'

'She's with the gift horse. Beautiful-looking mare, isn't she?'

'Hardly matters. It's not staying. We both know why.'

'Do we?'

'Don't be such a snowflake, Luca. Did you leave your spine in Canada?' Not waiting for a reply, she marched back to Lester, who was waiting regally in the Captain's old wingback chair, the flowered biscuit tin still resting unopened on his knee, tablet held aloft, freeze-framed on a small conker-coloured horse in mid-air.

'We *don't* need Bay as a patron, Lester. That's my final word.'

'This place needs a man at the helm.'

'Final word!'

Harrumphing, he set the tablet aside and tightened his dressing gown before pulling the biscuit tin closer to prise open its lid and offering it up to her, the burnt sugar scent rising from it like smoke. Viv's flapjacks were a tooth-breaking village staple cremated in her Aga for the elderly, infirm and fundraising events.

'Best not,' Ronnie valued her crowns too much.

'You may be right.' Lester took one and handed it down to Stubbs who carried it to his basket and started fussily burying it under the blankets. 'Your father used to say good baking won over clients better than a good bloodline. Pip Edwards made a very creditable shortcake.' He still lamented the departure of the Captain's housekeeper, a village busybody Ronnie could no longer afford to pay, whose far superior baking had sustained him through many long winters running the yard alone.

'She's not been amongst your visitors,' Ronnie realized

'Off travelling with her lady friend.' He gave a wry smile, Pip's recent whirlwind romance a pleasant surprise. 'We correspond on Facebook. She still knows more about what's going on around here than you or me.' An envelope rested on top of the flapjacks. He studied the name on it before handing it to her. 'Mrs Austen still buttering you up to be on her church roof fund committee?'

She thrust it in her pocket unopened. 'I'll get out of it.'

'It's an olive branch. You need to make friends in this village, Mrs Led— Ronnie.'

'I have. I am,' she exaggerated, aware the closest chum she'd made so far was fellow dog walker and oversharer Petra Gunn who spend most days locked in a garden shed making up stories and the rest of the time spreading stories.

Ronnie knew she should try harder. She'd been rather hopeful that she might ally with weekender Kit Donne, once married to her late, lamented friend Hermia, but while rewardingly bright and sardonic, he was terribly melancholy, his grief still raw, as though Hermia had been dead seven months not seven years. She personally felt the man needed to get out more.

A thought struck her. 'You're right, Lester! I'm going to offer a friend in the village some tickets I no longer want!' The Bowie musical was a sell-out; Kit worked in theatre and was bound to know somebody who'd take them.

The corners of Lester's mouth turned down. 'I gather Mr Robertson is unavailable again this evening?'

'Something came up.' She felt a fresh, familiar pang for Blair, sharp as a stitch. Then it hit her. The American horse was just his type. He had a lot of contacts over there. '*Who* did you say tipped you off about this stallion, Lester?'

'I didn't.' Lester's wrinkled eye shutters came down, jowls low.

'It was Blair, wasn't it?'

He didn't answer.

'I don't *believe* it!' she howled angrily, spinning round and raking her hair. 'What's he up to?'

Again, Lester said nothing.

'Lester, you're quite maddening! Please stop meddling.' She was furious with his newfound acquisitive bent, and with Blair too – if it *was* Blair – both bullheadedly believing they were helping with a gamble that could cripple the stud long before it paid out. 'The sooner we have you back on a horse, the better. I'm taking the dogs out.'

Seeing Lester creases deepen and dewlaps sag, she felt a pang of guilt. They both needed allies.

'Shall I take Stubbs?' she offered.

'Not if you let him run loose again,' Lester grunted back, then relented. 'Take a slip lead; he's a devil if he spots a squirrel. Want a walk, lad?'

The little fox terrier quivered at the prospect, gazing up at his master adoringly.

He gazed back, rheumy eyes turning down affectionately. 'Soon be on my feet again, lad.'

'Of course you will,' Ronnie's assured him, although she was starting to worry he might never be his old self.

In the kitchen, the flowers had been relocated from the sink to the bin and Pax was lapping the table at speed, a habit she'd picked up since the marriage split, along with muttering 'bastard!' at regular interval. Wild red curls everywhere, she was like a furious alpaca in breeches and a fleece.

Tomatoes sizzled on the Aga and music crackled from the radio while Luca wielded a spatula.

'Bastard!' Pax kicked the bin as she passed it.

This is about the mare, thought Ronnie. Atta girl! She should have trusted Pax wouldn't let Bay get away with this. 'It's all right, she's going straight back.'

'Who is?' Pax marched past.

'Lottie.'

'Wrong bastard!' Pax snarled.

'The flowers were from Mack,' Luca explained as he flipped a flatbread in a second pan. 'She loves the horse.'

Heart sinking again, Ronnie fished out the bouquet. 'Mind if I upcycle these?'

'Be my guest,' Pax flew past, her deerhound following excitedly. 'Bastard!'

Ronnie tugged off the label, reading out, *'To my beautiful Wee Bird of Paradise. You are my flame-haired goddess, my Lady Lilith, my Rapunzel. Let's try again, Tishy. Your Big Bad Wolf Man.'*

'Bastard!' Pax snatched it away to rip up. 'He only ever loved my bloody hair.'

Ronnie admired the flowers in her arms, which smelled delicious and were far too good for the bin.

'Off wooing?' Luca rattled the sizzling pan of tomatoes.

'Be*friend*ing, Luca, not wooing.' Ronnie whistled for the dogs. 'I'm making friends in the village. And Lottie *is* going back.'

'She is *not*!' Pax growled.

As Ronnie marched out, she heard her daughter add a 'Bitch!' to the 'Bastard!' and then 'Where are the fucking scissors?'

Ronnie hurried for her boots. Perhaps Pax was like her termagant grandmother after all. Irish-born Johanna, a wilfully outspoken Irish thruster, had taken on the stuffy Worcestershire farming set with tongue as sharp as a rabbit-gutting knife (and rumour had it she wasn't afraid to wield one of those either). Johnny had been proud of recounting that nobody could outride her.

Outside, Ronnie marched towards the drive, ignoring the mare shouting her head off on the yard.

The horse could stay, she decided. This season might just be the making of Pax.

Luca watched Pax pull the biggest scissors she could find from the utensils drawer before holding them up to declare, 'These will do!'

'Call me a spoilsport, angel,' he deadpanned, 'but I don't think you should murder your husband because he sent you roses.'

'You think I can't be trusted with these?' She waggled them.

'I trust you, but...' He hesitated. He'd already guessed what she planned to do.

'But what? I'm too wild and nutty and hot-headed and dizzy and crazy to know what I'm doing?'

He recognized those as the things Mack had said to her almost daily, that corrosive undermining of her confidence, years of chipping away her self-belief a casual comment at a time, couching insults as endearments.

Although Pax had enviable reserves of calm, Luca had seen her flip out more than once and knew that she could also be explosive, overthinking, hyper and impulsive. But she was never mad in the way Mack had painted her. And even if she was, it was a glorious, sparkling sort of mad.

'You're right. You go ahead, angel. Do your worse. It's about time you did what the hell you like.'

On the hotplate, the tomatoes hissed and spat over the sweeping swish of the blades opening. Lester was listening to Handel loudly in the dining room. They could just make out the mare still calling.

Luca watched in silence as Pax took the kitchen scissors, twisted her red curls up into a thick bunch, and cut it off. In seconds, her hair went from halfway down her back to ending above her shoulders, the curls springing tighter and wider.

'What do you think?' She stared at him, a wide-eyed and defiant pageboy, bunch in one hand like a fox's brush.

Luca stared at her in shock. To him, she'd never looked more beautiful, but he knew the deep, jagged cleft between the way she saw herself and how others saw her was too fragile to risk on a throwaway compliment. She reminded him all too acutely of Meredith at times like this, his insight still raw.

'You look stronger,' he said carefully, 'and newer.'

Her forehead creased as she let out an incredulous huff. Then she carefully set the scissors and the hair on the table and pressed her hands to her face for a moment, her shoulders high, ribcage shaking. Groaning, she shook her head, the unfamiliar hair springing out yet further.

Luca's heart turned over in pity.

But when her face reappeared, she was laughing, 'You have *no* idea how good that just felt!' She pressed her hand to her smile. 'Actually, you do!' She moved closer, reaching up to touch his blond tufts, recently shorn from the Viking pelt. 'Shall I cut mine this short?'

'If you like.'

'You'd still fancy me?' Her hands curled round his neck.

Luca loved her energy too much to point out that he couldn't abide the word 'fancy', like a fascinator or a cake. These moments she burst out through layers of self-doubt like a circus act through a paper hoop were glorious.

'Every minute of every day,' he assured her, not moving.

'I might do it before you leave and we'll see how long it grows before you return.'

They played this game a lot, dancing around his next job.

'Do you want your Valentine's gift now?' he deflected.

'You got me one?' She looked abashed.

'Just this,' he kissed her lips chastely, 'but I promise you *nobody* else in the world is getting one of those.'

'What a coincidence.' She smiled, kissing him back. 'I got you exactly the same thing.'

'And I bought a spare just in case.' He returned it.

'Mine was on a Buy One Get One Free.' She raised him another.

'Three for two.'

'Set of four.'

'Man alive, it's a five.'

Her kiss exploded with laughter. 'Where did you *get* that? Is that Bingo calling?'

Laughing and counting higher, the kiss got thoroughly out of hand as they ricocheted from Aga rail to sink to table.

This was when Luca adored Pax most, when the playful, reckless side of herself she'd repressed so long burst through its paper hoops again and again.

Then, at once, it was serious kissing, meaning-business kissing, the sort they'd shared just a handful of times, knowing where it would lead.

A bell rang from the dining room.

'Ignore it,' she urged as she pulled him with her, leaning back against the table, sending placemats scuttling sideways like shove ha'pennies.

'No ships,' Luca said it before she could, their kisses deepening, his hands in her strange, short hair.

When the bell rang again, more demanding this time, it took all their effort to back away.

'I'll see what he wants,' Luca told her. 'Don't move.'

Lester was dressed in his usual off-duty uniform of well-worn, well-tailored tweed, digital tablet on his lap, creased eyes fixed with a testy zeal. 'Need to take her slowly, lad. She's been rushed.'

Luca stared at him in shock.

'Blair always over-pressurises youngsters to get the quick return,' he went on, unusually conversational, 'can't risk her, or Pax, coming a cropper.'

He's talking about the mare, Luca realized with relief.

'Rare sort, isn't she? Should go all the way with the right pilot.'

'Absolutely.' Luca eyed the door, not just talking about the mare. He was already backing towards it. 'Is there something I can get you?'

But Lester had lifted the tablet. 'Tell me what you think of this chap, young man. Been competing in America. Looking for investors to campaign over here.'

Crossing the room, he watched the horse on screen for a moment, a familiar fist forming in his throat. 'Whereabouts is this?'

'A jumping yard, I believe. The owners are changing disciplines. Oregon, I think. Or was it Ohio? It's written down somewhere.'

'That's Ontario, Lester. It's Canada.' Luca recognized the arena he'd ridden in summer after summer, its white-painted rails, the red-painted buildings around it, and the legs squeezing half a ton of competition stallion over one metre forty fences as though they were cavalletti.

Seeing the place again was like having two hundred volts jolted through his system. He'd left Meredith there. If the gods weren't trying to tell him something today, his conscience was doing the work for them.

Pax checked her reflection in the small, cracked mirror in

the downstairs loo, her shock of newly shortened hair startling, a vampy Ronald Macdonald gazing back. Now *that* will fuck off Mack, she realized with satisfaction.

Back out in the rear corridor, she paused by the tall tableware cupboards to take a selfie as soon as she was in Wi-Fi range, updating her WhatsApp status with the all-new pouting Ron look.

Queued messages were landing, including Bay asking how his horse was settling, along with hands clapping and a galloping National Velvet gif. From the few messages they had ever exchanged, she'd realized he was big on memes and emoji, endearingly at odds with hard-nosed business and farming.

Lottie is fab-u-lous! she replied.

A smiling face came back.

Can't wait to ride her!

A thumbs up.

She waited for more. Nothing.

Mack was straight on her case. *Are you OK, Tishy? What have you done to yourself, wee bird? Do you need to talk?* (translation: what have you done to your hair?)

She typed: *Taken a weight of my mind. Please don't send me flowers.* Then deleted it. Helen had told her enough times not to engage in anything too personal. *I'm fine thank you.*

Her best mate Lizzie had sent *LOVING THE LOOK! YOU ROCK.* Thank goodness for friends. She sent kisses back.

In the dining room, Lester and Luca were studying a horse on screen, a mutual pastime on which they could waste happy hours, she'd noticed. She moved closer to take a look. 'Wow, now that *is* nice. Please tell me it's coming here?'

'Possibly.' Lester didn't look up. 'if your mother agrees.'

'She will,' Pax laughed, assuming it was a joke and glancing across to catch Luca's eye.

He swallowed awkwardly and looked down. Meanwhile, Lester harrumphed.

'What don't I know?' Pax looked at the horse on screen

again. It was fabulous, hurtling over technical, trappy big league fences for fun. 'Is that *really* coming here?'

'You look different.' Lester was eyeing her through his wrinkles.

'I pulled the wool from my own eyes. So, who owns this horse?'

Lester shifted his head in a slight nod. 'Mr Austen is keen on a share.'

Pax laughed incredulously, scaping back her short corkscrews of hair and rolling her eyes Luca. 'Give him a chance, Lester! He's just dropped one off. And I've not competed in over a decade. This one is *way* out of our league.'

'You might not get the ride.' Lester watched the little horse on screen and chuckled. 'If you ask me, Mrs Ledwell wants this little chap for herself.'

Pax peered closer, as in thrall as Lester now. 'It's so quick in front. Who's the jockey? Looks familiar.'

On the video, the rider was cantering the stallion in small circles, cranking the horse's head from side to side to try to get the stride shorter and bouncier, and shouting for the fences to go up. 'Put 'em higher, Ree! This thing can jump the wings!'

'That's not in the UK.'

Luca moved closer beside her, chewing his lip. 'I know him. They're showjumping pros, tough bastards—' He stopped as a small figure appeared on screen to put a jump up, no more than a flash of blonde hair and checked shirt before the camera panned away to the horse. 'I've worked that barn.'

'You've worked in half the world's yards, Horsemaker, and you always say that about your bosses,' Pax pointed out, excitement building as she watched the horse rubber-ball over a metre and a half as though it was a hay bale. No wonder her mother wanted to sit on it. 'Just wow!'

Unable to stand in one place for long, still feeling hyped, she took a lap of the room her grandparents had wined and dined key owners in, her eyes moving restlessly from picture to picture, past Compton Magna horses deemed victorious enough to capture in oil. If Bay's classy mare was the cream of the stud's hundred plus years of breeding experience, the horse on screen was a twenty-first espresso shot of speed and power.

'Standing a horse like that here could make all the difference.' She hurried back to Lester's side to ask about its breeding and ownership, competition record and veterinary history, progeny and fertility, all of which the old man had at his fingertips like an almanac. 'What other investors are interested?'

'That's all in hand,' Lester dismissed, eyeing her. 'You *have* changed something, I'm certain.'

She smiled and waited expectantly, tilting the hacked red corkscrews one way.

'What is it?'

'Can't you see?' She tilted them the other.

'No.'

'It's my *outlook*, Lester. From now on, I intend to be more like a pro and not care who's paying the bills so long as the horses get fed,' she quoted Luca.

'Your mother's favourite catchphrase!' Lester's eyes gleamed in their creased nests. 'That's the spirit!'

'You might have credited it,' Pax grumbled at Luca, who shrugged apologetically.

'Do I smell burning, young man?' Lester was watching him, gimlet-eyed now.

'Only bridges, Lester,' Luca said, sprinting back to the kitchen to rescue whatever had caught.

'What's that supposed to mean?' Pax wondered aloud.

'The lad's concerned Beck might be replaced, I should imagine.'

'He doesn't need to worry.' Pax followed Luca. Almost at the door she turned back, remembering to ask, 'Where exactly is the horse in the video based, Lester?'

'Oklahoma rings a bell,' he said vaguely, then fixed her with the same penetrating look that had just seen Luca off at speed.

'If I may be so bold, this morning is the finest I've seen you look in a very long time. Quite your old self, Pax.'

'Thank you, Lester.' Receiving a compliment from him was as rare as riding a Derby winner. She felt jet-propelled.

In the kitchen, Luca had taken a charred pan of tomatoes off the simmering plate and was leaning back against the Aga rail. He found a smile before she could question his hangdog look. 'Breakfast is ruined, sorry, angel.'

'It's OK, I've lost my appetite.' She paced around the table. Even from the kitchen, they could hear the Beck and Cruisoe still bellowing competitively on the yard. 'Beck's safe, don't worry. There's no way Bay will invest; he complained Lottie was overpriced.'

'So, you like the new mare?' Luca watched her.

'I *love* the mare. We were both bred in the purple right here. We're what this place is all about. We can do the job.'

'Owner might be tricky.'

'Competing was one of the only things I was ever good at, I mean *really* good. I can handle Bay. I know I've been out of the game a long time, but I can do this.' She stopped in front of him, putting her hands to her hot cheeks, seventeen again. 'It's really happening!'

He covered them with his own, the smile angling sideways. 'I don't doubt it. But you must pace yourself, angel. Don't rush everything.'

The sense of calm and well-being briefly flooded through her.

'You're right.' She leant into him gratefully, head heavy on his shoulder.

He pressed his lips into that newfound territory of pale skin on her throat, but she pulled away, uncomfortable with the way Luca always fast-shifted to physical when their secrets surfaced.

'That horse on Lester's iPad. Do you know it?'

'Never seen it before today.'

She studied his face, not doubting its honesty.

'You really don't have to worry about Bay, you know,' she said, trying to believe it.

'I know.' He smiled that big, easy smile, trusting her more than she trusted herself. It set off fidget spinners insider her. Luca who was so good. Luca who shared her weakness for self-destructive addiction and attraction.

She thought back to the local riders she'd caught up on the Three Mile Point that morning, all gossiping so loudly they hadn't realized she was there. *Part-man, part-Centaur, buttocks like marble, amazing hands, rock hard legs.* Reducing him to the sum of his perfect parts.

But it wasn't Luca she had spoken up for, defending the indefensible and snapping at poor Mo Dawkins before galloping away.

It was Bay.

7

Carly Turner liked Fridays. She juggled three jobs through the week, each day carefully timetabled to ensure she let nobody down and had childcare sorted. Husband Ash's morning gym routine was as inflexible as his late-night drinking one, so she needed to be organized.

It helped that so many of her husband's family also lived on the Orchard Estate. This morning, Nana Turner was looking after Carly's youngest two while six-year-old Ellis had joined his cousins three doors down to share breakfast before walking with them to primary school. Meanwhile, Carly had been at Lower Bagot Farmhouse since seven.

She'd only recently started as the Gunn family's Girl Friday – more accurately Girl Friday, Tuesday morning and Wednesday afternoon – and it was her favourite workplace.

Today, with boss Petra out riding with her friends from first light, Carly had been responsible for getting the Gunns' two daughters to the station to catch their train into Oxford where they went to school. The Gunn boys were older, one boarding, the other cycling to the local college where he was studying to resit his GCSEs.

Back at the farmhouse, Carly would usually have the place to herself: her magic hour, tidying away breakfast and making beds before Petra returned. Carly loved the Gunns' big house and liked to imagine it was her own.

But today Petra's husband was working from home. On the days Charlie Gunn shambled round the kitchen in gaping dressing gown and underpants, demanding fresh coffee and hot pastries and scratching his balls while eyeing her backside, Carly didn't like the job as much.

'I'll be based here a lot more now we're going to let out the London flat, Carly,' he told her chest. 'I'm relying on you to keep us shipshape. My wife neglects this place – and me – terribly when she's writing.' The 'poor me' face doubled his already double chin.

Hanging around to watch her work while he ate his croissants, he ordered Alexa to play obscure nineties indie tracks and told her about all the festivals he used to go to when he was 'young and free'. She wanted to squirt him away with her Mr Muscle bleach spray, especially when he asked if she was in the village Facebook group and had 'any idea who the Travelodge adulterer is?'

She busied herself wiping the surfaces and told him it wasn't her business.

'You *know*, don't you?' he teased, watching her. A gung-ho member of the village cricket team and Bardswolds social scene, gregarious Charlie shared his wife's nose for scandal.

'It's idle talk.' The husband's identity was an open secret on the Orchard Estate. Her sister-in-law had been gossiping about it for weeks, but Carly wasn't about to tell Charlie Gunn that.

'So talk to me idly,' he coaxed.

When she didn't reply, he ran through a few outlandish suggestions, from Brian Hicks to the vicar to old Mr Bentley, trying to make her laugh. Then the right name came up.

Her wiping cloth hesitated too long.

'You are *kidding*?' he gasped, letting out a whoop.

'Course I'm kidding!' She cocked her jaw and forced a laugh, wiping on vigorously.

He snorted. 'Nice one! Almost had me there.' He ran a hand through his thinning hair. 'Well, whoever it is, they have no bloody class. I'd take a mistress to a far cushier hotel.' He gave her a hot look, then seeing the ice in her eyes, added, 'If her husband wasn't a bare-knuckle fighter, ha!'

The wiping cloth stopped completely. 'Who told you that?'

'Facebook again. Terribly tribal, those amateur bouts. Do you sell tickets?'

Hearing hooves, Carly gratefully escaped outside to greet Petra, who was far later than expected. 'That turned into an epic! Local landowning tax dodger flew in like Logan Roy. Did you see the helicopter?'

In the Gunns' little stable yard, Carly helped untack The Redhead, a chestnut mare as temperamental as she was beautiful, her ears flattening furiously as she was rugged-up, ready to be turned out with the children's ponies.

'She's got a sore leg,' Carly said without thinking, reaching down with warm fingers to one knee. 'This one.'

'You're right.' Petra turned in surprise. 'Bridge's pony kicked out at her. Gill thought it looked fine.'

'It is.' Carly felt the mare's tight, velvet skin relax to her touch. 'She's not in pain, I reckon, just mad she didn't land a kick back.'

'You *have* been practising!' Petra laughed clipping together leg straps. Red-nosed from the cold, her wide, dark gaze gleamed, informal and gossipy. 'The Horsemaker's healing lessons are clearly paying off.'

About to mutter that it was the only pay she got at the stud, Carly stopped herself. Petra wasn't known for her discretion and was close to Ronnie. She wanted to keep the weekend job.

'Yeah, Luca's a pro,' she told her instead. 'Showed me how to lay on hands. Like this.' She held hers over the mare's knee again. Harnessing the gift Carly and Luca O'Brien both possessed was something Ronnie was eager to encourage. Carly's was far stronger, Luca said, but needed knowledge and experience to back it up and make it useful.

Carly loved horses and extra work at the stud had seemed like a dream job at first. But a month in and still unpaid, she needed to make it clear she wasn't doing it just for the fun.

'Feeling better?' Petra asked the mare who flicked back her ears and banged an impatient leg. 'How's our baby on board?'

'All good, I reckon.' Carly straightened up and patted her.

While the circumstances of the mare's pregnancy were regrettable – Ronnie's new star stallion escaping his field to pursue her into Church Meadow for a covering half the village had witnessed – Petra was thrilled at the prospect of the patter of tiny hooves.

'I loved being pregnant, but Charlie had the snip after four,' she sighed, patting the mare's belly fondly. 'Are you and Ash planning on more?'

Petra's open curiosity threw Carly sometimes, the way she casually asked very personal questions.

'Can't afford to right now,' she muttered.

'Not even for a King's Purse?'

It was the prize for the gypsy fight. Petra must have read the Facebook thread too. Carly's hope that it would just go away faded further.

The branch of the Turners that she had married into was settled, but theirs remained an old travelling family with long-standing traditions, including the bare-knuckle match for the title King of the Turners. This year, pressure was on Ash to challenge the holder, Jed, his mean-spirited thug of a cousin. Carnage was predicted.

'That's not happening while the title holder's inside,' she muttered, thinking *or while I have breath in my body to stop it.*

'Of course! I'd forgotten Jed's in prison. Poaching Austen venison, wasn't it?' Petra made it sound like a Nigella recipe.

'He's a nasty bastard, Jed.'

'Mo's rather fond of him. He's her SMC. All those bad boy tattoos.'

'She should pick a better one.' Carly found it weird the way Petra's riding friends ranked local men by fanciability – they called it the 'Safe Married Crush' – especially when they were as patently *un*safe and *un*fanciable as her husband's thug of a cousin. 'Jed's no better than her Barry.'

'You've heard the rumours too, then?' Petra eyed her.

Carly liked Mo Dawkins. Everyone liked cheery, hard-working Mo. It wasn't fair on her.

'It's just talk.' She repeated what she'd said to Charlie, wishing she believed it.

'Oh, I hope so.' Petra's dark eyes pooled with concern. 'Bridge says there've been some horrid comments online. I can't bring myself to look.'

'Facebook is bloody two-faced.'

'Isn't it just? I don't believe any of that nonsense about Ash and the steroids, by the way.' Petra beamed then, seeing Carly's brows lower, added that she really must shower before hurrying inside.

Carly didn't like the idea of Ash fighting one bit. She viewed the big Turner bout as outdated nonsense, a traveller tradition dating back long before the family had settled locally in the seventies. She'd tried talking him out of it, pointing out that they had a nice house in a good village, three small children, a dog and two guinea pigs to think about and, after his college course, he was going to work as a farriery apprentice with his mate, Flynn. He didn't need to trade punches with Jed to prove he was the better man.

But Ash just gave her the look she remembered from his soldiering days, his pale silver eyes telling her he could do whatever he liked.

She'd tried talking to Nana Turner about it. Ash's gentle little mother's agoraphobia – and television addiction – had confined her in her maisonette for decades, but back in the eighties she'd seen Ash's dad fight for the King title many times. Nat Turner's bouts had gone down in folklore; he'd never once been beaten. After he'd taken off on the roads, his long disappearances off-grid or behind bars had eventually lost him both the title and Nan's love. But he was still remembered as the best fighter the family had ever witnessed.

Nana hated the idea of her boy Ash fighting. 'It turned his dad brutal, Carly love,' she'd confided quietly. 'I found out Nat wasn't the king I thought he was at all. I got that very wrong.' And she'd looked terribly sad before pulling her cardigan tighter, saying, 'Ash is nothing like his dad, you'll see' and changing channels to watch *EastEnders*.

Carly felt sorry for Nana, who everyone took for granted as captive babysitter and soap expert. Like Carly, she was a 'Gorger' outsider who had married into the travelling clan, but unlike Carly she'd shared the road with Nat for a while when they'd first been together, travelling in a traditional vardo wagon pulled by a black-and-white Vanner pony with 'feathers as big as yeti boots'. Carly imagined Nana must have been very pretty once, with her big brown eyes and sparrow figure. The children doted on her. And she loved hearing about the horses. Nana loved horses.

When she turned out Petra's mare, Carly took a few pictures on her phone to show Nana, admiring her bucking around the field before sinking down to roll. The Redhead suffered no fools; her foal would be amazing. Luca had told her the sire had once sold for millions and that his few offspring were super-valuable.

Ash and his mates had laughed when Carly shared this. 'All that expensive jizz and he shags the girl next door!'

Unlike his mum, Ash wasn't interested in horses. Carly's weekend job up at the stud rankled her husband who said Captain Percy had treated Turners like scum, especially his dad Nat (although from what she could tell half the village had held feuds with Nat Turner and Jocelyn Percy, so it stood to reason the two had shared bad blood). 'Mean bastard was the Captain.'

Old money was always tight-fisted in Carly's experience.

She took out her phone to politely remind Ronnie about her unpaid wages again, but instead found herself opening Facebook, checking in on the village group for the first time in ages. The Turners were in the firing line as usual, although most of the bad press was predictably about Jed, Ash's no-good cousin.

Then an update on the Travelodge Adulterer made her start. He'd been named and shamed.

Three minutes ago.

'You'll never guess who's bought the manor!' Mo burst into her parents' farmhouse. 'Kenny Kay.'

'That's nice.' Joan was making a fried breakfast, hanging onto the Rayburn rail for support as she stepped over the elderly sheepdog and prodded at a frying pan jumping with fat, amid which swam black pudding, sausages, bacon and eggs.

'Mum, what did we say about watching yours and Dad's saturated fats?' Mo chided good-naturedly.

'There wasn't enough of Grace's hoopy cereal for all of us, and you know it disagrees with Jan's tummy.'

Mo started ticking her off that a diabetic woman with a BMI over forty and a man with a pacemaker should try to love muesli, but Joan went teary and said it was 'a special treat for your dad on Valentine's day, love. Enough for everyone. You'll have some won't you? You've been out so long in the cold you'll need a nice hot breakfast.'

Mo didn't have the willpower to argue. 'Just this once, then. Exciting about Kenny Kay, isn't it?'

'Believe it when I see it. They said Tom Jones was moving here last year. I even bought a new frock for church.' Pink-faced and cheery again, Joan started making eggy bread and singing along to an old Elvis number on the radio, accompanied by daughter Jan in her comfy chair.

Mo helped herself to tea from the pot. 'Grace said some woman called round? Was it about livery?'

'No idea, but she plonked herself down in here and refused to budge. I had to leave her to go up and get Jan dressed, didn't I, Jan?'

'Mum thought she was burglarising the place,' Jan laughed.

'And she told you she wanted to see me?' Mo hoped it wasn't a tax inspector or DEFRA, although she was sure the paperwork was up to date.

'Your Barry turned up and sorted it. He looked ever so pale.'

'Been up lambing,' Mo explained, quickly adding, 'and he's spending his days fitting that wet room in the bungalow,' (because it was good to keep mentioning it), 'big enough to park a car in, it is.'

'Why'd you want to park a car in a bathroom?' asked Joan, looking round as Sid appeared at the back door in a blast of cold air, climbing out of his boots, coat and muddy overalls, and shrinking from Goliath to wizened David. 'You hear that, love? Our Mo has a bathroom big enough for her car.'

'Bet that's chilly!'

In her chair, Jan whooped with laughter.

'No, it has underfloor heating, Dad.'

'Can't dry these on underfloor heating!' He pulled off his gloves and hat and put them on the range from which his wife was spooning out four big fried breakfasts.

The Stokes' kitchen had barely changed since ten-year-old Mo had fed rashers to little sister Jan before charging along Plum Run to the same village primary school that Grace went to now. It smelled of wet coats, wet boots and wet dogs, every surface crowded with clutter and paperwork, no two kitchen cabinet doors hanging at the same angle. The old dresser still played host to ancient county show rosettes and 'best China' only used at Easter and Christmas. The same painted plates spotted the walls, horse brasses on the beams and that year's corn merchant calendar on the back of the paw-scratched door.

Mo pulled a chair alongside Jan's so she could help her eat, her sister's cerebral palsy making her too shaky to keep food on a fork.

'Help me run the farm shop today?' Jan entreated.

Their farm shop – AKA Sid's Hut, a glorified garden shed by the farm entrance – was never going to rival the Austen family's overpriced Daylesford pretender at the other end of the village, but it was Jan's little empire.

'I'll see what I can do,' Mo promised, adding it to her list. 'Maybe an hour over lunchtime?'

'Too cold for me in there this time of year!' Joan made 'brrrr' noises, then chuckled when Sid gave a *Carry On* growl and offered to warm his wife up.

'Still flirting after forty years of marriage!' Jan nudged her sister. 'Just like Nan and Grandad.'

Mo grinned back, mouth full of toast. Their grandparents, who had once duetted 'Anyone Can See I Love You' over this kitchen table, had bought the smallholding after the Second World War when land was cheap, small-scale agriculture being actively encouraged to restock the nation and end rationing. Combining fruit and veg growing with rearing pigs, later adding a small Jersey herd and a Christmas tree plantation, the family had eked a modest living for four generations. Everyone mucked in. Those grandparents had worked into their eighties and sometimes Mo worried they'd set the bar too high.

For all his bravado, Sid Stokes was seventy-nine, his thin, stooped body wracked by arthritis after years bent double over his plots, his lungs shot from the endless roll-ups, his mind ever-more absent. Joan was a robust force of nature fifteen years her husband's junior, but her weight was starting to take its toll, her knees and hips crippling her, besides which, looking after Jan took so much of her time and energy.

Born with cerebral palsy five years after Mo, Jan was

wheelchair-bound and reliant upon parents who stubbornly refused outside help. Now in her mid-thirties, Jan was opinionated and often hilarious – but in just as much denial about her parent's increasing vulnerability as they were. If Mo tried to talk to her about it, she'd melt down and accuse her sister of wanting her locked up in the 'funny farm'.

The old Stokes' family joke was that they already lived in a funny farm, but it was starting to feel all too real. Her parents were struggling, their health and finances precarious. It was a hand-to-mouth livelihood. Try as she might to stop up the gaps, Mo knew something must change.

The farmhouse was draughty and damp in winter, its downstairs bathroom impractical. A solid fuel backburner still heated the water and the few ancient, silted radiators. The hoists that had been fitted decades ago to help get Jan in and out of bed and the bath were old and unreliable but her disability benefits had been cut to bare bones after the PIP review, and Joan and Sid were too proud and frightened to appeal for more help for fear the authorities would take her away, their daughter who still needed them, as opposed to the older one who they relied upon.

'Kenny Kay's moving to the village, Dad!' Jan told their father now.

'My arse he is!' he boomed.

'That's what I said,' Joan scoffed. 'Don't listen to chitchat, Maureen.'

'He is!' Mo waved a forked tomato. 'Gill Walcote says so.' Her parents never doubted the word of the village vet.

'Then I'll stand that man a drink at the Jug.' Sid slammed a calloused palm on the table, triggering the collie barking frantically. 'Your Barry know? Needs cheering up, he does. Grumpy bugger this morning.'

'Mum said as much. You should have offered him breakfast.' She watched her mother dish up seconds. Barry loved a fry-up.

'Stuff to do, he said,' Joan sighed.

'All that DIY!' Jan hooted.

'Who needs a bathroom big as a garage!' Sid cackled back.

Mo said nothing, but she felt her husband's pain.

Five years ago, when farm worker Barry had inherited a small lump sum from an aunt, they thought they'd come up with the perfect plan to help out her family and make their own dreams happen. Forfeiting the low-rent cottage that came with Barry's job, they'd bought a rundown bungalow in the village that they'd been doing up ever since, adapting it for her parents and Jan. When it was finished, the informal agreement was that they'd swap places, with Mo and Barry taking over running the farm while Mum and Dad enjoyed a quieter life in the bungalow with all mod cons and adapted living for Jan. But her parents had either misunderstood, or they'd changed their minds, because they now steadfastly insisted that they'd rather stay put, thank you.

Saddled with a hefty mortgage and a house they'd lovingly designed around others' needs, Barry and Mo – who never used to have a cross word – had started to bicker about it. Work had slowed to a crawl. In truth, the wet room was barely started, the marital squabbles far more heated than the floor. While Mo pointed out that her parents could hardly be expected to visualise themselves somewhere that still looked like a building site, Barry – who thought they should cut their losses and sell it – argued that adding Jan's adaptations would be costly and put buyers off, and complained that Mo was never there to help.

It was true that she was at the farm first thing every morning to help Jan up and was there last thing at night to see them safely to bed before checking on the horses. As well as running the livery yard, doing the pigs, and organizing produce and tree orders, she cleaned and shopped for them, all too often with poor Grace in tow. The small profit she made from her liveries all went back into the farm, but it was never enough. Sid could no longer keep on top of the market garden side, even assisted by local agricultural college students drafted in as work experience in high season. The fruit and veg had done poorly last year, rivals undercutting them, regular customers complaining about the quality, and Pick Your Own falling in favour. Their little roadside grocery stall, Sid's Hut, set up so that Jan had a job, was rarely open for more than an hour each day because Joan – who had to stay with her – found it too hard on her legs. Only the Christmas trees still made a tidy profit.

'You and Barry going out for a romantic meal tonight, love?' Joan asked, wiping her plate with her third slice of bread. 'Grace told us she and Bella are invited to a sleepover at Tilly's after school.' The three Pony Club friends were an inseparable village trio.

'Staying in for a movie and a shepherd's pie.'

'You two deserve a treat, love.'

After several rashers of bacon, a sausage, eggy bread and beans, Mo felt fatter than ever, worrying her good dress might not fit.

'The bungalow is *so* cosy and toasty we never want to go out,' she said, remembering to keep selling them the dream.

'Not like this place!' cackled Sid. Even in the kitchen – which was the warmest room in the house – they were all wearing two jumpers.

Mo seized the moment. 'You can move across there whenever you like, you know that. Me and Barry will take on the damp and the draughts here.'

'Wouldn't want to put you to the bother, would we, Sid love?'

'Your mother and I have got a few more seasons left in us before you put us out to pasture, Maureen. Tell your Barry he can sit pretty in Austens' tractors for now. You're not to fret yourself about us just yet.'

But Mo did fret. She fretted a lot.

'I'll still be over to get Jan into bed this evening, don't worry,' she reassured her mum.

Joan was cutting up an extra sausage for Jan. 'We can do that, can't we, Sid?'

'What?' He looked confused.

'It's no bother.' Mo watched her mother helping herself absent-mindedly to the pieces of sausage, feeding one to a collie. Last time they'd tried, Jan had broken a toe and Dad had put his back out.

'You take advantage of Grace being away, my girl,' Joan ordered.

Across the table, Jan was laughing. 'I'm ruining your sex life, Sis. Stay at home and have a shag!'

'What's she saying?' Sid demanded deafly again.

'That Grace might need a sleeping bag,' Mo fired back quickly. 'For her sleepover.' She caught Jan's eye, giggles bubbling.

'Grace did make us laugh earlier,' Joan joined in, faded blue eyes merry. 'She told us Tilly's mum's new house has lots of bunk beds so she can have friends over all the time because that's what you get when your parents separate.'

'Bunk beds?' Mo asked, confused.

'A second home.' Joan tucked in her chins. 'Tilly calls her dad's place her weekend cottage now, Grace says.'

'Doesn't do when a family breaks up like that, does it?' Mo thought about Pax Forsyth's little boy heading to school from one parent's house then going home to another's and felt a pang of sympathy for his displaced little life.

'He's a rascal, that Bay Austen.'

Mo had a soft spot for handsome, playful dad Bay, whose fierce Dutch wife by contrast treated her daughter's friends like school hamsters she was forced to look after. 'Petra says it was Monique who walked out on him after having a threesome with—' She stopped herself in alarm, the Saddle Bags' puritan turned family rumourmonger.

'Should count herself lucky, having three sons!' Sid said loudly, making Jan snigger, Mo realized with relief that their parents would have completely missed the point.

'Don't gossip, Maureen,' Joan was chiding. 'Bad enough you and those friends of yours loose-lipping Mr Kay.'

Mo coloured. She'd spent too much time with the Bags.

'Kenny Kay, eh?' Sid was chuckling again. 'I wonder if the Turners know?'

'What's it to them?'

'Kenny shot Nat Turner when he was out beating for the Eyngate guns, you remember Joan?'

'*That's* who got shot? Nat Turner?' Mo gasped. No-good Nat, errant head of the Turner family, was the village's wandering icon, its Keith Richards of free-roaming lawlessness, occasional incarceration and regular intoxication.

'Almost did for him,' Joan nodded. 'Shame it didn't, some say. A no-good bugger, that man.'

'Mum!'

'King of the Turners, Nat was back then. Never was the same after that day. Went on the road. Ashley and Janine hardly knew their dad. And as for that poor little wife of his…'

'Now who's tittle-tattling!' Jan laughed.

'Historical facts, Janet,' shushed Joan.

Nat was still remembered as a man who parented with his fists. A regular fighter at The Jugged Hare, he'd come close to killing his opponents more than once.

'Kenny shot Nat Turner?' Mo repeated, finding it hard to process. 'And Kenny's still alive?'

'He was a household star, love,' Joan chuckled, as though that excused a man from all earthly reckoning, which in the eighties Mo guessed it did. 'And he was friends with that Peter Sanson. It was his shoot, as I recall. *Nobody* messed with Mr Sanson. Nat worked for him.'

'*Sir* Peter,' Mo reminded her, thinking back to seeing the two men at Eyngate Hall that morning.

'They were like brothers, Sir Sanson and Kenny Kay.'

'Them were the days!' Sid sighed. 'Brought this old village

to life, them two. Always stood a few rounds when they was drinking in the Jug with the Captain.'

Once again using the vet's name for added authority, Mo said, 'Gill Walcote suggested they might have both been after Ronnie Percy?'

'No, that doesn't sound right,' Sid crossed his arms, tilting his head up, one eye closed in thought. 'Kenny was a womaniser, it's true, for all he was married before God, but Sir Peter only had eyes one girl as I recall, an Austen. The actress. Before she married that theatre fellow. Smitten, he was. Bought her a Porsche.'

'Flashy bugger,' Joan tutted. 'I'd rather have a bunch of wildflowers any day, wouldn't you girls?'

'Porsche!' Mo and Jan said together.

Remembering she had to check on Barry's whereabouts and get the shepherd's pie out to defrost for that evening's romantic cosying, Mo got up, hurriedly clearing the plates. 'Back in a jiff to wash up, Mum.'

'Pigs need doing.'

'That too.'

As she left, stepping into her boots in the porch, Mo could hear her father cackling, 'A Porsche! Silly girl went and married that grumpy Northerner instead.'

'And this silly woman married you,' Joan chuckled and Jan made the exaggerated 'Eeeew!' protest which meant their parents were kissing.

Mo hoped she and Barry were as loved up at their age.

8

Although Kit Donne had lost faith in God when his wife Hermia died, he still held the little Church of St Mary's in Compton Magna in great affection. It's yew-shaded graveyard was where Hermia lay at rest, just across the lane from the cottage that they'd shared for her final years after a riding accident reduced her bright, brilliant life to a small, painful one. Her headstone was now their meeting place, one-sided trysts in which he told her his woes, most recently his struggles to get to grips with his theatrical adaptation of Siegfried Sassoon's semi-autobiographical *Sherston* trilogy, a labour of love he was desperate to finish before directing *King Lear* at Stratford.

To work on it uninterrupted, Kit had relocated his desk to his ornate, wood-framed greenhouse, the closest approximation of a garret he could fashion. He liked its chilly simplicity. The Old Almshouse had too many distracting books, radio stations and snacks on offer, the log fire made him dozy, and WhatsApp messages buzzed in from London friends. Above all, it had memories.

Out here, Kit's focus was stripped back: his phone was off, only written pages lay amid the jungle of hibernating tender perennials, a small paraffin heater glowing close by.

Across the lane, St Mary's bell tower watched silently over him, its clock no longer striking each passing quarter in which he wrote nothing and thought too much. Until the roof was repaired, the bells would remain muted, scaffolding imprisoning them.

Setting a mug of green tea down on his desk, Kit gazed out at the metal framework now surrounding the spire, annoyed with himself. A born procrastinator, he sought outside distractions in direct proportion to the amount of pressure he was under, but even he didn't know what had possessed him to agree to join a village committee to raise funds to repair the bloody thing.

Hermia's jolly sister-in-law, Viv Austen, had caught him at a weak moment when she'd rung – halfway down a bottle of Malbec, not his first – and followed it up with a note, dropped through the door early this morning.

Having carried it out with him, he read it at his makeshift desk while he waited for the heater to come up to full strength. Her bold, round handwriting in blue fountain pen, reminded him all too vividly of his wife's. *So pleased you feel you can put something back into this village.*

'I never took anything from it,' he muttered, casting it aside. 'It killed Hermia.'

Opening his Moleskine book, he reread the last line he'd written yesterday, trying to make sense if it.

A salve in salvo: View Holloa and Howzat?

It made no sense whatsoever. Damned Malbec. Kit's ambitious attempt to weave Sassoon's war poetry through his prose was proving a struggle to reconcile and the cause of much rereading and woozy, late-night note-taking.

He rubbed his face with his hands before taking another swig from his mug, grimacing and pouring the rest into a potted fig. His kids, who were trying to make him cut down on coffee, had filled the cottage's cupboards with herbal teas, crammed together like fairies from *A Midsummer Night's*

Dream – Rosehip, Dandelion, Valerian Root, Elderberry Flower. He needed caffeine.

Inert with ennui, he glared up at the broken clock tower through the rooflights, fooling nobody that it was always twenty past three.

It had once been to Hermia, his lost friend and soulmate, whom he would talk endlessly about his work. He sometimes still did, imagining her here with him now, listening in quiet encouragement.

'Come on, man!' He slapped his cheeks, blew some raspberries, closed his eyes and started reciting the final part of 'The Last Meeting', Sassoon's beautiful lament to a slain friend, which always helped Kit capture the poet's spirit, this man of extraordinary insight and controlled anger.

'I know that he is lost among the stars,
And may return no more but in their light.
Though his hushed voice may call me in the stir
Of whispering trees, I shall not understand.'

It only took a few lines to find the voice he needed, the lament deep in his head, that urgent need for the deep root of nature and nostalgia to survive the eviscerating horror of war and loss. Sassoon's words inevitably made him cry.

And straight away he could see what his note meant and how it related to the scene he'd been wrestling with. As a coping mechanism, on occasions Sherston had imagined the Somme battlefield as a fox hunt or a cricket match, his mind visualising happier times, just as it did Kit's.

'It's a gift for a dramatist, don't you see?' he told Hermia.

Yes, Henry Higgins, she replied in his head, that gurgle of laughter in her throat.

Sobbing and laughing, he rubbed his eyes with the heels of his hands before looking up at the church clock for reassurance that time was standing still.

That exact same gurgle of laughter greeted him.

An amused face stared back through the condensation. '*There* you are!'

For a moment he thought he was looking at a ghost. Celestial and beaming, surrounded by blood-red flowers, his Hermia was back.

Then he heard dogs whining at ankle height and saw a small canine pack yapping at him through the lowest glass panes.

'Bought you some blooms and the hottest tickets in town as a peace offering!'

It took a beat to recognize his wife's childhood best friend, often mistaken for her sister back then. These days, Ronnie Percy was a strident, horsey type with whom he'd had only a brief acquaintance. Enough for one lifetime, he felt.

She was brandishing a glowing phone screen up at the glass. 'Isn't technology marvellous? Look! I promise I'm not going to share these with anyone else if you say yes!'

Guessing she'd just photographed him weeping in his greenhouse, Kit's face drained of colour even more.

The Church Meadow in Compton Magna formed a hilly, stony cushion between The Green and pastureland.

The meadow had been gifted to the Church of England by the Bingham-Percys of Eyngate Hall almost two hundred years earlier, when they'd also provided a pretty Cotswold stone church in which their workers could worship, and a school in which to educate their children.

No more than five acres in size, the meadow counted as common land, once grazed by locals' sheep and geese, also serving as a regular rest stop for the travelling community, many of them Turners. The oldest of the Roma families maintained it was a magic place – it was on the meadow that they traded horses, betrothed young couples and hosted fights – although the rowdy behaviour of more recent visitors had undermined that claim and they were regarded with suspicion by villagers these days.

Nowadays the gates were guarded by a vast tree trunk preventing vehicular access. Dog walkers and horse riders had to squeeze round it to climb up and admire the view across the village from the highest point, where three standing stones known as the Three Witches had huddled together for millennia, shortened to stubby, pocked boulders by so many centuries of wind.

It took a keen eye to spot the chalk marks that occasionally appeared on the witches' rough flanks. A circle with a dot perhaps, or three crossed stripes.

Roma signs.

Today, new marks had appeared to confirm a forthcoming gathering, a rare travellers' rite; a fight was in store. The whole Turner family was being called.

While this message was also currently being passed on more effectively by a smartphone app messaging service with end-to-end encryption, the traditional sign meant one thing: the travelling arm of the family was reuniting.

Nat Turner was coming back to the village.

Kit Donne's response to being offered the best seats at a star-studded, critically acclaimed, Bowie-inspired sell-out musical was less enthusiastic than Ronnie had hoped.

'For *tonight*, you say?' Scruffily patrician and pompously academic, the Cumbrian-born husband her best friend had once described in a letter as 'the funniest and sexiest man on earth' regarded her irritably.

'Are you busy?' she called through the glass.

'I'm working on a script!'

'You'll need a break then. This show's tipped to storm the Oliviers.'

'I didn't much go in for glam rock first time round.' He eyed her wearily over his round framed hipster reading glasses.

'Hermia worshipped Ziggy Stardust! We both did.'

'She was more of a David Grey fan latterly.'

'Who doesn't love "Suffragette City"?' She started to sing the words she and her friend had growled into hairbrushes as girls, both hopelessly in love with Bowie.

He held his hands up. 'Please stop.'

Ronnie had hoped he might offer her coffee to nurture their budding village allegiance, but he hadn't even come out of his greenhouse, redoubling her determination to liberate him.

Over the years, Hermia had written reams to Ronnie about how brilliant her husband was, how passionate and enthusiastic, how devoted a father, often repeating how well they'd get on, although the two never met in her lifetime. In rare, candid moments, she'd also written of his insularity, his overthinking slumps into depression, his intolerance of fools. Ronnie had been left with a strong sense that her childhood friend – the closest thing she'd had to a sibling in both their loyalty and their horse-mad, pocket-rocket blonde joie de vivre – had revealed Kit's self-destructive melancholia for a practical purpose. Hermia knew Ronnie's natural good cheer with grumpy horses, snappy dogs, savage cats and unforgiving children would spill effortlessly onto crabby widowers. Dogged good cheer was her legacy.

'You really should blow off the cobwebs.' She marched round to the greenhouse door and knocked on it. 'Get out and have some fun.'

'It's kind of you to think of me.' He opened it reluctantly.

'*First* person I thought of!'

'How extraordinary.'

'Have these.' She thrust in the flowers. 'Unwanted gift. I was going to put them on Hermia's grave – I know how much she loved roses – but I didn't want you to think some mystery man had done it, so I hope you don't mind passing them on?'

'Thank you, I will.'

She stepped inside and held up her phone screen again, taking advantage of his wistful look to show him the ticket Q Codes. 'And see *Ziggy* for her.'

'Will you leave me in peace if I agree?' He looked round for somewhere to put the flowers.

'You can't just hide away in here, although it's good to see you using the thing.' She peered around the greenhouse, which she'd been forced to pay for in cash to have delivered and erected so quickly after her old horse Dickon had accidentally destroyed the old one, a primary reason she now had no money. 'Goodness, you've made it into an office in here.'

Inside, it still smelled new with unexpected top notes of creative endeavour instead of the usual compost and wintering geraniums. Taking the cue, her dogs crowded in behind her, Pax's young deerhound Knott cocking his leg against a large potted fig. 'Sorry about that! No bloody manners.'

'Supposed to be a natural fertiliser.' He took it admirably in his stride. 'Or is that just humans. Can't remember. Do you?'

'Pee in my plant pots?' she asked vaguely, having spotted a familiar letterhead the desktop. 'I see you've been invited to C.R.R.A.P in the village hall too.'

'What?' He looked shocked.

'Viv's committee – the Church Roof Repair Action Plan. I'm trying to get out of it, aren't you?'

'It's important to put something back into a village,' he said grandiosely.

'I plan to put a successful stud farm back into it.' She turned to him. 'And get you out tonight.'

His gaze was unnerving. He had a very intense eyes – she remembered darling Hermia eulogizing about them in letters – dark and clever, with a Rochester twinkle to their sternness.

'*Do* say you'll see this show. The *Telegraph* gave it five stars. The *Guardian* probably did too,' she added quickly, for balance.

'Praise indeed.'

'You must have heard of it? It was written by that chap who does lots at the Royal Court. Terribly cool and clever.'

The smile was more withering than winning. 'I'm godfather to "that chap's" son.'

'Then I'm amazed you haven't been to his hot new production.'

'I saw it in preview. It's superb.'

Ronnie refused to be blindsided, her smile outshining his smirk. 'Good enough to see again, then!'

'You sound just like Hermia!' With a sardonic half-laugh, Kit looked at the roses. 'And you're quite right, she would have loved the show.'

They shared a split second of something close to a connection, united by the force of their mutual affection for a woman whose death still shocked them.

At forty, her children still tiny, Hermia's life had metamorphized overnight when a motorist had spooked her horse, leaving her unconscious on the road. Although she'd come out of the resulting coma, her brain injury was the fever dream from which she'd never awoken. She'd become dependent upon Kit for the seven years until her death, always believing she would recover her former self. Years that must have been agony for Kit, whose brilliant, vibrant wife haunted what was left behind. Years that had often been a living hell for Hermia whose loved ones lost sight of her self-belief, until the day a bleed on the brain took her away from them totally. Intensely private years, from which Ronnie – living abroad throughout, a Percy pariah in exile – had been tactfully excluded, the few letters they'd exchanged after a lifetime of lively correspondence distilled to a few lines remembering one another with love.

Ronnie reminded herself why Kit's morose manner, this skulking awkwardness, was nothing like the man her friend had written about. Kit Donne was still wallowing in widowhood. Drowning even.

They both jumped when her phone rang, shattering the

moment, its ringtone striking up with the intro to 'I Can't Get No Satisfaction'.

Saturday-girl Carly's name lit up on screen, no doubt after the money Ronnie owed her.

She rejected the call. There was no petty cash whatsoever at the yard, the accounts all far too overdrawn to risk a card in a machine or cashback from a till.

Kit was still eyeing her warily. 'You told me that you kept some of her letters that I can see?'

It took her a moment to realize he was still talking about Hermia

'Goodness yes, you're right, I did.' She'd quite forgotten that she'd promised to look them out. She'd only mentioned them in passing, but Kit – who had almost all her side of the correspondence, lovingly retained by Hermia – had fixed on the idea.

'Do that.' His brows lowered.

'I do remember Hermia writing to me about this particular theatre.' She held up her phone again, forgetting the tickets were no longer screen, just an incoming message from Carly demanding her wages. 'It's a lovely old place. You two went there a lot, didn't you?'

'That's right.'

'*And* she always said you needed prodding into action, like Hamlet.'

He looked even more discomfited, sucking in one cheek, as though she was offering him a filling without anaesthetic. Then he made a brief, gruff throat-clearing sound she realized was amusement. 'That is a very Hermia thing to say.'

'Isn't it?' Their eyes met again, warmer this time.

'Very well,' he said at last, resigned to his fate, 'as you are so insistent and I know how good it is, I'll go. Thank you.'

'Bravo! The list price is a hundred apiece, but you can have them for, let's say, seventy-five each?' It would just cover what she owed Carly.

The brows lowered again. 'Each, you say?'

'Or make me an offer?' Did he think she was *giving* them away? she wondered.

'You're selling me the tickets?'

Which was when it occurred to Ronnie that perhaps he'd thought she was inviting him on a date.

He was already pulling out his wallet. 'Hermia said you were a ruthless dealer. Cash?'

'Marvellous!' Shaking hands on it, Ronnie sensed that having allies in the village, while hard work, might not be a bad thing.

'Find those letters!' He waved her away, closing himself back in his greenhouse, calling through the glass, 'I'll pick you up at six!'

Ronnie hesitated. How disgraceful of her to give the impression that not only had she invited him out on a date on Valentine's night, but she'd made him pay for her ticket as well as his.

About to dash back in to explain that she wasn't intending for him to take her, she saw he was writing furiously into his notepad, Radio Three already back on, and she didn't want to interrupt the flow. Plus Carly needed her wages more than Ronnie needed to save face.

At least this way she'd get to see the show, with the bonus of an opportunity to redeem herself. And it would make Blair helpfully jealous.

As she walked home with the dogs, she sent him a message reassuring him she'd found a taker for the ticket and another to Carly to let her know she had her money. Then she called new friend Petra Gunn, who was in her plotting shed. 'Am I interrupting the muse?'

'Still warming up, scrolling the dark web for ideas on blackmail, damsel-distressing and infamy, AKA the village Facebook group. It's utter slander on here today, have you seen it?'

'Never look at it.' Ronnie nipped through the open gate into Church Meadow to let the dogs have a run, unclipping Knott's lead so the youngster could join her heelers bounding up towards the Three Witches. 'Now I'm going to ask a favour and you must say yes.' Covering the mouthpiece, she turned to call Lester's terrier who was dawdling in the gateway, 'Stubbs!'

'As long as you don't want me to take the Shetland back yet.' Her children's first pony was now serving as the stud's stallion companion.

'God no, Beck and Kes worship him.' Ronnie climbed the steep hill at speed. 'I've got myself roped into Viv Austen's church fundraising group and need to find a replacement.'

'Already roped in too, I'm afraid. Cable-tied to the chair with a gaffer-tape gag in fact. You know Viv.'

'Precisely why I want to duck out,' Ronnie sighed, whistling the dogs closer.

'And if Bay's not there to flirt with,' Petra went on, 'I'm resigning as soon as humanly possible to co-opt Charlie, who has far too much time on his hands, frankly. I think he's trolling the village Facebook page.'

As Petra started lamenting her husband's laid-back approach to working from home, Ronnie perched on one of the witches and looked out across the village. It was amongst her favourite spots, often shared with Hermia through childhood. Old Hezekiah Turner had taught the two girls how to spot Roma marks. Looking down, she started in surprise to see them here now.

She took it as a positive omen. Luck was turning. Travellers had always brought good fortune here.

The deerhound puppy had come to flop beside her, panting and smiling from a run with her heelers who were charging back down the hill to round up Stubbs, still the wrong side of the gate and poised to pounce into the verge brash, where a small rodent was no doubt cowering.

'Can you think of anyone else?' she asked Petra as she headed down after them. 'What about Gill Walcote?'

'Forget it, and before you ask that goes for Mo Dawkins too.'

Ronnie hadn't been about to, but Petra was clearly dying to offload. 'Have you heard the news? It's too awful. Ba... is... Tra... odge... ulterer.'

'What?' Ronnie's Call Waiting alert had started, beeping out most of this. Please let it be Blair – wildly jealous that she had a date, with a change of heart about putting them on deep freeze again and an apology for encouraging Lester's horse-trading.

'He's been... ving a... ide-hust... with... og groo...'

'Sounds painful.'

'For Mo, yes. So don't ask her.' Call waiting had stopped.

'I won't.'

'Anyway, the church thing isn't for ages, so I'll have written a book by then and you'll... spunk... Luca... foals.' Call waiting kicked in once more.

'Absolutely! Happy plotting!' Switching to the waiting caller, Ronnie covered the mouthpiece again and shouted for the dogs, three of them now out in the lane, the heelers joining Stubbs' roadside vermin hunt. *'Come back here!'*

In her ear, a familiar chuckle was curled through with smoky late nights. 'Your word is my command, Princess.'

Ronnie stopped in her tracks, bracing, as though expecting an earthquake's aftershock.

'Who is this?' She knew it was Kenny, but she wasn't going to give him that satisfaction.

The chuckle deepened, not falling for it. 'Long time no squeeze, Veronica.'

She managed a tight-lipped, 'Over thirty years, Kenny.'

'You heard we're going to be neighbours?' The chortling stopped, businesslike now. 'My assistant got your number from the stud's website. Surprised to find you living back there, if I'm honest. We're both tempting fate, eh?'

'What can I do for you, Kenny?'

'More a case of what I can do for *you*. I owe you one, after all.'

Ronnie watched her two little dogs play-fighting towards her. She might have guessed he'd try this. 'You shouldn't have come back.'

'C'mon, Ron. You don't believe in all this curse nonsense, do you?'

'You mean Daddy shouting the odds?'

'No – my condolences, by the way, Princess, he was a legend – not that, the Turner *curse*. That's why I want to make my peace in the village, make good.'

Ronnie had never heard of a curse and was quite certain the Turner family never threatened such things, but not one to let an opportunity go to waste, a thought struck her. 'Actually, there *is* something you can do.'

'Yes?' He sounded surprised.

'Take my place on the church roof committee.'

There was a surprised pause, followed by a baffled, 'You *what*?'

Her heelers had returned to look up at her expectantly. She craned to look for Lester's terrier, now dawdling in the opposite side of the lane.

An engine was approaching from the direction of The Green. 'Stubbs!'

'You what, Princess?'

The car engine was closing in fast. 'STUBBS!'

Kenny's third 'you what' trailed away as she started to run. 'Stubbs *come here*!'

The little fox terrier started trotting across the lane towards her. As he did, a pickup truck appeared round the corner, careering away from the village, its driver spotting the dog too late. The horn blasted, brakes screeching as Stubbs' small white body vanished beneath it.

'No!' she wailed, the thud of impact swiftly followed by agonised yelping and howling. Then silence.

Sprinting through the gate, Ronnie registered the pale, shocked face in the mud-splattered truck window. Unshaven, eyes wild, but unmistakeably local contractor and hunt devotee Barry Dawkins, a ruddy-cheeked barrel of a man in checked cotton and moleskin. He was holding a phone to his ear.

'Barry!' she cried, running towards the truck. Beyond it, Stubbs' immobile body had been propelled onto the withered grass and brambles of the verge like fly-tipped litter.

To Ronnie's shock, instead of getting out to help, Barry slammed the truck into gear and sped off towards the Fosse Way.

Call completely forgotten, Ronnie gathered up the little dog and sprinted up the stud's drive.

Mo had the Dua Lipa track she'd heard earlier as an earworm digging in, telling her not to show up or come out if she wanted to avoid seeing dancing. She hummed it as she hurried home. Having been waylaid by an escapee Tamworth pig who'd run for cover in the Christmas Tree plantation, then a livery pony who'd ducked under some broken electric fencing to cavort amongst the kale, she felt her day running away with her more than ever.

Squat and flat-roofed, Greenways (the previous owners had been golf mad) was the first bungalow in a cul-de-sac named Spinney End after the covert that had once stood there. Most outsiders mistook it for part of the once council-owned Orchard Estate it sat alongside, but it was older, some houses dating back to the thirties, genteel and conservative. Greenways had been pink when they'd bought it, and even though Barry had painted the pebbledash an attractive clotted cream, it still reminded Mo of a square of oversweet cake.

Inside, she raided the freezer, then went to the bedroom to check the sheets were a nice set, not the ones with the threadbare embroidery and bobbly undersheet.

That's when she spotted an envelope on her dressing table, propped up against the almost-full bottle of Eternity Barry had given her for Christmas – her favourite, he never forgot – and she felt a flush of affection.

It was the first time in years he'd remembered Valentine's Day.

Mo let the fuzzy warmth of being loved by a good man linger as she took out her best dress to hang in the bathroom for its creases to drop out. The last time she'd worn it was his birthday. They had eaten at Le Mill where they'd been so shocked by the tiny portions, they'd shared a pizza from the freezer when they got home then got frisky on the sofa. She missed those giggles. They'd been a bit off lately and it was important to make time for each other, especially on a day set aside for lovers.

Heading into the en suite, she ignored her daytime self in the mirror, red-faced, helmet-haired and roll-waisted in too-tight breeches. Instead, feeling like Marilyn Monroe in disguise and humming 'Anyone Can See I Love You', she hung the dress on the shower rail and shook out its full skirt, imagining herself in it later, soft music playing, flirty after a glass of rose, both knowing they could enjoy a bit of grown-up naughty time without worrying about Grace overhearing.

Unable to wait any longer, she hurried back to the envelope and ripped it open.

There was no card inside, just a few handwritten lines on one of the notelets she kept in the desk for writing thank yous.

Barry wasn't a man of many words:

Dear Mo,

There's no easy way to say this. I have been unhappy with our marriage for some time, and there is somebody else in my life now. Tell Grace I love her and I'll call when things are a bit more settled. Please don't be upset. This is best for all of us.

Yours,

Barry.

In shock, Mo sat down on the bed so hard the pillows jumped. She groped in her pocket for her phone in her pocket to call him, only to find she'd kept hold of Bridge's with its cracked screen, its battery flat. In her haste, she must have handed hers over by mistake.

If she'd got back sooner, she thought illogically, this wouldn't have happened. She could have stopped him. They had to talk about this. It made no sense. What about Grace? It was all her own fault for not getting back sooner.

Which was when the awful truth dawned.

The Saddle Bags knew. It's why they'd kept her out riding so long, why there had been so many awkward questions and strange looks. Her friends *knew* about this.

She hurled Bridge's phone at the wall, shattering it completely.

Carly went to the stud to collect her wages as soon as she finished her morning shift with the Gunns, only to find Ronnie had dashed to the vet with Lester's terrier and nobody else had any cash to pay her.

'Got run over, poor little bugger,' she told Nana later over a mug of tea. 'Needs an operation to put a metal plate in his pelvis, Lester says. He was ever so upset, poor man.'

'Can't you heal him with your magic hands, love?' Nana asked.

'They're not that powerful!' She pulled toddler Jackson up on her knee to stop him stuffing all the bourbon creams in his mouth.

In front of them, Sienna was glued to *Alphablocks* on

Cbeebies, pointing to the colourful animated S and shouting 'Ball!'

'Always drive too fast round here,' Nana was saying, holding out her arms to take Jackson. 'You've got to be careful. Too many accidents. Like that pretty actress.'

Carly handed him over. 'What actress?'

'Before your time. Came off her horse, she did. As good as killed her. I always told him he drove too fast, but would he listen?' She addressed this to her grandson, adopting a sing-song voice.

'Who are you talking about, Nana?' asked Carly.

'Nana didn't like going out no more after that day,' she told Jackson. 'They drive too fast round here. Should stick to horse-drawn vehicles. Clippety-clop, clippety-clop!' She bounced him on her knee and he let out a drumroll of chuckles. 'Grandpa Nat's coming home soon. Clippety-clop!'

Nana was always saying that. Carly marvelled at her long-suffering belief that he'd one day return to be head of the household.

'Has Nat been in touch, then?' she asked.

'We just know, don't we Jackson? And when he does, your Nana's going to lamp the lummock, yes she is! Give him a bell-oiling he won't forget!'

Jackson chuckled even more uproariously.

Perhaps not so stoical these days, reflected Carly, taking out her phone to distract Nana with the pictures of Petra's mare.

Having looked at the village Facebook page earlier, it was now sending her notifications. She swiped away all the gossip, although news that a celebrity was moving to the village caught her eye because she knew who would love it.

'Kenny Kay's bought the manor,' she told Nana, who never missed anything he was in.

The sound that came out of her mother-in-law wasn't like any Carly had heard her make before. A high-pitched cry of delight, like a bird, it made Jackson dissolve into yet more fits of hiccupping laughter. Nan was a big Kenny Kay fan.

On screen the Alphablocks were spelling out the word 'STAR', which Sienna pointed to and shouted 'Wish! Nana, wish! Look!'

'It says *star*,' Carly corrected impatiently.

'No, she's quite right my darling,' Nana told her. 'We sing it every day, don't we kids: *Star light, star bright…*'

'*Firstht thstar I thsee tonight…*' Sienna added her loud lisp while Jackson clapped his hands and burbled.

'*I wish I may, I wish I might,*' Carly joined in, remembering the little rhyme her grandma had recited to her too. '*Have the wish I wished tonight.*'

Nana wiped a tear from her eye. 'Oh, I wished for this for so long.'

For her sake, Carly hoped Nat really was coming back this time.

That night, when Ash had fallen into his war-torn dreams, she lay awake thinking about Nat's legacy, grateful his son hadn't inherited his wanderlust even if he had got the fiery temper. Eventually she got up and went to the window in search of a star bright enough to wish on, her gaze tracing a familiar line down from Orion's belt to find Sirius the dog star, as faithful as Nana.

And she wished that Ash wouldn't take part in the King fight.

PART THREE

9

'You make sure Nat gets this personally, Carly love.' Nana thrust deep-filled, sugar-crusted pastry tart at her daughter-in-law. 'Tell him there's plenty more where that came from. I know he likes his gypsy tarts, does Nat.' Her dark eyes gleamed.

Outside on the Orchard Estate, voices shouted, car doors were slammed, engines were revving and families hurrying past pulling on coats

'Wish I could come along,' Nana sighed as she saw Carly to the door.

'You can,' Carly urged, beckoning her through too.

'No, love, I'm best here.' Nana shrank back as a big truck roared past. 'Roads aren't safe round here. Tell Nat to come see me. We need words.'

The travellers had not long arrived at Church Meadow. The huge log that had been in the gateway was being chainsawed into burning wood, some of it already merrily aflame on a bonfire built at the centre of the circle of vardos and vans. Out on the village green, coloured horses were tethered, busy cropping circular Venn diagrams in the grass.

The visitors would be staying just two nights, but it was enough to outrage the village curtain-twitchers who were convinced their sheds would be cleared of tools, kerosene drained from oil tanks and koi lifted from their ponds. The Facebook page and WhatsApp groups buzzed with notifications. There might be no lead left on the church roof, but its scaffolding was kept under close surveillance.

The Turner family, by contrast, welcomed its wandering kin with a full-blooded celebration, marching along Plum Run with trays of steaming food and party packs of beer. Carly, who had only met her father-in-law once and knew his sobriety and sanity came and went, worried how Ash felt about it.

But Nat wasn't with them.

'Where's my boy?' wheezed Norm, having been driven there at speed in a van, eyes still watering from the potholes.

'Custody,' reported a wolf-eyed youngster, possibly one of Nat's grandchildren. Or a girlfriend. Hard to tell. She perched on a wooden mushroom under a makeshift tarpaulin gazebo and told them that Nat had got himself arrested again, this time for possession of an unlicensed shotgun. 'They reckon it was nicked in a raid, so they're keeping him banged up, but he bought it off a gadjo last week. I was there.'

'What's Nat want a gun for?' Norm was indignant. 'Turners don't use guns.'

'Protection,' she eyed Ash thoughtfully.

'From what?' asked Carly.

'He said something about coming back here to defend his prize,' she told them.

'My boy wants the king's belt again!' Norm wheezed excitedly. 'Best bare-knuckle boxer we ever had, was my boy Nat. You'll have to step aside, Ash lad.'

Star light, star bright Carly shivered with gratification as she turned to Ash hopefully. 'You hear that? Your dad wants to fight Jed.'

His face gave nothing away. 'With a gun?'

The girl was still looking at him too. 'It's not Jed he wants to fight. I know that much.'

When Carly broke it to Nana later why Nat hadn't come,

her big brown eyes went wide as a bush baby's. 'He doesn't need a gun.'

'Apparently he needs it to protect his prize, whatever that means.'

'Oh, that'll be me, dear.' Nana offered her a Jammy Dodger with shaking hands.

Barry Dawkins liked working for Bay Austen. He was a fair boss, organized and thorough like his father Sandy, but with an easier manner, less of a fastidious nitpicker and more of a motivator. He was also less high church and moralising, a man of earthy appetite who had strayed from the path himself, so when Barry had asked if he could rent a farm cottage again, Bay did his best to help him without giving him the lecture.

Barry was fed up with all the lectures. He'd had one from his parents, another from his sister, also his workmates, his drinking buddies, his five-a-side football squad, his in-laws and his daughter. The only person beside Bay who hadn't lectured him was Mo. She wasn't talking to him at all.

By contrast, Bay was practical, not judgemental. It made sense for Barry to live close to his work, plus Grace was pony-mad mates with Tilly Austen, often playing and staying at the farm, so the arrangement was kinder on her too. But all the farm cottages were currently tenanted, and Beverly, his girlfriend, refused to let him consider one of the static caravans the Austens provided for seasonal workers, so Bay offered one of the holiday lets off-season, 'Just until we can find something more suitable.' Beverly loved The Hayloft. It was full of chintzy, Farrow & Ball heritage touches, with a four-poster bed and a claw-foot bath. She said it was 'like being on honeymoon every day'. She bought overpriced sourdough bread, hand-churned butter and organic jam from the Austens' farm shop, arranged snowdrops artfully in empty Purdy's bottles and kept the heating at a simmering twenty-seven degrees so she could wander round in a basque, planning their future.

It was all a bit much for Barry who, missing his wife's cold feet in bed and mother-in-law's fry-ups, was secretly quite homesick.

Barry wasn't a man who made snap decisions as a rule. Patient, methodical and measured, he liked to think things over and weigh them up.

Beverly was the opposite. Once she made up her mind, then a thing was as good as done and gold-dusted. It had been Beverly who had declared their passion 'unstoppable' after a couple of flirty encounters; Beverly who had suggested they meet at the Travelodge where she got points on one of her loyalty cards, and Beverly who had told him his marriage was over.

When Beverly made up her mind that she and Barry should start their new lives together on Valentine's Day, he hadn't been given a lot of notice. Yet still he'd dithered and procrastinated. By then the rumours had started on Facebook, with Beverly threatening to take matters into her own hands, insisting that Mo 'deserved to know the truth' and she would tell her if he didn't. In desperation, Barry had mentioned his predicament to village drinking buddy Aleš, a Polish builder whose wife was one of Mo's mates and who had given him the first of his lectures, angrily telling him he must make his mind up what he wanted. Barry had agreed he would, then bottled it, hoping it would go away until after lambing. Two days later, Beverly had turned up at Mo's parents' farm.

Barry hadn't intended to walk out on his marriage the way he had, but his hand had been forced. The roller coaster had set off while he was still deciding whether he wanted to ride it. He couldn't bear to think what it had done to Mo and Grace.

And yet he thought about little else when he stayed up through late-night lambing shifts, especially watching the ewes all mothering so instinctively, that gift Mo had shared with him. They'd taken a long time to decide to start a family. How carefully they'd planned it, making sure they timed it right, then deciding to stop at one, because she already had so many others' needs to look after, plus the pre-eclampsia she'd suffered with Grace made it risky.

Barry moved between the three lambing sheds, the ewes divided into those expecting singles, twins and triplets, checking for signs of any about to give birth, helping those that needed it, penning the mums with newborns, and topping up the milk for the ones with too many mouths to feed on two nipples. He and Mo used to do this together in the pre-Grace days when Sid and Joan had run a little herd.

Beverly had decided she wanted a baby. She was forty-three so she said didn't want to hang about. She'd also decided to sell her mobile dog-grooming van and set up business in one of the Austens' little artisan trading units, with a full-time trainee so she could take a back seat. She'd already done a business plan and spreadsheets. She'd decided Barry would be a business partner.

The shepherd's room by the lambing barns had a kitchen area where they mixed the formula milk and kept the medical kit, and a rec area with old sofas, CCTV screens and a TV on which to watch Australian cricket or dumb movies to pass the time between herd checks. Although heated, it was blissfully cool compared to The Hayloft. Barry liked in in there, in the quiet of the early hours, thinking about Mo and Grace.

And that's where Bay found him just after six the morning, weeping quietly through an old repeat of *Cheers* where bartender Sam waves farewell forever to love of his life, Diane, before imagining himself dancing with her as an elderly couple.

Having checked round the lambing sheds, Bay made him tea and toast and asked him if perhaps he'd made a mistake walking out on Mo? It wasn't a lecture. But it was the first time anybody had guessed.

Barry wasn't a man given to revealing his innermost feelings – crying in front of the boss was bad enough – so he just shrugged.

But it was a momentous shrug, a confession from his deepest soul shrug.

'Just been out to do the rounds.' Bay sat beside him, staring at a nappy advert on screen. He drove around the farm tracks and up through the village before dawn most days, checking all the Austen land holdings, especially the shoots. There'd been a lot of poaching this winter.

'All OK?' Barry was grateful for the change of subject.

'Nothing awry. Our gypsy visitors all still asleep. Not like the stud. Everyone's up and at work there.'

Barry nodded.

'Always park up and look at it for a bit.'

Barry nodded again. He'd seen him there more than once.

'Keep finding myself asking why I did something so stupid, so selfish it changed the whole course of my life. And why I was just too proud and bullheaded to put it right at the time.'

Barry managed another shrug. A heartfelt one. Perhaps it hadn't been a change of subject after all, he realized, confessing, 'Just wish I could put it right.'

'If wishes were horses...' Bay murmured lightly.

Barry agreed and they drank their tea in wishful silence.

The travellers had no sooner trundled away from Church Meadow in their wagons and rusted Transits, leaving just a burned patch where their fire had been, than Kenny's chauffeur-driven Tesla led a cavalcade of liveried tradesmen's vans and a mini-bus full of staff to the Manor to mark his brand on it.

Now in possession of the keys to his new home and his Lord of the Manor title, Kenny wasted no time briefing his team how to adapt it precisely to his specifications. He'd brought enough people to throw a party, but still found the echo of emptiness of the house bothered him, like tinnitus.

'This place needs furniture! Rugs! Get some ordered, people!' he demanded before settling in a window seat in one of the smaller reception rooms from which he planned to host the day's meetings, like a booth in a bar. Before that, he was happy to let everyone take the guided tour with his project manager and leave him in peace to think.

Kenny might have bought Compton Manor sight unseen for a tidy knock-down price mistakenly thinking it was the stud, but he still reckoned he'd got value for money. While the Percy family stud was the village's undisputed crown jewel, Kenny remembered its manor house well enough, a creamy limestone showstopper amid sculpted topiary boastfully close to the lane. Being equidistant between his horses and the pub, it had often caught his eye back in the early eighties when he'd had perfect eyesight and zero hindsight. Now that the opposite was true, Kenny rather fancied the irony of being Lord of the Manor, certain Tina would approve, God rest her soul. He already had a statue planned for a new water feature, a nymph in her image, mounted on horseback. And there would be more horses. Tina had loved her horses.

The largest house in the village – conspicuous in its grandeur – it had been designed to show off the wealth of an upwardly mobile wool merchant, and it had once possessed a considerable landholding, stretching between here and the Broadbourne road, including the water meadow by Lord's Brook and the orchards alongside the Plum Run.

'This place needs its rolling acres back!' he ordered his team. 'Make enquiries, see what we can buy. And when that architect arrives, remind him I want old-fashioned radiators back too, none of this polished concrete underfloor-heating rubbish. And wood panelling. And that helipad can go. We'll put a Japanese gazebo there instead. The wife can do her yoga in it when she comes.' *If* she comes. With her wife.

He was keeping up the pretence for now – best way to avoid the press pack – but Mrs Kay mark five was past tense, as was his PA now that the two were a couple, eschewing misogynist patriarchs like Kenny to live their best same-sex life at his expense. Good luck to them. Kenny wasn't by nature a bitter man; he was all for finding happiness and good lawyers. This was his new refuge, and he was going to fill it with tributes to the one woman who had never asked for a penny of his money. He used to joke she'd left him with something most ex-wives can only dream of, his own tailor-made gypsy curse, but he didn't find that so funny four marriages and a heart attack later, plus the rest.

He shouted out a reminder, not sure anyone was listening, 'I want the best security money can buy!'

The previous owner hadn't been one for home comforts like carpets, handrails, or bathtubs that weren't two-metre-deep hammered metal design statements. The place was an overgrown playpen, full of boys' toys – not that Kenny was complaining about the indoor pool complex, six climate-controlled garages and His and Hers saunas. Although now that the current Mrs Kay had decided she preferred Hers and Hers, he might convert one into a walk-in tanning booth.

The Lord of the Manor liked the idea of a boys' own crib.

He'd also decided the manor would make a good base in which to write his third autobiography, *So Kay* (a follow-up to the super-successful *Oh, Kay* and *Doh, Kay*) which his British publishers had just politely reminded him was two years overdue. Earlier this week, his ghostwriter had given him a little digital recorder which he'd been chatting into ever since, mostly notes to his builders, but the occasional recollection or bon mot crept in.

'I'm minding my British manors,' he told it now.

Kenny was selling up his palatial neo-classical pile by the fourth-hole fairway on the same exclusive Surrey golf course where second wife and Iago both had their homes. Keeping it running and fully staffed was a ridiculous cost, and the place had lost its appeal now that he no longer played golf. His live-in domestic team, accustomed to playing house there without him eleven months of the year, were less enthusiastic about relocating to the Bardswolds. He'd brought them all with him today, certain they'd love the place as much as he did.

'It's beautiful!' they'd chorused upon arrival. But they were paid to.

'Cars, houses, wives and horses,' he told his digital recorder, 'are quick to lose their value in my experience. But loyal, well-paid staff are an appreciative asset.'

When he'd earned his first-ever million, Kenny had bought himself a Lamborghini and a new build in Edgbaston, a big step up from the mod scooter and rented bedsit he shared with Tina. To celebrate the next million, he bought a showjumper he renamed The Warm-Up Man. Kenny was more of a racing fan, but Tina liked the bright lights and glamour of showjumping, and it was a way of getting her out of the house. Kenny was pleasantly surprised how much he enjoyed the breeding side, Warm-Up Man going on to be a prolific sire, along with stablemate Funny Guy. Kenny had stood them at Compton Magna Stud for ten seasons, the profit from which bought a Spanish villa that he'd spent many happy family summers in after moving on to the second Mrs Kay, former Miss Colombia, Ria, mother to Santiago and his sisters.

'It all went a bit downhill after that,' he told his recorder, screwing up his face to peer back through the mental smoke at the after-hours bars, white powder and pole dancers.

'The architect's here, Mr Kay. I'll take this, shall I?' A hand tried to wrestle away the device into which Kenny had been reminiscing.

'He can wait five minutes!' he barked at the girl, a recent recruit that Iago insisted accompany him everywhere like a nanny or bodyguard. 'Get someone to show him round too, Sarah, bab.'

Now he'd lost his train of thought, asking the device, 'Where was I?'

His ghostwriter had asked him to go into more detail about the aftermath of his arrest in the late nineties. The public humiliation which had triggered the acrimonious and expensive end of his longest and happiest marriage – and killed his prime-time television career overnight – was not an event Kenny cared to dwell on long, although the vice squad lads had turned out to be fans, and all charges had eventually been dropped. Those were the days! Backhanders, fat red fifties rolled round wraps of coke. When the Operation Yewtree lot came sniffing round years later, there was no evidence that any girls were underage.

Sarah was still fussing around him, untangling his earphone wires. 'There's no food, so I've sent Ivor to the pub for a carry-out for lunch, OK, my darling?'

'It'll do.' Kenny would rather go to the pub in person – he'd had some good times in there – but he wasn't ready to meet the natives just yet. 'Burger and chips, yeah?'

'All the trimmings,' she promised.

'You're a diamond, Sarah, my darling. Remind me what you look like again?'

She sighed, and he heard her footsteps moving away. Perhaps she hadn't heard.

Sarah wasn't her real name, just as his driver wasn't Ivor. Kenny couldn't remember names, so he'd long since given his staff rhyming ones: Geoff the chef, Roddy the Dogsbody, Keith the brief and so on. Now Sarah. He resented the word carer, but that's what the Iago kept calling her, and she wasn't bright or devious enough to be his PA.

His clever, devious PA was still in America, shacked up with his wife.

He shuddered. Never again. He'd get the team to draft an advert for a replacement. He wanted someone local this time. A pretty one. The Comptons had always been full of pretty women.

'Next time, don't call her Gay the PA,' he dictated into his recorder, chuckling, trying to remember where he'd left off. 'Ah, yes! My downfall. After Tina and Ria, my reputation got a bit tarnished, readers, and the trophy wives were all tin pots.'

First had been Page Three Stunner and star of Live TV's topless darts, Chantelle Taylor ('Tell Tale' the press later dubbed her, the Kiss and Tell being her forte). Kenny's shortest marriage as it turned out, less than six months between exchanging vows and the tabloids exposing her affair with one of his Ivor the Drivers. He could hardly blame her.

To the delight of the red tops, Kenny Kay had behaved very badly from the naughty nineties to the noughties. Somehow, he'd held onto his career, his hard-drinking, blue-joke gigs a lot less family-friendly. But at that time late-night telly was booming along with cable, and he'd milked it well.

Until the first heart attack had stopped him in his tracks.

Kenny had been evangelical. He'd prayed. He'd jogged. He'd quit drinking. He'd played a *lot* of golf. Perhaps it was no wonder LA had embraced him so wholeheartedly.

It was a low-budget British comedy film that had turned him into a movie star in his fifties. Kenny only played a bit part as father of a bride as a favour to a mate but it became a cult hit. Almost overnight Kenny was America's new darling, the scripts flooding in. It was the easiest work he'd ever had. As well as playing himself in every movie he was offered, he was a gift to the chat-show circuit. They loved his Brummie brogue and wayward past, this reformed rogue who had once been as badass as Harris or O'Toole, but with a wheatgrass juice and keto lifestyle, recounting his stories to howls of audience laughter. Bigger roles followed, funding a fat pension fund, a house by the Pacific Ocean and an astonishingly effortless life. Also a deadly dull, dry, homesick one with another ill-judged marriage soon attached.

'Usual lunchtime drink, Kenny?' Sarah was back, keeping a safe distance away.

'When do I ever say no?' he chuckled, having taken up the sauce again – in moderation – after escaping Hollywood, where his fourth marriage has been as fake as his hairpiece and dental implants.

His LA management team had wanted to 'build the Kenny Kay brand'. Under their guidance he'd bought a vintage British car, became patron of a horse charity and started seeing an ageing pop diva turned soap star who shared the same team and was good for publicity, an old mate not a soulmate. For a while, it was a magic formula. With a reality TV crew following them, the couple stayed in the best resorts for free, bickered for fun and married in Vegas on a – carefully orchestrated – whim, their wedding episode garnering ratings to rival *The Osbournes*. Kenny was soon a family favourite again on both sides of the Atlantic, the nation's favourite naughty uncle. His wife had a comeback tour, collaborated with a rapper and won a Grammy.

Then she choked to death on an oyster at a fundraising lunch with her girlfriends. Terrible business.

Sympathy washed in. Poor old Kenny! He was cursed.

If only they knew he really was.

When it had happened, Kenny had been happily distracted in a Beverley Hills golf resort having his physical needs met thanks to a young Brazilian, baby oil and a watertight non-disclosure agreement. It was the last time he remembered feeling care-free.

'That architect knows I want them to wire in panic buttons into *every* room?' he demanded when Sarah placed a cool glass in his hand. 'Even the khazi?'

'I'll ask.'

'Never marry staff, readers,' he told the recorder as soon as she'd left the room again, 'especially if she's in love with someone else you employ.'

Terrified of growing old and dying alone – and pursued at the time by several superfan stalkers seeking to comfort him – Kenny had remarried in haste. His fifth wife was his holistic therapist and part-time bodyguard. She was behind Kenny's move to Florida for health and privacy reasons, backed up by his faithful PA, both promising they'd keep him forever young and out of trouble. Sight already fading, he failed to see they only had eyes for each other. In their luxury waterfront house, Kenny found himself occupying his own ground-floor suite, pampered like one of the French bulldogs: given regular exercise, grooming, a balanced diet and routine health checks. Except his wife and PA gave the dogs more love and found them funnier.

He'd barely been seen in public for five years. In private, as his world, future and field of vision shrank, Kenny had cast his thoughts back to happier times. He'd always felt bad about Tina, who had sought sanctuary with 'astral twin' Pete after Kenny walked out on her. He'd made attempts to contact his first love over the years, but the message always came back that she wanted nothing to do with him. Kenny gathered Peter had set her up in his ultra-private Riviera villa, where she'd lived very quietly. She was never one for going out. Kenny would sit in his own air-conditioned Florida Keys spa-for-one wishing they were sharing a settee like the old days, holding hands and laughing at *Some Mothers Do Have 'Em.*

It was the news of her death that had propelled him to finally break free and retrace his steps to the village Tina had loved. He'd been surprised when Peter had agreed to scatter her ashes together here. They barely spoke these days, but his childhood friend seemed keen for closure. Perhaps he knew how devastated Kenny was.

'And remember, kids,' he told the little machine, 'money can't buy you love. Trust your Uncle Kenny, you never know its true value until it's gone.'

He leant back in his window seat and downed a long draught of his drink, sucking the froth off his lip.

Lager and lime. Tina's favourite. Couldn't beat it.

Kenny sensed he could be at peace here in the Comptons. It had been a long journey.

'Hey, Siri.' He groped for his iPhone. After a couple of false starts, it was in his grip. 'Remind me I need to get horses. And land. And radiators. And hire a new bloody PA.'

She assured him she would, then he asked her to read out his messages.

Iago had called several times, checking he was OK. The boy worried too much. An old celebrity golfing buddy wanted to know when he when he was coming out with the gang now that he was back. Never. His agent told him *Strictly* had chased again. Ditto.

'Hey, Siri, call Ronnie.'

After a couple of false starts in his phonebook to a snooker pro and the widow of an old comedian mate, Siri struck gold. It went to voicemail, that husky welcome entreating him to leave a message or call the stud's landline.

Remembering she'd asked a favour that he'd done nothing about, he rang off. Always had been a bossy sort, Ronnie Percy.

He could hear his team coming back from the grand tour, ready to talk through the changes required to make the Manor safe for him.

'Let's get this over with quickly so we can move in here!' Kenny told them, pressing his foreshortened finger to the tip of his nose and casting his mind back to the eighties, to the fast cars and the horses, the excess and the fun. And the best of women. 'I want a bar, a flagpole, a Jacuzzi and *very* flattering lighting. I might want to entertain old friends soon. Also, tell me, what is going on with the church up the road?'

When one of his team read out the roof repair fundraising details from the official parish website, he cackled delightedly. 'Now that deserves something special!'

10

Ronnie had always disliked the gloomy dog end of winter with its cold and mud and self-denial for Lent. It might offer the best night skies of the year, but by day the harsh reality of running an understaffed stud farm with too few bookings made it hard to keep up a jolly demeanour, especially without Blair to look forward to.

Brought up to believe that fretting about one's finances was jolly bad form, Ronnie tried not to dwell on the size of the overdraft too often. She'd tried hard not to think about it as poor, uninsured little Stubbs went through a long operation to fix his broken pelvis; she also tried not to be alarmed when Pax – who had immediately clicked with turbo-charged Lottie as they all knew she would – reaffiliated with British Eventing and entered a clutch of spring competitions. Ronnie determinedly set the cost aside in her mind as saddle-fitters and dressage trainers arrived at her daughter's behest, despite Bay not yet paying a single livery bill. She quite refused to worry about a new stallion arriving – if Lester really had the backers he said he did – or that Luca kept badgering her about AI bookings, for which they still had no facilities or equipment because she was far too cash-strapped.

She kept hearing Blair's amused, gravelly voice in her head: *I'm so broke I can't even pay attention*, a phrase he'd coined when newly arrived from Australia, taking chance rides and living off friends' sofas, including hers.

It was pointless trying not to think about Blair, who had locked in on her straight away back then, recognizing a matching restless soul. They'd both come a long way in the intervening thirty years, but such was the feast and famine nature of working with horses, their fortunes still changed in the swish of a tail.

Just occasionally – usually in the bath when *The Archers* got boring – Ronnie missed having money, although she missed Blair far more, quashing the regrettable recognition that life was much more fun with them both in it. Blair had a smarter business mind than hers and would know what she should do to keep this place going, how to best use the opportunities he'd directed her way, and how to keep Bay under control. She longed for her sounding board.

But a break was total for as long as it lasted. Always had been.

She'd told nobody about Kenny Kay's call the day of Stubbs' accident, which had come as such a shock. To her relief, he hadn't tried again. Hardly surprising, given she must have sounded quite mad. After the poor fox terrier had come to grief, she had no idea which of the incoming numbers logged in her phone had been his. Not that she had any intention of calling it, but she needed a warning if he did make contact again. There was no sign of him taking occupancy at the manor yet. Contract gardeners had strimmed. A huge skip had been delivered. A fleet of dark-windowed cars and vans had been reported rolling in a week ago, then rolling away again. Local gossips suggested it was purely an investment, Kenny's life being in Florida now. This made sense to Ronnie. Like Knightsbridge or Chelsea, the Cotswolds were full of big empty houses, kept brochure-ready while quietly accruing capital.

News of the manor's multi-million price tag had certainly caught the attention of her older children, Alice and Tim, who viewed Ronnie as a wholly undesirable custodian. The stud was held in trust, something in short supply amongst her offspring. Communicating through Pax, they reported fresh interest from buyers and developers. They wanted a re-evaluation and a revised deadline by which to prove the business viable. The only thing preventing them selling was Ronnie's lifetime interest which was dependent on the stud farm side running profitably. For now, Pax had stalled her siblings, insisting it would take longer to turn its fortunes around, but Ronnie knew she was on increasingly borrowed time and borrowed capital.

Not that any of her children talked specific facts and figures, thank goodness. They'd been brought up as Percys, after all, taught to view discussing money as bad form.

As February gave way to March and the village gardens started to swell with a riot of clashing spring bulbs, Ronnie's mind remained determinedly focussed on its day-to-day tasks. When she wasn't with the horses, she was drumming up trade, her phone in constant use, her early morning dog walks with sociable gossip Petra Gunn a daily staple and a key part of forging village allies.

The novelist's retreat to her plotting shed had been hampered by an infestation of mice and a lack of inspiration, she explained, 'I need a new hero. Sean O'Shaughnessy, my super-sexy Royalist mercenary – based on Luca if you haven't guessed – isn't cutting it. Too much guilt. And even if I hadn't killed off my nefarious Bay character in book two, I'm simply off men. I blame Charlie working from home so much. He keeps bringing me out coffee and pastries. Kills the mood.'

'Make *him* your hero,' Ronnie suggested.

'My *husband*?'

'Why not?'

'You're talking to a Saddle Bag,' Petra laughed. 'Forget wedded bliss, we hack off the shackles.' She complained that all the Bags wanted to talk about was Mo Dawkins' marriage, then talked of little else herself. Barry Dawkins had now set up home with a new lady friend in one of the Austens' farm cottages, Petra explained. 'She's a dog groomer. I took Wilf for a trim to check her out. Predictably slutty, but surprisingly good at clipping claws. Terribly disloyal of Bay giving them safe harbour, don't you agree? Poor Mo's in bits. Won't come out riding. Won't come over for a drink. Won't talk about it.'

Ronnie wasn't surprised, given Petra's indiscretion, although it was gradually dawning on her that she was in a circle of trust, and nothing much had changed from village life thirty years ago. Petra was fierce in Mo's defence, her facts far more accurately backed-up than Lester raking through Facebook. When not dishing up the latest local scandal, the writer fished for gossip old and new. 'Builders started work on Compton Manor this week, did you notice? I wonder what Kenny Kay's planning?' she mused as they climbed up to the standing stones early one morning. 'He once kept horses at the stud, Gill says?'

'Years ago.'

'Weren't he and Peter Sanson terrible troublemakers?' Petra admired the view, first to Eyngate Hall one way, then the Manor the other. 'Wrong side of the tracks and all that? I heard someone got shot.'

'Did they?' Ronnie said vaguely, looking for more Roma marks, but there were none.

'C'mon, spill the beans!'

'Nothing to spill,' Ronnie lied, following Petra's gaze and seeing the scaffolding on St Mary's spire.

The first Church Roof Repair Action Plan meeting was taking place that evening, and she still hadn't wriggled out. She'd asked Kenny to take her place, she remembered, uncertain what had possessed her. Panic, on reflection. She would have to send apologies to Viv Austen instead.

But when she asked Petra what her excuse was, the response surprised her. 'How could we *miss* it? Come round for a glass of bubbly first and we'll go together.'

'I thought you were resigning?'

'That was before the rumours started about the Church shutting the school and flogging the buildings to fund the repair.'

'They wouldn't!'

'The Parochial Church Council are definitely discussing it. Bridge overheard head teacher Auriol Bullock shouting on the phone to the LEA that she wouldn't let them sell off her school.'

'Developers would snap it up,' Ronnie said hollowly, thinking of her older two children's desire to see the stud's stable yards converted. 'We have to stop it!'

'Which is why we need to raise lots of lolly. You must come!' Petra urged. 'Cotswold fundraisers are *the* place to network these days. I've a chum on a flower show committee with Kate Moss and the Beckhams.'

'Poor thing,' Ronnie sympathised.

'Celebrities are charity PR alchemy! They tweet, Insta, TikTok and Midas touchscreen everything to their followers.'

'Good job we've got a bestselling author like you on side.'

'Oh, I'm nothing,' Petra looked pleased, nonetheless. 'Kit Donne's ludicrously well-connected, so he's bound to pull strings and get some local luvvies on board. You two are old friends, aren't you?' She was fishing again.

'Not really. Hermia his wife was a childhood chum; I didn't know them as a couple.' Winning Kit's friendship had suffered a setback when she'd ducked out of the theatre date she'd inadvertently foisted on him. Frostily unsympathetic about Stubbs' accident, he'd been avoiding her since.

'I could weep when I think what happened to her,' Petra confided. 'I heard the car didn't even stop when her horse reared, just sped off and left her lying on the road.'

Ronnie looked down at the lane where Hermia had fallen, not far from the spot Stubbs had been struck by Barry Dawkins' pickup. When she thought about it – which she preferred not to – she'd always imagined that the driver simply hadn't seen it happen, like so many motorists who drove past riders too fast, not even glancing in a mirror to witness horses spooking and shying in their wake.

'No wonder Kit hates horses,' Petra sighed.

'But Hermia never stopped loving them,' Ronnie told her. 'Even afterwards, she wanted to know every tiny detail of the ones I competed and bred. She never once blamed the horse.'

'Try telling that to him.'

'I'm sure he knows.' Ronnie thought guiltily of the letters she'd promised to find, letters in which Hermia had handwritten excitedly about ponies from boarding school, then scratched out on whatever came to hand in theatrical dressing rooms and digs to ask after her eventing string, fountain-penned on headed paper from her beloved farmhouse with news of foals, and then finally and painstakingly typed through the fog and nausea of head injury from The Old Almshouse, still sharing their mutual love of horses.

Later, at home, she went in search of the old carpetbag she'd hawked up and down the country and halfway around Europe.

Kit's greenhouse was in darkness when Ronnie called by that evening. He answered the front door of the Old Almshouse looking baggy-eyed and bad-tempered. 'I'm about to go out.'

'To C.R.R.A.P,' she sympathised.

He looked affronted.

'The Church Roof Repair Action Plan meeting. I'm going too, remember?'

'Oh lord, is that tonight?' He rubbed his face. 'I meant out to a shop.'

Having passed a recycling crate on the path outside overflowing with empty wine bottles, Ronnie guessed at an off-licence.

'They're relying on you,' she said brightly, her previous reluctance swept aside. 'I thought I'd drop this off en route,' she held out the carpetbag, 'save us dragging it back and forth. It's surprisingly heavy.'

He looked at it over his reading glasses. 'Don't tell me there's a hatstand and pot plant in there, along with a tape measure to size up my shortcomings?'

It took her a moment to place the reference. 'Mary Poppins. Ha, no. I keep Hermia's letters in it.' She'd held on to far more of their lifetime of correspondence than she'd realized, much of it dating before her friend had met the complex, recondite theatre director who would become her great love.

He reached out eagerly. 'In that case, please give Viv my apologies.'

'I'll do no such thing.' She hugged it tightly to her chest. 'She needs everyone there. Plus, I promised Petra Gunn I'd invite you to have a drink with us beforehand.'

'In The Jugged Hare?'

'Their place. It's super. Have you been inside?'

'Not recently.' His eyes flashed, and Ronnie remembered too late that the Gunns lived in his old house.

'Thoughtless of me,' she apologized, realizing Kit was still looking at her as though she'd suggested joining a swingers' séance there.

By the time theatreland's young darlings Kit Donne and Hermia Austen had bought Upper Bagot Farm, Ronnie had been long gone from the village. Their bolthole had quickly become a hub for family and theatrical friends. Luvvie-bashing had been a popular media blood sport back then and, in exile, Ronnie had sometimes come across Sunday magazine profiles or caught television arts shows depicting the couple as the Oberon and Titania of Cotswold culture. But the many letters she'd received painted a different picture. Hermia loved raising their young children far from London's hubbub, being with horses again, close to her family, in the village she cherished, with the man she described as 'my heartbeat.' She often entreated Ronnie to come back. *Stay with us! You will love our house. It's like you – horse, culture, chaos, parties – only a house.* Somehow, it had never happened.

After Hermia's accident she and Kit moved to the

single-storey Old Almshouse, and the farm's new owner had wasted no time stripping it of its land, converting its farm buildings into dwellings and giving the handsome Georgian house a *Homes & Gardens* makeover to appeal to town-and-country incomers like the Gunns.

It was the same fear she had for the future of the stud.

'I'll try to join you later.' He tried again to take the bag.

She kept hold of it. 'You have to *promise* me on your honour that you'll be there this evening. Unless I have your solemn oath, I won't give you this until afterwards, possibly never.' She was sounding like Mary Poppins again, she realized.

'My solemn oath?' A spark of amusement warmed the rims of his reading glasses.

'It can be a cheerful oath if you prefer.'

'You have my word,' he promised, holding out his arms.

She handed it to him, wondering as she did if she should perhaps have tidied its contents first. 'There are a few other bits of paperwork and old letters in there, but please ignore those. Just don't lose anything.'

'I won't, and I'm really very grateful.' His smile was transformed, raven brows taking flight, grey eyes polished brightly at the prospect of being reunited with his wife, a reminder of how handsome his face must have been before grief masked it in shadows.

Ronnie's recent track record with personal correspondence wasn't good. Only weeks ago, Pax had stumbled across her father's letters to a secret lover, kept hidden in the stables' cottage in a shoebox which Ronnie had promised to retrieve then failed to do so.

It was only after she'd left the bag with Kit and been welcomed into Petra's luxurious, high-tech kitchen that it occurred to her that there were a few of Hermia's letters she perhaps should have taken out first.

11

My, my, my Delilah, how's things? It was Bay's new nickname for Pax.

If she scrolled back up their increasingly long message exchange, she could see how swiftly he'd moved on from emojis. Yet the biggest text boxes by far remained her own, raving about Lottie, whose boundless enthusiasm and talent had transformed her every waking day.

Lottie's doing great! She attached a few of that morning's photos of the mare in action, adding a polite *BTW it was Samson who had his hair cut off, not Delilah* along with a smiley face emoji.

Her new shorter, madder curls had delighted Bay the only time he'd come to watch her ride the mare so far. He claimed she reminded him of herself at seventeen, then having barely watched her warm Lottie up, he'd declared the pair a 'perfect match' and disappeared into the house with another tin of biscuits to talk to Lester.

He was, as he'd promised, a very undemanding owner.

Pax was the one who couldn't stop telling him how brilliant his horse was.

A habitual texter, Bay now messaged most evenings to check on his mare's progress, for which Pax had to hang around close enough to the dining room router to WhatsApp video footage

181

or photos. Modern horsemanship was a high-tech business, she was learning, owners expecting constant 4K feedback. Clients enquiring after stallions standing at stud demanded the same. She'd invested in a plug-in signal booster to try to keep in the loop at the stables cottage – and for Mack to video call Kes as bedtime – but it failed so spectacularly often that she seemed destined to spend the twilit hours skulking here by the back stairs, breathing in the wax and dubbin of a past era.

Bay's reply landed. *Call me a Philistine, but I love a neatly pulled mane. How soon can I come and take another look?*

Anytime. She replied accommodatingly.

Now?

Ha ha.

He signed off with a laughing emoji.

Stepping out into the corridor, Pax gazed along it, past the rows of old boots and coats, remembering how fast she'd once raced its two-wicket length to greet Bay in a flying leap of kisses and laughter at the back door. They had lived in each other's pockets when she'd been seventeen. There had been no cell signal or Wi-Fi, no slow-texting using her clam-phone's number pad, and no need for it. This threadbare carpet runner had seen them kiss from one end to the other in a joyful, stumbling, breathless hello snog.

The serried ranks of boots lined up against its walls held a darker secret too. They were where her father had stored his empty Famous Grouse bottles after a hard-night's drinking, a temporary holding place until he could sneak them outside to the dustbins. By the end, he often forgot they were there, until almost every boot was testament to his hollow legs, like a procession of champagne coolers.

Pax badly needed a drink, the craving shifting within her, clawing and urgent.

She looked at her phone screen again, at all those messages to and from Bay forming a tall tower of bricks, rebuilding trust, and giving her a little jump of joy each time an alert chimed.

Behind her, Looney Tunes boomed from the dining room, where Kes was watching television with Lester after an early supper. Pocketing her phone, she joined Luca in the kitchen, saying over-brightly, 'Bay's happy with the way the mare's coming on!'

He pocketed his own phone and smiled. 'That's grand!'

The look they shared felt like an electric shock. Guilt. Desire. Game faces on.

It wasn't unusual to crackle with sexual static when alone together, but Pax was adept at damping the spark when her son was home.

'I'll quickly wash this lot up,' she started piling up their pasta bowls to carry to the sink, 'then I must run Kes a bath.'

'Sure.' He put a stack of plates alongside and turned with that happy-go-lucky smile full beam, dropping a kiss on her shoulder. Then another, higher and longer.

A vampire bite of lust made Pax close her eyes, only to hear Tom Jones crooning 'Delilah' in her head.

Crack, crack, *crack* went her libido's warning shots.

'God, but I love your neck,' he breathed into it.

Now she heard Looney Tunes again. 'Not here.'

Crack. A serving plate landed against the old enamel sink.

Luca ducked away, laughing. 'Sorry. I've stopped.'

Pax could feel her heartbeat in her throat and between her legs.

'My grandmother dished out suppers on this.' She gathered up the two broken halves of a hated, much-chipped platter.

They washed up in uncomfortably charged silence.

'No relationships,' she reminded him priggishly, aware of his body heat alongside hers as she handed him a colander to dry.

'No ships,' he repeated, nodding, tea towel whirling. 'That's a big old empty sea, so it is.'

'Full of other fish,' she pointed out pragmatically, waiting for him to argue.

Instead, he held the colander up to the light, his handsome

face freckled with bright little dots. 'D'you know horses swim in a straight line? They find it hard to turn. Ride them into the waves and they just keep going, far out to sea until it's too late to stop them drowning.'

Turning back to the sink, Pax scrubbed a saucepan vigorously, trying to shake the image. 'That's just awful.'

'We're a long way from the sea here,' he reminded her, the smile still in his voice. 'In dry dock.'

'Sober, you mean?' Pax couldn't bring herself to steal that smile away by admitting how much she wanted a drink. *I am dry*, she reminded herself. *We are dry.*

'Sure, I get drunk enough on you, angel.' He cast her a sideways look. He had all the lines.

'No ships,' she repeated firmly, 'not even ones that pass in the night.'

'Break my heart, why don't you?' he laughed, all easy come, easy go, walk-on-water indifference.

Pax felt her own heart splinter a little. Filling the pan up with suds to soak, she threw the scrubber into it and retreated to the cottage to run Kes's bath.

There, paddling Mr Matey to a foamy froth, she pressed her hot forehead to the hard edge of the bath and groaned, even more desperate for a drink. She wouldn't do it with Kes here. That was non-negotiable.

Luca didn't get the divide between Kes being around and not. Hers was a Jekyll and Hyde consent.

Heart and face on fire, she pushed open the tiny casement window for a few deep gulps of frosty air, searching the horizon for Orion, out on one of his last evening hunts before the hour change chased him west through the night sky. She'd always thought of it as her father's constellation, the great huntsman watching over her.

Pax had long suspected she'd inherited some of the demons which had driven Johnny Ledwell to his untimely death, perhaps his famously wild mother, Johanna, to hers as well.

She shared her paternal grandmother's red hair, so why not the same madness? Had Johanna been unhappily married too, was it that 'madness'?

Secrets were stitched into their family fabric, and Pax was an expert seamstress. She patched over her feelings daily.

Every time Luca checked how she was, she buttoned up and said she felt great, and each time they stole a kiss, she pinned a bright smile over the deep, dark desire building inside her, increasingly doubtful they were cut from the same cloth. Sometimes, like now, she unravelled, squirming with anxiety and longing, worried she was being as dishonest with herself as her father had been.

They both knew what it was to deny oneself the thing you crave.

In her case, it wasn't just a cool, numbing slug of vodka fresh from the freezer.

It was Bay.

Bay who had stayed rooted in the village, living and working here, constant as an oak. Bay, who had given her a horse, then kept his distance just as she'd asked. A hands-off owner whose hands she dreamt of undressing her at night.

Turning the taps down to a trickle, she found enough signal by the little casement window to call best friend Lizzie. 'I think I need sex.'

'What are you waiting for, darling? Luca's divine. He puts you first and he's not fazed by your exes hanging round.'

'Dirty, no-strings, guilt-free sex.'

'I refer you to my comments above. Get bumping and grinding right now. That's an order.'

Confidantes since their teens, Lizzie was one of the few friends Pax unburdened to. The two had been on Young Riders teams together in the early noughties, rattling around Europe with hot crushes and a desperate urge to lose their virginities to sexy cads in breeches like young Jilly Cooper heroines.

An early survivor of a marriage that had withered on the vine, now replanted on a Dorset farm with a devoted second-chance love and a blended family, Lizzie empathised evangelically and outspokenly. 'Do what comes naturally! You're living in a stud farm. Sex is mandatory.'

Even so, Pax struggled to explain to her friend how shredded her confidence was these days, marriage to Mack stealing her sexual joy and self-esteem. Luca, who had enjoyed a notoriously uninhibited sex life – including his passionate ten-year affair with wild-child showjumper Meredith – was bound to be disappointed. 'I'm terribly out of practise, and what we have is special. We're friends. I don't want to ruin it.'

'Having dirty, no-strings sex with anybody else *won't* ruin it?'

'We're in each other's pockets here. That's a lot of strings: apron, purse, bow, horses.'

'Sounds a perfect match.'

'I have to think of Kes.' She looked round to check the bath.

'Your son is five and needs lots of love, play and sleep. You're in your thirties and need all that, plus sex after bedtime. C'mon, you fancy Luca rotten, don't you?'

'Hopelessly.' Pax looked out at Orion again. 'It's just hard to trust someone though, isn't it, when you know they...' She groped for a euphemism.

'Shagged around a lot?' Lizzie suggested cheerfully.

Having been about to say 'have another job to go to', Pax kept quiet.

'Not if they've grown out of it,' Lizzie went on. 'The man is adorable, Pax. I know plenty who would love to be in your shoes.'

Pax glanced down at her mismatched socks with a disorienting sense of being in the wrong Cinderella fantasy. At the other end, she could hear Lizzie pouring wine, felt her own mouth crave the slake of alcohol, her body yearn for the simplicity of just sex.

'Have a weekend away together,' her friend urged after a swig. 'Take the horsebox somewhere picturesque to rock its axels, steam up its windows and have a gallop.'

'Now galloping I *can* do,' Pax told Lizzie about the mare she had so many weekend plans for. 'Bay's got a trainer friend with an all-weather gallop on offer to get her fit. Can you believe he's being so generous? He just keeps saying "do what you want with her".'

'Please don't tell me you're falling for Bay Austen again?' Lizzie had been frontline when Pax's teenage dreams were bulldozered.

'Of course not,' she replied far too quickly. 'He just owns the horse I'm going to campaign this season, possibly a leg of another if I'm lucky.' Grateful to change topic, she told Lizzie about the experienced little American-bred stallion Lester was trying to syndicate. 'If he does come here, I'm back in the big league.'

'Now that *is* something you are dangerously out of practise with, darling.' A note of anxiety crept into Lizzie's voice. 'You can't just step back in at top level.'

'I've checked my rider accreditation with BE, and I can still compete at the same rank I was previously.'

'Almost fifteen years ago?' came an incredulous wail. 'I compete every *week*. It's tough out there.'

'I know it is,' Pax reassured her, explaining her personal training and fitness programme at such length and with such enthusiasm, she didn't notice the bath overflowing until her socks got soaked, her wail of horror making Lizzie laugh.

'Maybe I've got this all wrong,' her friend admitted. 'It's not Luca you need to ride, it's Luca you need to beat.'

'Remember when we used to say competing was better than sex?' Pax perched on the loo seat to peel off her wet socks.

'You're about to find out for yourself, darling. Promise me you'll be careful? Take it slowly on both fronts. But bloody well do it!'

'I will!' Pax promised, nerves ends tingling with such anticipation that when she put her hand in the water to test it, she half expected it to blow up like a toaster.

Out of habit, she checked her messages from Bay again before she headed downstairs, studying that final laughing emoji. Before she could think too hard about it, she sent one back, sharing the joke.

Plied with sparkling English wine at Upper Bagot Farmhouse – but without so much as a crisp in sight – Ronnie regretted not eating any of Luca's pasta high tea before she'd set out. He was always cooking up great pans of food and only ever seemed to eat out of bowls, like a pet. She shared this with Petra, who had decided to reinstate Sean O'Shaughnessy as the hero of her latest historical romance and wanted to hear more about the stud's work rider. She'd just presented Ronnie with a copy of her latest book – 'please just gift it if you don't want it; I always get sent a stack' – so Ronnie felt she should give something back.

'Luca's so modern and does so many things differently, it's like he's time-travelling back to try to educate us,' Ronnie told her. 'He's aghast we don't have CCTV or foal alarms, says we're prehistoric.'

'He's an innovator, a revolutionary,' Petra nodded eagerly, although Ronnie sensed giving Luca's yoga-loving vegan good cheer a swashbuckling, rakish seventeenth-century makeover rather lost his poetic soul.

'He goes out to check the due mares constantly. He's terribly sweet. He and Pax have charts and notes everywhere, like primary school teachers.'

'Yes, I heard they're *very* close,' Petra said leadingly.

Ronnie glanced round for a diversion, determined not to jinx it for them. Various Gunn children were milling about, tweens and teens, music thumping in distant rooms, but she had yet to spot Petra's raffish husband. 'Where's Charlie tonight?'

'London, the slippery sod. Buggered off this afternoon. He gets so bored here. He's probably up to someone.' She lowered her voice. 'I was hoping I might have another fun flirt with Bay tonight now that he's footloose. Just for fun. Cheer us both up.'

'Good plan.' Ronnie would be happy to see him distracted.

'The trouble is Bay's stopped playing. No more naughty texts. I've sent him two *Dirty Dancing* gifs and a lot of winking emojis this week. Nothing.'

'He must have a lot on his mind.' Ronnie hoped it wasn't her daughter.

'The end of a marriage is torture, isn't it?' Petra's dark eyes melted into a sympathetic smile. 'I can't stop thinking about poor Mo. Pax going through it all must bring back painful memories for you?'

'Not a bit.' This wasn't entirely true, but again Ronnie stayed schtum, reluctant to shine light on her past's darker secrets. Johnny had never been a bully like Mack. Quite the reverse. He'd hated conflict. Domineering, aggressive personalities overwhelmed him – countless owners, particularly garrulous ones like Kenny Kay, found themselves avoided – and when he was forced in contact with them, he drank himself numb to cope. But ultimately the conflict Johnny could never escape had been in his head.

It's what she feared most for Pax.

Pax paused to gaze up at Orion as she crossed back to the main house, wishing he could step down from heaven. 'Why did you have to drive into a bloody tree?'

Her father glittered back impassively.

Her senses thrummed with the desire for something more, a tangible sign that the universe was listening. She could smell woodsmoke in the frosty air, hear the dogs barking in the house. And then she picked up the faint sound of an all-too familiar engine on the lane below.

Please don't turn, she prayed as it slowed at the end of the drive.

It turned, Bay's big, bullish Land Rover idling up the drive, its headlights strobing between the poplars, strains of Nina Simone on the stereo.

You asked for it, Orion glittered down at her.

Panicked butterflies rose inside her when it rattled onto the cobbles, the arrival's yard floodlights coming on. She caught the glint of Bay's eyes blazing over the steering wheel. Then, to her relief, she spotted Viv Austen in the passenger's seat, solidly dependable in headscarf and vintage Husky as she lowered the window.

'Here to offer Mum a lift to the church committee!' she called, breath clouding in the cold air like vape fumes. 'Thought she might have forgotten it was on.'

'You missed her.' Pax hugged herself for warmth, stepping closer. 'She met up with friends first.'

'Bravo! Tell me, how's Lester?'

Behind Viv, Bay's face gave nothing away, quite unlike the laughing, smiling emojis he sent every day.

'Back on his feet and driving Mummy mad with all his plans,' Pax told Viv, bending lower. 'It's hard stopping him doing too much.'

'That's the spirit! Must call by properly soon, take a look at you on this horse of Bay's.'

Unable to stop herself, Pax caught Bay's eye. He half smiled, blue gaze still burning brightly. And she found she couldn't look away.

Clicking on the handbrake, he was out of the car in a plume of steamed breath, saying, 'That reminds me, I need to have a quick word with Pax about the mare, Ma.'

'Be quick! The meeting starts in ten minutes.'

Leaving Viv listening to 'Don't Let Me Be Misunderstood', he strode through the archway onto the main yard and disappeared from sight.

Pax set off in pursuit.

She caught up with him by the feed store. 'Lottie's in the next yard if you'd like to see her.'

He turned to face her, face in shadow. 'It's you I need to see. Anytime, you said earlier.'

Orion watched them from above the clocktower while Pax waited for more, cold and nonplussed. After a while, her teeth began chattering. 'I was expecting a quick word, not a long silence.'

'We've had the quick word. I told you I needed to see you not the mare. Now I can see you.'

There was another long pause, his silhouette a tall statue, studying her.

'Do you just want to *look* at me?' she laughed doubtfully.

His eyes gleamed in the near-dark.

She'd never known Bay lost for words.

'Is this a wind-up?' Her skin prickled, the thrill seeker getting what she'd asked the stars for moments earlier, summoning wilful, wayward Bay. But his conceit angered her. 'You enjoy seeing hypothermia in real time, is that it?'

'Here.' He uncoiled the striped woolly scarf from around his neck and hooked it round hers, his warmth and smell against her skin, that vampire bite of lust back at her throat, this one far deeper and deadlier.

She stepped back sharply, forcing him to let go of the ends. 'Stop being weird.'

'I'm not being weird!' He sounded affronted. Then he looked down, half-laughing. 'Sorry, yes, maybe I am.' He pressed his fingertips to his lips, signet ring glinting, before touching them lightly to her cheek, their warmth a surprise. 'Forgive me.'

'Stop that.' She stepped back further. 'This must stay professional, Bay.' The emojis had been a big mistake. 'I think perhaps my messages are a bit informal.'

'Mixed messages.' He sucked his teeth, moving closer again

as if to tuck the loose ends of the scarf round her neck, before stopping himself. 'I like your informality – and your terrible typos too.'

'I do not make terrible typos.' She could see is face in the light now, surprised to find his eyes turbulent, not amused at all.

This time he was the one to step back, glancing towards the sound of Nina Simone. 'I must go. Look, I really am sorry about this. Stupid idea. Idiotic of me. I just assumed you knew.'

'Knew what?'

'This… affliction I have. It's bloody painful, actually.'

'Are you ill?'

'I'm not sure.' He glanced towards the arch again, eager to leave now.

'*Tell* me Bay!' She couldn't bear him to be ill.

'Promise you won't laugh?'

'Why would I laugh? What is it?'

He held his hand out towards hers. 'May I?'

She shrugged, suddenly wary, guessing this might be a big practical joke at her expense after all.

'It's this…' He took her hand and quickly drew it inside his coat, holding it against his chest. Even through layers of lambswool and merino and cotton, she could feel his heart pounding.

She snatched her arm away and laughed to cover her shock. He wasn't allowed to change the rules like this.

'You should get that looked at,' she muttered, staring fixedly up at Orion.

'Yes, I thought so,' he muttered, gaze locked on the arch.

In the brief silence that followed, Pax's own giveaway heart thundered, the vampire artery in her throat pulsing wildly and offering up enough blood to make her dizzy.

'I don't feel the same way you do, Bay,' she told him, barely able to hear herself over the treacherous roaring in her ears.

'Of course not.'

'All that was over years ago.'

The car horn beeping made them both jump out of their skins. Viv was getting impatient.

When Bay reached out towards her, for a panicked moment, Pax thought he was going to put his palm against her chest to feel her heart crashing around in there like a weasel in a snare.

'No!' She grabbed his hand, her fist tight around it. 'You do *not* have my permission to do that.'

One eyebrow shot up. 'I need to ask for permission to get my scarf back?'

'Yes,' she bluffed, feeling her cheeks flaming.

He looked at her incredulously, his eyes moving between hers, swinging back and forth hypnotically.

Her fist was still clamped around his, Pax realized, watching transfixed as he drew it to his lips and pressed his half-smile to it with a courtly, apologetic bow before turning to stride back beneath the arch.

Moments later, the red taillights were streaking away along the drive, Nina Simone singing 'I Put A Spell On You'.

Pax's teeth might be chattering like castanets, but her chest was on fire, her recently kissed knuckles like a hot coal.

Kes's bath forgotten, she hurried through the second arch to Lottie's stable. The bright V was already waiting, bobbing eagerly, a low rumble of a whicker greeting her.

Letting herself in, Pax leant into her warmth, breathing deeply, the heady hay-sweet scent of horse combining intoxicatingly with the Bay-smelling scarf around her neck.

There was no point denying it. The thing she longed for most didn't need Orion's hunting skills to unearth it. It was hiding in plain sight.

12

The inaugural meeting of the St Mary's Church Roof Repair Action Plan took place in the Bernard Ugger Memorial Hall, an unprepossessing Bradstone-clad municipal slab on the outskirts of Compton Bagot, named after its benefactor whose coach business had been even more of a village eyesore. Known locally as the Bugger All, it had achingly uncomfortable chairs, unflattering neon lighting and always smelled of pensioner's lunch club gravy and sweaty Lycra.

This evening, it was also incredibly cold, the heating turned on too late and too low, the cold March snap blowing in an icy chill with each new arrival. The participants all kept their coats on as they scraped chairs up to trestles tables arranged in a big square and studied tonight's revised agenda.

Kit read it without great enthusiasm, still mentally in front of his fire, the bitter frosts having driven him in from his beloved greenhouse in recent days, which had done his wine habit no favours. Having polished off the last of the red before coming out – Sassoon cast aside while he sorted Hermia's letters into date order – it was only the possibility that there might be some plonk on offer at half-time here that had finally convinced him to come. He glanced hopefully at a couple of bottles of red on a side table.

The agenda, hastily retyped by Parish Council secretary

Chris Hicks, now included an address by the vicar and a proposal to call the C.R.R.A.P campaign *Raise the Roof*, Kit noted with relief.

'Also, coincidentally, the name of a popular entertainment show hosted by our new village celebrity in the nineties,' a voice whispered as the seat beside Kit was occupied by Viv Austen, a pepper-haired, gappy-toothed gusher. '*So* glad you could make it, dear man! Absolute trooper!'

Kit had often bellyached to Hermia that her sister-in-law was insufferably jolly, but after his wife's death, Viv had been such a backbone of practical support, childcare, cooking and kindness, that he'd developed a grudging admiration for her boundless good cheer and charitable largesse. It took a robust personality to be married to boorish Sandy for forty years, after all. Her joie de vivre was the Teflon coating of rural middle-class marriage.

'Are you chairing?' he asked her.

'Leaving that to Brian.' Viv tilted her head to indicate their white-bearded village elder, Brian Hicks, a Captain Mainwaring in Cotton Traders, who also served as their church warden, chair of the Parish Council, website moderator and annual Santa. 'I'm just a collie rounding up the flock. And selling raffle tickets.' She brandished a booklet. 'Shall I put you down for a strip? There's a brace of rather nice Shiraz up for grabs.' She pointed at the bottles on the side table.

Guessing it was the only way he'd get a drink tonight, Kit bought five strips.

'Here we go!' Viv hushed as Brian started calling for everyone to be seated. 'We can't wait indefinitely. You *did* say Mrs Ledwell is coming, Vivienne?'

'Yes! Absolutely! And Petra Gunn too.' She beamed, muttering to Kit. 'Frightfully flaky but well-connected.'

Kit exchanged a polite hello with an ageing blonde who was scraping her chair in on his other side, recognizing her as the opera-loving head teacher of the village's primary school,

Auriol Bullock, sucking on a mint to diminish top-notes of gin and looking round fiercely as she banged down a spiral pad full of handwritten notes.

Kit rather liked the formality of community meetings, the self-conscious hierarchy and positioning; it was the perfect platform from which to observe people. As well as worthy bore Brian and his silent, worried wife, there was the somewhat less holy local vicar, the Reverend Hilary Jolley, a guffawing snorter of indeterminate gender who did a lot of 'grateful for your support' back-slapping as the meeting gathered and said 'bloody good' repeatedly once it kicked off.

Apologies were read out, of which one from the elderly Stokeses was greeted with much muttered sympathy and Kit distinctly heard a 'bastard!' from the end of the table.

'The daughter's husband walked out last month,' Viv confided in an undertone. 'He works for us. All a bit awkward actually. Ran over a dog on his way off and didn't stop. There's always a rash of them, isn't there?'

Kit stiffened. 'Dog hit-and-runs?'

With an awkward half-laugh as she realized this might have touched a raw nerve, she hurried on, 'Marriages falling apart. Terribly tough when children are involved.'

She looked pained again, and Kit recalled that her son's was amongst the latest Compton broken homes. 'There'll be more divorces than weddings in this village at the rate we're going, especially without a functioning church. We *must* save it, Kit!'

'Hear bloody hear!' Auriol flapped open her spiral pad on his other side and uncapped a pen. 'And no more talk of selling the school!'

This roused a few cries of support and surprise from those who hadn't heard the rumours.

'We'll Raise the Roof!' Viv sounded like a hockey player bullying off, and yet more committee members joined in with rowdy agreement.

'Order!' Brian called, and they quietened down as he

introduced everybody around the table, starting rather alarmingly with Kit – 'one of our longest-standing and must illustrious Compton Magna residents' – whose smile froze as 'multi award-winning' was added to his job title, along with an exaggerated 'RSC veteran' a spurious 'Hollywood favourite', and a downright fictitious 'friend of a many A-list actors.'

Beside him, he spotted Auriol jotting down *Ask KD to talk to Year 6 About Drama?* which grounded him somewhat.

As the faces around him gained names, Kit was reminded how few of the slowly shifting drift of the village population he knew, and yet how little they changed, its dominant demographic remaining white, reactionary, over sixty. Apart from a couple of media-savvy Londonshire types drafted in for social networking skills – because none of the Compton Facebook Page administrators could remember how to log in, and the Parish Councillors all thought Twitter and TikTok were bird and clock noises – most of the committee was made up of elderly stalwarts.

Brian's turgid reading of a surveyor's report and repair estimates reduced most of them to a soporific stupor. Kit was regretting the red wine. He longed to be back home reading Hermia's letters. And he was furious with Ronnie, who had insisted he come in the first place and hadn't turned up

Auriol was writing a shopping list now: *Laundry Tabs, Firelighters, Tena Lady.*

Then a flurry of blonde apology in a squashy coat, Ronnie arrived, and the energy in the room changed completely. With her was a glamorous brunette with tired, smoky eyes who Kit recognized as the writer now living in the farmhouse he and Hermia had once shared.

Alert once more, Kit observed them with interest, the brunette impassive while Ronnie fidgeted, spinning a big silver ring around her middle finger and rolling her eyes at the table like a bored schoolgirl. He guessed she was unaccustomed to sitting down or staying still. Her gaze soon moved around the room in search of interest, as unafraid of staring at people as Kit was. But whereas he quietly watched, she inevitably caught eyes and engaged, sharing amusement or surprise. When they met his, they creased into a warm, conspiratorial smile. He looked away without returning it, even more irritated that he'd so obediently come here.

He knew he should be conciliatory for Hermia's sake, grateful to have the letters at last, and quietly relieved Ronnie had bowed out of the Bowie musical a fortnight earlier. Her unwanted theatre tickets had even rekindled an old friendship when he'd passed them on to married musicians in a neighbouring village.

He was here to re-engage with his neighbours and renew just such connections, he reminded himself. It shocked him how anti-social he'd become when staying here, and that's why he needed to show willing. Not because a bossy Mary Poppins had said 'spit-spot'. He stole another glance at her. She stole one back, amused.

Other committee members were now listening in frozen horror as Brian outlined an ancient chancel liability which could be enacted to make all those with properties close to the church share the hefty bill for its roof repair.

'How much are we talking, exactly?' Kit asked, aware that he lived closer than most. 'A couple of thousand between all of us?'

'Add a zero and multiply it by five, maybe?' the vicar suggested cheerily.

'Of course, we want to avoid that at all costs,' Brian insisted, aware that his own house also fell into the chancel tax category, 'and we are indebted to the church for getting right behind us on this. I will now hand over to the Reverend Jolley to explain the nature of the repair and the outline funding options.'

Kit saw Ronnie stifle a yawn, now discreetly flicking through photographs of horses on her phone beneath the table edge, attaching them to texts that she fired off with swiftly thumbed messages. He had begrudgingly to admire the guile of the woman, horse-trading at a parish meeting.

When she caught him watching and beamed across at him, he smiled back this time. A tingle crept from his scalp to his toes, as unexpected as it was unwelcome.

'Percys are born sexy and Austens are born charming,' Hermia had once told him. 'It's why we love to hate each other. Outsiders just fancy us both.'

Did he count as an Austen, he wondered now, or an outsider?

Luca's globe-trotting life meant he'd missed out on having a dog of his own since childhood, although he inevitably fostered one with each job. At the stud, it was Pax's dog, Knott. He'd grown accustomed to the young deerhound following him about, and he liked the company. But he knew the transference of loyalty hurt her. His 'we should tie the Knott' joke hadn't gone down well.

The dog was watching him now, young brown eyes anxious under their old-man brows. He seemed to see straight into Luca's shadowy conscience as he picked up his phone, staying at his side when he wandered down the back corridor to the spot where Pax messaged Bay. The irony wasn't lost on Luca as he checked for new messages from Meredith.

There were two; the first was a photograph of a horse jumping, almost clearing the wings. *Tell them I wanna keep this one here!* The second photograph was of her, a mirror selfie *And I wanted to keep you here too.*

He deleted it, almost dropping the phone as Knott scabbled away to join Ronnie's dogs barking at the back door, his bass boom echoing.

Pocketing his phone, Luca followed, glancing from the side window, watching Pax's long shadow emerging from the yard gate and hurry towards the cottage.

It wasn't the first time she'd set off the dogs. Barely fifteen minutes earlier, Luca had witnessed her staring up at the sky. He always loved the way she talked to it, just as she talked to the horses when she thought he wasn't listening.

He'd also seen her talking to Bay. He loved her a tiny bit less for that.

He owed her the truth, quietly and alone. But as he pulled on his boots and reached for the door handle, he heard Lester bellowing, 'It's stopped working again, Luca, the infernal Wi-Fi!'

'Daffy Duck's stuck!' Kes confirmed, storming into the hallway.

The big smart TV in the dining room was vastly superior to the ancient little one in the cottage or the Captain's elderly, boxy Sony in the snug. Loaned by a hunt crony so that Lester could watch the racing, it was a magnet for Kes. It also regularly blew the tech.

Luca reset the router and waited until the cartoon burst back into life with a loud, 'Youuu're dethspicable!'

The dogs were all now roasting flat-out in front of the blazing dining room fireplace, the old man and the boy equally supine in front of the glowing screen.

'Duck feathers are nature's best waterproofing,' Lester informed Kes as Elmer Fudd was strapped to an alligator on-screen, 'so much so that when they dive the plumage by their skin stays completely dry.'

'Like Nanna Forsyth's hair!' Kes launched into an explanation of his grandmother's magical swimming hat, telling Luca that, 'when she takes it off her hair is all fluffy and you can see her pink head.'

Luca lingered by the door as they all watched the cartoon hunter's come-uppance, held by the silly talk and old-fashioned companionship. Elmer Fudd pursuing Daffy through the bayou reminded him of Bay with his tweeds and his guns.

'Youuu're dethspicable!' Kes shrieked, sitting cross-legged on the floor beside Stubbs' crate, where the little dog was recuperating away from his canine housemates and three-a-day rodent habit.

Kes loved hanging out in Lester's temporary digs. The old man welcomed his exuberance, not minding if he talked all the way through television shows, marched around the room enacting battles, or asked an endless stream of questions, a sharp contrast to his dour Scottish grandparents who expected puritanical focus and politeness, or Ronnie, who bored quickly.

Lester was clearly relishing his newfound grandfatherly role. Still furious with Ronnie – he blamed her entirely for Stubbs' accident – the old man had loosened up considerably since communal meals, followed by cartoon hour, had become a regular thing, these post-prandial fireside chats with Kes his favourite hour part the day.

'Top-up please, young man?' He held his small glass up to Luca.

'Of course, sir!' He took it to the kitchen where he'd hidden Lester's home-made plum gin beyond easy reach.

Lester liked a small tipple or two after supper each night.

The smell of it reminded Luca of cold mornings and hunting flasks in Ireland in boyhood, of the tip of a slithery slope he'd found himself hurtling down, latterly alongside Meredith. Rye whisky was her drink, which she'd consumed by the quart before still jumping faultless rounds. She could always outdrink him.

He now wished he hadn't deleted the photograph.

Luca diverted along the back corridor to check for more messages – none – and look out for Pax again. Quietly shadowing, Knott lent against him, warm from the hearth. The smell of the plum gin he was carrying rose like Elmer Fudd's swamp as they waited, but all remained dark outside.

Back in the dining room, *Daffy Duck* had given way to a noisy advert break and more chatter. Luca felt a pang for his rowdy, generation-spanning Irish family shouting at the TV. And for his adopted Canadian one that had always talked over it, for those layered summers of love and affection, for his lost daughter. For Meredith.

Why had he deleted the bloody photograph?

A Tom and Jerry cartoon started, and Pax's face appeared around the door at last, bright-eyed and pink-cheeked, making Luca start guiltily.

'Time to say goodnight, Master Forsyth.'

'Just *one* more cartoon, Mummy, pleeeeeeeeese?'

'I've just had to run your bath again and there's no more hot water left after this.'

'I like cold baths!'

Pax laughed, crossing her arms and watching while he determinedly pretended that she wasn't there. Luca tried to catch her eye, but she avoided his gaze just as Kes did hers. There was an excited energy coming from her like gamma rays. He could see the joy in her face when Kes and Lester hooted with mirth as Jerry untied bulldog Spike to chase Tom. She looked down at her watch.

'C'mon darling, we're half an hour behind already. Daddy will be calling to say goodnight soon.' The moment she said it, the familiar ghost of panic stole her smile. Mack's rigid timetable still ruled their evenings: bath by seven, pjs and story seven fifteen, lights out seven thirty.

'Five more minutes, Mummy, pleeeeeeeeese!' Snorting with giggles when Spike swapped his false teeth to giant snarling ones, Kes began explaining loudly to Lester, 'Cats and Dogs are like Mummies and Daddies but the mouse isn't really like me because they both want to eat it, like when Gronny's dogs chase rats in the hay barn, and Mrs Bullock says there are feral cats in the village too but I haven't seen them, and if I did, I'd make friends with it and keep one as a pet and call him—'

'C'mon, Kes,' Pax interrupted. 'It's time to leave Lester in peace.'

'Let the lad have his five minutes,' Lester urged, launching into a story about the Captain's old stable cat, Mulligan, who'd had a taste for stoats.

Pax finally caught Luca's eye, her nervous energy crackling against his.

'Big as a dog fox he was,' Lester was saying.

'Like Laurence?' asked Kes, who was fascinated by the orphaned cub the old man had rescued this winter.

'Much bigger'n that. He'd stand up on his hindlegs and box your great-grandad's gundogs like a hare.'

'*Five* minutes, no more,' Pax told Kes, holding Luca's gaze before heading out to the kitchen.

He followed, finding her lapping the table, her customary displacement.

'Bay came round just now.'

'Is that who it was?' He played it down, heading to the sink again – his own customary displacement – and reminding himself this was the perfect opportunity to start the conversation, share some truths, clear the air.

Instead, he turned on the old radio on the windowsill in front of him before setting about scrubbing out the big pasta pan Pax had put in soak earlier, hips moving to Prince growling 'I Would Die 4 U' from the speakers.

She stopped lapping to watch him. 'I should be doing that.'

'Think you can do this?' He exaggerated the dance to make her laugh.

'Here, let me dry. You cooked.' She moved beside him, her hips moving in time as Prince told them he was neither lover nor friend, their shared energy crackling again.

When she reached for his drying cloth, he flapped it away like a matador's cloak.

'Sure, it was only *spaghetti alla Norma*.' Luca boogied away, hanging the pan over the Aga then pulling a smile together before looking back over his shoulder. Flirt your way out of trouble, O'Brien. 'Besides, you get to turn on the dishwasher if you like.'

Taking a while to get the joke, Pax flushed and laughed. 'My luck's in tonight.'

Prince sang that he'd make her good when she was bad.

Luca danced closer again. 'What did Bay want?'

'Mummy,' she said, her gaze not quite meeting his.

'*Dethspicable*.' He tilted his head and chased it, until they were looking at each other, the crackling static back.

'He and Viv were here to pick her up for this charity meeting,' she danced opposite him, 'but she'd already set off.'

They were hamming it up like hop pickers at a Young Farmers disco now. 'What's it in aid of again?'

'The church roof. Mummy needs God on side.'

'We all need Him. Nice scarf, by the way.' Luca watched the blush rise through her freckles as Prince sang that he was her conscience, he was love.

'Actually, it's Bay's,' she blurted.

'Sure.' On they danced and on he smiled. *Tell her!*

'I was cold so he lent it to me.' She sounded nervous as though, like Othello, he was about to scream 'a handkerchief!' and try to suffocate her with an oven mitt. Mack had been insanely jealous, he remembered, her anxiety now habitual.

'Good of him.' Luca tossed the tea towel onto his shoulder and cupped her face in his hands. Pax's fragile trust was too important to mess with. *Tell her.*

'I'll call round later, shall I, when Kes is asleep?' He kissed her mouth lightly.

Put it off why don't you? You can't flirt your way out of this one.

Pax hesitated. 'For a little bit, maybe. Not too late.'

'Just to talk.' He kissed her cheeks in turn, each barely more than a breath, then bit his lip ruefully. 'No shipping, I promise.'

Her eyes didn't move from his. And he knew she was thinking of things that they categorically, absolutely should not do together later.

She reached out her hand and held the palm flat against his chest at arm's length, taking him by surprise. 'That's fast.'

Was this some sort of truth test, he wondered, reaching out to hold his palm over hers, which was beating quick as hares' feet. 'So is yours.'

Now he was the one imagining anything but talking.

Prince was repeating 'I would Die 4 U' with funky abandon. Kept at arm's length, Luca swayed in time, polite as an officer at a military dance.

Pax laughed, that gratifying explosion, eyes still too bright. Then she danced closer and her hips met his, like two magnets snapping together in a kitsch kitchen rhumba, mutual attraction sizzling, warm breaths of laughter against each other's skin.

Luca had flirted his way out of danger after all.

Sarah Cox's creamy Lancashire voice took over the airwaves to remind listeners that Prince was a right sexy blighter, and so was this god of the dance floor.

David Guetta's 'Hey Mama' started grinding its way through the room, all Dutch House Jam and prison blues, Nicki Minaj singing that she was all theirs whichever way they wanted her.

It was a *seriously* sexy song. Luca let his guard down, shoulders rolling and faded denim hips swaying in time.

'Enough!' Pax ducked away, hot-faced. 'Tonight, I'm the only Mama in this house, and I bang the drum. I must get my son into his bath.'

Calling through to the dining room for Kes, she hurriedly gathered up his abandoned drawing pad, pens and cuddly rabbit, not looking at Luca. 'That was unforgivably stupid of me.'

Luca watched her, angry with himself too. He owed her the truth, not a cheap O'Brien seduction. He'd just blown it.

They could hear Kes saying a loud goodnight to Lester.

'He will be fast asleep by nine,' she whispered quickly, 'come round then.'

Before Luca could reply, Kes appeared in the door, wide-eyed with excitement. 'Lester says he's well enough to give me riding lessons and I'll soon be as good as Luca!' Then remembered to add, 'And you, Mummy, only you're a girl so you can't be a cowboy or a highwayman or a knight.'

'Women can be all those things, Kes,' Pax corrected, catching Luca's eye, emboldened now.

'Don't you doubt it,' Luca agreed, 'your mother can do just about anything she wants.' A ricochet of anticipation rattled through him, David Guetta's track chanting through the kitchen, loaded with sexual innuendo and power play.

'That's what Mrs Bullock always tells the girls,' Kes told them earnestly as Pax hurried him out before Nicki Minaj dropped an f-bomb, 'Except for having a wee-wee standing up, although Grace Dawkins says Victorian ladies used to do that too.' Their voices drifted away along the corridor.

Luca reached down the plum gin.

'I don't need another one, young man,' Lester told him when he carried it through,

'You might. Because I want you to tell me exactly what the deal is with the American stallion, and what he's doing in Canada.'

13

'Our faithful flock has an abundance of pasture in the Comptons, dear friends.'

Half listening, Ronnie discreetly fired off more messages from her phone beneath the table as Reverend Jolley brought the same animated kindness to addressing the village fundraisers as if reciting the parable of the Good Samaritan to Compton Magna primary school's Reception class.

The village hall Wi-Fi was usefully quick. Ronnie had managed to send out videos of Beck to several interested mare owners and was once again studying footage of the American stallion.

'Damn it!' Her 'battery low' warning came up.

'What was that, Mrs Ledwell?' asked Brian Hicks, his eyes narrowed because he'd already reminded committee members twice to put phones on Do Not Disturb.

'Just swept up in the thrill of it.' She held hers in her lap and listened to the vicar, head tilted.

'As I was explaining, the Church of England was already looking to reduce their land holdings in the parish,' the Reverend Jolley revealed with pink-cheeked glee, 'so when St Mary's roof came down, one might say this really was an Act of God, ha!'

Ronnie tried to catch Kit's eye, but he wasn't playing along. Beside her, Petra was half-asleep.

Her phone buzzed in her palm and she glanced down to see Blair's name on screen with a heart-jolt of surprise. He was always rigidly self-controlled when they were 'off'.

She opened the message.

Don't call.

Ronnie felt a rib nudge of irritation. She hadn't been going to.

'Don't you think Mrs Ledwell?' a voice broke her focus.

The vicar was looking at her earnestly.

'Absolutely!' Feeling like the naughty girl at school, she pocketed her mobile and nodded vigorously.

'As Mrs Ledwell concurs,' the reverend told the room, 'land is God's own no matter who holds its legal title.'

Forced to listen, Ronnie soon found herself sitting up in shock.

'We must all make sacrifices,' Hilary Jolley pronounced, before adding with a convivial flourish, 'and to save St Mary's and the souls she guards, let us be prepared to part with something very dear to us.'

The discovery of deathwatch beetle in the church's roof joists had pushed the cost of repairs way beyond the scope of even the most ambitious fundraising committee, it transpired and there was only one thing for it: the rumours were right; the church was selling up.

Ronnie listened carefully as the reverend outlined the assets that the church owned in the village, all once gifted to it by her Percy ancestors at the Eyngate estate.

'There is the church itself of course,' the reverend told them. 'Also, the school buildings and playing field—'

'Over my dead body!' roared Auriol.

'—and finally, Church Meadow.'

Ronnie glanced across at Petra who was now wide awake.

Reverend Hilary pressed on. 'It is the consensus of the

parochial council that the meadow should be disposed of by means of land auction to fund the repair.'

Ronnie felt her gaze lock onto their vicar with unswerving focus, willing for a trident to come plunging through the ceiling with a Celestial cry of 'Never!'

When it didn't, she interrupted Hilary reading out a land-valuation report. 'Absolutely not! That meadow is of enormous historic value. It's always been for the use of villagers with the church acting as custodians, not land agents.'

'The Church of England has a legal right to sell it, Mrs Ledwell,' intoned the reverend. 'And it will take more than a few coffee mornings to see off our little wood-munching friends, alas.'

'What about this chancel tax you mentioned?'

'That's still under consideration, yes.'

Which had Kit Donne reaching for his reading glasses to look down at his notes. 'Is this repair figure right? This quote is extraordinarily high. Have you put the work up to tender?'

'It's a specialist historic restoration, Mr Donne, not a conservatory.'

'Still, this is insanely high. Doesn't the Parish Council have a say whether the meadow should be sold to fund it?'

'Already approved in principle at last week's extraordinary meeting,' Brian informed him.

Mutters of surprise burbled around the table at this. Ronnie and Kit weren't the only ones who suspected something didn't add up.

'Please be aware,' the Reverend Jolley was looking slightly less jolly, 'that I'm not here to request the committee's permission, merely inform you of our intention.'

'God's own land knocked down to the highest bidder?' Ronnie's blood was up. 'The summer fete's held there, and a gymkhana was too until the parish council got in a flap about health and safety.'

'The fete moved to the old cricket field years ago,' Petra whispered aside.

Ronnie heard but forged on. 'Local travellers venerate that little plot; they used to come here from miles away to have their babies because it's full of rare herbs and wildflowers and considered lucky.'

'Bloody gypsies,' grumbled a local elder. 'Did you see them on it last month? Lighting fires and all sorts.'

Ronnie refused to be deflected. 'And villagers have the right to graze sheep and drive geese and whatnot there, don't they? When I was a girl, a friend and I ran a little animal sanctuary on it, raising money for the church!' She turned to Kit for backup.

'I hardly think your *Whistle Down the Wind* memories are relevant.' He seemed reluctant to be drawn in when he was in the Chancel Tax firing line.

'Your wife was the friend who ran it with me,' Ronnie pointed out. 'And if Hermia was still with us, she'd be arguing loudest to save it.'

The room fell uncomfortably silent.

'Church Meadow is of great historic interest,' Petra pitched in kindly. 'I researched it when I used it as a setting for a Civil War encampment in my last book. Royalists were billeted here on the way to Edge Hill. The Percys were very pro.'

'No surprise there,' murmured Kit.

'We lashed commoners like you to the witch stones and pelted them with roast swan,' Ronnie murmured back.

'Let's not get sidetracked,' Brian interjected firmly. 'The meadow serves no practical role. While it may have historic ecclesiastical ties, it falls just outside the village conservation area and is not an SSSI.'

'It *should* be SSSI,' Ronnie insisted. 'There are green-winged and bee orchids, dragonflies and swallowtail butterflies.'

'You've made your point, Titania,' Kit muttered.

'Mrs Ledwell, all God's meadows are in His care,' the vicar reassured her.

'And what about the standing stones?' asked Petra. 'The Three Witches are ancient monuments, surely?'

'There is no documented proof of that,' said the reverend. 'I've checked the records. More likely they're a glacial relic, a bit of geological clutter.'

'Druids performed sacred rights on them according to my research,' Petra said firmly. 'Something sexily sacrificial at *Litha* – that's the Midsummer's Day festival, involving naked maidens on horses.'

The room perked up, listening more attentively now.

'Ronnie should know all about that!' cackled one of the old guard.

'*Litha* comes from Bede's *The Reckoning of Time*,' Kit told them. 'In Druidry it's known as Alban Hefin, mother nature heavily pregnant with the seed of the horned god.'

'Don't put that in the minutes, Chris,' Brian ordered his wife.

Ronnie caught Kit's eye again, unable to determine if its glitter came from amusement or irritation.

'Isn't this all a bit nimbyish?' interjected another of the Bagot old-timers. 'The land in question is directly opposite your stud's entrance, Mrs Percy.'

'And that meadow adjoins Percy fields!' another voice protested. 'No wonder she don't want it sold.'

'Actually, the Austens own the adjoining fields now,' she pointed out.

'And I certainly don't want a bunch of gyppos setting up camp next door to them,' a voice drawled.

For the first time, Ronnie realized Bay was in the room, slouching at the far end of the table, uncharacteristically taciturn, tweed flat cap lowered to his waxed coat collar.

'I think they prefer to be known as the travelling community,' Petra corrected kindly.

'And they'll try to buy it if it goes to auction,' he muttered. 'Always have a surfeit of cash in need of laundering. Best tactic is to secure a pre-auction offer from a buyer sympathetic to village interests.'

'Like you, I suppose?' Ronnie laughed hollowly.

'I'd love to, Ronnie darling, but as you know I'm saving up all my pennies to buy a horse.' The blue eyes glittered beneath the flat cap.

She returned his gaze. 'That doesn't wash with me.'

'Unlike gypsy cash.' Arms unfolding and big shoulders squaring, Bay pulled off his hat with a tumble of oaky hair and straightened up. There was a perceptible brightening amongst the Church Roof Repair Action Plan women.

Ronnie, who found it too easy to dismiss his charisma, hadn't forgotten how much Bay enjoyed the devilry of debate as he smiled round the table now. 'You might have fond memories of the days all Turner babies were born there amongst the oxeye daisies, Mrs Ledwell, but Church Meadow is hardly Ayers Rock.'

'Uluru,' Petra said. 'And perhaps to our travelling community, it is?'

'The children did a project about nomadic cultures last term!' a voice announced theatrically, and Ronnie recognized the head teacher of the village school Kes now attended. 'It's said that if a Romanichal man spits on a piece of land it's cursed, if he spills blood it's claimed, but a single tear landing from his eye means he will never return.'

'I'm much the same with public hostelries and nightclubs!' Trying to inject some jollity, the reverend stunned most of the committee into silence.

'If we raise enough money, can C.R.R.A.P prevent it being sold?' Ronnie broke it first

'We've proposing to change the name to Raise the Roof,' Brian reminded her, 'but I believe so. Reverend?'

'Yes, as Mr Austen so wisely pointed out, anybody can make a pre-auction offer,' the reverend beamed coquettishly at Bay, 'but they will need *very* deep pockets.'

Across the table, Kit Donne cleared his throat. 'The Church of England currently owns two billion pounds worth of land,' he told them, his voice carrying. 'That buys an awful lot of charity.'

The committee watched him with interest, sensing insurgence.

'Let's weigh the benefits…' He took advantage of the lull to address the whole table as though it were a university debating chamber. 'The meadow is bound to be scheduled and have a multitude of covenants attached to it, being Church land, meaning that whoever buys it will be very restricted in what they can do with it, and the villagers will still have a right to roam or whatever.'

'There *are* strict covenants on the land, Mr Donne is right,' the reverend pitched in smoothly. 'Developing it for housing would be nigh on impossible, and the Church takes a very dim view of commercial enterprise.'

'Rewilding is all the rage,' Auriol Bullock announced to nobody in particular. 'My little ones rewilded a corner of the playing field last summer using seed packets donated by the PTA. Turned out it was full of hemp!'

'On the *other* hand,' Kit carried on in his *Question Time* voice, all gravitas with a Cumbrian accent, 'that land was given *precisely* for the people of this village to use to share together, to replenish our larders, celebrate our joys and host our travelling friends – nature's church, if you like – and if we have the power to save it by using that same collective spirit to buy it back for the village, isn't that why we're here? The Church will get their money to mend the roof and we'll get control of our meadow.'

'Brilliant!' Ronnie cheered, others joining in, her opinion of him soaring.

He stood up. 'I therefore propose we change the name of this committee from the Church Roof Repair Action Plan to Buy Our Meadow Back!' This time he was the one to catch Ronnie's eye and wink.

He really was rather impressive, she conceded, a small bomb going off deep inside her in his honour as she cried, 'Seconded!'

Brian silenced them all. 'If you check your meeting Agenda, you'll find there's already a proposal to change it to Raise the Roof, Mr Donne.' He was withering.

Kit was more so. 'I propose we change the proposal, Mr Hicks.'

'In that case I'm afraid you'll have to wait for Any Other Business to suggest it,' Chris pointed out, making a note in the minutes and adding, 'if we have time left. Shall we get on?'

Kit looked dumbfounded, sitting down.

'Very rousing nonetheless, Mr Donne,' the reverend beamed.

'What we need is a famous patron,' Viv piped up eagerly. 'A local pop star or presenter? A celebrity gardener maybe? What about that TV chef who looks like Jesus? Doesn't he live near Broadbourne? You mix with lots of rich, famous people, Kit. You can find us someone!'

'Or maybe you can ask one of your famous actor friends to *buy* it?' Auriol looked excited.

'Can you get us a Twitter activist with a blue tick?' Petra asked.

Ronnie watched the theatre director's discomfort with sympathetic amusement as Viv leant across him the tell the head teacher, 'Kit's *terribly* well connected. He's chums with the Redgraves, Foxes and Wests, plus lots of Dames.'

'I'm no more than a wandering minstrel,' Kit held up his hands. 'A mere player.'

'As is Ronnie!' Viv said brightly. 'With all her aristocratic horsey connections.'

'Hardly,' Ronnie dismissed as Bay snorted with laughter nearby.

To everyone's surprise – not least Ronnie's – the reverend cried 'Amen to that!' and stood to pronounce, 'Mrs Ledwell is indeed very well connected! Quite the village saviour!'

Brian cleared his throat. 'Perhaps we could stick to the agreed agenda, Hilary? That's *confidential* information.'

'Of course!' The Holy nose was tapped, a wink aimed at a perplexed Ronnie.

'Who *have* you been fraternising with this time, Mrs Ledwell?' Bay chuckled again, and she snapped at him to shut up.

'How about Jeremy Clarkson?' One of the old-guard suggested.

'There's an obvious candidate right under our noses!' Petra banged the table in recognition. 'Kenny Kay!'

'Of course!' cried Viv. 'He is *marvellously* funny. When does he move in? What a feather in our caps to get the great man on side.'

'BUT WE DO!' The reverend's hands clapped together evangelically, unable to contain the secret a moment longer. 'Thanks to Mrs Ledwell, we already *have* Mr Kay on board.'

'*Reverend!*' Brian hissed.

'We *do?*' Petra's mouth opened.

Hillary Jolley bowed towards Ronnie. 'And we are so *very* grateful!'

Ronnie was open-mouthed, having never imagined Kenny would act on her suggestion. Around her, the committee started oohing and aahing excitedly, the volume in the room rising fast.

Bay was laughing uproariously. 'Another skeleton, Ronnie dearest?'

'*The* Kenny Kay?' Auriol gasped. 'Who has starred with Meryl Streep?'

'And Dwayne 'The Rock' Johnson!' cried a voice.

'And *The Muppets*!' added another.

Brian had to stand up and ask repeatedly for silence.

'This must not go beyond these walls,' he told them in a discreet undertone when he retook his seat. 'A few days ago, Mr Kay's representative approached the Parish Council in confidence, saying Mrs Ledwell had asked him to join the Church Roof Repair Action Plan committee.'

'He's coming here tonight?' Viv reached for her raffle ticket book.

'No!' Brian blustered, clearing his throat before explaining. 'Mr Kay has requested absolutely *no* publicity, and while he apologized that he can't attend meetings in person, he did offer our cause a very generous contribution.'

'Don't tell me he's buying the meadow?' Bay asked in shock.

'Not exactly.' Brian cleared his throat again. 'Mr Kay personally arranged and paid for roadside signs, posters and publicity material for the campaign. Show them to the committee, Chris.'

Stacked up against the wall at the back of the hall were some large rectangular shapes covered with sheeting that everyone had taken to be sports equipment or scenery. But when Chris tugged off the first one's cover, it turned out to be a billboard, expensively produced with a huge photograph of St Mary's Church and the headline WE ARE C.R.R.A.P. A second read HELP YOUR VILLAGE C.R.R.A.P. another C.R.R.A.P HERE TODAY.

'OK, that's enough, Chris love!' Brian called, turning to address the guffawing, tittering table. 'I think we all agree Mr Kay has been more than generous, although these are sadly of no use to us if we change the campaign name.'

Ronnie kept her hand clamped over her mouth so nobody could see how much she was laughing. *Oh Kenny, you rogue.* He hadn't changed one bit. Which spelled trouble.

'We are indebted to Mrs Ledwell for asking Mr Kay to help...' The reverend still looked thrilled. 'And hope she will continue to nurture the acquaintance with our celebrated new neighbour for the good of the village.'

Ronnie patted her cheeks and took a deep breath to stop the laughter aftershocks. 'From a safe distance, perhaps.'

'Of course!' Viv remembered, 'Kenny Kay stood stallions at the stud. Quite the local hellraiser, I gather.'

'And a womanizer,' called another of the older villagers. 'Lock up your daughters!'

'Worse than Bay here!'

'I bloody resent that!' Bay put his flat cap back on and crossed his arms angrily.

'Was Kenny Kay really as naughty as they all say?' Auriol asked, patting her hair.

Ronnie sucked her teeth. 'The devil himself.'

The vicar's jolly smile froze.

She found herself once again catching Kit Donne's eye. This time he held hers for a long time.

It was all in the letters exchange with Hermia, Ronnie realized. Every last, shameful secret of it.

14

Each time Mack rang the cottage to read Kes a night-time story, Pax felt physically anxious, as though he was in the room with them. She avoided engaging in conversation, a self-protection made easier by appalling telecommunications: if he made his punctual bedtime calls to the shared landline, they klaxoned across the stud's fields and were all too often intercepted in the main house; trusting the patchy mobile signal was even more hit and miss. Since the arrival of the plug-in Wi-Fi gadgetry, however, father and son had started FaceTiming, which Pax dreaded but Kes loved.

'I can see Daddy! Look! There's Daddy!'

It felt like an invasion, Mack's eyes on the room, searching for something to criticise. That sanctimonious voice. 'Is that a television I can see on your chest of drawers, son?'

'It's a tank! Aunt Alice gave me a pterodactyl, Daddy.'

'Terrapin,' Pax corrected, trying to stay out of shot.

'He's from my cousin,' Kes waved her phone at the tank, 'the one who's away studying flossy feet at university.'

'Philosophy,' she corrected again, alarmed to find the phone pointing her way, a small glowing rectangle of co-parent glaring at her.

'The light will keep the wee lad awake,' Max's digitised face lectured.

'No more than his nightlight.'

'I *love* him, Daddy,' Kes reclaimed the screen, his father's face reflected in his big, dark eyes. 'He's called Wedgie.'

'Reggie,' Pax murmured.

'Whatever his name, it's unhygienic having a reptile in there with you. I want a word with Mummy after our story.'

'I can't tonight,' she said quickly.

'You will,' Mack corrected. 'It's important.'

She wished she had the steel to refuse, but she didn't want to upset Kes. The familiar tick of guilt was clicking its fingers in her head, reminding her that she was the one who'd brought all this about, who wanted to gallop away from her responsibilities.

When Mack wanted words, it inevitably meant a telling-off.

She longed to shout: Go away, Luca's coming round!

He'd already launched into a *Just So* story for Kes.

Grabbing the wet towel, she escaped to put it on the bathroom radiator, catching her eye in the basin mirror and sharing a moment of déjà vu with her reflection. When her marriage had been at its unhappiest, the bathroom had become her safe place. She'd stared at this reflection so often, at the woman reduced to Mack's wee bird, his Tishy, his flame-haired lunatic, in search of her old self.

Had she found it? She still looked far too like passive, pensive Mrs Forsyth for comfort, the cloud of hair unrulier than ever since the home-cut, now with a permanent riding helmet-head kink above the ears like a mullet.

She scraped it back into a ponytail so tight it made her temples ache. She could hear Mack's voice next door describing how the camel had got its hump. That same, self-assured brogue had once told her she was beautiful, precious, his wee angel.

Heart thrumming, she paced the tiny room, familiar demons returning, raw memories guaranteed to extinguish any tiny new spark of self-confidence and sexual reawakening with a wet slap of shame.

They'd met when she was barely twenty and partying her way off the rails in London, still heartbroken over Bay. She'd been Mack's lodger at first, in awe of the blues-loving, dapper surveyor whose compartmentalised life seemed so frictionless. Urbane and successful, he was almost twenty years her senior, an undeniable father-figure whose single-minded, attentive pursuit of her made Pax feel more cared for and cared about than she'd ever been. It was only after they married, when he'd increasingly controlled and belittled her, treating her like a sexually available employee, that she started losing her sense of self. He insisted on calling her Tishy and repeatedly told her who she was: his wee doll, wee bird, a fragile wee thing. All too soon that self-assured voice was also convincing her that she was weak and hysterical, clumsy and paranoid, and that she was nothing without him. Drink had numbed the pain, but never enough, and it took more each time, until that controlled her too.

Kes was her one bright spot, the longed-for child who had made her loveless prison of a marriage somehow tolerable through his toddling, giggling, adoring early years, until Mack had revealed plans for an education that would take her sensitive son away from her to 'toughen him up'. The lad was spoiled, he'd told her, a mummy's boy she'd overindulged with affection. He'd repeatedly called her a bad mother. He still did.

How unhappy she'd been, demented with self-loathing, lying awake in the small hours while he slept, her phone glowing dimly as she planned the escape it had taken her years to pluck up the courage to follow through.

'It's stopped, Mummy.' Kes appeared at the door, thrusting the phone at her, its screen frozen grotesquely on Mack pretending to be a harrumphing camel.

She checked the plug-in link then tapped it a few times and it unfroze, Mack letting out a bark of alarm as he found her giant finger jabbing at him. 'What are you *doing*, Tishy?'

Tempted say she was trying to break through and squish him, she handed the phone back to a yawning Kes.

When the camel had finally got his hump and Kes was almost asleep, she reluctantly reclaimed the phone to take the video call downstairs. 'I can't talk for long.'

But instead of bellyaching about Reggie and his glowing terrarium as she'd anticipated, Mack thanked her politely for agreeing to speak. 'I want to get this thing on a more civil footing, wee bird. We need to stop paying lawyers a fortune to fire off a letter every time there's a diary clash. Have you cut your hair again?'

'No.'

'That's good. You're beautiful just as you are.'

'Just say what it is you need to, Mack. I have things to do.' She deliberately sat with the light behind her and angled the phone screen so all Mack could see was her right ear and a picture over her shoulder of Lester showing a foal in hand at the Bath and West.

'Don't be like this, Tishy.' His playful growl made her uncomfortable. 'Let me see that pretty wee face of yours.'

'It's Pax.' She kept the phone camera trained on Lester.

When their marriage had first fallen apart, Mack's phone calls had all been angry rants, bitter with hurt recrimination, him blaming her drinking, blaming her mother, blaming her for insisting they move down here from Scotland, blaming her, Pax, *Tishy* (and as soon as he found out about Luca's interest, him too). But lately he'd switched tactics, adopting a daytime tv presenter approach, all fake smiles and sincerity. It never lasted long.

'So...' He paused, then, 'I want you to reconsider couple counselling.'

'No, Mack, I—'

'Shh, wee bird, calm yourself and hear me out.' The magnanimous mask was already slipping, his conciliatory tone undercut with the businesslike urgency she knew so well. 'There's been a cancellation at the practice I told you about. They're holding next week's appointment for us.'

'I'm not going to change my mind, Mack.' Her solicitor Helen had advised her to be unambiguous in response. 'Counselling won't alter my decision. Maybe in future family therapy will help Kes adjust to his parents living apart, but—'

'I want you both back, Tishy!'

'I prefer Pax now.'

He peered into the camera, one eye huge on screen. 'Is lover boy there with you, is that it?'

'We're not lovers, Mack,' she whispered, 'and no.'

Not yet.

'We've talked about this, remember, wee bird?' Mack reined in his tone to sound determinedly cheery, as though still reading Rudyard Kipling. 'We neither of us want Kes getting hurt by your fly-by-night flirtation, do we?'

'Of course not.'

'You owe it to the boy to try to make this work again.' His voice was already losing its levity. 'You can't just break his family apart. Don't do this to him, Tish— *Pax*, to *our son*.'

They were back to familiar territory; Pax the homewrecker who was ruining Kes's life.

She longed, longed, longed for a drink. These conversations were inevitably circular, each round bringing more blame and shame.

After conciliation came pleading: 'I've given you everything you ever asked for, Tishy. What more could you possibly *want*, tell me?'

She closed her eyes, remembering Luca telling Kes that she could have anything she wanted.

Mack advanced rapidly to sermonising. 'I'm going to *fight* for this marriage, you hear? For the sake of *my son*, I'm going to *fight* for *us*. I'll do whatever it takes. You *need* me, wee bird, and I'm here for you, every *step of the way*. This is for *you*.'

And as he spoke, she curled tighter into herself, feeling her resolve start to crumble.

The term 'coercive relationship' was something Pax was still trying to get to grips with, just as it had taken her over a decade to summon the strength to break free of hers.

The split had come as a shock to many who viewed the Forsyths' marriage – and business partnership – as a success, not least Mack himself. The product of a strict Calvinist Scots' upbringing – his elderly parents still providing the old-fashioned and controlling blueprint he followed – Mack had no intention of losing this battle, his army ready-assembled.

'This counsellor came highly recommended.' He'd circled round as predicted, anger once again in check, conciliatory voice re-engaged. 'My mother put a lot of time into researching it. We're all committed to getting this marriage and the business back on its feet after your... wobble.'

It had been a 'blip' last time, before that 'a phase'.

Mack launched into his penitent speech, yet another familiar feature of these conversations, cut through with croaky regret and passive aggression. 'I've changed, wee bird. I've been a bullheaded, selfish beast, I know, working too hard trying to make a legacy for this family, neglecting my beautiful wife. No wonder you drank so much, all those hours I was out grafting. I want to make it up to you, to treat you with the respect you deserve, Tishy – Patricia – I mean Pax. Christ, I can't call you that. Sounds like a loo cleaner.'

He would never change, Pax acknowledged sadly. The rock ballad of self-pity would come next, then the passive-aggressive financial threats.

'If you want to respect me, Mack, please start with my decision to leave this marriage,' she said quietly, glancing to the stairs, although she guessed Kes would already be asleep, his ability to conk straight out enviable.

'But it's the wrong decision, don't you see? I am not that man anymore, wee bird. I am a man who's travelled that lonely road too often...' Off he went again, sounding like a Bruce Springsteen lyric.

A bark from Knott caught her attention and she pulled

out one earbud, craning round, worried it was Kes coming downstairs.

The small rectangular window in the corner of the kitchen had lit up, its lowered blind glowing bright blue. That meant the working lights had come on in the yard. Luca must be checking horses, topping up water and hay, keeping a close eye on the broodmares now they were closer to foaling.

She felt her belly hollow out with anticipation

In their first few weeks of mutual attraction, he'd often checked in on Pax too, sharing quiet talk, much silly flirtation and unhurried, laughter-laced stolen kisses before she'd panicked, realizing this was dangerously close to love, and that taking it so fast had given her headrush.

By mutual agreement, for Kes's sake, they'd backed off.

Until tonight.

Just to talk, she reminded herself. And because she didn't want to be alone.

'Are you listening?' Mack was barking. 'I'm saying something important here.'

'Yes. Sorry.' Her ears were on elastic, one craning for sounds on the yard while the other listened to Mack droning on about trust again. 'We both know how much that trust is worth, but I won't take any more than I'm owed, than our child is owed.'

There was a light knock at the door.

'Mack, I must go.'

'Why?'

'Mummy's here to talk through plans for the stud,' she lied, pointing the phone away so he couldn't see her blush.

'That's what *I* am talking about.' He sounded irritated.

'We'll speak about all this again soon, I promise.' Ringing off with indecent haste, she rushed to the door, Knott dancing beneath her legs, as eager to greet the visitor as she was.

The frosty air was like a slap.

Luca was on her step, face shadowed beneath a woolly hat.

'Just here to talk,' he reminded her, teeth flashing white through the dark as the big smile came out.

Pax was about to tell him she'd heard more than enough talking from Mac, but then she smelt a familiar heady tang and started in shock. Surely not?

She was almost certain she could smell alcohol.

Lester could always tell when Kes's father had finished his virtual bedtime story in the cottage because the Internet got faster again.

He'd messaged Blair Robertson twice to alert him to a new complication with the American stallion and was holding his tablet in readiness for a reply.

Nothing so far.

Lester didn't see there being a big problem. While Luca might have some bad history with the yard in Canada – he'd been tight-lipped on the subject, but Lester intended to find out more – that didn't affect this deal.

But Luca had got to the truth quickly enough. He now knew that Bay wouldn't budge on money and they were still a significant investment short, with the horse the wrong side of the Atlantic. And Blair, who was supposed to be lining somebody up, had gone ominously quiet.

Lester disliked all this subterfuge.

Yawning, he looked at Facebook while he waited, liking a clutch of new photographs that Pip Edwards had posted of her travels with her lady friend, and noticing that the Compton village page had tamed down considerably of late, mostly posts about the church roof repair, potholes and a missing cat. The fact Pip was still away might not be unrelated to the drop in sensationalism, he sensed. He sent her a brief message asking when she was returning?

He must have nodded off, the ringing he could hear a part

of a complicated dream in which Johnnie was alive and pulling all the old servants' bells in the house.

He jumped awake to grope for his tablet, touching the pulsing green circle and finding a familiar round face beaming on video chat, the stud's former housekeeper, demon cake-baker and busybody.

'Les!' she greeted him in her flat Brum voice which he'd missed more than he'd ever admit.

'It's Lester, Pip,' he re-established, quietly bursting with delight. 'Where are you?' There was a sunny beach behind her.

'New Zealand with my lady love! We're having breakfast by the ocean.' She shifted the camera to show girlfriend Roo waving eagerly beneath a Black Ferns baseball cap. 'I just got your message. When did you hear the news? Roo thought it was family only. She only heard about it herself an hour ago.'

He tried to ask what news, but Pip was still talking, 'I bet Ronnie's relieved she's passed, eh Les? This changes everything, doesn't it?' she predicted excitedly. 'There'll be a new gaffer at the stud soon, mark my words.'

Again, he tried to interject to remind her to call him Lester and to ask what Ronnie had passed – some sort of test, maybe – but she'd never been one to leave gaps for breath or conversation. 'It's so beautiful here, Les! Can't believe we've got to come back to England already. Roo's brother's farm is three thousand acres, can you imagine? We've been talking, and now Roo's coming into money, I might sell the bungalow and we can buy a little smallholding over here and breed fell ponies. Are you in?'

Lester cleared his throat, pointedly this time, intending to ask if they'd ever considered investing in an event horse? But Pip was still chattering on. 'That's a nasty a cough! Don't even *try* to talk. Poor Les, they don't look after you like I did, do they? That's why I wanted to make sure you know there'll always be a room made up for you with us, no matter what happens next. Stay calm. I'll message soon as we're back. Bring you some cakes round. Ta-ra, Les – kia ora! Ta-ra! Kia ora!'

'Kia ora!' Lester echoed as they vanished from screen, still none the wiser.

He selected an old *Midsomer Murders* on the giant TV and Googled New Zealand.

'Believe me, angel, tea and your company are all I need – although sex would be great too,' Luca's presence always seemed to fill this tiny cottage with its low beams, his high-octane cheer now laced with a peppermint martini scent that made Pax's senses spike.

The smell of alcohol was from was a home-made muscle liniment, he explained. 'Mint, juniper, ginger and comfrey which my ma would steep in poteen, but I make do with Aldi vodka. I've been treating Beck with it.'

'On the rocks with a lemon wedge?' Pax found it hard to imagine unscrewing a vodka bottle without pressing it to her lips. Not that she wanted anything pressed to her lips but Luca's mouth right now. Their combined nervous energy had reached a pitch that could boil the kettle he'd just filled.

They both knew nothing would happen with Kes asleep upstairs, but that just added to the frisson.

Luca had made himself straight at home in the kitchen, teabags in mugs, legs on springs. 'Beck's got a hot tendon off hind, worse since the ground froze again. Sugar?'

He must know she didn't take it. Pax had seen him in this wired mood more than once before, switching from restless to buzzy to flirty like a radio dial. Especially flirty.

'I can't stay long, so get your kit off,' he joked, heading to the fridge for milk.

'Propose first,' she deadpanned.

'Marry me.' His green eyes brimmed with amusement, but he was preoccupied with the yard. 'Just don't let me forget to go back out in a minute, check on one of the mares. She's not right. Might be colic.'

'Which one?'

'The chestnut.' He was lousy with names.

'Nancy,' she groaned. 'It would be.'

Her grandfather had given all his broodmares stable names related to historic political doyennes: Maggie, Barbara, Shirley, Constance. Nancy – Astor, not Reagan – was the most valuable mare on the yard, a highly-strung high-flyer bought off the racetrack by the Captain not long before he died, her first foal justifying the expense by being both exceptionally classy and a rare buckskin like his father, the stud's old stallion Cruisoe. In foal to him again, Nancy was carrying the most exciting prospect of this year's crop.

He splashed milk in the tea. 'She's a month off her foaling date and she always box walks so it's hard to tell what's up. But I don't like how she's sweating up. Here,' he thrust a steaming mug at her, 'is the wee man asleep? Can I kiss you all over and make you mine?'

'Sparko.' Kes was a hibernator like his father – deep in the duvet, immobile for ten hours straight at this time of year. 'And no, because sex would be a ship.'

'Sure, sex is just a sport.'

'What about sportsmanship?'

'Does that mean friendship isn't allowed either?'

'OK, let's forget the ship thing.'

They looked at each other, enjoying that silent shock of attraction. We're just talking, Pax reminded herself. Luca said it. He's come over to talk.

Like mirror mimers, they both put their mugs down at the same time, stepped out of view of the staircase just in case, and kissed. Chaste as it was – full of minty-mouthed, sea-breeze, close-lipped child-in-the-house self-control – it fizzed with bottled-up emotion. It was a kiss Pax badly needed, a kiss that put Bay back in his box, kicked Mack far over the horizon and ignited a flurry of horny sparks that lit up her sky with a firework show.

They'd been here before. They knew this kiss. And they knew how it ended.

She pulled back. 'Not in the cottage.'

'Sure.' For a moment, his fingers stayed on her face, his mouth still so close she could feel his breath on her lips, and she found herself wishing he'd defy her, kiss her once again, to hell with it.

But he stepped back, hands dropping to his sides, and smiled. Because Luca always smiled.

Except there was something different about it tonight. His eyes kept leaving it behind, darting away, his tongue running along his teeth, a soft laugh playing in his throat. This was the wild other coming through, the bad boy Luca he'd warned her about.

She watched his mouth, longing to be kissed again.

'Pax, we need to talk.' The smile faltered like flickering neon.

'Of course.' Stray fireworks were still detonating inside her. *Stop* staring at his mouth. They must put Kes first, the stud first. They had plenty to discuss. No more kissing.

He looked at her through a mood-killing pause, eyes creased in worry, lashes veiling their greenness. 'Meredith and I have been messaging. A lot of messages.'

The sexy spark dampened in an instant.

If she ever wanted to torture herself, Pax Googled Meredith Belanger, who looked like a starlet and rode like a Cossack. Meredith, who Luca had loved longest and hardest of all.

She was grateful for his honesty.

'You can message who you like, Luca.' She moved to the back to the kitchen, leaning against the Rayburn rail for warmth. 'You don't need my permission.'

'I don't want it coming between us.' He followed, putting his hands on her shoulders. 'She knows how I'm crazy about someone new.'

His eyes drank in hers. The spark reignited dimly inside her.
'But she has this, this – *hold* over me, y'know?'
Extinguished again.

He touched his forehead against hers, eyes so close she could count the gold flecks on his irises. 'I should never have replied; I wanted a clean break this time. But I'm worried about her. I'm sorry, angel.'

Pax knew she was in no place to judge, not least with Bay always in the wings, his emojis in her inbox and his scarf on her coat hook. 'How long have you been back in touch?'

'A few weeks. She's in a 'mare. Her marriage is at endgame and she says I'm the only one who can help her through it.'

He'd warned her this would happen. 'Wake up, Luca. She's just being controlling again.'

His restless gaze took another tour of the room. 'She says she's going to leave him this time.'

'And what does she want you to do? Carry her bags? Call her an Uber? You told me she always says this and you always fall for it. It's why you keep going back.'

'I'm not going back.' He looked down at his feet.

'You will. It's why you tramp round the world with a pair of spurs in your backpack. You need to know you can drop everything at a moment's notice. Like you'll drop us.'

'I will not!'

'You're the kindest man I know, Luca, but you're anchorless. You've ridden so many horses, they're all one to you. You're a gun for hire.'

The smile flickered back on, 'You know I have more loyalty than that, angel.'

'Yes, but you live in the moment. You've no sense of ownership.'

'That's a ship, so it is.' He affected a thick brogue. 'And we don't all have your privileges, your ladyship. Another one!'

She wasn't falling for it. 'Oh c'mon, Luca, Meredith is the boss's daughter too.'

The smile worked its full repertoire. 'I'd like to see you walk a mile in my shoes.'

'Or hers? Because that's what you want me to fill, isn't it?'

'Tell you what, try it now.' He started tugging off his boots angrily. 'Humour me.'

'Keep your voice down!' She glanced up at the beamed ceiling, anxious he'd wake Kes. 'And I'd rather not join you both strolling down memory lane, thanks.'

Luca had crouched down on the quarry-tiled floor to wrestle off the second boot, sliding both in front of her feet. 'Try these for size and tell me what *you'd* do if you were standing in them, your ladyship.'

'Let me demonstrate.' She prised off her mules and stepped in his big boots, two warm, sheepskin-lined caves. But when she opened her mouth to tell him to get lost, she couldn't say it.

Still sitting on the quarry tiled floor, he was looking up at her, eyes bottomless with worry. 'She has our child, Pax.'

She glared down at his big boots like clown shoes on her feet, unable to shake the image of them walking away from her forever, of those loping strides that had taken him back to Canada again and again. And of his pain because no matter how many times he did it, it never worked out.

Lizzie's voice echoed in her head from their earlier call: *The man is adorable, Pax... I know plenty who would love to be in your shoes!*

They should try wearing his, she thought numbly. And she could hear her own voice, deep and calm like a recorded emergency evacuation message, reassuring him that she knew just how much it hurt, that they were alike. Pax the peacemaker guiding them back to their happy place to flirt and talk and kiss like teenagers.

Slowly he stood up and put his arm around her. His lips brushed her forehead, nose tip then cheeks, fingers lifting her chin, his kindness making her feel worse. The smile was back, conciliatory and concealing, his whisper even gentler. 'I knew you'd understand, angel. You've gone through it yourself. How can you not understand?'

Her thoughts ran to Bay and away again.

'You could be good for Meredith,' he went on. 'You've left behind a bad marriage. You've been where she is.'

Pax understood too well to trust herself to say it. She understood just how Luca's innate goodness must draw Meredith back in times of crisis, how having him around made a broken marriage bearable. And Luca was right, they had a child together, which changed everything. Their lives were so tangled up that cutting free took more than a one-way flight.

And she understood, because she always had, that he still loved Meredith. That she was borrowing him, just as everyone borrowed him.

He'd moved closer still, wrapping his arms tightly around her, breath on her neck. 'You know it's you I think about night and day, angel, you I long to have in my bed.' He pressed his lips to her throat. 'You know how crazy I am about you. I adore you, Pax. Completely adore you.'

His voice in her ear made every little hair stand on end, sending a beat pulsing downwards.

The spark was back with vengeance, petrol bombing her libido, burning into her conscience. 'And I'm crazy about you,' she whispered back, fingers curling through his, 'but two crazies just make this situation even madder, don't you see?'

'I know, I know. No ships except friendship and horsemanship, and sex doesn't count.'

'Forget the ship thing.'

'That ship has sailed.' He kissed her mouth.

'Stop it.' She started to laugh.

'Permission to torpedo the ship.'

'As long as it doesn't wake Kes.'

'That child would sleep through the Battle of Trafalgar.'

'True.'

The smile was at full force once more, green eyes back to playful default as he repeated, 'And sex isn't a ship. It's sport.'

They almost kissed again before stopping themselves with stifled laughter. Luca backed away, holding his hands up. 'I shouldn't have come round tonight, angel,' he confessed. 'I knew I'd just want to kiss the life out of you. I think we need to—'

'Cool off, I agree.' She pulled off his boots and pushed them towards him. 'Go and check on that mare.'

'No listen, I think we really need to—' He paused, eyes widening, hand flying to his mouth with a muffled, 'Fuck!'

'That's candid.' Swallowing more nervous laughter, Pax felt the same spike of urgency, the fireworks back, bright as gunfire. 'I prefer *make love.*'

'No, I mean fuck, what an eejit!' Spinning away, he rubbed his face and raked his fingers through his hair. 'How long's it been?' He strode to the door, then doubled back and cupped her face in his hands. 'Sorry, angel, I want to make love too.' He was stepping back into his boots as he said this. 'But you're right, I need to check Nancy. It looked too like colic for my liking. I'll be back as soon as I have.'

'Go!' she told him without hesitation.

He was already gone in a blast of cold air. She hugged herself tightly, trying to stop all the heartbeats still fluttering in awkward places

15

Kit stifled another yawn and took a discreet look at his watch as the committee got sidetracked debating the Health and Safety implications of welly-wanging. He tried to catch Ronnie's eye, but she was reading phone messages under the trestle table again. Then he realized it wasn't her phone, it was a book, which Kit founded splendidly rebellious, even if it was one of Petra Gunn's bodice-rippers.

Beside him, Auriol Bullock added more jots to her food-free shopping list: *Fizzy water, Cheap white, Ovaltine, Gordons*. She tapped her pen on the page, as if remembering an important item, fished in her pocket and drew out a hip flask.

'Swig?' She offered it to Kit, who wished he had the willpower to refuse, but desperately needed anaesthesia from all the paper shuffling beadledom.

It contained limoncello, a pleasant surprise.

He found it ludicrous that while the reverend had made it clear the sale of the land would cover the repairs to the church – the whole thing reeking of backhanders – parish bureaucracy dictated they were there to talk tin-rattling, not palm-greasing. The past forty minutes had been devoted to agreeing upon a revised strategy and name, Kit's uprising cast side.

Now rechristened Raise the Roof – with a Fix the Clock sub-committee proposed to repair the long-broken timepiece – the fundraising suggestions struck him as a lot of time-wasting hot air: head-shaving, bake-offs, sponsored walks, silent auctions, quiz nights and Auriol's ambitious offer to abseil from the church tower. 'I had a go at it on last year's PGL excursion, great fun!'

As they moved on from welly-wanging to sponsored knitathons, he watched Ronnie reading. She was a quarter of the way through the book already, with the feverish focus of somebody trying to blot something out. He noticed Bay Austen kept glancing at her uneasily from beneath his flat cap. Realizing he was being watched, he studied the raffle prizes on a nearby table instead.

Kit's memory stirred. Years ago, Hermia had been furious with nephew Bay for causing upset between Ronnie and her family, he recalled. It might explain the frisson between them. Kit had noted the way they kept snarling at one another, the tension historic and Oedipal. Perhaps that was where her affection lay? Then he told himself off for wondering.

The limoncello was thrust at him again, Auriol hissing, 'We need something *much* bigger. Like *The Secret Policeman's Ball* or *Live Aid*, agreed?'

On his other side, Viv hadn't yet given up hope of a famous patron. 'I heard you're directing at the RSC this summer. Any celebs in that?'

'No, talented actors.'

'One of my school parents is in *The Archers*,' Auriol muscled in, handing Viv the flask.

'What about friends in Hollywood?' Viv asked Kit eagerly then took a swig.

'I mostly just do theatre.'

'Oh, me too!' Auriol agreed. 'The Broadbourne Light Operatic Society, I don't know if you've heard of us? I directed last year's *Iolanthe*.'

'That's *it*!' Viv clapped her hands as realization struck. 'You two must stage a play! Petra can write it. It will be our banker.

We'll put it on in the field. Everybody! Auriol and Kit are going to direct outdoor theatre!'

The committee ruminated animatedly at the prospect.

'I'd be *thrilled*!' Auriol shuddered with joy as Petra and Kit both gave emphatic 'noes' in unison.

'Far too busy, I'm afraid,' Kit said emphatically.

'Me too,' Petra nodded.

'In that case, shall I direct *Mamma Mia!*?' Auriol offered, breaking into spirited Abba medley as she turned over her shopping list page to start a fresh one entitled *CAST*. 'I hope you'll audition for Donna, Mrs Ledwell?'

Kit noticed Ronnie didn't look up from her book.

'Let's not get ahead of ourselves,' Brian urged, wiping sweat from his brow, casting an anxious look at the reverend who was humming 'Dancing Queen' with the church warden. 'There are significant Risk Assessment and licensing considerations involved in putting on a public performance.

'And the new owner might not want a performance staged on his land,' the reverend pointed out cheerfully.

The room fell silent.

Ronnie's book was carefully placed back on the table. 'Are you telling us that Church Meadow has *already been sold*?'

'Not at all!' Brian Hicks blustered. 'What the Reverend Jolley is saying is that—'

'I am *delighted* to be able to inform you all that thanks to our good Lord's gracious provenance, there is already *considerable* interest in the church plot!'

'*Already?*' Ronnie cross-questioned.

'From whom?' demanded Bay.

'All I can say at this stage is that they do have close associations to the village,' the reverend beamed around the room, 'and a great love of its land.'

'How did they know about it coming up for sale?' Ronnie asked suspiciously.

'God?' suggested Bay.

Kit Donne covered his mouth and coughed 'stitch-up', which everyone politely ignored, apart from Ronnie who caught his eye again, and coughed 'Couldn't agree more.'

'Sir Peter Sanson's been back recently,' Petra stage-whispered. 'Just saying.'

'Tell me it's not Sanson Holdings?' Bay looked outraged.

'My lips are sealed,' the reverend said, smiling with such open-mouthed joy that they all knew it had to be the super-rich investor who owned thousands of arable acres locally.

'Sanson Holdings will just plough it up!' Petra pointed out.

'The man's a corporate landowner, not a farmer,' Bay joined in.

'Better him than the gypsies!' piped up one of the older committee members.

'Sir Peter is a very philanthropic man,' the reverend calmed the alarmed chatter. 'And remember, the Church will consider all offers to restore our mutual place of worship to its flock.'

'Which is why we're here tonight!' Brian reminded them, tapping his pen on his agenda. 'Now, are there any other fundraising suggestions from the committee before we move on to the next item, the election of the Fix our Clock sub-committee?'

'I like the church clock telling me it's always ten to three,' Kit said honestly, having heard enough talk of charity commission governance and accountability to last a lifetime.

'I quite agree!' Ronnie's voice rang out. The book had been put away, Kit noticed, sensing she might be about to stir things up. She addressed the room impatiently: 'All this talk of weekenders throwing their Les Chameaux around is a smokescreen! We'll never make enough money. *Surely* the committee must be able to stop the meadow being sold to a crook like Peter Sanson?'

'That's not a foregone conclusion, Mrs Ledwell!' Brian gritted his teeth.

'Of course it bloody is! It's exactly how that bloody man bought so much of Daddy's land, offering him more than he needed to bail himself out so greed got the better of him.'

Kit admired her tenacity. She really was Westminster's loss.

'Aren't there natural springs under the meadow?' Viv stood up. 'Old Zeke Turner was always wandering round up there with a dowsing twig. Biggest natural chalybeate spring under it this side of Cheltenham, he'd tell us. Pure alpine water. We could bottle and sell it!'

'As the church still owns the land, that would be Holy Water,' the reverend pointed out kindly, making a note.

'Straight into the sale details,' sighed Auriol. 'That just *adds* to the land's value, Mrs Austen.'

'Does it? Sorry!' Viv sat down.

'Tenner says Sir Peter puts a socking great spa resort on it!' one of the old-timers called out.

'Who *is* this chap they keep talking about?' Auriol whispered to Kit, offering limoncello.

Before he could answer, Viv leant across him to whisper back, 'Peter Sanson, agri tycoon. Owns most of the productive land around here. Lives in the Caribbean. Rough diamond, but not unattractive in a Russell Crowe sort of way. Whisked my sister-in-law clean off her feet back in the day. *Yummy.*' She accepted a nip of Auriol's flask, leaving Kit uncertain if the tycoon or the limoncello were yummy.

'Wasn't it Sanson who hosted the most dangerous shoots in the Cotswolds in the eighties?' Bay called along the table to his mother.

'They were very drunken,' Viv agreed, 'and usually full of businessmen who had no idea how to handle a gun. Your father shot Kenny Kay's finger off at one, didn't he, Ronnie?'

'He did not!' Ronnie looked furious. 'That's an urban myth.'

'Village myth, you mean,' Viv corrected. 'And what a shame. Sandy loves that story. Always claims Captain Percy did it to stop Kenny taking a potshot at Sir Peter.'

'Would have done this village a favour if someone *had* shot Sanson.' Bay pulled his cap low on his face before lounging back in his chair. 'Wake me up when it's time to go home.'

'Shall we stick to the point?' Brian pleaded. 'Volunteers for the Fix our Clock Sub-committee! Anyone?'

Everyone was looking fixedly at the raffle prizes now.

'Bay's not himself, poor love.' Viv whispered to Kit, reaching across him for Auriol's hip flask. 'Been under a lot of strain. This marriage break-up of his has shaken all the family.'

Kit was worrying over something she'd said earlier.

'Which sister-in-law did Peter Sanson sweep off her feet?' he whispered back.

'Didn't Hermia say? Before your time, of course. He was besotted with her for a while. I say, are you OK? It's jolly hot in here.'

But Kit felt ice cold, even though the hall's heating had finally kicked in, coats being peeled off and sweat glistening on Brian's furrowed pate as he tried to sneak a detail past them. 'Let's take a vote, shall we? In the light of the church's intention to fund its own roof repair through a sale, this committee agrees to repurpose our primary fundraising for the restoration of St Mary's Tower clock. All those in favour?' He counted the hands that shot up obediently despite Ronnie leading a shout of protest. 'I make that a majority in which case the motion is carr—'

'Hang on!' Kit interrupted, standing up. 'I think this village deserves more transparency, don't you?'

'Not again!' Brian muttered through gritted teeth.

'We are as transparent as God's good air,' the reverend soothed, catching Brian's eye.

Still trying to reconcile the fact his late wife had once been 'whisked off her feet' by Peter Sanson, Kit was in no mood for soft-soaping. 'With the greatest respect, I'm not sure we're in possession of all the facts yet.'

'Hear, hear!' Ronnie cheered, which he needed.

'Let's discuss this another time, shall we?' Brian cleared his throat awkwardly.

'We'll discuss it now!' Kit couldn't wave this one past. 'We still don't know how the "interested parties" found out about the sale of the meadow before the rest of us. When did *you* hear about it, Brian?'

'I hardly think that's relevant.' Looking furtive, their Chair turned to his long-suffering wife. 'Chris! The printouts!' As she leapt up and to distribute Raise the Roof fundraising forms, Kit walked round to stand in front of the raffle table. It was only when he shouted, 'This is a whitewash!' that he realized quite how tipsy on limoncello he was.

'It's the beginning of the end!' Auriol stood up, swaying slightly. 'My little school may have been spared, but for how long?'

'Buy Our Meadow Back!' Kit gave it his best Brechtian agitpop.

'Buy Our Meadow Back!' Ronnie also stood up to join in.

'Buy Back Our Meadow!' Auriol held on to the table for balance.

Petra and Bay were scrambling up as well when Brian told them all crushingly, 'If you want to call yourselves that, you'll need to resign and start a new committee.'

'Then I resign,' Kit said with relief.

'I resign too!' Petra offered eagerly.

'As do I,' Ronnie added.

'Make that four of us!' Bay held up a hand.

'Five!' Viv rallied loyally, beaming at her son, then ruined it by adding, 'What am I voting for?'

'Six!' Auriol pronounced grandly.

The rebel alliance stood united briefly, only to be shushed back into their seats by Chris. 'You'll all need to submit formal resignations in AOB at the end of the meeting.'

'Oh good, we can stay for the raffle!' cheered Viv.

Kit reluctantly sat back down while Chris handed out the last of the fundraiser forms. He eyed the raffle prize bottles with a faint glimmer of hope. His odds of winning were too good to storm out.

'Any Other Business!' Brian announced when Chris finally rejoined him.

'I regret to inform the committee I wish to resign immediately,' Ronnie said without hesitating. 'Conflict of interests.'

'Me too,' Kit followed. 'Conflict of disinterest.'

'You can't just yet...' Chris checked her notes sucking her lips. 'We have the prayer and refection time already scheduled in AOB which takes priority.'

'This is bloody Kafkaesque!' Kit muttered, looking at Ronnie again, gratified to share their horrified amusement. Her eyes really were astonishingly blue.

But when the reverend launched into a thank-you prayer and blessing, she stayed in her seat like an obedient Sunday School pupil, head bowed during the prayer. She had more faith than she let on. Hermia had been the same.

Knocking back the last of the limoncello, feeling woozy enough to send a silent request up to God to tell his wife he loved her, Kit thought instead about Peter Sanson sweeping Hermia off her feet. He'd never met the man, but he already hated him.

Luca had been gone over half an hour. Pacing round the cottage, anxiety mounting, Pax had drunk both their cold mugs of tea, trying to stay focussed on Nancy's predicament so that she didn't keep thinking about Luca and Meredith, and about Luca and no-strings, guilt-free sex, and about Bay, and about no-strings, guilt-free sex.

Think about colic, Pax. It could be extremely serious in pregnant mares. While mild colic was relatively common close to full term – big foals kicking and changing position put such pressure on their dams' stomachs that fodder often became impacted – more acute causes could quickly prove deadly for both mother and foal if left untreated.

Now Pax's imagination was playing overtime to keep other thoughts at bay – mustn't think about Bay – and she kept imagining their best mare in agony, Luca battling to save mother and foal, pulling off his coat and shirt like a sexy Irish

James Herriot to splash soapy water up his arms and around his neck. Oh God, she was thinking about no-strings, guilt-free sex again.

Stop it!

She went up to check on Kes, who was fast asleep, terrapin tank glowing, Rab, the threadbare toy bunny, under his chin. From the casement window in his room, she could see the glow of the broodmare barn, just beyond the garden wall. A shadow of man leading horse briefly fell across its entrance, distorted like a prehistoric hill carving, before moving away.

If Luca was walking Nancy, that meant his suspicions might be right. Keeping the horse moving was a familiar method to help dislodge an obstruction in the horse's stomach before the gut twisted or ruptured, both potentially fatal.

She needed to know for certain.

Kes was deep within the ten uninterrupted hours sleep Pax envied. She kissed his cheek. 'Be right back.'

Grabbing her coat from the hook downstairs, she was through the door in seconds, grateful for fresh air and focus.

Nancy was housed in the middle of the three modern barns beyond the Victorian yards, more practical labour wards than the dark old foaling boxes, already sub-divided into pre-partum stalls, each thick with straw providing comfort and privacy.

Luca had just put Nancy back in hers and was closing the pen gate behind him when Pax hurried up. 'How is she?'

'No better, no worse.' His focus remained on the horse. No sign of stripping off and soaping, Pax was relieved to note.

She could see the mare was in discomfort, neck and sides darkened with drying sweat as she paced around, pawing at the bedding.

She slipped inside to run a hand over her big pregnant belly, checking for changes of shape, heat or tightness. There was no sign that her milk was coming, or any other indication early labour was imminent.

Nancy seemed amenable enough, her eyes still bright, even nudging for treats. 'She finished her last feed, you said?'

'Every last scrap.' He climbed in with them, leaving Knott whining in the aisle. 'And she's had a drink.'

'You're probably right – it's a touch of colic.' She looked around for fresh droppings, seeing none. 'Just pray there's no torsion. Perhaps we should call Gill Walcote to be sure?'

'You're the boss.'

'Let's see if we can't move it on first.' Pax was aware her mother's economy drive meant after hours vet call outs were a last resort. 'Walk her again, will you?'

Grinning, he gave her a sideways look, doffing a pretend cap and thickening his brogue. 'Yes, your ladyship.'

'Thank you, O'Brien.' Pax played along, adopting an imperious tone, grateful the privilege jibe was now a joke.

'Begging your pardon, ma'am,' he put the mare's headcollar on, glancing over his shoulder as he fastened the buckle, 'but do I have permission to kiss you out here, away from the big house?'

'Not while there are sick animals around, O'Brien, no.'

'Very well, Lady Patricia.'

'But if you make her better,' she unlatched the gate, 'you can ravish me in the haybarn,' she held it open, 'just as long as you're quick.'

Laughing, Luca led the mare through. As they passed Pax, his hand brushed hers, fingers threading together for a moment.

Pax watched him lead the mare away, hot sparks firing again, lighting an all-too rare little blaze of self-esteem. Or was it a prickle of guilt?

'Need to check on Kes!' Leaving him to walk the mare up and down the barn aisle, Pax slithered back across the icy cobbles to the cottage. Kes was still deep asleep, Rab now across his face like an eye mask, Reggie the terrapin swimming dimly lit lengths nearby.

Downstairs, Pax paced the small warren of rooms, reluctant

to leave Kes alone in the cottage again, however close it was to the foaling barns. She could hear her grandfather's familiar bark in her head, telling her to toughen up. He and Granny had abandoned Pax and her siblings at all hours to be on the yard in foaling season, but there had been three of them, all packed off to boarding school as soon as they were old enough. Pax had been the most homesick, grateful to be given special dispensation during term time to come back and compete.

There were pictures of her on horseback all over Lester's cottage. She took a tour of them now, drawing strength from the determined little character whose spirit – and heart – had yet to be broken back then. And here she was at sixteen, a Union Jack stitched to her hat silk, newly capped and madly in love, glowing with the thrill of it.

Pausing by the stairs, she relived her kiss with Luca here. His instinctive touch – with women as with horses – kept catching her by surprise, turning her back into that sixteen-year-old again.

Was it so wrong to borrow him for a little bit? She could think of herself as one of his projects, no different from a horse like Beck, a defensive, neurotic pain in the backside at first, but one Luca drew pleasure and strength from putting right and making good before seeing it thrive and prosper elsewhere.

Lizzie was right. *What are you waiting for, darling? Luca's divine.*

She had to step off this cliff edge sometime.

She made more tea, overfilling the kettle so its spluttered and juddered when it came to the boil, rocking hotly in its base. She knew how it felt.

Out in the garden, a fox bark made her jump, the clench in her belly digging its nails deeper. She looked down at the teabag floating in the mug for a long time, steam rising to warm her face, the beat between her legs still insistent and unwelcome, too closely associated with Mack taking his fill, with shame and pain. Unable to stand still, she went outside into the little walled garden to check on the young fox Lester kept there, rescued from death's door last year.

He was pacing the boundary of the run they'd constructed beyond his cage, flame orange eyes looking past her to freedom.

'And I know how you feel too,' she told him. She'd be empathising with the moon and stars soon. Anything but a horny, thirty-something, newly single woman.

Laurence chattered at her for food. Now that the hunting season was over and he was a strapping adolescent, she longed to set him free.

Stored in a metal dustbin beside the fox's cage were kibble treats that she fed him through the chicken wire, enjoying his bright-eyed greed, the wildness in him. Hidden in sackcloth beneath the kibble bag in the storage bin was a bottle of Lester's plum gin, kept for emergencies.

She reached it out, opened it and sniffed its contents, feeling its alcohol tang beneath the jammy sweetness. Then she screwed the lid back on, hid it again, eyes scrunched shut as she galloped, galloped, galloped in her head to get away from the thought of it.

She hurried back into the cottage for the tea, stewed brick-red now, splashing in milk before carrying it across to the mares' barn, slopping it everywhere and scalding her wrist in her desperation to get away from the plum gin.

'I can't leave Kes long,' she told Luca breathlessly. 'How is she?'

'Still no change,' he took a mug gratefully, eyes glassy with cold.

The mare looked brighter, but her coat still curled with fresh sweat, and the telltale stamp of her hind legs indicated ongoing discomfort.

'I think we're going to have to call Gill,' Luca sighed. 'We can't risk it. She's too valuable. Best check with your ma first though. I'll ring her now.'

'I'm in charge when she's not here,' Pax said, then corrected herself. '*We're* in charge.' She sucked her lip. 'OK, *you're* in charge. Is there nothing else we can try first?'

'There is an old Irish trick my pa taught me, but I've never seen it tried on a mare in foal.'

'Is it dangerous?'

'Only to me if she kicks my bones to bits.'

'Try it.'

He looked at her askance. 'You sure?'

'I'll take full responsibility.'

Handing her back his half-drunk tea, Luca led the mare into her stall again and unclipped her headcollar.

'Is it quick?' She glanced in the direction of the cottage, only half-watching as he took a handful of tail in one hand and laid his hands on Nancy's withers so that he could rock her gently back and forth, huge belly swaying.

The mare let out an ecstatic moan.

Turning in surprise, Pax watched entranced as the horse lowered her head, eyes glazing, lower lip drooping.

On Luca rocked, the movement soon so exaggerated it seemed impossible the mare wouldn't fall over.

'How does she let you do that?'

'Sure, she knows she's safe.'

Nancy groaned in blissful agreement, her entire weight – and that of her big foal – pivoting between his hands.

Pax could only guess at the strength it took a man to do this, yet it was far more subtle than simply manhandling half a ton of thoroughbred. The rhythm, the balance and the trust were magical.

'Is this your miraculous healing touch in action again?'

'No more miraculous than a warm hand on a tendon or a few herbs steeped in mountain dew.' He was grimacing with effort. 'It's just knowledge, horse-sense.'

Pax was still watching the mare. 'She looks in ecstasy.'

'You want me to try this on you later?' He flashed the big Luca smile shot over his shoulder.

Catching his eye, Pax felt the sexy spark strike afresh, burning new paths, fizzling up to the rafters, threatening to ignite the straw underfoot. 'Is that an offer?'

Which was when the mare let out a volley of wind followed by a small wet pile of droppings.

'Just not like that,' Pax added quickly.

'She should feel a whole lot better now.' Laughing, Luca climbed out of the stall to stand beside her to watch as Nancy indulged in a thorough ear to tail shake, then swung round her head and flattened her ears at them to tell them to get lost.

'I don't think we'll be needing a vet.' Luca took his tea back and drank it, steam pluming.

Without her mug handwarmer, Pax pressed her cold fingers under her armpits.

'Hey, you're frozen stiff.' He put an arm round her, warm and weighty, adding a brogue 'Your ladyship.'

'Granny used to say cold feet and hot heads run in the family...' She adopted her upper-crust voice.

'May I suggest your ladyship needs warmer socks?' He hammed up the Irish accent even more, eyes staying on the mare. 'Or you can take my shoes. Walk that mile in them. O'Briens have warm feet and soft heads.'

They looked down at their feet. 'Where exactly would walking a mile your shoes take me, O'Brien?'

'At a guess, I'd say a mile from here, Lady Patricia. Unless you walk to the car first, in which case considerably further'

She swallowed back laughter, still looking at his feet. 'I think they'd take me somewhere that you don't share with anybody.'

He said nothing.

'I think that's why you always keep walking.' She glanced across at him, still playing it in character. 'Because while you do you can always tell yourself you're moving on and not waiting in vain.'

He nodded briefly, eyes sliding away, cheeks hollow with tension, and she knew she'd pushed him as far as she could.

'So, tell me, O'Brien,' she gazed up at his profile, staying in character, emboldened by his vulnerability, 'are we going to the haybarn now, or will you ravish me later?'

'That's a joke, right?' He flashed the trademark smile.

Oh, to be reckless, to release the drumming beat inside her. But this was just an outdoors game of make believe before she raced back to Kes. She nodded exaggeratedly, and he rolled his eyes in mock disappointment and they let out a short, shared breath of laughter that steamed between them in the cold, both pretending it was fine.

She reclaimed the mug, its warmth gone. 'Best check on Nancy every half hour.'

'I'll do that.'

Their faces were just inches apart. Neither could bear to turn away. They moved together without thinking, this kiss no longer than the last, but not nearly as polite, cool lips parting to quick warmth, the kick fantastic, sharing that magical tilt, a roller coaster tipping over its apex. A sex kiss.

Pax pulled away first, nerve-endings thrumming so much she half expected her skin to glitter like fibre optics. 'I must get back for Kes.'

'Stay a moment longer.'

She shook her head. 'It's too easy to forget who I am out here.'

Knowing she shouldn't, she kissed him again, sharing one short, sweet intake of breath that blotted out guilt, blood rushing in her ears so loudly she stopped hearing the other mares munching hay nearby and Luca whispering that she was an angel, a beautiful soul, his Pax. His mouth was all smiles and sweet nothings against hers.

The chestnut mare watched disapprovingly as they necked like teenagers by her stall. Pax kissed him harder, loving the kick of letting her mojo uncoil just for a moment, feeling Luca's touch finally melt through the walls of fear and self-loathing that had iced her in for so long.

When he whispered in her ear that they'd take this slow, she wanted to shout no, let's hurry up, let's get naked right here on the straw. The ravishing is back on! Miss Patricia and O'Brien are heading for the haybarn!

As the kiss got even more out of hand, the mare turned her head, ears pricking up. The sound of a car engine only registered with Pax when a horn beep brought them rapidly up for air. 'Was that from the lane?'

'Could that be your ma back?'

'She went on foot.'

'Maybe she got a lift?' Luca started kissing her again.

Her fingers entwined in his like a lightning bolt needing an earth, but she knew she had to get back to the cottage.

There was another horn beep. It was closer than the lane.

'They'll wake Kes.' She turned and hurried towards the barn doors, fingers still threaded with his. 'Come too'

High on mutual attraction, they slipped and slithered back across the icy cobbles, unable to resist pulling each other into the shadows beneath the middle arch to snatch another lightning-quick kiss, heartbeats slamming together through the many coats and jumpers they longed to rip off.

Emerging, they were briefly blinded by full beam headlights in the arrival's yard. These dimmed and Pax recognized the silver Mercedes in the glow of the Tungsten lights. She heard a sound come from her throat that she didn't recognize until she realized it was fear. Pure fear.

Mack's silhouette approached the yard entrance gates, a plume of steamy breath caught in the backlight.

Something in his hand glinted, another small bright light, and Pax realized he was filming her on his camera phone.

'Tell me my son isn't alone in that cottage while you're out here with lover boy, Tishy? Because he's coming straight home with me if so. And you're gonna have to fight *very* hard to see him again.'

16

In the Bugger All, Reverend Jolley had finally finished sharing God's love and appreciation for bringing them such good fortune in their roof repair mission, and Brian had droned through a lengthy summing up of Matters Arising, Due Diligence and Next Steps.

The raffle was being drawn at last.

Ronnie discreetly re-examined the text from Blair: *Don't call.*

It irritated her more each time she read it. He knew she had an iron will. If she offered the village a sponsored Don't Call Blairathon, she'd raise a small fortune.

Not that there had been any shortage of suggestions tonight, including Auriol Bullock's outdoor *Mamma Mia!*, which she'd already cast in her spiral notepad, hissing across at Ronnie now, 'Do you think your friend Kenny could be available? He's a bit old for one of the exes, but he might make a creditable Father Alexandrios. Will you ask?'

Ronnie smiled non-committedly, not wanting to think about Kenny. She rather liked her grandson's egocentric Head, despite the fact she was a bit of a dipso. Plenty of those around here. Kit and Viv were clearly eager recruits, tonight's hip flask not escaping Ronnie's eagle eye. Being married to a drunk had taught her to be alert, mothering another had refreshed her skills.

She thought anxiously of Pax whose drinking had been so secretive and self-loathing, just like her father's. Having hoped Luca might bring her more out into the open, Ronnie sensed their secrecy growing instead. Their generation's rules were so different to her own at that age, theirs the modern courtly dance conducted behind the fan of a smartphone, whereas the aftermath of Ronnie's marriage had been a procession of naughty affairs and rackety one-offs spun in the full truth or dare glare of close friendship circles. Secret calls from phone boxes; liaisons in quiet little pubs, stolen afternoons in someone's borrowed cottage.

She thought about Kenny again, then pushed it quickly away.

She glanced along the table at Bay who, for all he had graduated to this digital world of emoji semaphore, remained more accustomed to passing the port left than swiping right, a naughty squire. She might not trust him, but she was starting to understand him better, to see his unique charm. Hermia's favourite nephew, meddling with the stud like a child playing with toy soldiers.

That boy will go far by staying right here, her friend had once written.

Ronnie sensed Hermia's memory close tonight. It made her unsettled, the fate of Church Meadow inextricably linked to that childhood friendship. She wished she'd reread some of her letters before rashly handing them over to Kit. They'd shared every awful truth.

'Orange *THREE... SIX... THREE!*' Brian bellowed and she snapped back to the present.

Ronnie's singular raffle ticket was still abandoned in front of her, reluctantly purchased from Viv at half-time after a telling-off when she'd refused to fork out on a strip.

'Oh, that's me,' she realized, soon in possession of two bottles of good Australian wine she would have to hide from Pax. Blair's favourite vineyard, she realized, reading the labels and feeling aggrieved again. *Don't call me.* As if!

She picked up the phone to read it again, but the battery had died.

At last, the meeting broke up, resignations accepted, her reputation as a troublemaker refreshed.

'We're giving you girls a lift!' Viv called woozily across the car park as Ronnie and Petra emerged from the hall.

'It's OK, Bay's driving,' Petra whispered, 'and we can find out what he *really* knows about this land sale.'

'I'll trust you with that one.' Suspecting Bay might try to invite himself in for a drink to sniff round for Pax, Ronnie insisted the walk would do her good. While a pink-faced Petra leapt eagerly into the Land Rover, she marched off towards the Plum Run, sticking to the verges to avoid slipping on black ice.

Her boot soles crunched down hard frozen grass, cracking open memories with each yard. How many times had she and Hermia cantered this verge on their ponies, practising for bending races between the old fruit trees, talking and laughing non-stop?

More memories crowded round her in swift succession. The ghosts of dogs she'd walked here clipped her heels, long gone companions to an only child. Her father, her husband and Lester pitching drunkenly back from the pub or riding out with hounds, Johnny's hunting horn ringing out to the river of liver and white, sterns waving, the spark of horseshoes striking tarmac behind.

Hermia again, careering along in a red Mini Metro the day she'd passed her driving test, declaring 'I'm going to drive straight to London and ask Peter Hall to give me a job at the National Theatre, Ronnie!' And off she'd set, only to run out of petrol near Aylesbury.

Ten years later, her Medea would reduce the Cottesloe Theatre audience to shreds.

Ronnie walked faster, breathing in the frozen past, blowing it out hot and alive. As she did, car headlights behind her threw her shadow down in front of her, a puffa coat mushroom. Then it was briefly eclipsed by another shadow – someone walking behind her, taller and thinner – before Bay roared past in his big Land Rover, Petra waving from the back seat.

Ronnie turned to see a figure dimly illuminated by red tail lights.

Kit Donne was walking home.

It would be rude not to wait for him.

He caught her up. 'Let's please not talk about fundraising.'

'I wasn't going to.'

They fell into step.

'What are you directing next?' she asked as they trudged on.

'*Lear* in Stratford. Donald Samuels.'

'Oh, he'll be wonderful. I saw his *Othello* at the National in the nineties.' She sensed that surprised him. 'What's his take?'

'Mugabe meets Maxwell.'

'How thrilling.'

'Should add in Peter Sanson as inspiration?'

Uncertain how much he knew, she echoed a vague 'perhaps'.

'Tell me why he'd be so interested in buying our little meadow?'

'I thought we weren't talking about that?'

'Humour me with the politics behind it.'

'Officially,' she sighed, 'it links two of his largest local landholdings. He'll pay way over the odds, and they know it.'

'And unofficially?'

'It smells like a grudge to me, and he bears plenty of those about this village. What did Hermia have to say about him?'

'Before. My. Time.' He said it with curious resonance, as though quoting.

'Not before hers,' Ronnie reminded him, uncomfortably aware that the letters would fill in any gaps he might have.

He put on a burst of speed, now walking so fast she had to jog to catch up.

They were passing Upper Bagot Farm, where Kit and Hermia had lived for so many years, its big, sixteen-pane

Georgian windows glowing behind thickly lined drapes, Petra safely back inside and Bay's car gone.

Ronnie noticed he didn't look at it. 'D'you hate the idea of going back in the house so very much?'

'I've no interest in it.' Kit sped up even more as they passed the Gunns' electric gates.

Accustomed to walking fast, Ronnie kept pace, marching together past the shared entrance drive to the barn conversions. 'You must miss the old place, surely?'

'It's no longer here.'

'Yes, I suppose it's so altered, it could be a different building.' She glanced over her shoulder at the glowing doll's house. 'Sanson Holdings bought your land too, didn't they?'

'Not my land by then.' He slowed to normal walking pace again. 'It changed ownership twice more before they acquired it. Not that it stopped some villagers giving it me in the neck for selling out. Called me a rich Londoner.' His accent thickened.

'You're a half-blood now.'

'I'm a working-class Cumbrian and proud of it.' His eyes gleamed, illuminated as they walked into a pool of light.

They were alongside the Manor, where the road forked right into Church Lane or left round the green towards the stud. Behind its high gates, the big house was illuminated inside and out, two hulking removals lorries parked on the gravel carriage circle. Voices shouted from deep in the house.

Ronnie stopped and looked disbelievingly. 'Who moves in at this time of night?'

'The devil himself,' Kit reminded her.

She hugged away a shiver, sensing a ghost walking across long-quiet graves.

Kit was watching her in the light from the manor.

'Come back for a drink,' he urged unexpectedly. 'Make up for earlier.'

'Thanks, but I should get home.'

'I was hoping you might provide the drink.' He glanced down at the raffle prizes she was carrying.

Ronnie suspected he craved the wine more than her company.

'Be my guest.' She thrust them at him, grateful it solved one dilemma. 'Even if I regrettably can't be your guest.'

He didn't take them. 'I have a wide selection of herbal tea if that's less brazen?'

She hesitated, still sensing Hermia on her shoulder, pointing out his melancholia, urging her to keep him company.

'I'd like to know more about my wife's relationship with Peter Sanson,' he admitted.

'Ah...' She offered an uneasy smile.

'And if those letters reveal she danced with the devil, I'd rather hear that from the hor—' He stopped to rephrase. 'From you first.'

'Do you have peppermint tea?'

'Probably.'

'Because if you're going to hear it from the *horse's* mouth,' she set off purposefully along Church Lane, 'you'll bloody well need to sweeten it.'

Luca checked on Nancy again, now dozing contentedly in the corner of her stall. Knott had come with him, slinking low in the shadows, upset by the recent confrontation.

The mare woke as they approached, regarding Luca impassively, no longer in pain; one yard crisis averted, another domestic one raging.

Mack had just taken Kes away, the boy still half-asleep, wrapped in a Thunderbirds duvet, Rab in his arms.

'Mummy got the dates wrong again!' Pax had told her groggy son. Everything was fine, she assured him. Nothing to worry about. 'Think of it as an exciting adventure.'

She'd refused to make a scene or reveal how upset she was

in front of Kes. Pax the family peacekeeper, a role she'd played out since childhood. Her self-control astonished Luca.

But it was the first time he'd seen how overwhelmed she could be by Mack, especially when her ex used their child as leverage. She would do nothing confrontational in front of Kes. A blade could slide between her ribs and she'd tell her son everything was OK.

It made no difference that Luca took the blame, telling Mack that she'd left Kes asleep for just a few minutes to help him out with an emergency on the yard.

'Too right it's your fault! And I'll see you suffer for it,' Mack had snarled, a string vest and machine gun away from Rambo.

This was also the first time Luca had witnessed just how righteous Mack could be, this self-assured bully, convinced he was the hero evacuating his child from an immoral danger zone of neglect and depravity, running to the car with his son in his arms, shouldering a small, hastily packed rucksack containing clothes, toys and his school uniform.

It was only after they'd driven away that Pax had let loose, setting about the arrivals yard kicking and thumping walls, fences and planted troughs, wailing like a banshee. She'd paced the cottage afterwards, messaging frantically, too upset to speak, except to ask him in a monotone if he'd mind checking Nancy again.

The door was unlocked when Luca returned. He let Knott in ahead of him and called her name. A tiny white toy horse lay on the mat, dropped on exit. He picked it up and placed it on a side table. It reminded him of Beck, with whom his bond was as fragile and fleeting as the one he had with Kes and with his extraordinary mother.

He found her in the garden by the fox's run, tears gleaming wet on her face in the half-light.

'I let him go,' she said hollowly.

It took Luca a moment to realize she was talking about the fox.

'At least one of us can run away,' she said and her breath steamed in the cold air. There was a clank as she turned away, her boot catching an empty bottle underfoot.

Luca stooped to pick it up, recognizing the handwritten label of Lester's plum gin, part of a huge haul they'd unearthed under the cottage stairs, now locked beyond easy reach, and which he dosed out medicinally to the stallion man each evening upon request.

'I poured it out!' she sobbed. 'You must believe me, Luca! I couldn't, I wouldn't!'

'I believe you.' He put his arms around her and she leant her forehead against his breastbone momentarily for before shaking him off.

'I'll do *anything* to get Kes back: Mack's couple counselling, AA, rehab, anything!' Her voice cracked to sobs again.

'Shh, it won't come to that, Pax angel. He had no right to take him. Talk to your solicitor first thing and she'll have Kes home again by school pickup for sure.'

'You and I have to cool it completely, d'you understand?' She was animated now, marching around faster, eyes huge in her pale, moonlit face. 'No more kissing, no flirting, no *us*. There can't be an *us*.'

'You need rest.'

'I don't! I need Kes. This is *all* my fault.'

'Mine too.'

'You can't share this with me, Luca. We don't share anything anymore, understand? Not till Kes is back, perhaps not even then. I just want you to go. Just *go!*'

When he didn't, she bent down and wrestled off her shoes, throwing them at him. 'Walk a mile in those, why don't you? And just keep walking, like horses swimming at sea. Get away from me, Luca. I'm no good for you. Just go away!'

It was only when Luca was back in the main house, grateful to find Lester's light was off so he could head straight up to his run of attic rooms, that he wondered whether Pax meant him to leave completely.

He took a shower, as much to warm up as clean up – although the water up here was never much hotter than tepid – dressing swiftly again afterwards because he had to check on the horses soon, adding two extra jumpers. Uncertainty gnawed deeper into his bones than the cold.

His phone had good signal up here, messages waiting from old bosses and colleagues demanding when he was free to work, from friends wanting to know when he was free to play and from family eager for him to come home to rest.

Luca was accustomed to being on the move, to warm welcomes cued by quick texts and even swifter exits triggered by hot heads. A nomadic career of lifelong loyalties and fast friendships had provided plenty of experience with ungrateful, aggressive, impulsive and bloody-minded charges, but he knew when he was needed, as was the case here. Lester needed him to be his legs; Carly needed him to help her heal; Ronnie – whose message to say she'd be late home was amongst many – needed him to work as hard as three men.

Luca had always taken pride that he needed little himself beyond a bed, food and work, riding for his life and singing for his supper. After meeting Meredith – and perhaps because of her – that evanescence had become an art form.

Leaving here would be easy enough, and he was all for an easy life, but he was going nowhere.

For the first time in years, he sensed a need that was shared. That he needed Pax as much as she needed him right now.

Walk a mile in my shoes.

And he couldn't leave Beck.

If she wanted him to leave, she'd have to convince him.

17

'That's huge and *not* peppermint flavoured!' Ronnie's amusement that Kit handed her a large glass of wine and not herbal tea was an unexpected tick in his opinion. 'Petra's Prosecco almost finished me earlier, so this will floor me. I'm trying to lay off.'

'For Lent?'

'Something like that. How very neat you are.' She regarded the piles of letters on the coffee table in front of her. 'You've already made a start, I see.'

'Just put them in date order.'

She set down her wineglass with a throaty chuckle. 'Hermia told me you were a piler and filer – in a letter somewhere around *here*!' She plucked out an envelope post-stamped 1990, pulling her reading glasses down from her head. 'Which was about the time you moved in together.' She began leafing through its contents. 'A flat in Finsbury Park, wasn't it?'

'You have a good memory.' Another plus point.

'Hermia wrote about you *a lot.*' She took off her reading glasses. 'As you know, we were great confidantes.'

Kit had skimmed enough of Ronnie's end of the exchange to appreciate there were no secrets too salacious for the two friends who had corresponded regularly from boarding school until his wife's accident thirty years later. After sharing an idyllic seventies' childhood in Compton Magna, the two were rarely in the village at the same time, long letters and postcards flying back and forth, full of news and stories of theatre life, the horse world, families and romance. An analogue mutual devotion.

Their close friendship had always mildly irritated Kit, existing as it did offstage from his marriage, a secret confessional of which he was no part. Yet in person, so much of Hermia's psyche resonated with Ronnie that it was hard not to be drawn to her.

'Actually, this one was written before Finsbury Park.' She had her glasses on again, reading the letter with obvious joy, as though it had only just arrived. 'She's rehearsing *A Streetcar Named Desire* – that was the first time you directed her, wasn't it? She calls you a brilliant maniac.' The glasses were lowered again. 'I booked to come and see it, but something went wrong. It usually did. Bloody horses.'

'Where were you living?'

'The Dales, I think,' she said vaguely, reading a line and laughing in delight. 'She's *so* funny. God, I loved her.'

'Touché,' he said, surprised to feel more allied than possessive. 'She valued laughter far higher than applause.'

'And giggling above that. She was a terrific giggler.'

A memory jogged, of Hermia unable to speak for glee, tears pouring down her face and a stitch doubling her up, one hand waving at him to stop making her laugh.

He'd been mistaken to imagine that sharing her memory with Ronnie would be hard. Reconnecting with the vibrant woman he'd first fallen in love with all too often eluded him, its memory tarnished by her tortured final years. Tonight, it was Technicolour again.

'She was an absolute hoot after you moved to Compton Magna, describing village antics,' Ronnie went in, 'but in this one she's all method acting and realism, telling me off for gallivanting around with turf-mad toffs.' Throwing him a knowing smile, Ronnie turned the page over to read on.

'She loved your adventures,' he told her, mildly ashamed

that he'd tuned them out when Hermia was alive. 'She thought our life very boring by contrast.'

What Kit had seen of Ronnie's half of the correspondence mapped an unexpectedly Quixotic route from galloping girldom to globe-trotting femme fatale, whereas motherhood had brought Hermia back to her roots to raise their children here in the Comptons amid horses and dogs on their farm. Her stage career had burnt all too briefly, albeit brilliantly, like her life.

'Her letters kept me sane.' Ronnie put it back in its envelope, slotting that carefully back in order. 'And she was so infectiously happy after she met you, I lived rather vicariously through that.' The blue eyes shone bright over the rims of her reading glasses

'I can assure you the vicariousness was mutual.'

'Oh, I made a lot of mistakes, especially with men. Still do.'

'You're quite safe here with me,' he said stiffly, hoping his invitation wasn't misconstrued.

'And you're perfectly safe with me too,' she laughed, watching as he poured himself another glass of red.

Kit realized she had yet to touch hers. 'It's good, try some.'

She obliged, closing her eyes as she savoured it. 'Who can resist a deep, complex Australian from the Hunter Valley?'

He checked the label. 'Spot on.'

'Full of vines and horses,' she said, that growly laughter lacing her voice again. 'One grows richer and more complicated; the other stays dangerous at both ends, but you gotta love both.'

Kit sensed she was quoting.

The smile turned onto a frown. 'You *mustn't* let me have more than one glass,' she warned, raising hers and gazing into it. 'Never had a head for wine, especially when aggrieved.'

'About Church Meadow?'

She looked nonplussed for a moment. 'Oh, that, yes. The Devil's plot.'

'Tell me about Hermia's run-in with Sanson?'

Her fingers rested on the envelopes and walked left, turning back time, until she reached a large creamy pile. She lifted several and held them to her collarbone. 'These ones aren't such easy reading.'

Kit listened as she told him about the stud's long acquaintance with Kenny Kay, who'd stood his own and first wife Tina's beloved showjumping stallions there in the early eighties and often brought his mistresses to visit them. 'He was incorrigible, but Daddy adored him. Peter Sanson sometimes tagged along too and was a frightful thug. They were likely lads, Kenny all showbiz, Peter a ruthless wheeler-dealer running protection rackets or some such. The summer Hermia and I left school they tried to bed us both.'

While gregarious flirt Kenny took a shine to the Captain's racy eighteen-year-old daughter, it seemed silent, brooding Peter set his heart on her pretty friend. 'He wouldn't give up, sending Hermia flowers and chocolates and teddy bears with balloons tied to them, turning up at all hours. She simply wasn't interested, but when she told him to back off, he started shouting the odds about her thinking she was too good for him, and this village looking down on him. Thankfully, she headed off to RADA and Kenny bankrolled Peter to start up some sort of property business which kept him occupied, so it seemed to be forgotten.'

'Only it wasn't?' Kit refilled their glasses.

She took a sip from hers, explaining that their paths had crossed again some years later. 'By which point Peter had made a mint transforming rundown YMCAs into luxury hotels. Kenny had just convinced him to buy the Eyngate estate and everyone thought he was going to turn it into a golf club. Daddy was furious.

'That summer, Hermia was here with the family for a week or two "resting" as you theatre types say. Typically, I was away on a ghastly Greek holiday with Johnny, toddlers in tow, trying to patch up our silences, so we missed each other as usual. But she wrote it all down here.' She fanned the letters in her hand, casting him a look over them like Mrs Erlynne.

'The day the Eyngate deal was signed, Peter and Kenny got

three sheets to the wind at The Jugged Hare. Their behaviour went down in village history. Kenny's first wife was there. She was a little mouse of a woman from memory, but Peter protected her fiercely. They'd all been in care together. The tabloids were full of stories about Kenny carrying on with a glamour model or Miss Universe or some such, so the atmosphere was charged. Glasses were thrown, box brownies confiscated. Pete was particularly out of control, making some noisy wager with Kenny about buying the village back for the estate like feudal lords which put local noses out of joint.' She took a large swig of wine, leaving an endearing red moustache. 'Afterwards, Peter drove back across country and smashed his big, flashy car straight into a tree on the drover's byway, narrowly missing Hermia riding out on a horse.' Her hands went up. 'Unfortunate connotations all round, I know.'

Kit reached for the second bottle, shocked his wife's life-changing accident had been foreshadowed, uncomfortably aware also that Ronnie's ex-husband had died in a car crash. It was the first time he's put their experiences in parallel, and while there was no real comparison, they sat unnervingly close.

'Hermia gave them merry hell for it.' She went on. 'When he recognized who she was, Peter sent her enough roses the next day to carpet a room. Then the presents started again – a Cartier watch, diamond earrings. He even bought her a sports car. She sent it back. She couldn't afford to insure it for a start.'

'She never told me any of this.'

'It would have been a couple of years before you met.'

'What a creep!'

'The thing is, she *did* rather fall for the whole Jay Gatsby thing this time. Only *very* briefly,' she hurried on. 'But long enough to go with him to the French Riviera.' She plucked a postcard from the coffee table pile. 'Then New York.' She pulled out another, followed by a third. 'And a couple of weeks in Antigua.'

Kit's jaw hung open, his mind's axis shifting as his wife's single life gained more chapters.

'The curious thing is he didn't lay a finger on her the whole time. He'd even booked them separate rooms. She was going wild with frustration.' She looked at the postcard, reading, '*No HP Sauce here either* – that was her code for hank-panky – *Starting to think PS prefers Daddies.*'

'Hermia thought he was gay?' Kit asked, feeling relieved.

'She suspected it. But then that week they were in the Caribbean, Kenny finally left his wife for the Page Three model or Miss World or whatever in a flurry of flashbulbs and red-top news exclusives. Peter dropped everything to fly back and comfort Tina, leaving Hermia high and dry.'

'I knew none of this!' Kit drained his glass in one.

'It wasn't her favourite anecdote.' She swigged back most of hers. 'I feel awful for spilling it, but she was blameless and it shows how volatile he is, how bullish. Hermia thought he was having his revenge for snubbing him once.'

He poured yet more wine. 'I could lamp the bastard.'

'I wouldn't stand in your way.'

'What did she *see* in him?'

The blue eyes gleamed over her glasses rims. 'Don't pretend you don't know the attraction factor, dear Kit. You've cashed in plenty, as did I back in my day. Gorgeous girls, powerful men; it works both ways. I envied her. She was footloose and fancy-free.'

Kit snatched up his glass, glaring at her. It was true that his well-publicised track record with leading ladies since widowhood was evidence that he knew it well and practised it often. But Hermia...

They drank in silence for a while. Ronnie was looking pink-cheeked and glassy-eyed, the wine going down much faster now.

'Did she – was she – have feelings – upset?' he asked eventually, his words refusing to come out in order.

'She was terribly hurt, yes; she felt used.' She picked up her glass again, surprised to find it empty.

'But she didn't ever sleep with him?' He drained the last of the bottle into it.

'I'm pretty sure not, although her letters seldom went into that sort of detail.'

'Yours did.'

She choked on a mouthful. 'You've read them?'

'A few, and you certainly don't hold back.' It came out more accusingly than he intended.

'They're hardly Anaïs Nin! Anyway, that's me. The thing with Hermia was all ancient history, just a bit of fun that went sour. You two hadn't even *met*.'

'You think I'm a fool for being jealous?'

'Not at all.' Her voice dropped a soothing half octave, a slightly woozy edge to it. 'It's natural, rather admirable in fact. You loved her. Our pasts, those other lives, are tricky to navigate, aren't they?' She stared down into her glass, swilling the last draught of wine.

Which was when it registered at last: *a deep, complex Australian from the Hunter Valley*. Was she thinking about her married man? A sinewy rockface of outspoken Aussie testosterone, Kit had met him and didn't much like him.

He wondered if they were still together. Then he felt angry with himself for even caring. This was about Hermia, his clever, kind wife who he'd loved so intensely he still ached from losing her.

He snatched up the letters and put them in the carpetbag. 'You can take these back.'

'You don't want to read them?'

'It would feel like grubbing around in your friendship.' Standing up, he walked to a small mother-of-pearl inlayed chest on the desk and took out another thick pile of blue Airmail envelopes. 'These are yours to her. The older ones were lost in the house move, I'm afraid, but there must be ten years' worth here.' He thrust them in the bag with the others before plonking it in front of her. 'Please take them all away.'

'Are you sure?' She pressed her fingers to her mouth for a moment. 'I think I might have done a terrible thing telling you all this. So disloyal of me. I thought you'd soon read it anyway, but—'

'I'm grateful,' he interrupted crossly.

'Please don't feel you have to be gallant about it.'

'I can assure you gallantry is not in my repertoire.'

'It's never too late.'

With a roll of laughter that took him by surprise, the anger left him. He perched down beside her. 'I can't keep trying to construct a hologram of her from memories. It shapeshifts too much. I have to learn to leave her in my past.'

'Then I'll take them away.' She regarded him pensively, much thought going on behind the eyes, reminding him again of Hermia, which was all wrong. Cut-glass, kick-on Ronnie didn't have this softer side. It was much easier sparring with the gung-ho flirty version.

Their glasses were both empty. He sensed her taking her cue to leave.

'How's it going with your rider friend, Blair, isn't it?' he asked before he could stop himself, still sounding angry and defensive.

'It's not at the moment.' She placed her wine glass neatly beside his, standing up.

He found this news strangely uplifting. 'I have some brandy somewhere if you want to drown those sorrows?'

'I honestly can't touch another drop.' She picked up the bag. 'I'll need to sober up on the walk home as it is. This village turns us all into dipsos'

'Have that tea!' He leapt up to put on the kettle.

Her voice stayed too low, too kind. 'I do know how lonely you must feel, Kit.'

He stood in the dark kitchen, his back to her, wishing he could argue otherwise.

She stepped closer. 'And it's probably no comfort, but I feel it too. Often. Daily. Different, certainly. Lesser, perhaps. But she was my greatest friend, the most loyal and loved.'

He turned to face her, this strident, Sloaney little Mary Poppins with her carpetbag. Kit had never been much of a hugger, reluctantly enduring the backslaps, caresses and air kisses of theatre life. But he wanted to wrap his arms gratefully around Ronnie for bringing Hermia alive, just briefly, so that he could finally let her go.

And to his utter humiliation, he sobbed.

The carpetbag was quietly laid back down. 'I'll make the tea...'

There was nowhere Pax's mind could gallop to escape reality.

Kes wasn't here...

She had nowhere to run to. Nowhere to gallop.

Kes was gone...

There wasn't a drink in the house to fall into. She'd searched everywhere, angry herself for pouring out the emergency ration in the kibble bin, then grateful, then angry again.

Kes was gone, taken by Mack because Mack was still in charge. She'd been fooling herself to think she'd ever be free of that. She had no control.

Kes wasn't here and it was all her fault.

She stood in the dark kitchen, the small window glowing behind its blue blind as Luca crossed the yard again, checking on Nancy first. Luca who was so good. She could hear the horses greeting him: Beck's demanding bawl, Cruisoe's nicker. More distant, Lottie's shrill delight.

Horses made sense. She needed horses. Luca understood that.

Knott was whining at the door, desperate to join him.

Pax found she couldn't move. She closed her eyes and tried to gallop.

Kes was gone...

Beyond the window, Beck whinnied again and Luca soothed him, voice soft as a shanti.

Still Pax couldn't move. She felt as if she was trapped in an airlock chamber between marriage and another life entirely. No longer a wife. Half-mother, half-child. The door hatch was in her grasp, its wheel ready to turn, but she wasn't sure she had the breathing equipment to swim to the surface and she needed to know Kes would be with her and be safe out in this new ocean.

Knott barked at the door.

Forcing herself to move, Pax let him out, watched him race away, envying him, letting her breath cloud, her eyes sting, the cold bite her bones.

Then she saw them on the doorstep.

Luca's boots.

She swallowed a sob, a laugh, another sob, remembering him playing the stablehand. *Walk a mile in my shoes.*

She needed his kindness.

She stepped into them and walked. Jogged. Ran. Sprinted, tripping over their clownishly big toes to search the yards, the barns, the hay store, the tack room. A mile in Luca's shoes.

The main house was the only place left to look. The back door was unlocked. Pax stepped out of the boots, tiptoeing past her forefathers' mahogany-topped ones to the back stairs and stopped dead in her tracks as she remembered.

Sex isn't a ship. It's a sport.

It wasn't kindness or goodness she craved. It was the oblivion of abandoning herself to something forbidden to her for so long.

She heard faint music from the kitchen behind her.

Luca was sitting at the table, Knott at his feet. The big, easy smile was wider than ever, but the green eyes glinted as she'd not seen them before, his voice matching their devilry. 'They walked you here, then?'

She hesitated. 'Are you drunk?'

'On you, definitely.' He stood up, emitting an amused 'oof' as she hurled herself at him.

The kiss was a headrush, not remotely coy anymore. She knew what she wanted, already undressing him. He was covered in hay, his jeans hems wet and muddy. And how could he be wearing so many sweaters? He was like a sexy Babushka doll.

'What if Lester hears?' he whispered, laughing, as she tugged them off over his head one after the other. 'Or Ronnie comes back?'

'This is the only warm room in the house,' she insisted, grappling with his belt. He was fantastically proportioned. 'You always turn me on in here, O'Brien.'

'I think you're mistaking yourself for an appliance, your ladyship.' He helped her wriggle out of her fleece, tee and sports bra in one swift movement before lifting her onto the table edge, taking a small, hard nipple in his mouth.

Which was when Pax fell through the rabbit hole, lost in a new world.

The sex was a body shock: intimate, hushed, urgent. She didn't come – it was too rushed, she was too tense – but her senses span and sky-dived and flew with such a G-force of sexual attraction and energy, the hot buzz diffusing through her was sensational.

While the dogs slept on in their beds, the Aga burbled and the fridge juddered, she and Luca found a delicious, shared new secret addiction

'It's just sex,' she whispered into his hot neck afterwards.

'Yeah, I thought I recognized it,' he joked breathlessly.

'There is no us,' she reminded him. 'We can't do this again.'

'You've walked in my shoes, remember.' He took her chin in his hand, tipping her head back to look at her, smiling, those strange sparks in his eyes she'd seen earlier. 'We're so doing this again.'

Shivering with delight, Pax knew he was right. She'd got what she wanted. Dirty, guilt-free, no-strings Luca. 'No shit.'

'Don't ever say ship,' he ordered, adding 'your ladyship.'

18

One of the anomalies of being the Other Woman for so much of her life was that Ronnie rarely spent a night alone with a man. Since her marriage, she struggled to remember passing the small hours in a dark room together without sex before sleep and an alarm call booked. And never a night talking this much, certainly. She felt like a teenager.

Kit spoke of his workaholic life, of his children who told him off for drinking too much and wanted him to find a soulmate. He talked of plays and books, travel and music. He was breathtakingly well read and refreshingly self-deprecating. The stand-offish pomposity was social awkwardness, she realized. He'd confessed to a bad stutter growing up. He was a man who said very little until he trusted he'd be listened to, and then found it hard to shut up.

In turn, she talked of her struggles at the stud and with her children, confiding some of her worries about Pax. And she told him of her three-decade friendship with Blair, during which their love affair had ebbed and flowed, currently dammed up behind his wife's awful illness. She ranted a bit about the *Don't call me* message she'd received earlier. 'I *never* call! Verity's family are always around – that's his wife. She doesn't really know who any of them are any more, poor darling, let alone me, but they know what I am to Blair, and I have every respect for how they feel. Why would I call?'

It was such a relief to have someone to spill it all to.

This was a kinsman. He was no moralizer. He didn't judge.

They talked only a little of Hermia, her memory allowed to doze peacefully close by while they remained wide awake. But they both knew she was the reason they could talk like this. Without her still alive to confide in, they'd finally found the next best thing. Lost ground rose up to meet them.

It was almost one in the morning by the time he offered to walk her home, the log burner still roaring merrily, both wrapped in blankets pulled from the sofa backs, a bowl on the coffee table between them piled high with spent herbal teabags.

'Or you can sleep here?' he offered. 'I'd love the company. I'm going to write.'

'What, *now*?'

'Stay and rest up here. Go home when it's light.'

Ronnie was suddenly too tired to argue, pulling her feet up onto the sofa and snuggling deeper.

When he added his blanket to hers, she reached up to pat his shoulder in thanks but instead found her fingers against his cheek, its stubble reassuring.

He covered her hand with his for a moment.

His pen had just started to scratch busily in his play script notebook when she fell asleep.

The next morning, Kit was snoring ripely on the opposite sofa when Ronnie awoke, the room freezing, her hangover morbid.

It was almost seven. She'd be late on the yard

She stumbled round, bones aching from sleeping on a sofa, furious at herself for thinking she could carry on as though she was still eighteen. What had possessed her? How was staying out getting slewed going to help Pax or the stud?

They must be going frantic not knowing where she was.

The carpetbag was still abandoned in the kitchen. She

tracked down her phone plugged into Kit's charger by the toaster.

Leaving a dashed farewell note, she hurried outside. It was getting light, the frost a white-out, the village mostly asleep. Sticking to the verge again, she hurried towards home, speed-dialling the stud's landline to let them know she was on her way. There was no answer. A voicemail notification buzzed the moment she rang off, date-stamped late the previous evening.

It was from Ronnie's old friend and one-time landlord, Bunny, a Wiltshire landowner and near neighbour of Blair's. His voice was low and grave. 'Ron, darling, I'm calling you before you hear this from somebody else. Verity died this afternoon.'

She stopped walking.

Don't call.

She looked hurriedly at her messages. So many messages. All saying the same thing. Verity Verney has died, have you heard?

And missed calls from Blair. Multiple missed calls until the early hours.

Don't call. Sent in haste because he wanted her to know he would call her. He knew she'd hear the news from others, and he'd call her as soon as he could. Only she hadn't answered.

She pressed Call Back.

He picked up in one ring. 'I said don't call me.'

'I'm so sorry, I just heard.'

The deep, gruff voice was so hollow with tiredness and sadness, it was ashes. 'She wouldn't have known a thing. Another stroke, way too big for her to see this one off. Over in a moment.'

'You must all be in terrible shock.'

'Too much going on for that. The Verneys have been readying themselves for this for months. It's a full-scale military operation to evacuate her soul to God. It's what they do. Saves on grief.'

'There's no discount on grief.'

There was a long pause.

'Where were you last night, Ron?'

'I got waylaid.' As soon as she said it, Ronnie wished she'd phrased it differently. Her waywardness appalled her. Another glass or two and she might even have got laid. Or done the laying.

Blair, who could X-ray a soul with one direct question, whose wife had just died, left another gaping pause. Then, 'I called the stud, woke that Irish fella. He went to look and said you hadn't come home. No one could get hold of you.'

'My phone packed up; I was just with a friend in the village.' Drinking herbal tea, she wanted to add sanctimoniously, but didn't. He could already see the lie coming and had too much on his mind to hear it out.

'I'll let you know when we have a date for the funeral.' He rang off.

Another voicemail from the previous evening landed, voice like a Brummy cement mixer. 'Ronnie, princess! Kenny Kay! I did what you asked, so we're even. Now we're back in business, I might be in the market to put a few hands between your legs and jump off against the clock again if you get my drift?' The laughter explosion hadn't changed, a double barrel of cheek and irony. 'Call me, bab. Be good to catch up.'

This time, she saved the number.

Bad Ronnie was back in town. Bad wife, bad mother, bad friend. The scarlet woman who'd betrayed her family. There was no hiding now.

PART FOUR

19

Ronnie had no time to process Blair's loss, its impact swept aside by the force of Pax and Mack yet again picking up the sharpest fragments of their broken marriage to hurl at each other. Her failure to come back overnight had barely registered at the stud. Unsurprising, given the high drama there, the phones almost melting with solicitors' calls and family interventions to soothe the situation.

Ronnie was furious with herself. If she'd been there, she would have dealt with the colicking mare; Mack wouldn't have found his son home alone; Kes would still be with them.

But Pax saw it differently, and her face remained a mask of rigid defiance when Ronnie apologized for not realizing what was going on, a warrior mummy armoured against her own mother's love. 'You weren't needed. You're still not.'

It didn't help that Mack's parents got involved, the judgmental Muir and Mairi Forsyth appealing to Ronnie directly 'as grandparents to get these two poor souls back together for the sake of the wee boy'.

Although Ronnie refused to collaborate, the fact she'd even spoken to them got Pax's back up further. 'My solicitor Helen says grandparents getting involved just inflames things, so please just *back off*. It's all under control.'

Ronnie could see just how raw Pax was beneath the calm

veneer, something she was uniquely positioned to understand having lost custody of all three of her children to their over-zealous grandfather. Yet this history simply drove a greater wedge between them, the darkest shadows of the family's past raked up for comparison as Pax looked for somewhere to lash out. 'I'm not giving up like you did, Mummy! Mack's not backing me into a corner, nor his bloody parents. I'll do this differently – and I'll get my son straight back.'

In the ensuing twenty-four hours, she did just that. Kes came home after school the next day as though nothing had happened. Pax retained her equanimity, masking the torrent beneath and all was quickly smoothed over, apologies made, but there were scars.

Over coming days, Ronnie sensed a seismic change in Pax, a hardening and distancing, tightening the armadillo shell her daughter had always rolled into as soon as she felt greater threat. She privately suspected there was more to the story behind Mack taking his son away, intrinsic details missing, but nobody was telling her anything. Her fragile bond with Pax had come unstuck.

'It's all sorted, Mummy. Just leave me alone and let me get on!'

Pax worked harder than ever, rode longer, talked less, ate less, withdrew more. Only Kes got to share in his mother's explosive laughter, that wellspring of kindness, a forcefield surrounding them when they were together.

With Luca preoccupied as visiting mares began arriving ahead of foaling, and Lester glued to a screen or sweating out his physio exercises, Ronnie felt a sense of isolation engulf her she'd not experienced in decades, ever more aware of the need to put things right at the stud after all that she had forfeited here: her children's innocent years, Johnny, her parents' old age, her freedom, her youth. Talking to Kit Donne had brought it all back. Like Pax, she worked harder than ever, rode longer, talked less, ate less. Too often, she found herself thinking about Blair and hoping he was OK.

Six days after Verity Verney's death, Ronnie sat in her father's old study staring at her funeral notice.

A tsunami was ripping through Blair's life which she could only follow through third-party reports. Ronnie knew just how hard he would find grief, her lone wolf who renounced pity. Her heart ached for him. His wife's quick, quiet death, one hand resting on her favourite spaniel's head, was so typical of Verity's kind-heartedness, a generous French exit before the dementia had entirely robbed her of physical dignity.

The funeral was to be a small private ceremony. A larger memorial would follow later. Ronnie worried her presence would be too controversial, but the fact that Blair had put her on the guest list left her no choice. She'd spoken to mutual friends over the past week, all of them expressing a combination of shock, sadness and quiet relief, all stressing how much Blair would need her there. Her carefully worded letter of sympathy had taken hours and said nothing. But they'd always read between one another's lines, especially now they were older and the lines ever more plentiful, worn deep by shared laughter and sadness.

Having unearthed an old box of her mother's embossed Smythson stationery on which to write it, Ronnie had made good use of its deliciously thick, woven-cream good manners in recent days. She'd penned old-fashioned notes to Petra and to Kit, thanking them for their hospitality, and an apology to Viv for deserting the church roof committee. She'd also discovered a gold cigarette box crammed with unfranked stamps, most now so ancient that she had to mosaic half the envelopes with them. There were too many to let waste. Inspired by her old correspondence with Hermia, she'd spent the past hour writing a chatty letter to son Tim in South Africa, like the ones she'd once sent to him at boarding school. Let him think she was a mad old Boomer if he wanted.

She liked sitting at her father's old desk, where she could keep an eye on the arrival's yard. Today there was a red pickup parked there. Older daughter Alice was visiting, and Ronnie was diplomatically keeping her head down because, as Pax had pointed out matter-of-factly, 'she still hates you'.

Must dash, Alice is visiting! She sighed off the letter to Tim, wryly aware that any dashing would involve running away while Alice charged after her, accusing Ronnie of gambling with her inheritance. Last time, she'd called her mother a heartless, scheming fortune hunter who used her knickers to keep her ankles warm.

A pocket-sized, pony-tailed termagant, Alice had plonked a pot plant in on Lester earlier before marching across to the yard, no doubt to tell Pax she thought she should try to patch things up with Mack and try for another baby, which was her usual line. That, and trying to persuade her they should sell up the stud.

Ronnie longed to be out on the yard keeping busy, but Pax insisted she keep away during Alice's visit. 'She's watching me ride Lottie. Can you go shopping or something? I'll help Carly.'

She was far too broke to go shopping, besides which, Luca had borrowed her car, taking advantage of his day off to visit old friends, setting out before anyone had got up.

Ronnie picked up her phone to check for messages, but there was no signal, nothing new since a flurry of gossip from Petra about the goings-on at the Manor, where delivery trucks and tradesman's vans had been coming and going all week.

On a whim, she also wrote a polite welcome note to Kenny Kay, hastily addressing it when she spotted Mitch the postie's red van on the drive.

Outside on the doorstep, she exchanged her letters for an unwelcome stack of bills from suppliers who knew going paperless meant they'd be ignored.

'He'll not be moving in there for a while longer,' Mitch said, reading Kenny's address on the top envelope, always abreast of the village SP. 'He's having the place wired for extra security. All high tech, like something out of a Bond movie, the guys there tell me.'

'I wonder who he's afraid of?' Ronnie had a vision of Kenny in a swivel chair with a Persian cat.

'The *curse*,' Mitch chuckled. 'It's all in his book. He got shot at round here years ago, lost a finger – his Dave Allen tribute he calls it – and that was the start of it.'

'Absolute nonsense!' Ronnie huffed, tempted to ask for her letter back. Kenny Kay could never resist spinning truth with lies for the sake of a good yarn.

'Keeping busy here, are you?' Mitch asked.

'Very!' she assured him. 'Business is booming.' Kenny wasn't the only one.

In amongst her post was a reply from Kit Donne, written on a postcard of Gielgud playing Prospero at the RSC, which she read while standing in the front door, still waving Mick away.

It was a delight to spend time with you. I'll drown my book. More please.

It wasn't yet eleven. Ronnie needed to get out of the house. Lester was watching a YouTube video about hedge laying so loudly that she could hear every word.

She took her dogs up to the woods at the highest point of the stud's land where she was guaranteed five bars of mobile reception and called old friend Bunny, who had Blair's ear. 'How is he?'

'Bad tempered, but that's nothing new,' Bunny's port-soaked voice reassured her. 'Ready to kill Verity's family. There's a big hoo-ha about her final resting place. You know he's decided not to ride at top level this coming season? All his advanced horses are being farmed out to deputies.'

She'd heard. 'I don't blame him. My mother used to say riding with a heavy heart is like carrying a ten-pound penalty.'

'And there was me thinking he was making himself light on his feet in case he needed to do a flit!' Bunny chuckled before demanding to know how she was. 'Is that ravishing daughter of yours really coming out campaigning again? And why not you? Everyone's talking about it.'

Ronnie was careful not to unload too much. Just enough to salve her soul a little, admitting to Bunny that she thought Pax needed more autonomy. 'She must feel this place is her future not just my pet project. That's why competing will be so good for her. Good for the stud, too. God knows, we need more mares coming in this season.'

'Stay with me before the funeral,' Bunny insisted. 'I have a lot of favours to call in, and you have a very smart stallion arriving soon. Heard Blair found it for you, so it must be good. We'll fill your book up in no time.'

Ronnie laughed, although she rather regretted telling so many people about the little American stallion when negotiations were still ongoing. But Lester had assured her the deal was as good done, and despite Bay being in the syndicate the horse would be too good for business to miss out on.

Much cheered, she walked back down. The red pickup was still parked in the arrival's yard so she darted inside the house.

Minutes later, Alice tracked Ronnie down in her grandfather's study, looking furious. 'There you bloody are, Mummy! Been looking everywhere. I need to talk to you about the Trust and this can't go in a letter.'

She threw herself down on a chair, hands on knees, as though posing for a rugby team shot. 'Strictly hush-hush, we think Mack will go after half Pax's interest in the stud if they divorce.'

Ronnie's first thought was that her son-on-law hated horses, so why want to part-own a stud? Then she felt sick. Property-developer Mack had been the first to rave about the goldmine potential in converting the stable yards. 'Surely he won't get it?'

'It's a dirty trick, but not uncommon when one party has a significant interest in a family holding like this.' She started leafing through the paperwork on her mother's desk. 'He'll argue it's a marital asset.'

Alice explained that, unlike Ronnie's lifetime trust which

had no monetary value, each stake held could be bought and sold: 'This is Pax's only tangible asset. She has no income, no home.'

'The stud will be both those for her and Kes.'

'For how long?' Alice was a pragmatist. 'She needs a guaranteed future. She's a single mother in her thirties. All this talk of competing again is madness.'

'I was competing up until I came here and I'm—'

'A dreadful mother!'

'— in my fifties,' she finished. 'Nobody's future is guaranteed, dear Alice, as you'll start to realize when yours gets shorter and your past longer.' She thought of poor Verity, old age stolen from her.

'You're quite right,' Alice said sharply, 'nobody's future *is* guaranteed. The Trust has discretionary control over your life interest, don't forget. We can force the sale and find you somewhere more modest to live out your days.'

Ronnie sensed she longed to add 'on Mars'.

A thought occurred to her. 'Can I transfer it to Pax, my life interest?'

Alice looked baffled. 'I suppose it might be possible with the Trustees approval. Why would you want to?'

'Because a life interest trust can't be considered as a part of a divorce settlement,' Ronnie explained. 'Your grandfather was very emphatic on the point when he drew up his will.' After her mother's death, they'd met regularly for lunch midway between the Comptons and Wiltshire, during which her father – increasingly frail and irritable – outlined his intentions to safeguard the stud's future. 'Just as he was about it preventing the stud's sale so long as it's running profitably.'

Alice's berry eyes darkened from sloes to deadly nightshade, lips tightening, nostrils flaring.

'That's simply not going to happen!' She stood up and marched to the fireplace to strike a pose as though dancing a Paso Doble. 'You must give up on this idea that you can recreate what Grandpa had here. Face facts, Mummy, it's never going to return to its glory days of Captain Percy.'

'It was your grandfather who lost control of it. You've seen the estate accounts. It's all there.'

'That was your fault for buggering off.'

'And I've never stopped regretting it, Alice! But there was no way back, the door was closed on me for decades. Pax deserves a different future than I had. I'd like her to bring Kes up here. I believe she has what it takes to run this place profitably long-term.'

'Pax couldn't hope to run it!' Her daughter stomped closer, chin flicking up. 'And she'll never stay on here with you around. She hates you being here. We both do. You gave up on us.'

Alice had finally said something to hurt Ronnie, pulling claws through her conscience, swirling her red cape at the bull.

Ronnie kept her voice low and calm. 'I never gave up on you. Any of you. And I'm not giving up on you now. That's why this place matters so much. This,' she threw her arms out, joining in the Paso Doble as she turned around, pointing out the walls covered with photographs and pedigrees of Percy horses, 'is *your* security, *your* heritage, *your* land, not mine. You're a farmer now, Alice, you know what land means to families. Tim runs a vineyard; *he* knows what it means. The stud is our family land and Pax needs this chance more than I do. Let her take it on.'

'She's a drunk!' Alice spiked the banderilla.

'She's stopped all that.'

'Nonsense. She's a lush like Daddy. That was your fault too.' Another spike.

'Give her a chance to prove herself.' Ronnie stood firm. 'Mack can't do anything if we pull together here.'

'Don't be so naïve!' Alice flared, marching forward for the kill. 'None of this will stop him going after Pax's original share.'

'It will if she puts that share in Kes's name,' Ronnie blocked.

'He can hardly argue that's not in their son's long-term interests.'

Alice hesitated, regrouping. 'That's not the path we envisage.'

'There's an Aboriginal saying, *there are no paths, paths are made by walking.*'

Alice looked peeved. 'You know perfectly well public rights of way are there to stop ramblers trampling everywhere in this country. You're not some bloody tribe elder reclaiming this land.'

'Aren't I?' Ronnie loved the idea of standing by the top coppice, wrists resting on a wooden staff across her shoulders, knowing the place would be safe for future generations.

'I'll talk to Tim about it,' Alice muttered tightly, picking up her bag to leave, 'but with Pax's personal issues, I doubt he'll want her in charge here anymore than I do.'

'By chance, I've just written him a letter mentioning how well I think she'd run the place,' Ronnie said, feeling kismet charge up alongside, aware her son was far more sentimental about both the stud and Pax than his older sister was.

'You really should tidy all this up, Mummy,' Alice grumbled as Ronnie saw her out along the back lobby, past the rows of dusty hunting coats and cracked leather boots towards an ungracious parting of ways. 'This place really is a bloody museum piece. Don't tell me that's been here since Daddy's time?'

That's when Ronnie spotted it too, the glint of something reflecting in a boot top, and it took her back thirty years in an instant, her heart hammering.

It was an empty Famous Grouse whisky bottle.

Pax, who always found her sister exhausting, was grateful to see Alice's red pickup storming back down the drive, meaning she didn't have to endure another lecture about marriage being a job one didn't resign at the first sign of trouble. She'd barely shut up, even going on about it while videoing Lottie for her, Pax now realized as she reviewed the footage on her phone, hearing her sister's loud Pony Club DC voice behind the camera, bellowing that Mack was safer being in the family than outside it. She'd have to mute that out before she sent it to Bay later. At least the mare looked fabulous.

Her calendar app popped up on screen, reminded her she had to be in Broadbourne for twelve thirty.

Kes was playing in the straw barn with Ellis, some elaborate *Star Wars* make-believe neither boy wanted to end. When Pax gave the half hour warning he roared with fury, a new noise she disliked intensely.

'We need to set out at midday!' She kept it bright. 'Lunch in the Big M! McFlurry too if you're good!' Best not mention the dental appointment.

'I'm NOT hungry!'

'It's Power Rangers Happy Meals this month,' Ellis told him. 'I've got three.'

Pax loved Ellis, who was five-going-on-fifty to Kes's five-going-on-fifteen, with manners to match.

'Shall I ask Ellis's mum if he can come along?' she suggested, rewarded with cheers.

Carly was brushing hay from the cobbles with sharp, deft movements of her broom. Wearing earphones, chin bobbing, woolly hat pulled low over her blond extensions, she had an enviable ability to live inside her own head. 'Don't want tea thanks!'

It sometimes irked Pax that Carly viewed Ronnie and Luca as the bosses and her as the kettle-boiling intern.

The two women got along for the boys' sake and because they were mutual friends of the effervescent Bridge, but it was a mismatch, worsened by the work dynamic. Carly was a dervish who hated taking orders, Pax a perfectionist adept at organizing people. Yet despite this, the Saturdays they worked together were by far the calmest and best coordinated on the yard.

Pax waited patiently until Carly pulled out an earphone.

'I'm going into Broadbourne with Kes,' she explained. 'We can take Ellis if you like, get some lunch while we're there. My treat.'

'You're all right, thanks.' Carly pulled the earbuds out. 'We have plans.'

'Of course.' Her heart sank.

'His grandad's calling by.' Her eyes flashed. 'Ash's Dad.'

Pax knew Nat Turner by reputation. Everyone in the Comptons did.

'He's got a bee in his bonnet about something, Norm says.' Carly glanced up towards the fields where the boys were now charging with their light sabres. 'Reckon it's the rumour about Church Meadow, you know?'

'I don't talk to anyone much.'

'At the meeting last week. Your mum was there.'

'You'd have to ask her.'

'Petra says Bay Austen called us Turners gyppos, said we'd buy the field with dirty money.'

'*Bay* said that?' she asked, shocked.

'Somebody needs to tell him to lay off. Especially if Nat's around.' Her eyes narrowed, and Pax wondered if she was supposed to pass this on personally?

'I'm sure it's been exaggerated,' she said distractedly as Ronnie bore down on them, her heelers up bounding up first.

'Doing a super job, Carly! I'll come and help in a minute – I just need a quick word with Pax.'

'Actually, Carly wants to know something about the church roof meeting?' Pax ignored Carly's urgent headshake. 'Did Bay suggest the Turners want to set up a travellers' camp on Church Meadow?'

'It's all nonsense!' Ronnie waved a dismissive hand. 'The Austens are just showing their NIMBY roots.'

'I can't believe Bay would say something like that!' Pax was outraged.

'It's Sir Peter Sanson we should be worried about,' Ronnie said darkly. 'But *nobody's* selling the meadow if we have our way. There's a breakaway group trying to save it. Kester's head teacher is staging some sort of mini-Glyndebourne. Now come into the tack room for a minute.' She set off across the yard, beckoning for Pax to follow. 'I need to talk to you about all this fresh semen you've been offering clients. Luca will never manage it all.'

Beside Pax, Carly snorted with laughter.

'She's talking about stallion semen,' Pax explained tightly.

'I know that. I've read up on it all.' The earphones went back in, sweeping resumed.

Ronnie was waiting in the tack room, her voice low. 'I don't want to talk about AI. That was a ruse. What's this about Mack going after a share of the stud?'

'Alice promised she wouldn't say anything,' she groaned, not wanting their mother involved.

'Well, she did, and I want you to know I am right behind whatever you decide to do. I'm in your corner.'

About to defend herself, Pax shut up in surprise.

'My thoughts, for what they're worth, are that you should put your share in Kes's name,' she went on matter-of-factly.

Pax smiled to herself. She might have known her mother would be unable to resist an opinion. What surprised her was that it aligned with her own. And she'd said nothing to her sister.

Ronnie's voice dropped even lower. 'But I should also warn you that Alice saw the empty Scotch bottle in the riding boot in the hall.'

Pax tried to make sense of this.

Ronnie was looking at the pictures on the pinboard above the desk, amongst them a cutting from an eighties *Horse & Hound* hunting report, yellow with age. Still just visible was a picture of Johnny Ledwell leading out the Fosse Vale pack, horn to his lips, devastatingly handsome in his red coat. 'Your father used to hide his Famous Grouse bottles in the boots. Full ones to the right, empties to the left.'

Pax was nonplussed. 'Do you think it's his *ghost*?'

'Don't be facetious.'

The penny dropped like ice fired into a tumbler. 'You think I'm drinking again?'

'Are you?'

'No!' Pax was insulted.

Ronnie huffed disbelievingly. 'Who then?'

Pax racked her mind, thoughts racing.

'Lester's visitors are always bringing bottles and then drinking it themselves,' she pointed out, not trusting herself to say more. She didn't think it was Lester's visitors. Nor, she was sure, did her mother. But suggesting it was Luca out loud made the fear too real.

'Perhaps you're right. I'm sorry I had to ask,' Ronnie was rubbing her face tiredly. 'It's just that when Alice told me what Mack is threaten—'

'It *won't* happen,' Pax said emphatically. 'And I'm *not* drinking.'

'Good!' Hands still either side of her chin, Ronnie's brightened into its customary good cheer. 'In that case, let's talk about stallion semen!'

Pax found her mother's ever-jolly, antiquated schoolgirl gumption maddening. Before she could gather her thoughts, she was being grilled in excited detail about this year's stud bookings which had finally started to pick up thanks to the promise of the American thoroughbred arriving. While they couldn't officially market him until the syndicate was guaranteed and an arrival date nailed down, the rumour mill was already generating enquiries and social media was buzzing. As a result, Pax had wasted no time offering Beck and Cruisoe to long-distance mares via AI, something the stud had traditionally never done.

'Which is all well and good,' Ronnie said now, 'but natural coverings are our speciality.'

'You make it sound like we're selling floors.'

'Ha! Brilliant. The point is that we still have no practicable way of fulfilling this promise of all the fresh, frozen and chilled goods you're offering on the website. We're not Ocado.' Ronnie took nothing seriously, the twinkle remaining in the blue eyes throughout the heated spat that followed because she was backing Lester's caveman insistence that the stud must continue to service visiting and home mares the old-fashioned way. 'We have no other means, darling.'

'We'll get "other means". That's where Luca's gone today. He knows people with "other means" we can borrow.'

'Gratis?'

'I believe so.'

'Good for Luca. You two still getting along?' Ronnie's fishing line whizzed down.

'We get on just fine.' Pax swam rapidly back to safe water.

The truth was she was at sea with Luca, in a shark cage of her own making, with no ships in sight, not even a lifeboat. Neither of them knew what to do with all this newfound sexual energy, apart from have more sex. It was exhausting. All she thought about was sex with Luca. Then all they talked about by day was stallion sex. Semen was their thing.

'We're limiting the market if we don't expand into AI,' she told her mother for what felt like the hundredth time. 'The profit margin is huge. Luca has lots of experience, so let's use it. He thinks he can get hold of a dummy mare from the people he's seeing today.' She dropped the name of the country's biggest sports horse stud, whose owner Ronnie had once competed alongside.

'They have three hundred mares coming through their gates each season, Pax. The place is an out-and-out foal factory, offering embryo transfer as well as AI. There are tens of staff including full-time vets. We're just an old family stud.'

'*They're* a family business too,' she pointed out. 'And I don't expect us to follow that blueprint, but we must move with the times. *You've* always said that.'

It frustrated her how antiquated they were, how reliant on faded reputations. The mares coming here to foal and be covered again were mostly returning customers. For all the increased interest, they had only a handful of confirmed new bookings for the two stallions already in situ at Compton Magna, one pensionable and the other unknown in the UK with a questionable temperament. There was no future planning: Cruisoe was a spent force and Ronnie still planned to stand Beck for just one season before returning him to his previous stud when Paul Fuchs finally agreed a price.

'We should be maximising the advantage of having Beck here now by freezing his semen, and Cruisoe could bank his for loyal customers too,' Pax pleaded. 'Both horses are barely covering their costs the way we do things. We need to widen the market.'

'Cruisoe's dance card's almost as full as last year,' Ronnie pointed out. 'He's an old boy now. Once a day is more than enough.'

'But Beck's biggest market is on the Continent.'

'Where he'll be standing from next year. This season is all about building our own line from his so that we're future-proofed, a British Sports Horse dynasty from a German one, like four-legged Windsors. Approved mares only. Keep it exclusive, building an elite like his current progeny. Rebuild the stud's reputation from the ground up. Blair's idea, and quite brilliant.'

Pax was getting to know this expression. Blair's brilliant ideas often featured, although the man himself had retreated. Her mother's face was fixed, a freeze-frame mask, lips rolled together, emotions in check. She'd been doing it a lot since news of Verity Verney's death.

'We need cash not caché, Mummy,' she sighed eventually.

'For that, we need to be competing, making winners, standing proven stars. The American stallion is the banker.'

'He's not in the bank yet.' Ronnie's eyes were laser sharp amid their laughter lines. 'Frankly, I'm amazed the sellers are waiting on us. I'm half afraid Lester doesn't have a syndicate at all, just Bay bagsying a leg. Has he said anything to you?'

At the mention of Bay's name, Pax looked away, starting to count in her head to keep calm. Her mother knew how much she hated talking to her about him.

'We need to agree how Bay fits into all this,' Ronnie pushed.

Pax was already up to twenty.

'You're letting him buy you,' Ronnie pushed harder.

Thirty.

'We both know what Bay did and why we can't trust him.'

Fifty.

Pax glanced out of the door to make sure the boys and Carly were well out of earshot. '*We* don't trust *him*? You haven't even sent him a contract for Lottie yet.'

'A contract?' Ronnie made it sound like a dark web deal with a mercenary.

'Yes, we need a contract. Put him through the books, Mummy, stop making him pay cash. You're the one treating this like a dirty deal in a backstreet bordello. I'm trying to keep it professional. His mare is fabulous – and so long as the horses get fed, I don't care who's paying the bills. But I want a signed, legally binding agreement.'

Ronnie's eyes flashed as she recognized her well-worn line which Pax now suspected had been Blair's line before that. A wide smile emerged at last. 'Perhaps you should do the contracts and invoices, darling?'

'If you want me to.' She already had the proformas downloaded on her laptop.

'Let's trial it.'

'I can't be bought, Mummy. We'll take Bay's peace offerings, and I'll compete horses for him because this place bloody well needs it and I need it and you've stopped doing it because you no longer have the...' She was going to say 'nerve' but knew that was wrong, her mother's gung-ho ebullience being the most fearless of them all.

'Spunk?' Still Ronnie's eyes burned, the smile now fixed.

'I keep telling you that's exactly what this place needs!' Pax wailed in exasperation. 'More spunk. Fresh, chilled and frozen.'

'And you want to prove to me that you have what it takes?' Her mother's voice sounded odd.

Pax suspected the spunk line had triggered an indigestion of swallowed giggles. This infuriated her even more. 'I have nothing to prove to *you*. Nothing at all.'

'Prove *that* then.' Ronnie held her gaze for a long time, her expression strangely excited. 'Because if you do, I think we might just save this place.'

Lester could always tell when Ronnie was on the warpath. She walked differently, marching through the house like a drum majorette. He could hear her on the back corridor now: thud, thud, thud, thud.

He quickly started streaming a loud How To video about trenching and ditching.

Lester's new tactic for keeping the boss away from the dining room with her awkward questions was proving surprisingly effective. Playing instructional YouTube videos about countryside skills at top volume on the smart TV – dry stone walling, turf cutting, lime pointing, chain-sawing – could keep Ronnie at arm's length for hours.

But he had no doubt he would be interrogated about the American stallion's arrival again soon. There was only so long he could keep waving her away with a vague 'it's all in hand'.

It wasn't in hand, The only thing Lester had in hand was his iPad, the thing that had briefly made him feel as if he had the world at his fingertips and now meant his wrists were tied.

Ronnie had been right all along, of course; he was no horse trader. Blair Robertson had been the one with the contacts who had brokered the deal and put down a deposit, but he was now understandably preoccupied. It had given Lester a tremendous sense of power at first to liaise with the sellers, but now he just felt exhausted panic.

He knew how valuable a championship-winning son of Master Imp would be to the yard, and Ronnie had put extraordinary faith in him, and but he'd fallen short. He still hadn't got a syndicate together and time was almost up. The Canadian was threatening to walk away if he didn't get the rest of his money.

Lester had a small nest egg set aside himself, but it wasn't nearly enough to secure this purchase, a realization that made him feel rather insignificant and mortal. His life savings wouldn't buy one leg of this horse. Bay Austen could buy more with loose change, but he was no fool and drew the line beyond a 20 per cent share, which still left Lester 70 per cent short if he went all-in.

Earlier, Alice had bent his ear again about a quieter life and retirement, trying to pension him off so there was one less obstacle between Ronnie's older children and selling the stud. Well, he wasn't having it. They'd have to sell it with him in it, a permanent fixture like the panelling or the carved stone fireplace in here. Above it, the Captain's father Major Frank Percy looked down at him from a smoke-darkened portrait, a dapper old gent – far more temperate than his son – who had bred horses for the Queen. He'd thought Jocelyn positively libertine with his parties and celebrity owners.

Lester messaged Bay again, who had promised to ring around some more friends: *May I enquire if anybody has expressed further interest in the American stallion, Mr Austen?*

He scrolled Facebook despondently while he waited for a

reply, the village page predictably obsessed with the goings-on at Compton Manor.

An inspired thought struck him and he hurriedly opened a new tab. But Googling the contact details for the rich and famous appeared to be a great deal trickier than for horse professionals and farmers. Damn it! Ronnie kept all hers on her phone.

The ditching video ended and Lester froze as heard the drum majorette marching from the direction of the Captain's office across the flagstones of the entrance hall. He hastily scrabbled for the tablet to cast another YouTube video on the big television. *How To Make a Besom Broom.*

The little heelers barked shrilly from the stairs, following Ronnie up to change for afternoon yard work.

Relieved, he stood up uncomfortably, reaching for his crutches. He was vigilantly doing his exercises, but healing was taking a long time and the stiffness was troubling, especially on cold days when the pain seemed to sit deep his bones.

Stubbs was whining in his crate, hopeful they might go for one of their slow, lame potters to the courtyard, but Lester hushed him, making his way instead out though the big doors to the main entrance hall, rubber grips squeaking against the parquet.

He crossed past the huge carved bear Ronnie had shipped over to her parents as a peace offering when working in Germany, and into Captain Percy's old study.

The desk was covered with clutter and unopened envelopes. He waded through it quickly, and then through the drawers, in search of the Captain's address book. There! Thick leather covers, that distinctive spiky hand striping its pages with the names of mare owners and breeders.

He hurriedly flicked halfway through to K-L.

There were several numbers listed, daring back to the eighties, London still 01, Selly Oak 0472, and a number listed as Car Phone began 0370.

It was quite hopeless, Lester realized.

Stubbs was howling for him from the dining room. The besom broom video had stopped.

Then he spotted Ronnie's phone lying on the desk.

Lester wasn't a dishonest man, but desperate times called for 'a certain military daring', as the Captain would say. Her unlock code was the same as the combination padlocks on the yard.

He had the number in moments. Now all he had to do was steel his nerves to call it.

He hurried back to put on video about foot-trimming pygmy goats and picked up his tablet. Bay had sent two of his little smiling faces, one with dark glasses and the other with one eye bigger than the other and its tongue out, which Lester didn't understand.

Best call him given the urgency. He could sound out Bay's thoughts on the bright idea he'd had to sell the remaining 70 per cent. He tapped the little phone symbol on the messaging app, the trilling sound starting. It wasn't like a proper telephone, Lester had learnt. It wasn't very reliable for a start, taking several repeated attempts to get through, and then the sound was distorted when Bay picked up, lots of weird thumps and hollering, as though he was in the middle of a buffalo stampede. 'Is it urgent, Lester? Is everything OK?'

'Yes, Mr Austen! I don't understand the tongue.'

'The what?' The line was awful. More roars and thumping interference.

'The tongue, sir. What does it mean?' The television screen had frozen now that he was calling over the Internet, the little buffering circle going around, the room silent.

At Bay's end, there was a lot of bellowing interference. 'I'll call you back, Lester.'

'Wait!' He could hear Ronnie's dogs barking on the stairs again, the thud, thud, thud of the majorette marching back down. 'I have a plan!' he hissed urgently. 'I'm going to ask

Mr Kay to join the syndicate because he always loved owning horses, only—'

'I really can't talk,' Bay interrupted. Then there was a deafening roar and a 'Get back!'

'—there was some very bad blood between him and the Captain so I thought it might be better coming from—'

'Lester, our Jersey bull's got loose and jumped in with the Wagyus,' Bay gasped. His valuable beef herd was his pride and joy. 'I'll have to call you – holy fuck!'

The green phone icon on Lester's tablet turned red.

'Lester!' Ronnie marched in. 'What news of the American stallion?'

'All in hand,' he said weakly, grateful for the foot-trimming video burst back into life.

'Was that Bay on the phone?' she shouted above it.

'It was! All in hand!'

'Super!' She marched away again.

Lester took out the piece of paper with Kenny Kay's number on it and saved it onto his tablet.

20

Pax still used the same Broadbourne dental practice she'd visited as a child, located in a tall Cotswold stone townhouse around the corner from her solicitors. The Percy family had been going there for generations, loyalty dating back to an era when their old dentist had hunted with the Fosse Vale. Most of the local rural families still went there, even though the partners were now metropolitan and Asian, with far less enthusiasm for pipe-smoking and boozy lunches.

This waiting room had been old-fashioned and chintzy when Pax was Kes's age, a pile of well-thumbed *Country Life*s on the coffee table, a dried flower arrangement in the fireplace and brocade cushions arranged on bum-swallowing Laura Ashley sofas.

Now it offered free Wi-Fi and an Interactive Kids Corner. The fireplace housed a mood-lit zen stone pyramid, a huge wall-mounted flatscreen TV above its mantel showcasing the before-and-after tooth whitening, Botox and filler treatments on offer.

Pax sat on a firm slug-grey leather banquette eyeing her watch. Kes's annual check should only take a few minutes to count milk teeth and put a sticker on his jumper, but there was a delay for an emergency patient, the receptionist had apologized.

The wait stretched on.

Kes was enjoying the Interactive Kids Corner, cleaning a massive white tooth with a giant buzzing electric toothbrush. Pax took advantage of the Wi-Fi to start editing together the latest Lottie video for Bay, slotting one earphone in and trying to work out how to remove the sound. Alice was a superb live-action camerawoman – trained in the field at Pony Club rallies – but her voiceover skills were distinctly Gogglebox. 'YOUR problem is you should have married BAY AUSTEN,' her voice boomed through a sequence of Pax jumping the two big fallen logs in the front paddocks, too far away to hear, 'he was FAR better suited to you, but you chose MACK and THAT'S who you vowed to STAY with for richer and POORER, in sickness and in health. Well JUMPED! Dammit, she is a BLOODY nice sort.'

In her other ear, Pax heard a familiar smooth-barrelled voice emerging from an adjoining treatment room: 'Shank you sho much – I really apprechate thish.'

Familiar yet very odd. She snatched out the earphone and turned to look.

Standing there was the man her sister thought she should have married. Tweed, checks, denim. Thick oak hair, broad shoulders, narrow hips. Manners, charisma, privilege. Missing tooth.

Bay could be a show-boating scene-stealer, but even he couldn't have planned this.

Spotting her, he smiled, a pirate gap where one front tooth had recently completed his perfect smile. Behind him, a white-masked dentist in bright turquoise scrubs blinked up at him coyly and indicated for him to take a seat. 'I'll just examine young Master Forsyth here while your numbing takes effect, Mr Austen, and then we'll fit that temporary tooth.'

'What happened? Are you OK?' Pax asked as she and Kes were ushered past him. Her expression must have been more horrified than she realized because Bay closed his mouth and nodded vigorously.

In the treatment room, she perched in the plastic chair in corner while Kes reclined on the big padded hot seat, telling the dentist and nurse about his wobbly front tooth, talking so much the dentist couldn't get much of a look at it.

Pax's phone buzzed, a customary heart-leap at Bay's name. *A bull ran into me. Are you free later?*

Taking Kes to McDonald's after this.

Ah, the Scottish restaurant. Good choice. I mean later, later? Why?

Why, why, why did he have this effect on her? She was all shiny and new. She'd finally begun standing up to Mack and organizing her life into neatly separate labelled boxes, was having secret no-ships sex with Luca, and she knew Bay was a bigoted bad lot. He should have no effect. Yet even partially toothless, he broke her.

Worried about Lester. Call me when you're free to talk.

OK.

Appreciate it. He sent a Tom and Jerry gif of Tom smiling widely before his teeth fall out.

A loud giggle made her jump.

'That is *soooooooo* funny!' Kes was beside her again, sporting a large Disney Cars sticker and watching her phone screen.

They were ushered back out to the waiting room where Bay looked up from a grey leather banquette and smiled – lopsided as well as piratical now – before remembering to close his mouth. His blue eyes shared a short, intense conversation with hers that, sitting in McDonald's a few minutes later, Pax played on a loop in her head, her own private gif. This must stop. She was determined to keep it professional.

Opposite her, Kes and his small plastic Power Ranger were swooping down on French Fries in their own parallel ketchup-dunking universe. Taking advantage of free Wi-Fi once again, Pax sent Bay the video of Lottie, followed by a screenshot of their first affiliated entries, a contract and an invoice.

By the time Kes was inhaling his McFlurry a few minutes later, a Power Ranger saving the galaxy on its lid, her phone screen was already lighting up with Bay's reply, her heart palpating.

It was a horse gif and *speak later.*

Professional, she reassured herself.

She scrolled back up their messages, up and up and up, their column of talking bricks now crazily tall. Her rectangles remained far bigger than his emoji-dotted ones in this teetering tower of trust. Her own many typos kept catching her eye. Embarrassed because she'd denied them so ferociously, she quickly slid her thumb back down to double-check herself. There were three bloopers in today's message and she'd attached the wrong contract. She clicked on the sent video. Alice's voice rang out: 'Till DEATH us do PART should mean something, Pax. Lovely shoulder in!'

She'd sent him the unmuted version. Not so professional.

Mad at herself, she watched Kes's Power Ranger freediving from the McFlurry lid, fighting the forces of evil, and she longed for something as straightforward to fight.

She grabbed her phone and typed: *Btw stop saying bad things about the travellers. They have every right to Church Meadow.*

Within seconds, Bay sent back namaste hands and a love heart emoji. *Couldn't agree more. Ronnie already convinced me on that one. My bad.*

Which should have helped, but only made her angrier. *Never* put my mother and a love heart together, she wanted to message back furiously. Not with our shared history. But that would be disrespectful to Carly and her family because there was a bigger point at stake: *Land is what our feet stand on and our eyes see, not a piece of paper.*

She and Kes had left McDonald's and were buckling up in the Noddy car when he replied: *Marriage is a piece of paper.* Swiftly followed by *Off my tits on painkillers.* And finally: *Can't find my car.*

She texted *grow up* and drove home.

Carly had never seen a purple and pink themed buffet before, but she had to admire the ingenuity – and extensive use of beetroot – with which her sister-in-law had created it. At first she'd assumed it was another of Janine's many faddy diets, but she now realized it matched the décor of her front room, nails and outfit.

'He should be here by now.' Janine was gazing out of the lounge window that overlooked the Triangle, the car-covered grass epicentre of the Orchard Estate. 'You don't think he's been arrested again, do you, Granddad?'

'More likely picked up a pretty girl on the way!' Norm wheezed. 'Chip off the old block, that boy.' He reached for a handful of pink popcorn.

'Sticky hands off the buffet, Granddad!'

Carly and Ash exchanged a glance.

Nat was aways going to be late. It was family tradition.

They were waiting at the house on Apple Rise that Granddad 'Social' Norm shared with Janine and her kids, a homage to nail-artist Janine's love of restricted palettes as well as palates. Its front room was dominated by a flowered pink and purple feature wall, to which she'd not only carefully colour-matched today's food, but every rug, throw, scatter cushion, book, DVD and carved wall-art letters spelling out her kids' names, names she was shouting at regular intervals today, followed by '*Stop* eating the food!' 'No, you can't go back to Nan's to watch TV!' 'No you can't play Xbox!' 'Granddad'll be here any minute!'

Beside herself with excitement that her dad was coming home, Janine had even done her nails to match her feature wall and dressed in a pink bodycon dress than conned nobody.

'Do you think he'll want to move back in?' she asked now.

'He'll want to borrow money!' Norm sneaked a ham sandwich up his sleeve.

The Turner family rented several houses on the Orchard Estate from the council, although none of them lived in the ones they'd been allocated, swapping and changing round according to need, legal status and family feuds. Carly and Ash's house on Quince Drive was in Janine's name, this one on Apple Rise was still in Nat's, although he'd never lived in it, and neither Ash nor his sister had been raised in it. After Nat had abandoned his wife and two young kids to go back on the road, Nana had been shunted around the least desirable properties in the family portfolio – including a caravan parked on the Triangle – before ending up behind thick net curtains in her maisonette on Medlar Avenue. No wonder she refused to come back out.

'Is he coming in the vardo or the van?' demanded Janine.

Saying nothing, Ash clicked his knuckles. He always got super tense at the prospect of seeing his dad.

'I don't think he's coming, Auntie Janine,' said Ellis, their voice of reason.

'He bloody is!'

After another hour, when Nat still hadn't arrived, they started on the pink and purple buffet.

Carly made up a plate to take down the road to Nana who was glued to the *Four in a Bed* omnibus. There was a strong smell of rolling tobacco in the maisonette.

'Lovely, dear!' She took the food gratefully. 'What a feast! Could have done with this half an hour ago. Nat's as good as cleared my cupboards out. Had all the fishfingers, two tins of potatoes and all the kids' favourite biscuits. I forgot he had such an appetite.'

'Nat was *here*?'

'Checking I'm still alive, cheeky bugger,' Nana selected a slice of pork pie. 'He'd heard a rumour I'd pegged it, can you believe? Did he not come round to you after then? I told him to.'

'No, Janine's doing her nut over there.'

'Poor girl.' She chewed on the pie appreciatively. 'That's

probably my fault, asking him for a divorce and all. You should have seen his face!' She watched her TV again, still chewing.

Carly stared at her in shock. She'd always imagined Nana had been waiting for Nat to come home for good. 'Where'd that come from, Nana?'

'I saw a programme about it, saying you can do it all online. Not like it used to be. Horrible back then, it was.'

'What did Nat say?'

'He said we never got wed proper in the first place, but I kept the certificate, so there's proof, in there, see?' She pointed to the big sewing and knitting bag by her feet, her patterns' folder poking out of it. 'It's all in there. Take a look.'

Carly did as instructed, finding its concertina pockets full of neatly folded vintage patterns pulled out of *Prima* magazine. 'Did he agree to get divorced, then?'

Nodding, Nana selected another slice of pie. 'On condition he can have the house.'

'Which one?'

'The big one over the road.'

'On Apple Rise?'

'No!' Nana chuckled so much, pork pie got stuck in her throat and Carly had to slap her on the back until it flew out. 'The *big* house, love. Eyngate Hall!'

'Oh, right.' Carly managed a humouring smile.

'I never liked it. Too big and creepy.'

'Yeah, me too,' Carly let her have her flight of fancy. 'So Nat's gone again, has he?' She found a marriage certificate poking out of a back pocket. Except it was nothing like the one she and Ash had been given, that one was printed on cream paper with a green crest and had formal column for names, addresses and father's profession. This was a beautifully illustrated page of handwritten vows, signed by the couple.

'We were travelling with New Agers when we wed,' Nana said. 'Lot of them around back then. The old-timers didn't accept me at first, see, being gadji. He was such a force of nature, was Nat,' she sighed, 'I thought the sun shone out of him back then.'

Carly turned over the certificate, saying as gently as she could, 'I'm not sure how legal this is, Nana.'

'No?' Nana looked delighted.

'You should get it checked by a lawyer,' Carly was studying the certificate again and laughing. 'Is this your married name?'

'Nobody calls me that.'

Still laughing, Carly put it back in the pocket with the more official-looking papers. 'You want me to make you a cup of tea before I head back and break the news?'

'You're a good girl, Carly. And tell Janine not to worry. Her dad'll be back soon enough. He's getting ready for a big fight, he says.'

'The King's Purse?' Carly felt her smile stick.

But Nana was focussed on the television once more as the *Four in a Bed* contestants sniped about inferior breakfast trays. 'There was talk of turning the big house into an hotel. Who'd want to stay in a spooky old place like that, I ask you? Bound to be ghosts. I can't abide ghosts.'

Pax studied Lester closely throughout supper and cartoon hour. He was grumpy, fastidious, melancholy Lester, but she saw nothing new in that to worry her. He complained about the lack of meat as usual. As usual, he defected all Ronnie's questions about the syndicate with a determined 'it is *definitely* in hand' and even an excited 'mark my words, it'll be just like the old days!' Then he had three plum gins and reminisced about how consummately her father Johnny had understood husbandry in hounds and horses.

'Feels like he's still here sometimes,' Lester sighed mistily, 'just in the next room, writing down bloodlines in those notebooks of his. Nobody understood breeding so well as your grandpa, Kes.'

Kes listened agog to the much-repeated and embellished tales of celebrated stallions and prize-winning foals, another family generation learning the legends. Having grown up with them, Pax valued the old man's regular flights of nostalgia and his undying loyalty above any photograph of her father in the house, more so than ever now that she knew of his and Lester's secret love for one another.

Ronnie, who enjoyed these conversations less, sloped off early, soon followed by Luca pleading tiredness from his day out. Pax caught his eye as he left, sharing their own secret, his half-wink teasing. His mood had been withdrawn since returning, as though he was barely in the room, the big smile on autopilot, his long absences to top up Lester's plum gin hinting at messages being written and read by the coats.

Herding a reluctant Kes along the back corridor, Pax remembered her mother's accusation and glanced down. There were two empty Famous Grouse bottles in a pair of her father's mahogany-topped boots.

Lester was right. It *was* sometimes as though he was in the next room.

After she'd put Kes to bed, she collapsed on the sofa, hugged Knott, girded her loins and rang Bay. 'Are you still looking for your car?'

'Hello!' He sounded shocked. 'You never call.'

'You wanted to talk about Lester, remember?'

'Did I? Sorry. Had a bit of a knock on the head earlier. Turns out dental anaesthesia and concussion don't mix.'

'Oh goodness, did you get home OK?' Pax felt ashamed for abandoning him, realizing guiltily that her *get lost* message must still be on his phone. Maybe he hadn't noticed.

'No idea how, but I now have a beautiful smile and no memory after the mid-noughties so I'm happy. Come over and we'll drink WKD blues and watch a DVD box set. I got *Lost* for you.'

He had noticed.

'Listen,' he sounded serious now, 'I think Lester's way out of his depth with this horse deal. He needs our help.'

'He seems fine. Really chipper in fact.'

'Are you sure?'

'He was on good form tonight, talking about the old days when Daddy was still alive.'

'Ah, the glory days.'

'Some of them.'

They fell silent for a moment, both knowing how bad Johnny's drinking had got. Pax had been eleven when her father's car had careered off the Fosse Way, his bloodstream steeped in alcohol, hitting a big oak so fast he'd been killed instantly. Bay had been incredibly kind to her afterwards. It's when the first shoots of her crush had started growing, something bright and hopeful emerging from the darkest of places.

Speaking to him on the phone brought back how devotedly she'd hung off his every word then, an ugly red blush creeping up her neck whenever they spoke. She put her hand to her throat now, shocked to find it burning hot.

'You think we should leave Lester to it, then?' he was asking.

'I think he'll be furious if we don't. He's very excited about this horse.'

'And are you excited, Pax?' He still sounded cheerfully matter-of-fact.

She flapped her jumper neckline to fan her reddening face. 'Very.'

'I want you to promise Lottie will get just as much attention when the flash Yankee arrives. Thank you for the video, by the way.'

She fanned harder.

'Still there?'

'Yup.'

'Alice is right, isn't she?'

'Mmm?'

'We should have married, you and me.'

She stopped fanning and got up to start pacing the room as Bay talked on, his voice more urgent now. 'I know what happened killed it dead, and I know it was entirely my fault and I will apologize again now because I can never apologize enough, but it doesn't stop Alice being right about us.'

Pax stopped walking started fanning again.

'And I'm probably only saying this because I've had a knock on the head, novocaine and one too many codeines, but I have never stopped regretting it and wondering what might have been. And I want to tell you this now because you keep blatting off across country on half a ton of horseflesh with a brain the size of a walnut, and you might get hurt, and I'm the one paying for you to participate in one of the most dangerous sports there is which makes it even worse if you *do* get hurt.'

'I won't get hurt.'

'And promise I will be a hands-off event-horse owner with regulation red Hooray trousers and tailgate picnics and dogs on slip leads just as I promised, and I won't ever embarrass you like this again, but I can't bear to think of either one of us dying without me having said it.'

'I'm not about to die either.' She resumed walking in circles, still fanning.

'Well, there was a moment today when I thought I might peg it. And frankly, being flattened to pulp by expensive Japanese beefsteaks on legs is an undignified enough ending without the added ignominy of dying a coward who can't tell someone how he really feels.'

Pax turned and paced the other way.

He'd gone very quiet.

'Go on, then,' she urged, still lapping the room at speed.

'Go on what?'

'Say it.'

'Say what?'

'How you really feel.'

'I just bloody did!'

She thought back through the cattle trampling, red-trousered, walnut-brained sport, opiate-overload confession to find the crux of it. 'That Alice was right, you mean?'

'Yes! I mean no!' He let out an impatient huff. 'I'm saying that I love you, of course. Loved you then, love you now. Never stopped loving you.'

'Right.' She realized she was standing in the kitchen in complete darkness.

'Thought it best to tell you. Declaration of interest and all that. Not sure I made myself clear last time.'

'Right.'

He'd tried the night of the village meeting, she remembered, standing out in the darkness together. The night Nancy got colic and Mack took Kes and she and Luca found a new sport.

There as an achingly long pause. The working lights on the yard went on, the illuminated blue square from the little kitchen window landing on the floor directly where she was standing, as though she was about to be beamed up by an alien spaceship. She half wished she could be.

'I won't say it again, I promise,' Bay said quickly.

Pax's mind raced, remembering the yearning she'd felt through her marriage to be here again, amongst horses, in the place she'd first known love and trusted it completely. Her safe place.

Outside, Cruisoe was whickering greedily from his corner stable as Ronnie went round topping up hay and water and checking the broodmares, her thirty-year banishment from the stud's century-old day-to-day routine of no interest to its horses whose every need was always met here, even when the Percy family's were not.

She thought again about her father, a man mourned to this day by his soulmate, yet too tortured by the prejudice of his upbringing and rural community to grow old here.

Pax might not share her father's conflicted sexuality, but she had his addictive, self-destructive personality. She couldn't let Bay hurt her again. It had been too devastating, too life-destroying. She wouldn't survive it another time.

'You're right. Don't ever say it again.' She closed her eyes, her jaw aching with effort of not letting the rising tears into her voice. It took several seconds before she trusted herself not to sob. Calm voice, low voice, Pax the peacemaker voice. 'But in case you die under a sheep stampede tomorrow, Bay, I have something to say too.'

That's when she realized he'd already rung off.

She looked at her phone screen, where the photo had to be the one from his Google account, at least ten years old, a blurry shot of him outside the farm shop, laughing and squinting into bright sunlight.

Just this once, while nobody is listening.

'I never stopped loving you either,' she told it.

The square of blue light at her feet went out abruptly.

21

Verity's funeral took place in the private chapel attached to the stately Wiltshire pile she'd run for three decades. Organized by her former husband Tony, Earl Verney – who had always stubbornly refused to acknowledge his wife's remarriage – the ceremony was a full-throttle requiem. Old school smells-and-bells devout, it was presided over by the elderly bishop who had christened six of their eight children and multiple grandchildren thereafter.

Crow-backed in their pews, the chief mourners were tight-knit and insular, locked in grief for the woman they'd lost in three acts: first her reputation to adultery, then her mind to dementia, and now her body to the death that let them offer her soul up to God for absolution. To be seen to do so, the last twenty years of her life must be piously overlooked. The cordial bridge that had once been extended between the Grade I moated ancestral home of the Verney family and the life its former matriarch had later made for herself was all too quickly drawn up upon her death.

Arriving late because Bunny had decided to take an off-road short cut across the Wiltshire by-ways and misjudged the depth of a ford, her boots still sodden inside, Ronnie crept in as the last verse of 'The Lord's My Shepherd' was being belted out by a small, tightly packed congregation of mourners:

*'... and in God's house forevermore
my dwelling place shall be.'*

All eyes were tearfully focussed on the flower-strewn wicker coffin in front of the alter.

Poor Vee. The wicker looked out of place amid all the glittering papal pageantry, yet it suited her perfectly. She had loved simplicity, been at her happiest in the ugly modern farmhouse she and Blair designed together.

Ronnie spotted Blair's familiar silhouette as everyone sat back down and felt a lurch of pity and deep, angry affection. Relegated to fourth row amid the family's third generation, he looked out of place: wiry, weathered and pewter-haired amongst a throng of pale and pasty little Verneys, his head bowed while they gossiped over his broad, suited shoulders.

Ronnie had hesitated about coming, aware how controversial her attendance might prove, but Blair was emphatic he wanted her there, and that meant she'd brave lions – and Verneys – to support him. The family were immune to lorry-park gossip. It was Verity who had been the eventing devotee, first as rider and later owner, none of her offspring sharing their mother's infatuation with the sport beyond their teens.

Blair was the one with whom Verity had shared her great passion in life, for horses as well as each other. After such a dutifully dull marriage, it had been her awakening.

Before that, Verity's first husband Tony – who had nobly married the most eligible debutante available from a small pool of recusant English families to keep the Verney line and faith, landing himself a duke's youngest daughter as his Countess – had spent much of the ensuing thirty alternately years impregnating or ignoring her.

Now in his eighties, Tony was stooped and frail, his octet of grey-haired daughters to either side, sons-in-law beyond, and grand and great-grandchildren fanning out protectively on surrounding yew pews, a patrician closed order.

Penned in with the standing-room-only outsiders at the

back, mostly horsey cronies and fellow latecomers, Ronnie's heart went out to Blair, relegated to his mid-ranking bench, indignation bubbling within her. Throughout the many impersonal prayers and readings, the tributes to Verity were almost entirely limited to her high birth and her role as mother and grandmother, only brief lip service given to her adoration of horses and eventing, and no mention whatsoever was made of the fifteen years she'd shared with her Australian soulmate or the joy those years had brought her, that dazzlingly, rebelliously happy sunset before illness struck.

Ronnie's fury compounded when Bunny whispered during the Recessional that all this whitewashing family forgiveness didn't stretch as far as a full-sized slot in the Verney mausoleum. 'Thankfully the darling girl insisted upon cremation, so they're all hoofing off to the local hothouse now. Blair had a furious ding-dong with Tony because Vee wanted to be scattered on their gallops at home and the Verneys insist her urn stays top-shelved with the family stiffs here.'

'Why's he letting them take over like this?' she breathed back, knowing it wasn't like Blair at all.

'Vee was Catholic to the last, darling. This is for her children, so they know she won't be burning in hell like you and me. Or him.'

Blair caught her eye just briefly as he passed by, a glint of gratitude so intense that Ronnie felt it linger long after he'd left.

She was wrong to imagine none of the family would recognize her, a cry coming from lower down the orders: 'Bloody hell, Ronnie! That's a fucking turn up! Aunt Vee would be thrilled you're here! Bet Uncle Tony's pissed off, though!'

It was Verity's small, solidly blonde niece Roo, a foul-mouthed family rebel and countryside activist. With her, to Ronnie's surprise, was her late father's housekeeper and Compton village busybody, Pip, equally small and solid, berry-bright eyes challenging. Ronnie had heard from Lester, who was absurdly fond of them both, that they were now a couple.

'Did Les tell you we're engaged?' Pip showed off a ring with a green gem, identical to one Roo was wearing. 'It's a New Zealand Pounamu stone.' Without apparently drawing breath once, she launched into a catch-up monologue that covered Lester's well-being, Pax's marriage, the church land sale, Kenny Kay's high-tech security system and several of Compton Magna's bigger domestic scandals in less than sixty seconds, finishing in her flat Brummie drone, 'Lester says the stud's not the same without me there. Between you and me, he's desperate for a decent baker on the team again. On the down low, I hear Mo Dawkins has got money troubles since her Barry's run off and she's looking for extra work. She always wins Victoria Sponge at the Food and Produce Show, plus she knows her way around a horse and your veggie garden could use her green fingers, so bear her in mind.'

With a polite, 'I will', Ronnie made a mental note to wean Lester off Facebook.

'Anyway, lovely to chat, Ronnie. Shame we can't catch up more over a cup of tea in the house later, but it's family only.' She said this with satisfaction, taking Roo's hand. 'Have a think about Mo. Time younger legs took over. Les deserves to take it easy. He might come and live with us in New Zealand, did he say?'

Lester's tablet could not call or message Kenny Kay's mobile telephone number, he'd discovered. It lacked something called a SIM card. The Captain had never believed in mobile phones. Up until his death last year, the stud had survived on one shared landline. Now that the magical box of worldwide wizardry was glowing in the corner of the dining room and Lester communicated with Facebook friends on Messenger by voice, video and text, he'd imagined he'd be able to contact any smartphone he had the number for, but he was wrong. They had to be on a compatible app. Kenny Kay was not on a compatible app.

Just having a phone number meant Lester had to take his chances with the shared line.

Ronnie had been monopolising it for days, making and taking calls, trying to drum up business. He'd managed just two attempts to call Mr Kay, both nerve-wracking, neither successful.

Today she was away at the funeral and it was his best chance. The need was urgent. The Master Imp stallion's Canadian bloodstock agent – who had several compatible apps – was lighting up Lester's iPad night and day.

He'd agreed to let Pax show him around the yard's new AI facilities later – a guided tour he was *not* looking forward to, sharing Captain Percy's lifelong opinion that horses should do what comes naturally – so his window of opportunity was small and his mood not good.

By the time he made it to the kitchen to take the walkabout phone off its cradle, it was worse. The pain in his hip was excruciating and Stubbs was howling in his crate.

He dialled clumsily, mistakenly getting through to a woman who thought he was a crank call first: 'I'll give you "Can I speak to Kenny Kay?"! Who do you think you are, Lenny Henry?! Tosser!'

He tried again, carefully this time, getting his puff back at last.

It rang for an interminably long time before it was answered. 'Ronnie, Princess! You found me a—'

'It's Lester from Compton Magna Stud speaking, Mr Kay. You may not remem—'

'What d'you want?' The tone was far less friendly. He'd anticipated as much.

'I am calling with an offer I'm certain you'll find hard to resist.' He'd practised this line many times, emulating Ronnie's horse-trading charm.

The bellow of laughter was so loud he had to hold the phone away from his ear. He glanced nervously out of the window, but there was no sign of Pax or Luca. Stubbs was still howling. Kenny was talking again, he realized.

'I'm all ears, Lester. You've given me the best laugh I've had in a long time. The least I can do is listen.'

'Let's go to bed for an hour,' Luca urged Pax, loving the fire in her eyes when she pulled Cruisoe's half-door closed and turned to share a smile they both knew meant mischief.

The morning yard work was done, Ronnie was out for the day, Lester was inside the house, Kes was at school and a black cumulus was about to dump a heavy rain shower on them. It was the perfect moment to step away into their secret world before they began riding.

But Pax worked on a far more rigidly-timetabled schedule than Luca, and she held none of his affection for a comfortable mattress and convenient shower. Taking his hand, she pulled him into the tack room instead, dropping the latch on the door behind them.

'We have twenty minutes,' she instructed between kisses, already pulling off layers of clothing. 'Then I've promised Lester a guided tour of the new AI equipment.'

'Say that again, baby, you know how much work-talk turns me on,' he teased.

Luca had quickly learnt not to let Pax's down-to-earth, curiously feral, sex drive put him off his stroke. After all, he was the one who had told her that sex was sport, he reminded himself. He just hadn't expected her to take the concept quite so literally. Given how competitive Pax was, he supposed he should have known better. She treated it like High Impact Interval Training.

It was often thrilling, occasionally risky, surprisingly chatty, and rarely ever romantic. And while she often led the way, was vocal and greedy and laughed a lot, Luca sensed she got a lot less pleasure out of it than she should. She never allowed any time to talk about what it meant. Talking was something they did elsewhere: about the yard, about family, about their heartbreak and the no-ship rule, but never about sex, unless it was equine reproduction which they discussed all the time. Their sex just happened with sportsmanlike gusto.

Half an hour later, both still flushed from a quickie in the tack room, they showed Lester how the stud would service remote mares, the parallels between work and play uncomfortably close together.

'The racehorse industry is the only one still fixated on sires performing a natural covering,' Pax reminded the old man as they showed off the newly installed dummy mare in the covering barn. She wanted to take advantage of her mother's absence to introduce the stud's retainer to her new ideas without Ronnie and him constantly butting in with recollections of the old days.

Lester simmered with disapproval and mistrust.

'This – *thing* – fools them all?' He waved a crutch at the padded pommel horse that stallions would mount instead of a live mare for semen to be collected.

'Not all of them,' Luca conceded, 'but most can be trained to accept it easily enough, especially with a mare teasing behind the boards. It's safer and more time-efficient than a natural covering.'

'But it's not *natural*,' Lester emphasised the word.

'No more than IVF in humans or routine insemination in dairy.'

'Horses are neither babies nor cattle, a rudimentary mistake many inexperienced owners make.'

Luca could see pain puckered round those tightly creased eyes, the heavy way Lester was leaning on his crutches, but when offered a seat, he'd refused it. 'How do we know our stallions will take to it?'

'Beck covered his mares this way on the Continent,' Pax assured him. 'We've already tested him with it and he remembered exactly what to do.'

'He was a legend at Gestüt Fuchs,' Luca recounted, having broken in the stallion in Germany as a three-year-old. 'He actually got a bit too good at it. There were a couple of competition venues where you had to steer a wide path round full-size horse sculptures, and those life-size plastic horses they use to model tack, you know?'

Lester looked scandalised at the thought.

It amazed Luca that the old boy had so little knowledge of modern stud work, although Pax had explained that he'd never worked anywhere but Compton Magna, recruited by the Captain straight from National Service at twenty and trained on the job. The farm was his life, and its old-fashioned ways were all he'd ever known.

He had to be well past retirement age. When Luca had asked her why Lester's approval was so important, she'd said, 'Because he's the closest thing to Daddy and Grumpa we have; that makes him family.' Given the old man was such an enthusiastic new adopter of the Internet, there was every hope of converting him to more modern practices, she promised.

But Lester had been glowering so much at Luca lately, he suspected he had more to prove besides. Lester knew something was going on between them, and he didn't approve one bit.

They showed him the yard's former laundry room which they'd just cleaned up, scrubbed, sterilised, and equipped with a second-hand fridge-freezer and microscope, explaining how each collection would be filtered, analysed, split into doses and cooled ahead of transporting via courier to mare owners.

'The costs are low,' Luca explained. 'Pax is brilliant at the logistics side, so she can liaise with mare owners and vets to make sure the timing is spot on. It triples the income if one collection can be split three ways.'

'For a stallion like our American boy, that's essential to time in with his competition commitments,' Pax took over, explaining that his AI bookings could be make or break for the yard that season. 'Have you any more detail about when he might arrive, Lester?'

'Soon enough.' Lester gave Luca a frowning, sideways look that caught him unawares.

His stomach knotted, wondering if Meredith might somehow be stalling the deal. Surely not? The Flying Maple Leaf sold hundreds of horses a year. Deals were deals.

'So much is riding on this horse,' Pax said anxiously.

'*You* will be riding on this horse, Pax,' Lester corrected, adding that perhaps he should sit down after all. Luca found him a chair, feeling quite like sitting down with his head in his hands himself.

Luca was astonished Lester hadn't made more of the connection between the big jumping barn in Canada and his recent past. Blair knew all about its potential to blow up in their faces – he and Luca both had a chequered past with the Flying Maple Leaf – but he had clearly stayed tight-lipped.

He knew he should have told Pax, but somehow the opportunity hadn't presented itself. She was supremely edgy around the subject of Meredith, who she was aware Luca now messaged frequently. She also knew that Meredith's marriage was also unravelling, but she never asked about it, just as she never questioned her exchanges with Bay, although she'd spent a lot less time in the back lobby scrolling emojis this week, he'd noticed.

By contrast, he was frequently in amongst the coats offering quick-thumbed moral support. Pax might be aware that Meredith's marriage was as good as over, but she had no idea that her tough-talking father sided with her husband, who was also his business partner. Pax didn't know how impossible her situation was becoming, that Meredith had moved out of the family home and yet she still rode ten young horses a day for her father, sometimes more, because if she didn't, she knew they'd suffer. She didn't know Maple Leaf had threatened to cut his daughter out of everything, including her children's lives, if she didn't fall back into line. Or that it wasn't the first time this had happened. The parallels with Ronnie's past made him especially cautious saying anything to Pax, who was so judgemental. The fact the American stallion was located with Maple Leaf had seemed the least important detail to worry about. Now he wasn't so sure.

'Our stallions will all be on standby for a mare coming into estrus on or off site.' Pax explained to Lester how they would work with owners and their vets, monitoring fertility cycles remotely as well as at home, and that the moment they had warning a mare was ready, the semen could be transported for insemination within twenty-four hours. 'For frozen, it's six hours, but they will already have it there, although the fertility rate is lower. To tap the international market, we must offer frozen. It's almost pure profit, so by far the best new income stream.'

Lester's face softened a little as he listened to her enthusiasm and dedication, appreciating how thoroughly she'd done her planning and costing. Ronnie had handed her a baton and she'd hit the ground running. Luca was unsurprised by her zeal, that typical mercurial passion she threw into everything.

Like sex, for example. He could still feel the aftershocks of it.

He caught Lester looking at him again and forced a smile.

It wasn't returned.

'Ultimately, by far our best option is to take the competition stallion route,' she was saying. 'We can't rival the big studs, but we can offer a unique tailored package and trade on reputation and heritage. This place still has a name that really resonates.'

'So it should...' Lester nodded approvingly, then asked if she would mind fetching him another jumper from the house?

As soon as she was out of earshot, he turned to Luca, his eyes still pain-pinched, but his voice soft, 'Tell me, young man, when you get on a horse that's been badly ridden, do you ride it the same way as the previous jockey did?'

'Of course not.'

'Yet one sees it with so-called tricky horses all the time, don't you agree? The poor things are sold on, over and over, their bad habits returning in each new setting despite well-meaning adjustments. Like that stallion out there, Bechstein.'

'Like Beck, yes.'

'And do you know why that is?'

Luca had no idea where this was going. 'Because it's easier to ride them the way they have always been ridden, I guess.'

'If you say so.'

He tried to explain it better. 'Most riders think that's what the horse wants, not realizing that all those "bad habits" are just barriers built up to protect themselves.'

'Exactly so.' Lester stood up slowly and stiffly. 'If you treat your young ladies with as much respect as you do that stallion, you'll be doing well.'

Luca realized he had just been pep-talked. 'I'll bear that in mind.'

'Mr Robertson was right...' Lester limped towards the door. 'You're not a good fit for this place.'

Luca was shocked. Had Blair really said that? The Australian might have been crabby at first that Ronnie had hired someone with Luca's reputation for flirting his way around the best yards in the world but they'd cleared that up swiftly enough.

Following Lester out to disagree, he found Pax striding back, jumper in arms, face alight with smiles. 'I just checked the stud's email and we have five more provisional bookings for our American boy! They love him.'

Leaving them talking embryo transfer by Lottie's stable, Luca went into the neighbouring yard to see Beck who was bellyaching as usual, head snaking behind his bars. 'You're better than he is,' he told him softly. 'You just need to be somewhere that recognizes that.'

They both did.

*

After the funeral Ronnie joined Bunny and the eventing cronies for a brief drink in the Verney Arms in the nearby village where they toasted Verity.

'Always rather fancied having a pub named after me,' Bunny confided, cueing a barrage of jokes about queens, their brand of old-school eventers being far from woke.

With so many of their ageing horsey rank also still being die-hard puffers, they sat outside to accommodate the smokers. Spring sunshine flashed brightly between buffeting, shower-filled clouds that were moving past too fast to catch them out. Talk swiftly moved on from the funeral service, descending into the usual pre-season badinage, a round-up of holidays and hunting just had, and plans for competing and breeding to come, full of good-natured sparring.

Cross-questioned about the stud's future, Ronnie remained indefatigably positive, talking up Luca's brilliance, Pax's ambitions and their exciting new stallions. 'Compton Magna is back on the map the year, chaps! Our powerhouse German and American hot-blood are going to sire a generation of five-star champions.'

'Tell me about this American stallion? Master Imp's son, isn't he?' demanded a senior national squad rider who bred extensively. 'I might be interested in using him.'

In the past fortnight, she'd had more interest in the one horse not actually at the stud than anything else.

'Cracking little thoroughbred. Come and have a look when he gets here, or he's entered at Maumesby if that's easier.' It was next month's big showcase international, a season opener they needed the horse to run at. Ronnie was banking on it.

'Is he still over the Pond?'

'Better get it here in time!' Guffawed an old rival.

'The buyer's sorting the details out,' she said smoothly, wishing she knew what the hell Lester and his mysterious syndicate were up to. The stallion was in pre-flight isolation and competition fit, he insisted. This one would win Badminton, he promised. Bay was putting up a considerable amount of capital. But the horse had not materialised.

Last night the saintly Bunny had rung round a few old contacts and drummed her up six new visiting mares, but she had no idea what they were going to cover them with if the American deal fell through.

Excusing herself, she took a pee and fired off a text to Bay from the cubicle. *What news of the new stallion?* Remembering he was an owner, however testing, she added *Got lots of interest!*

There was a new voicemail from Kenny Kay, one of the few people she knew who still recorded anything after the beep. The two had played phone tag so far – she never left a message – and his cigar-smoke voice was more corrupt than ever, cackling that he wanted to talk business over dinner. Ronnie remembered him well enough to box clever, especially without Blair around as a sounding board and plus one. The 'lots of hands between your legs' message had set her alarms ringing.

This one was even odder, panting from what sounded like a gym treadmill – or a brothel – that he didn't want half a horse, he wanted a whole horse. 'Two eyes, four legs, both kahunas, you get me? I don't do nothing by halves, Princess.' He gave his smoky cackle, then coughed a lot. 'You've seen the crib, bab. No half measures.'

While Kenny's oversized furniture, cars, security staff and a brace of giant Japanese guard dogs had variously arrived at Compton Manor at anti-social hours over the past fortnight, the star himself had yet to be seen. Each time Ronnie had ridden past, the place still teemed with workmen and interior designers.

The message continued: 'And why d'you get the bloody ostler to call me? Talk to the stablehand, the face ain't listening, is that it? Call me, bab. Personally.'

She rang back, composing a polite message in her head, only to get Kenny in person. 'Princess!'

'I'm confused.' Honesty was the only way.

'Comes to us all, bab, and you're no spring chicken.'

'Am I right in thinking you want to buy a horse, preferably entire?'

'What d'you think I wanted?'

She replayed 'lots of hands' line in her head without the trademark innuendo and realized her mistake. 'I thought you were propositioning me.'

He laughed uproariously at this, coughing a lot and sighing with exaggerated delight. 'You crack me up, bab, That's priceless that is. I'm done with all that bed-hopping, especially posh birds like you. Too athletic. Bad for the back. Retiring to the country is my game. Should have got a place round your way when I was with my Tina, God rest her soul. Might have saved myself a lot of bother.'

'I wasn't aware she'd died. I'm sorry.'

There was a pause which spoke volumes, sad silences all the louder on a sad day.

'She moved to the South of France after we split. Pete looked after her. She liked a quiet life, did Tina, a real homebody. Loved her rose border and her kitchen. I still dream about her scones.' He gave another exaggerated sigh. 'Most of all, she loved her horses. Whole horses. Not 70 per cent of a horse.'

This time the silence was a quick-thinking one as Ronnie pieced the clues together. The 'ostler' had called him, Kenny said. He must mean Lester, who had clearly offered him a share in the American stallion, seven tenths of an entire horse. Not a whole horse.

'Syndicates are absolutely the way to go these days,' she said carefully, surprised by Lester's enterprising guile.

'Like I told the old fella, the only bit of the word syndicate I like is the sin.'

Ronnie felt kismet giving her a leg up. Getting into bed with Kenny on stallion ownership wasn't something she was keen to repeat based on previous experience, but it had its advantages. It would put Bay out of the picture for a start, and his desire to get into bed with Pax kept clouding her judgement. This stallion was too good to leave for Lester to broker.

'What if I can get you this horse without any other owners involved?' she offered, adding 'a whole 100 per cent' for clarification.

'Then it's a done deal. I trust you, Princess. You know your horses.'

'I'll get right back to you.' That would kick Bay back into the long grass.

At the table, conversation had moved onto Blair's precarious future, an old friend confiding, 'He could be forced to give up the farm, have you heard?'

'Surely not?' she gasped.

'Family kept a tight grip on Vee's finances, especially after she got ill. They were the ones with power of attorney. Place was leased in her name from the estate.'

'She'd never have wanted him to lose it!'

'You're rather the wrong person to speak on her behalf, Ron darling.'

Although she was more than accustomed to being ribbed by mutual friends, Ronnie found it in poor taste today, her irritation mounting as the good-natured jibes grew boisterous: 'Planning to move in there yourself are you, Ron?' and 'We all know it's his horses she's after!' then 'He'll never marry you, darling, you're not rich or old enough.'

'Will you all SHUT UP!' she fumed. 'You're all utterly vile.'

'Yes, leave her alone...' Bunny stood up for her gallantly, then left a comic pause '... or you won't be invited to the wedding.' He left another one: '... and neither will she.'

They all fell about.

'We're no longer together,' she snapped, deciding she preferred Kenny's innuendo and sentimentality.

'Of course not.' Bunny was diplomatic. 'If he wants to keep

the farm Blair must be seen to tow the family line for a period of mourning.'

This riled Ronnie more. 'He rides his own bloody lines quite brilliantly. Vee loved that about him. Why should he pander to the Verneys? That family treats him appallingly.'

'He has got thirty-odd horses to feed,' Bunny reminded her.

'Blair doesn't have to suck up to them. I have that many, and I'm nobody's whipping boy.'

'Whipping and sucking being your forte,' goaded one of the nastier of the pack.

Only Bunny defended her, blustering that Vee had been Ronnie's friend too. The awkward silence that followed reminded Ronnie that death changes everything, that losing one of their own always left the others scrabbling for the moral high ground. Even amongst their close-knit circle, she'd defaulted to Bad Ronnie, a lifetime of infidelity's knocks teaching her that Oscar Wilde was right – *one can survive everything, nowadays, except death, and live down everything except a good reputation.*

When Bunny drove her back to collect her car from his country pile where she'd once rented a cottage a few fields from Blair's yard, she found herself wishing aloud that she could turn back the clock. 'We were so happy and so naughty; I always had my weekend bag packed.'

'You know you can move back anytime, my darling,' Bunny insisted, 'but I don't think Mr Robertson will stick around these parts long, do you? My hunch is he'll go back to Australia for good. He's talked about it often enough.'

'Don't give away the honeymoon destination,' she joked flatly. The thought of Blair decamping was like an ice bath, but it made sense. He often went back several months each year, had a breeding programme there, four generations of family, old friends. And there were no memories of Verity halfway around the world. Or cash-strapped mistresses.

'You two have always said you'd be hopeless full-timers,'

Bunny warmed to his theme. 'Why fuck up a fuck-buddy friendship?'

'I loathe that term,' she said, shuddering.

'You're a tough bird, Ronnie. My advice is to cut your losses. Move on. It doesn't do to trespass on grief.' She saw the worry in his watery eyes, realized this was a lecture she needed to hear, from a friend she'd known even longer than she had Blair. And he was right. Given free rein, Blair would gallop for open country. They were far too alike that way.

She drove for home, listening to Bowie at full blast, refusing to stew. Stopping for fuel and a pee break between Marlborough and Swindon, she checked her phone messages, willing him to break cover if only to confirm Bunny's warning. She started composing one to him then deleted it.

A break was a break, especially now he was a widower. She knew the rules. She must wait, even if that meant waiting while he flew halfway around the world.

They weren't over yet. Ronnie just had to believe it.

Showering in the cottage after riding, Pax had company and a freshly made tea, which Luca left steaming on the back of the basin as he climbed in with her.

'How long until you fetch Kes from school?' he said, moving behind her to soap her back.

'Half an hour.'

They'd done this more than once, for practical as much as sensual reasons. They both usually wanted to wash off traces of sex, and the water in his little attic bathroom in the main house only got lukewarm at best.

The cottage bathroom was as far from a fantasy as Pax could imagine. It had a small, cracked enamel bath with an octopus-themed shower curtain, a rattly extractor fan and mouldy grouting. Kes's bath toys were group around the taps like a brightly coloured dogging crowd.

They'd had sex in here twice, both times ending in squelchy wet laughter rather than a crescendo of mutual pleasure. Pax was constantly too tense for crescendos anyway.

So when Luca's soapy fingers slid between her legs, she pushed them away. 'There's no time.'

'Twenty minutes.' He kissed her neck. 'And you do nothing, got it? Do not move an inch.'

She grumbled that her tea would get cold in twenty minutes.

'Humour me, here.'

She did as he asked.

After twenty minutes, Pax knew she'd never look at it the cottage's dingy little bathroom the same way again. The little tub was a boat in which Luca had rowed her through the gin-clear waters of a Caribbean atoll, the curtains its coral reefs, Kes's toys its colourful sea life and the extractor fan the swish of the oars.

The cold tea tasted as good as champagne, her hands shaking so much she had to hold the mug with both.

She didn't want to spoil the moment by asking Luca where he'd learnt to do that or why they hadn't tried it before, she was just grateful he had. Still no ship, but her boat had come in.

'Next time,' he told her as he towelled her dry, 'I want a *lot* longer than twenty minutes, angel.' He dropped a kiss on her shoulder. 'I adore you.'

'And I'm crazy about you.'

You're just borrowing him, she reminded herself, more than happy to settle for adoration and a bathroom that made her blush.

She knew he was messaging Meredith. What worried her more was the fear that he might be drinking again.

22

Driving into Compton Magna at dusk and glancing across at the stud's fields from the village lane, the sharp, familiar pain in Ronnie's chest told her that she couldn't face going home right now. The atmosphere there was too tense: Pax was on self-destruct, Luca distanced and distracted, Lester back on his feet and determined to wrestle back authority. She longed even more for her carefree little cottage on Bunny's estate and secret trysts with Blair in the woods.

She turned to glance up at the standing stone witches in Church Meadow, remembering Hermia quoting Shakespeare there with a pageboy bob, decrying life's brief candle.

Once the foals started arriving, she knew everyone would cheer up, but she felt down in the dumps today, past mistakes haunted her waking thoughts like eye floaters. Funerals always depressed her, that sharp reminder of one's insignificance and brevity.

She drove on to the manor house to see if there were any signs of Kenny in situ, but it was still crawling with workmen. On impulse, she swung the car into Church Lane and parked beside The Old Almshouse where Kit was, predictably, in his greenhouse, wrestling with Sassoon just as she'd hoped he'd be.

He seemed gratifyingly happy for the interruption, explaining that he was struggling with the Western Front, and inviting her into the house to take pot luck with the herbal teas.

'Have you got anything stronger?' she asked as she followed him in. 'We've hidden absolutely everything alcoholic at the stud and these yardarms are sunning themselves on a rare day off.' She thrust her hands wide, watching his wry smile as he fetched a brandy bottle from a cupboard.

'Are you sure you want to break such devoted Lent abstinence?'

'It's not my abstinence to break,' she took the glass gratefully, 'although I blame you giving me a taste for it.' She shot him a mock-reproachful look, taking a sip which burned blissfully deep and tasted of good memories

'Tough day, I take it?' He eyed the black dress beneath the formal coat.

'Buried a friend.'

'To your friend, then.' He chinked his glass rim against hers and crossed the room to flop onto a sofa, indicating for her to do likewise. 'I was hoping I might see you. That head teacher woman is on my case about her ruddy *Mamma Mia!* production and still scouting round for a Donna.'

'Absolutely not! I'm far too busy and at least ten years too old.' She prowled the little room, looking at its many pictures of Hermia onstage. 'She would have been quite brilliant, of course.'

'Utterly.' He smiled. 'And she'd have loved doing it.'

'Whereas I am merely well-suited by virtue of wanderlust and a racy reputation.' She paced on restlessly. 'It was Blair's wife. The funeral.'

'Ah.'

'She's been ill a long time. I think I told you that.'

'Does that leave the field clear for you two?'

She winced. 'Less bluntly put than some, but still...'

'Sorry, far too soon.'

'It most certainly is.' She strode up and down his hearthrug.

'And the thing is, we're neither of us very good with empty fields, Blair and I, we prefer obstacles. It's the competitive horse riders in us.'

He regarded her with amused interest. 'You really are just as contrary as Hermia always said.'

'Oh God, d'you think so?' She perched on the sofa opposite. 'Isn't it awful? And I'm rather afraid my daughter's the same. There's the most glorious, available, kind-hearted suitor right under her nose, and Pax holds a torch for the screwed-up, duplicitous one.'

He continued to regard her with psychoanalytical interest. 'Tell me, which screwed-up, duplicitous individual do *you* hold a candle for, Mrs Ledwell?'

Ronnie admired the directness. He was good at this. Hermia had said as much. Then again, he had read some of her letters. He probably already knew. 'Who do you think it is?'

He held the gaze with a weighted, Pinteresque pause for dramatic effect, one eyebrow lifting. 'Me?'

Ronnie snorted with laughter, grateful for light relief. 'You are *so* dry. I love it! Goodness, that would be funny, wouldn't it?'

'Hilarious.' He smiled thinly.

She looked into her glass, shocked it was empty, its fireball heat still unfurling inside her. She needed to unburden to somebody and Kit was the only one who knew at least a part of the story. 'When I told you about Peter Sanson wooing Hermia, I omitted to mention something rather important.'

'What?' He glowered.

'You remember I said that he and Kenny had a laddish wager about deflowering us both that first summer?'

'Go on...'

'Well, Kenny won it hands down.'

He set his glass on the table in surprise.

She gave him a rueful smile. 'I've always had rather a weakness for being laughed into bed, you see.'

'How old were you?' the eyebrow arched again.

'Eighteen, and already thoroughly deflowered. He was married to the saintly Tina, and an utter rogue. Hermia gave me a frightful telling off. I put a stop to it pretty damned fast after that, although Kenny never gave up asking for second helpings, even after I married.

'By the time Peter Sanson bought Eyngate and wooed Hermia with flowers and fast cars, my marriage was firmly on the rocks. I'd had two babies in quick succession and Johnny was tiring of us all – in hindsight, he was driving himself mad with living a lie. We went on a make-or-break holiday without the children, which was a disaster. Kenny was busy working his way through Miss World contestants a continent at a time – and still miraculously married to the saintly Tina – but it didn't stop him trying it on when I got back with a mahogany tan and a balsawood marriage. And in a moment of weakness, I succumbed again. I needed cheering up. Then I found out I was pregnant.'

'Are you saying Pax is Kenny Kay's daughter?'

'No! She was conceived on that awful holiday with Johnny – once is enough, drunken as it was – but Kenny refused to believe it. He and Tina had been trying for ages, and he got obsessed with the idea he was going to be a father, that he had proof of his own fertility. He told Daddy he would look after me, spare the family any scandal, and like the fool he was my father swallowed it for a large cash incentive. Then Kenny changed his mind and ran off with one of the Miss World contenders. According to village legend, Daddy shot him.'

'Did you say *shot*?'

'It's been wildly exaggerated over time. There was an accident at an Eyngate shoot. There's no way Daddy would have taken aim at a fellow gun. Even if he did, he missed, thankfully. At least, missed most of him.' She repeated Kenny's Dave Allen tribute finger line, which made Kit laugh.

'Sorry to dump all this on you.' She picked up her glass, remembered it was empty and set it down again.

'Dump away, it's sensational,' he said, pouring her another. 'A much-needed contrast to the Western Front.'

'Sensational?' She weighed the word.

He rephrased it for her drily, 'Indulge my senses – please don't stop.'

Ronnie looked down at the brandy. 'I'll have to leave my car here if I drink this.'

'Good, that means you'll come back for it. Or just not leave.' He smiled, reminding her how single-mindedly attentive he could be. 'Now tell me about your father shooting Kenny's finger off?'

'I wasn't there. Lester was loading and Mummy was picking up and they both swore it was an accident.'

'But you don't think so?'

She decided to have another sip after all. 'Ancient history.'

'My forte. Set the scene.' He steepled his fingertips and looked over them.

'Stop being a director!' Ronnie laughed.

'I'm the audience.' He was rapt.

'All right.' She set her glass down. 'My father – who was perennially cash strapped – leapt at the idea of lots of lolly when Kenny told him he wanted to invest in the stud and buy his unborn child a future. Johnny was too far down a bottle with the black dog for company to pay much heed, but Mummy was apoplectic. She believed me when I told her the baby was Johnny's. The dates matched up, and I'd always used my diaphragm with Kenny.'

'Mmm?' Kit's steepled fingers interlocked, his eyebrows reangling.

Suspecting she'd overshared that detail, Ronnie took broader brushstrokes. 'It was a well-worn local rumour that Kenny and Peter both wanted to buy the stud as part of their wager to return the village to feudal ownership, so there was clearly a coup d'état at play. Their reputation as hellraisers was atrocious. Everyone knew poor Mrs Kay was keeping the home fires burning in the Brum gin palace while Misses Costa Rica, Brazil and Peru were Monday, Wednesday and Friday respectively. And Peter Sanson was feeding Hermia caviar in an Antiguan beach hut at the time.'

'Is that relevant?' He looked pained.

'Very.' She patted her hot cheeks. 'You remember I said Peter dropped Hermia like a stone and came rushing back when Kenny walked out on Tina?'

'So Kenny left his wife for you?'

'No, thank goodness. Ha! Here's the twist. The tabloids were full of another story. It turned out Kenny had got Miss Venezuela or Colombia or somewhere pregnant at the same time as claiming my bump was his. And there was no doubt about the parentage, her being a seventeen-year-old global ambassador who loved children and believed in world peace. That proved the final straw for poor, saintly Tina, who ironed a month's worth of Kenny's shirts, packed them between tissue paper in his Pierre Cardins, and told him to sling his hook.'

'So she threw him out?' Kit was finger-steepling again, gaze intent.

'Cue Peter's exit from the Caribbean, leaving Hermia swinging on a hammock. My guess is both men had been in love with Tina since childhood. Flash Kenny might have been the one to win her heart, but best man Peter never gave up hope. That's what the wager was all about. They'd tried to outdo each other lavishing her with gifts. She adored horses, so the moment Kenny got rich he bought her showjumpers. When she'd set eyes on Compton Magna Stud and said she'd always dreamt of living somewhere like that, it became a big boys' game to them to get hold of the place for Tina. Peter bought Eyngate instead, which was frankly just showing off, while Kenny still had his eyes on the real deal. He was forever telling Daddy he'd take it off his hands, making ridiculous offers, and joking he'd convert one of the stable yards into garaging for his supercars. The answer was always no, but there's no doubt his leading sires helped prop up the stud farm for much of the eighties.

'When Tina realized the showbiz stud she'd married had sired his own line, Peter swooped in like a knight in shining armour to gather into his arms, and Tina became chatelaine of Eyngate. Meanwhile, Kenny shacked up with his pregnant Miss World; I hung onto my marriage such as it was and Hermia was free to marry you. It was all remarkably civilised. The Kays' showjumpers even stayed at the stud.'

'A Shakespeare comedy fifth act?'

'Tragedy's fourth. Kenny got shot, don't forget. And he wasn't the only casualty.'

'Of course, the shooting accident. How did that come about?'

'It must have been a few months later because I was quite pregnant by then and didn't go. Peter was hosting a big charity shoot at Eyngate to which he'd invited some serious movers and shakers, as well as a few local guns like Daddy. Sanson's shoots were notoriously over-catered and unruly, with too many game birds and poor sight lines on the drives. Daddy kept telling him off. Kenny was there for showbiz glitter – their friendship had survived Tina changing sides – and behaving particularly badly, I gather. Daddy was still fuming that Kenny had welshed on their deal. He'd already spent half the money in anticipation, you see. According to witnesses, Daddy started shouting at Kenny never to darken our door again. Somehow Kenny got shot, along with a local man. All hushed up of course.'

Kit pressed his glass rim to his chin. 'D'you think Kenny's now back for revenge?'

She shivered. 'Please God, no. He's made a career out of that missing finger. And I wasn't there that day so can't vouchsafe anything, but Daddy always insisted Kenny was the one who lost his cool and started waving his gun around like John Wayne. It was Nat Turner who was most badly hurt that day.'

'The traveller?'

'He was out beating for the shoot. I think he worked a lot for Peter back then, a factotum bodyguard-come-driver. He was always with them, chauffeuring Tina around in those big souped-up cars – she was too frightened to drive any of them, I remember. After he got injured, Nat was never the same, always getting in trouble and disappearing for weeks on end. Took to the road year-round in the end, only coming home to unpack his wagon when he wanted to dump his two kids and their mother on the Turner elders. His poor little wife just hid at home, and the children were feral, especially Ash. Daddy was always catching him up to no good on our land – although it soon became Sanson Holdings land.

'Daddy started selling parcels to Peter Sanson. Lots of them. It went on for years. I tried to talk to him about it – we'd begun building bridges after Johnny's death, particularly once Pax was competing. But Daddy was absolutely trap-tight on the subject of Sanson. In hindsight, the stud must have been running at a catastrophic loss. I booked to come down and stay so I could see Pax after she'd finished her lower sixth year and planned to have it out with him face to face, but – well, I didn't stay as long as I intended.'

'I know what happened between you and Bay.'

'Of course. It's in my letters.' She looked away, too bruised by the episode to linger on it.

'Hermia was furious with Bay...' Kit wanted to linger.

'I was equally to blame.' She shrugged. 'I wanted to see off my thirties with a bang. It should have been what Erika Jong called a zipless fuck.'

'You really didn't know who he was?'

'Not a clue. Bay had been a small child when I left the village. Hermia wrote about him in her letters, of course – and then Pax was besotted once they started going out together, so I knew he must be something special – but our paths hadn't crossed again. Not till I spent a night in one of the Austens' holiday cottages, and a gorgeous young blood stumbled in expecting to find somebody else. There was no romance to it whatsoever, it was just thrill-seeking. We hardly even spoke. If we had, we might have got on first names terms and worked out that his girlfriend was my daughter.'

'Hermia blamed Bay totally.'

'It takes two...' Ronnie sighed ruefully. 'I knew what we were doing, I just didn't know who he was. Neither of us did. Pax was devastated.'

'Hermia said they'd have been perfect together.'

'No, Pax was far too young and inexperienced,' she said hotly. 'Bay was a horny twenty-one-year-old with a lot more wild oats to sew, and she was fresh out of school. Their timing was wrong.'

'She said that too.'

She pressed her fingers to her mouth for a moment, staring at the glass on the coffee table until the tempest in her head circled away again. 'Hermia was so kind about it when my family were utterly unforgiving. We wrote to each other a lot that year – it would be the year before her accident. Pax had run off to London and my parents were in a frightful state. It was like losing me all over again, their flag-bearer and jockey, and in Pax's case the sanest business head around. She was only seventeen but knew far more about running the stud on budget than my mother who lived to hunt, and Daddy who merely flogged land to Sanson to survive. They just left it all up to Lester, who is encyclopaedic on bloodlines but quite hopeless on bottom lines.

'Hermia sweetly kept an eye on them all and kept me in the loop. Sanson used to make regular grand visits to Eyngate in those days, piles of hangers-on in tow. Always made a big show of bringing them to the pub. Daddy would go along, suited and booted in his county show best.'

'I remember it,' Kit shuddered. 'They used to take over the Hare. I never understood why your father was there. They were all so lawless, so self-entitled.'

'He was very corruptible. I'll never forget Hermia's letter when she found out Daddy was selling the old gallops. It really was the final straw. Mummy wrote to me too, burying her fears amid the usual starchy news, but it was obvious, reading between the lines, that she thought Daddy was spending too much time with Sanson and his cronies. They were all rich knuckle-scrapers, drinking champagne and careering off in supercars. She thought they'd crash into a tree like Johnny or—' She stopped.

Kit was looking at her with such compassion she had to look away, because she wasn't thinking about Johnny at all.

She took a breath, quashing the thought that had just ripped through her conscience. 'Poor Mummy. Pax was up to all sorts in London at the time, a complete wild child. I let them both down horribly.'

Kit watched her through a long pause, then said carefully, 'Tell me, did you ever have a paternity test for Pax?'

She switched sofas to plonk beside him, clinking their glasses together. 'She has Johnny's mother's hair and she rides like a gypsy. Of *course* she's his, although I did have a bit of a flirt with James Hewitt around then. Post Diana. He hunted with the Fosse Vale occasionally. Thick as two short planks, but super lower leg.'

'You know, I *really* think you should reconsider playing Donna in *Mamma Mia!*.'

She laughed. 'Oh, you *have* cheered me up. Now I want you to tell me all about your Sherston play and what you're stuck on – if it's not too painful to explain to an ignoramus. I've been reading the trilogy.'

'You have?' He looked terribly pleased and she made a mental note to start reading it that night.

Except she didn't get a chance to, because at that moment, he kissed her.

And it shouldn't have felt as good as it did, but it was wonderful.

23

Mo thought it was high time everyone stopped talking about her and Barry. She'd had enough of the curtain-twitching on the cul-de-sac and elbow nudging at the school gates. He was now living with his new lady friend and that was that.

He'd been gone long enough for it to be old news, if moving to the far end of the village constituted 'gone'. To his credit, he'd kept a very low profile. Mo's friends insisted she should hold her head high but facing scrutiny and humiliation each day was a cold, hard shock. Poor Grace was being ever so brave, saying that lots of her school friends' parents went through difficult patches too, and it was like Tilly's mum and dad splitting up and that Tilly had just got a new pony, lots of clothes and was going to have two foreign holidays this year, so it wasn't all bad.

Mo hadn't the heart to explain that you couldn't put a price on lost pride.

It was her next-door neighbour who had told her the unabridged truth about her husband and Beverley, AKA the Dog Tart, a thirty-something married pooch groomer who lived on the far side of Broadbourne. She said it had been the talk of the Orchard Estate for weeks, where Dog Tart's sister lived, one of the single mother brigade who had adopted Barry as unpaid handyman. The Don Draper and Midge Daniels of the Comptons had first met when he fixed her jammed washing-machine door. Now Mo was the latest recruit to the single mum brigade and Barry was getting his smalls washed by Dog Tart in the Austens' farm cottage that came with his job.

The village scandalmongers still wouldn't let it drop. The Orchard Estate kept buzzing with it, the school mums still shot her embarrassed, sympathetic looks, nobody knowing what to say to her face, although they were chatty enough behind their hands to one another: 'She really didn't see it coming, did you know?'... 'Been going on for months'... 'It was all over Facebook.'

His betrayal hurt more than a perforated ulcer, broken leg and concussion all rolled into one, but Mo didn't want the world and his wife knowing that, so she kept her chin up. She was a pragmatist, and she had her dignity. She wasn't one to have public shouting matches, hire expensive lawyers or throw herself into new love affairs, lifestyle choices and funky new haircuts like Pax Forsyth. She couldn't afford to for a start.

Barry had stopped all his automatic payments into the joint account, insisting Mo must message him whenever a bill was due so that he could transfer the funds. Their marriage had become a gig economy.

He'd built quite a chip on his shoulder that so much of his contracting income had been diverted into renovating the bungalow he hated on the promise of taking over a rundown smallholding that never materialized. It was only now Mo realized quite how much he resented propping up his in-laws' farming income and Jan's well-being when it meant missing out on holidays, boys' toys, nights out and Netflix. A few weeks living the high life had opened his eyes.

Now he'd tasted all these luxuries in swift succession – along with enough forbidden fruit to satisfy his five a day for years to come – he wanted more.

Mo thought he was behaving like a small child, but she guessed this was his way of feeling in control now he'd triggered the eject button (or his lady friend had; she didn't dwell on that side of things). Their real child was far too important to let her own feelings get in the way, so Mo kept things practical for Grace's sake, avoided conflict, and kept a careful note of bills so that she knew when to message him.

They communicated almost exclusively by messaging app. She hadn't realized how bad his spelling was until now. But his maths was improving wholesale. He even used spreadsheets. And he seemed increasingly obsessed by money.

She tried not to keep totting up the cost in her head when he started buying Grace 'presents' to be kept at his place: a smartphone one week, an electric guitar the next. Mo had to keep her opinions to herself, determined their daughter mustn't be made to judge, that she needed both parents' love, her natural kindness and good cheer already sorely tested. Enough of Grace's tears had been shed.

She dealt with her own upset swiftly and privately – a quick cry in the bath, or when she was feeding the pigs was all she allowed herself – and she took everything one week at a time to keep things simple.

Mo avoided all those caring, sharing friends who wanted her to open up about it. Talking about her feelings wasn't her style, besides which, most folks couldn't help themselves gossiping. She'd dropped hacking out with the Bags for that reason, as well as not trusting their partisan offers of revenge. The village Facebook page was firmly out of bounds.

Occasionally, she caught herself wondering when the stupid idiot would realize it was all a mistake and come home.

Growing up on a farm had also taught Mo that when something broke free – be it animal, vegetable or silly sod – nine times out of ten it found its own way back. The trick was never to force it, give it time and patience.

Regrettably, her parents had never adopted this approach

to agriculture or to husbandry, which could be the reason the place was on its knees.

There was no telling Sid and Joan Stokes to drop the subject. Every day they demanded Mo knock some sense into their son-in-law. They said she was too soft on him. They said she should send the vicar round to talk to him. They even offered to pay somebody to threaten him. 'Old Norm Turner can find a man'll duff him up a bit. Put the scarers on. His Nat used to be handy like that.'

Today, Dad needed help sowing the broad beans, and she'd been so busy all day that it was almost dusk by the time she could lend a hand. Having given Mo a thirty-minute lecture across the furrows on why she must go straight round and fetch Barry home, he grumbled she owed money to both Flynn the farrier and his old farming crony who supplied their straw. 'You're giving us a bad name. I could hardly hold my head up in the pub last night.'

'Yeah, and how big's your bar tab at the moment, Dad?' Now a gastro-pub gunning for a Michelin star, The Jugged Hare herded locals into one small, dim corner like petting zoo attractions with a full sawdust and tankard backdrop. The prices were ridiculous, but weathered oldies like Sid who had drunk there over forty years refused to go elsewhere on principle.

Dad stepped across a seed row to pat her coat arm with a mud-crusted glove. 'You're no good without your Barry checking your figures.'

Or my figure Mo though hollowly, the weight dropping off her unnoticed beneath all the layers. She was furious people were talking about her finances. It was true – and unfortunate – that they currently had three vacant livery spaces, and another two were behind on payments. Times were tough for everyone right now, so she'd let that pass when she could afford to and now it was a lot to ask back. Plus, the tractor gearbox had bust again, there were leaks in stable roofs and broken fencing. But she still kept a tight eye on things. Didn't gamble her money like Dad, who had a wager on the Turners' bout.

'Put fifty quid on Nat Turner winning,' he boasted.

'*Nat?*' she scoffed, horrified. 'Who even says he's fighting? It's Ash versus Jed.' Her one-time Turner bad-boy crush felt like a distant comfort.

'Not what I heard.' He tapped his red-veined nose. 'Nat is planning on setting up on Church Meadow and fighting till the last, according to the lads in the pub.'

When they went inside the farmhouse for a cup of tea, Mum was lying in wait with Jan, both cornering her over a garibaldi.

'We've had words with Barry,' Joan announced in a hushed voice. 'Well, your sister has. She went on the pill again. Told him she needs him here right now.'

'You did what?'

'Mum means my tablet.' Jan's shakes were bad, a sure sign she felt stressed. 'I went on my tablet, sis. Messaged him on Facebook.'

'Why d'you—'

'Playing Cupid,' Joan interrupted eagerly. 'Jan told him how much you're missing him. That he needs to come home to be a husband and dad. Asides, her bed hoist needs fixing again.'

'Locking pin got stuck as usual,' Jan nodded.

'The council will come and fix it, you know that.'

'Don't trust them lot,' Sid grumbled.

'What did Barry say?' Mo sighed.

'He's upstairs fixing it right now.'

The news smashed the safety glass on Mo's heart. 'Then I'm going out.'

'You are *not*, Maureen!' Mum ordered. 'You'll stay and you'll sort this thing out. Come on, Sid, Jan. We're opening up the Hut for a couple of hours, get the last of that kale sold.'

'It's getting dark, woman!'

'So, you never heard of late-night opening? Grace can come and help.'

'Where *is* Grace?' Mo looked round.

'Up there with her dad, but we'll take her with us. She loves playing shop with her Auntie Jan. GRAAAACE!'

Pink-faced with happiness that her father was back, Grace bounced downstairs.

Before she could protest, Mo found herself sitting opposite her husband in her parents' kitchen, a collie panting to either side, tasked with 'sorting this out'.

Barry couldn't look at her at all and Mo found herself as tongue-tied as she'd been on their first ever date, albeit a lot keener to hit him over the head with a saucepan. It was the first time she'd been alone with him since his departure. She felt ambushed.

Barry looked alien these days. Beard gone, sideburns neatly clipped, red face smooth and shiny – had he been *moisturising*? – and eyebrows plucked, he looked like a drag queen on her day off.

'You keeping well, are you?' she asked tightly.

'Can't complain.' His ruddy cheeks were truly aglow, eyes downcast.

She didn't recognize his clothes, crisp with newness. The discreet little Burberry and Ralph Lauren labels on them came as a shock. He'd always lived in Dickie farming workwear, bought from the feed merchant. His nails were the cleanest she'd ever seen them. She stared at his hands, unable to stop herself imagining them exploring another woman's body, taking pleasure from it in a way her hefty barrel no longer offered him. Even a stone lighter, she had yet to find a waist.

She forced her head back into the room, here, today. 'I didn't see your car in the yard.'

'Got a new one. It's parked on the lane. Nevada hybrid. Got to save the planet. It's leased.' He added quickly, 'Beverly has a friend in the business.'

'Course.' She kept her gaze fixed on his hands cupping the mug, trying to stop herself visualising them on the Dog Tart's thighs. Did she cry out in pleasure like in the movies? Mo was a squeaker, her surprise at bed pleasure still thrilling her when the mood stuck. Or it had. Barry had been her first, her only, lover. Who would want her now?

He was talking about money, she realized. Something about the Austens putting rent up for the farm cottage. 'We need a more formal arrangement about the bills and stuff. I can't keep shelling out.'

'As long as Grace always comes first,' she said quickly because that was most important right now.

'Course she does. I'll be there for her just as much. It's not like I'm far away.'

Yet it felt like he was a continent away to Mo, the husband she'd known setting sail for a new life without warning.

Looking at him, she had a curious sense that he was just as much at sea as she was, but to say so would be foolish. Instead, she said. 'She misses you. God knows why.' She clamped her mouth cat-bum tight to stop herself adding *I miss you too*. God knows why.

There was a glassy look in his eyes. He excused himself to the loo.

She checked her phone, ashamed to find her hands shaking. Petra had left three messages in quick succession offering a box of her girls' old books for Grace, the most recent one *I'll call round about five*.

She looked at the clock. It was ten to.

Don't, she typed hurriedly, *Barry's here*.

When a line of shocked emoji faces came back, she wished she'd been more circumspect.

He came back from the loo looking even redder and shinier, smelling strongly of cheap hand soap. Sitting down, he still couldn't look her in the eye. 'I need to fetch some more of my stuff from the bungalow today. I've told Grace she should pick out a few things to keep at mine too. We've also bought her some new clothes, did she say?'

Why that, in particular, ignited her, Mo had no idea – Grace always needed clothes – but at once she was molten, murderous with anger. There was a pause through which she determinedly stared at those big, familiar too-clean hands, still imagining them on another woman's skin, and refused to let herself shout that nothing of her daughter's would go to his dirty love shack.

'Bev's looking forward to getting to know her better,' he went on. 'We're planning a few days away soon, all of us together.'

It was the 'we', she realized: *we've* bought her some new clothes, *we're* planning. She counted to ten before asking his clean hands, 'She got kids of her own, has she?'

'Not—'He stopped himself. 'No.'

Mo's own knuckles whitened in her lap, guessing that he had been about to say not yet. 'Just dogs, then?'

'She grooms them, but she's not got one right now. Too busy building the business. She's worked hard.'

The pride in his voice felt like blades in her side. 'We all do that.'

'Yeah.' She sensed he was smiling. That superior smile she hated. The one that he flashed when she talked about the little livery yard where she undercharged everyone and let those who were struggling miss the odd bill, which was why it made so little money, almost all of it going to Mum and Dad, to the farm her parents wouldn't give up.

'You'll still keep paying the mortgage, though?' she asked, looking up worriedly. Which was when she realized that he wasn't smiling at all. That shiny, hair-stripped face was quilted with tension.

'It might not be easy, love. Like I say, the Austens have put the rent up and Bev and me, we want a place of our own where she can run the grooming business.' He looked down at his hands too, the big thumbs rolling round each other.

She forced her eyes up to glare at the top of his head, where his hair was thinning on his thick skull, beneath which was a selfish, scheming mind that had thought this all through in secret, talked about it to his mistress as they planned his getaway.

So why couldn't she stop a nagging question mark dangling from her subconscious? Why did she sense something wasn't right, and found herself fighting a desire to cover those thumbs with her hand and say are you OK, what happened to us, this isn't just about money is it?

Instead she just talked about money. 'I can't afford it on my own, Barry. The business here hardy covers its costs, you know that.'

'More of a hobby though, isn't it?'

'I can't believe you just said that.'

'You could move back with your mum and dad, like Ronnie Percy's daughter did when she and her fella bust up.'

This didn't sound like him at all. She wondered how scripted it was, whether she was hearing another woman's words. 'You suggesting I should move in here?'

'Just saying that's what she's done. She and her bloke were doing up a big place over Stow way. Bet they sell it quick. Buyers like a project.' He cleared his throat, looked up at her, and she knew the words he was struggling to put together in a line.

'You want to sell the bungalow?' She felt weightless and hollow, as though gravity had suddenly stopped working.

'Well, neither of us like the place.'

'It's our *home*, Barry. Our daughter's home. I'm not parting with our home!'

'Of course not!' He held up the big hands. Hands that had lifted their baby seconds after her first cry to her new world. Hands that had laid their new pipework, plastered their walls, fixed the leaking flat roof. Hands that now rested on Bev's body every night. Hands that might never hold hers again.

Why did she want to grasp them, squeeze them, not let them go?

'You've barely been gone five minutes,' she pointed out.

'It's been over a month.'

'That long?' She started at the realization, felt the steel cage of self-protection clamp round her. 'Well, don't you worry, I'll get another job, I'll be fine.'

His big face softened, off script now. 'Course I worry, love. You've no time as it is.'

'Yeah, what with all my *hobbies*.'

'You're an unpaid carer.'

'I don't need paying to look after my loved ones! Why's it all about *money* with you?' She counted again to calm herself down.

His gaze trailed round the familiar kitchen she loved, 'This place will fall apart before we ever get our hands on it.'

'Not your problem anymore, Barry.'

He hesitated, cleared his throat again, went even redder. And she felt it as surely as a blast of cold air from an open door, his fear. Surely he wasn't frightened of Mo?

'Mum and Dad think I'm asking you to come back right now,' she told him, forcing a laugh.

'And you're not?' He stared fixedly down at the table.

If she begged, would he, she wondered? What if she pleaded for Grace's sake? Would he agree to try again if she promised to lose weight, wear sexy lingerie, get a spray tan and be sexually available every night? Perhaps if she offered to get formal care assessment for Jan and her parents, to push them into choosing between a quieter life in the bungalow and endless nosy intervention from social services? Would he come back if they got to run the farm at last? Had this always been about the farm?

She would never know because she would never ask. Pride and scalding anger kept her mute as she watched him drink her parents' tea from a cracked mug in their warm, well-worn kitchen, waiting on her to speak again.

Her phone rang to fill the gap. She snatched it up. 'Mo Dawkins.'

'At last! The right number!' rasped a ridiculously Brummy voice. 'Name's Kenny Kay.'

It was 100 per cent a wind up, Mo realized.

'I'm sorry, did you say *Kenny Kay?*'

Across the table, Barry's mug landed back on the table with a thud at the mention of his idol's name.

'That's right, bab.'

Whoever it was was good. The Bags were bound to be behind it.

She gazed at her husband's wide-eyed face. 'I'm just putting you on speakerphone, Mr Kay.'

Barry sat up straight and smoothed his hair, as though the great man was stepping into the room.

'What can I do for you?' she asked when she had.

'More what I can do for you, bab,' his famous voice boomed out like a podcast clip. 'I hear from a good friend you might be looking for a spot of work?'

Now Barry was scoffing in disbelief, looking round the room as though it was bugged.

'I am, Mr Kay, what a stroke of luck,' Mo told the caller, realizing it had to be Petra's husband Charlie, demon impersonator and confirmed prankster. This was typical Bags' mischief, hastily organized by Petra after reading Mo's message saying Barry was here. Normally she'd be livid, but right now she was too mad at Barry to care. 'I'm just saying goodbye to someone. Let me quickly see them out and we'll talk more privately. Can I call you Kenny?'

'With pleasure, sweetheart. That accent of yours is Caramel Bunny gorgeous. You as pretty as you sound?'

Barry looked furious, especially when Mo started to chivvy him out, enjoying this now. He got up and stomped to the door, muttering that they'd speak again when she and her friends had stopped playing silly buggers.

As soon as he'd gone, Mo leant over the phone, telling the

caller, 'You should have *seen* his face! I don't know who you are, but I love you forever for this!'

'And I love you, bab. Just Google Kenny Kay and you'll find out who I am. Been in the States too long, but I'm due a cult following amongst you younger generations. Now, where was I? Oh yes – job interview.' He lowered his voice. 'Tell me, what d'you look like, Caramel Bunny?'

Charlie Gunn was being a cheeky sod, but she had his measure. 'Petite, blonde, size six, huge knockers, get mistaken for a young Kylie a lot. Flat head for resting pints on.' Realizing this would incur the feminist sister wrath of the Bags, she quickly added, 'Helps with deportment and it keeps my hands free for more important things.' Was that any better? 'Like wrestling.' There.

The boom of laughter almost took her ear off. 'You've got the job! Officially, you're my PA. Hours to suit.' He named a rate that proved it was a prank. 'Confidentially, I need you to be my eyes in the village, OK, bab?'

She sighed, feeling sad again, because all the eyes of the village were on her. 'OK, Charlie.'

'No, bab,' he threw in an extra-seedy chuckle, 'it's Kenny.'

24

'Come at it again... one... two... three... four... five... super! Another time... steady ... shorten... good... good... brilliant! Feel that? She's got some scope!'

An afternoon's training with a showjumping coach Lizzie had recommended was just the respite Pax needed.

Jumping down a grid of fences, each successive one larger, blew away her worries.

Don't think about... Bay

Don't think about... Luca

Don't think about... Mack

Don't think about...

Don't think about... who?

Pax fed off Lottie's boundless eagerness to please and her physical toughness. It was like getting a part of herself back. Aside from the youngstock, Lottie was the only mare at the stud not heavily in foal and seemed oblivious to the stallions' competing charms. Not for her the sexually charged shrieks of mercurial Beck, constantly boiling over with excess and past trauma, or the come-hither bellows of seen-it-all Cruisoe, their pampered old player. She had her future ahead of her and she was taking Pax there as fast as their six legs and two hot heads could spirit them.

A morning on the local gallops pounded her worries deep

into the silica sand and left them there as she started to feel the pure nuclear reactor power at her fingertips.

A lesson with a shouty local dressage pro helped her rediscover muscles she'd forgotten she had, unlocking paces she didn't know the mare possessed.

Each training day brought more magical discoveries – the mare was afraid of nothing, she adored travelling, she got fit quickly, she was a water-loving mudlark. She was Pax's most functional relationship right now.

In Lottie, Pax had found a small pocket of safe haven amid ever-shifting chaos. Lottie was her soul sister, just as desperate to prove herself as Pax was. They outclassed the field in their first few outings, part by luck, largely by breeding, with a hefty dash of chemistry. Both were tricky, opinionated, fearless perfectionists. As they got fitter and stronger, it was getting harder to contain their enthusiasm, the mare's lack of experience and Pax's long absence from the saddle making for the queen of all adrenaline rushes. Yet blazing through open country was also the only time Pax felt truly at peace.

When she was galloping, she couldn't let herself think about anything.

As March swelled tree buds, bleating lambs began filling local fields and the clocks went forward to steal an hour of everyone's sleep, Pax found her own less interrupted by demons. By taking herself to the brink of exhaustion each day, she'd created a portal to dreamless nights, no longer craving alcohol's anaesthesia. And by compartmentalising her life into as tight and uncompromising a timetable as possible, she felt in control at last.

Kes came first, always. Mack had once more cooled his fire, his official line yet again that he wanted reconciliation, and failing that mediation, the unofficial one that he wanted to stay in control.

But Pax was the one in control now. She was going it alone.

On the large paper planner on the tack-room wall,

traditionally used to mark out the foaling due dates, mare covering dates, stallion duties and vet visits, she had added her competitions in pink highlighter, training days in yellow. The pink stripes were taking over. An identical planner in the kitchen of the cottage was also marked out with colour-coded *Daddy Days* and *Mummy Days*, along with *Gronny Afternoons*.

Ronnie insisted that it was unhealthy to separate everything in life so obsessively, comparing it to the childhood years when Pax had fussily pushed the food on her plate into zones. Pax disagreed, pointing out just as sharply that living a double life was exactly what Ronnie herself had done for years as a mistress and absentee mother.

Their relationship remained strained, Ronnie pushing more and more of the stud administration her daughter's way, her bossy desire to prove herself super-granny a mixed blessing. But Pax needed hands-on help too much to deny her, and Kes needed all the support and stimulation he could get. Also written on the chart were her son's weekly swimming sessions, sporting clubs, play dates and – Kes's absolute favourite – *Riding Lesson with Lester*.

Once more out and about, the old stallion man was on a mission to pass his knowledge onto a fourth generation of family, the sound of Handel and disparagement of all things modern once again ringing out through the yards. He was also Pax's champion, approving wholeheartedly of her regimented approach, her mercurial return to competitive riding and her obsession with the highly-strung, explosively talented Lottie. 'Now that's an out-and-out Compton horse!' He often joined them on their new adventures, briefing her en route to baby competitions in Ronnie's swish little horsebox, a legacy from a previous life. Sprung from his dining-room prison, Lester made it up into the cab with the aid of the plastic mounting block, waved away by Luca who held the fort at the yard.

But she couldn't let herself think too much about Luca.

Competitions were her little parallel world, where Pax

appreciated Lester's unswerving support and endless thermos flasks of strong tea, his Lawrence Olivier dressage test calling, and snappy advice when she and Lottie boiled over. Because his hip wasn't yet strong enough for walking long distances, his hunting buddies had come up trumps once again with the loan of an electric mountain bike which he used to walk courses with her. He was her lucky mascot and advisor, minding Kes when he came along too, boosting her confidence and – most useful of all – reporting back in detail to Lottie's owner afterwards to spare her typos and emojis.

She definitely didn't want to think about Bay.

In this newly compartmentalised life in which she determinedly tried not to think about her marriage or Luca when she was out training and competing, Bay went everywhere with her in a small, locked flameproof tin marked Do Not Open. It was only at night in her dreams that it sprang open of its own accord like a jack-in-the-box.

Until the day he came along in person.

Enter at A. Slalom along the centre line in power trot without halting. Career left at C, spooking left at E, triangle left fifteen metres at X, then canter large with great gusto and a big smile, ignoring your bellowing dressage test caller and feeling the sheer buzz until the judge honks their car horn to tell you that you've made an error of course.

It was Lottie's first affiliated event and she and Pax were delighted to have a small crowd to show off to, albeit too energetically for the dressage arena. The weekend horse trials near Banbury turned out to be a far bigger gig than Pax had anticipated, her decision to start the mare a level above entry grade perhaps unwise in hindsight.

For all her rediscovered toolkit and the mare's newfound paces, their dressage test was an over-exuberant disappointment.

She didn't doubt Lottie's talent. It was her own nerves that were boxing her in. Leaving Lester to mind Kes, she walked the course a second time after her test, trying to remain rigidly focussed alongside an eager foot army of cheery amateurs, grateful nobody knew her. But she felt isolated by her renewed ambition. In her twelve-year absence, the sport had swelled its ranks tenfold. She no longer belonged to the small elite of pro riders she'd known as juniors. They now arrived in big HGVs packed to the gills with team and equipment, all setting up base close together in the lorry park, forming their own gated community. Having never graduated to those hardworking ranks that competed six in a day, Pax didn't belong there. All her hopes rode on Lottie's shoulders. Today, she was grateful for her obscurity.

Then Bay rolled in like a circus ringmaster.

Heads turned when he swept loudly into the lorry park, a cavalcade of expensive tweed, children, pouty au pair, dogs on slip leads, folding chairs, air-kisses and large Fortum and Mason hamper. Alienated yet further from the grass roots rank and file who didn't have loud, glamorous owners demanding champagne flutes and cake forks, Pax ushered them hurriedly into the cramped horsebox living.

'Good job we're here – you'd starve!' Bay exclaimed when he peered into the empty fridge.

He was wearing red trousers, Pax realized, recalling his promise.

She watched him, his flop of oak hair and chuckle of good cheer, blue eyes creased with amusement, aftershave brightening the smell of wet dog. Memories were crowding her. They'd crammed together in horsebox living many times that heavenly last summer together, Bay always charmingly generous and without ego: catering, grooming, cheering, dog-sitting, coffee brewing and mixing stiff drinks, nursing bruised bodies and egos.

He was a natural at this, playing the Hooray owner to perfection.

She felt like the outsider. 'Why didn't you say you were coming?'

'Lester and I thought it would be a nice surprise.' He didn't quite catch her eye.

She mustn't think about their last call, when he'd told her he still loved her and she'd told him never to repeat it. They'd messaged only a few times since, photos of Lottie from her and emojis from him.

Pax crammed the lid back on the little flameproof tin she kept her thoughts about him in. *Must stay focussed on today's competition.*

At least pony-mad Tilly and boisterous little livewire Bram were company for Kes on a drizzly day. And Lester was delighted by the upgrade from garage sandwiches to deli counter delights from the Austens' farm shop.

'Bit wayward on the dressage, she was,' he told Bay, cheeks bulging with smoked salmon and cream cheese.

Pax couldn't eat a thing, her jittery focus splintering more. Escaping through the groom's door, she shared an apple with Lottie, longing to gallop.

'I think wayward dressage is vastly underrated...' Bay followed her out, eating a sausage roll.

'Just wait until our louche showjumping,' she joked, grateful that Lottie never touched a pole.

Half an hour later, the mare toppled two showjumping rails through rider error, and Pax's stomach twisted tighter still. In the old days with Lizzie and the gang, she'd have nipped back a bolstering swig of alcopop. She needed something to dilute the bubbling nerves.

The rain began drumming in earnest at the cross-country start, and Lester's take-it-steady pep talk fell on deaf ears, although Bay's order to show them what she was made of steeled her nerve. She then distinctly heard his yell of, 'Don't bloody fall off!' as she blazed away from the starter's countdown which put her blood up with perfect timing.

Now they could gallop. Pax's mind locked on target, each fence counting down, the mare on fire. This was her forte. Lottie the mudlark paid no heed to rain. They scorched round so fast she Pax had to reel back to a trot for part of the last half mile to avoid being penalised for going too quickly, her arms aching.

Whooping through the finish, she drummed pats down onto the hard, wet brown neck, loving the pricked ears ahead, between which she could see Bay's wide smile.

'You bloody stayed on!' He cried, delighted.

'Of *course* I stayed on!' She pulled up, panting and still patting.

'Set off far too fast,' Lester grumbled 'Looked better anchored by the water.' He fed the mare a mint and clambered back onto his electric bike to keep up as they walked back to the lorry.

'Beautifully ridden!' Bay strode along on her other side. 'I was *seriously* impressed.'

She waved the compliment away. 'That I didn't fall off?'

'That you took my advice.' His blue eyes creased up at her. 'Mare was a springbok out there wasn't she, Lester?'

'Needs better brakes,' Lester mumbled, then conceded, 'It was a creditable start, and we are very grateful to you for your support today, Mr Austen, aren't we, Pax?'

'Of course.' Finally letting the body-rush of joy from the ride register, Pax found she was bursting with gratitude, because it registered afresh that Bay had made this happen. That it was Bay who had helped her rediscover the greatest fun she'd lost. That Bay trusted her with his amazing horse. Bay, who remembered the person she'd once been.

For a heady moment Bay's blatant, flag-waving support felt more than good. It took her back to what he'd once meant to her. To just how much she'd thrown her heart over first and loved him.

He had his hand resting the mare's neck just in front of the wither as they walked, its fingers strong and square-ended, scrubbed and tough, familiar signet ring on his little finger. She'd worn it on a chain as a lucky charm once, tracing her fingers across the Austen family motto engraved inside before each ride. *Dum Spiro Spero.* While I breathe, I hope.

'It means a lot you're here,' she said with feeling, and a deep breath of hope.

'Entirely Tilly's idea.' He dismissed breezily. 'Mad keen on all this sort of thing. Main reason I sent the horse to you is to stop her trying to ride her. That and to put a zero on the value.'

The hopeful breath gasped back out. 'You're surely not selling her yet?'

'Not if Tilly has her way and gets the ride at sixteen.' He tilted his head, squinting up at her thoughtfully. 'Same age you were when I started chasing you round the countryside like this. Brings it all back, doesn't it?'

'A bit.'

'You're just as good, just as fearless. Just as bloody wet and muddy.' There he was again, the man she'd once loved, underplaying it with a throwaway aside, while his eyes beamed a thousand lumens.

Then he looked away as he was hailed by a passing farming crony, resuming his red-trousered Hooray-owner role, while she locked him tightly back into his flameproof Do Not Touch tin.

The rain had eased off to light drizzle, a promise of spring sunshine glowing through distant clouds.

At the horsebox, rosy-cheeked devotee of all things equine, Tilly was waiting eagerly with a bucket to help cool off the mare, breathless from running back from a hillside vantage point with Knott. 'Lottie was brilliant! Daddy says I can groom for you because I've done my Pony Club B test and you're stony broke.' She had her mother Monique's ice-blue eyes and abruptness, along with Bay's irrepressible cheer. 'Did you really compete for Team GB?'

'Long time ago. Just juniors and young riders.'

'And she'll do so again for the senior squad,' Lester predicted, wobbling away on his bicycle with Stubbs in the basket to check the scores before Pax could argue.

Embarrassed by his loyalty, she busied herself unbuckling the mare's breastplate.

Bay was back after catching up with his friend.

'Good to see the old boy on form again,' he said, watching Lester's retreating figure. 'Tells me he'll be back in the saddle too soon. Not the British squad maybe.'

'He's overdoing it.' She unbuckled the girth red-faced, realizing he'd heard Lester's boast and aware today's performance didn't match up.

'Nonsense.' Bay lifted the saddle off for her. 'YOLO, as Tilly says, you've only got one life.'

'That's YOGOL.'

'Is it?' His baffled surprise made her laugh.

'*That's* totally LOL, Daddy!' Tilly joined in underfoot, sponging the mare's legs so enthusiastically she was soaking all their ankles.

'With a ROFLMAO on top.' Bay gave Pax an old-fashioned look as she took the saddle from him.

'You even *talk* like a text message.'

'I'm better on the phone,' he said lightly.

The tin box burst open, the memory of their last call playing on a loop. Again, she slammed it shut.

'How could I deprive Lester? Calling you makes his day.' She carried the mare's tack to put in the lorry locker before checking in on the living compartment where Kes and Bram were glued to a screen, building a Minecraft world with the pouty au-pair, who Bay sent off with a tenner to treat herself to coffee.

'Poor thing came here to improve her English and found herself fluent in Dutch insult-singing,' he told Pax. 'She goes back to Hungary next months. Until then, I get weekend custody of her along with the kids. Monique likes the new place to herself when they're with me.'

'Mummy needs "me" time,' Tilly explained loyally.

Pax watched Bay suck his lips, a sarcastic quip held in check, saying instead, 'Too right. How about you, Pax? Will you move into the house when Lester wants his cottage back?'

'No.' She threw a wicking rug over the mare's back.

'Not bunking up with Luca, then?' He pronounced it with a deliberate pause between 'loo' and 'ca'.

'Or my mother, no.' She stooped down as Tilly fed the straps to her under Lottie's belly from her opposite side.

'I live with *my* mummy from Sunday to Wednesday,' the ten-year-old told Pax brightly, 'which is super tricky if you have knickers with days of the week on them.' She scooped up the discarded boots to carry to the locker.

Bay stepped closer to Pax, glancing round to check Tilly was out of earshot. '*Do* you?'

'Doesn't everyone?'

'Ever go week at the knees?'

'Never in a month of Sundays.' She said, poker-faced. 'And that is a truly awful line.'

'Yes, you could do better,' he poker-faced back, making her laugh.

Grinning, he buckled up the rug's chest straps. 'Are you looking for somewhere local? One of our barn conversions will be vacant soon if you're interested.'

'Thank you, but it would be way beyond my budget.'

She was determined their next home would be a separate haven just for her and Kes, who came bounding out of the lorry now, crying, 'Bram's invited me for a sleepover. Can I go, *can* I, Mummy?'

'You're too young for sleepovers.'

'Nonsense,' Bay overruled cheerfully. 'Come over to supper later. We'll celebrate today's triumph. You can look at this barn coming up for rent.'

'I've not even been placed today. And I can't afford one of your barns. And Luca's cooking something special for supper.'

'Luca is my best friend,' Kes told Bram, 'then Ellis from school, then Coll my pony. But you can be my next best friend if you like?'

'I have too many best friends,' Bram said, his blue eyes earnest, 'but I can put you on the wait list?'

'Cool!'

'He's very like you,' Pax told Bay as they watched them charge off.

'Isn't he just?' Bay's voice deepened. 'Come to supper later.'

'Not tonight.'

'What's Loo-ca cooking up that's so irresistible?'

'A stable diet?'

'Another truly bad line.' He stepped closer. 'What's the deal between you two?'

'He never criticises my bad lines.'

'Then he's not to be trusted.'

'We're mates.' Pax stepped away.

Compartmentalising Luca had been her biggest challenge, but they had a rule: friendly workmates when Kes was around, and when he was with his father, they mated. And when she was out competing with the horse, she tried not to think about him at all. In Bay text speak, they were FWB.

Not that she'd confide in Bay. He was looking at her with the expression she remembered from childhood, back when he'd been her raging crush, summer after summer, from twelve to fifteen. Then she'd turned sixteen and he'd returned from agricultural college and he'd looked at her just like this.

'Fuck it, I've missed you,' he said, too simply and unromantically for it to be a line.

And she said 'yup' very quickly and quietly because she'd missed him too.

Both were grateful to hear a shout as Lester made his way back from the score tent, electric bicycle overshooting them and making Lottie spook before he looped back around. 'Made up a dozen places with that cross-country! Eighth in her section!'

'You bloody superstar!' Bay kissed her cheek, making her heart spin like Lester's bike spokes. Then he leant closer, kissing her other cheek and leaving behind two hotspots as he added so quietly, only she heard it, '*Dum Spiro Spero.*'

A moment later, he'd dived into the lorry and produced a bottle of champagne from the hamper.

Pax was just as quick on the draw, whisking it away before he could rip off the foil 'Thanks. I'll save this for later!'

'To share with Loo-ca, not likely!' He whipped it back. 'Let's have it now.'

'Absolutely not!' She wrestled it from him. 'We're both driving.'

'You're right. Naughty of me. Come round for a glass later. Or anytime: breakfast, elevenses, 2 a.m. I'm easy...' That look again.

Bay doesn't know I'm a drunk, she registered giddily. Like riding Lottie, realizing it made her feel her old self again. As did catching his eye inadvertently everywhere she looked.

He put the bottle back in the hamper. 'Bloody annoying being cut out of the deal for the stallion, eh Lester?'

'Yes.' Lester's face puckered into deeper creases. 'Mrs Ledwell found a single investor in the end.'

'I'm a single investor, just saying,' Bay pointed out idly, and Pax could tell from the tick pulsing in his cheek he was deeply annoyed about it.

'It was taken out of my hands,' Lester reminded them.

Bay turned to smile at Pax again. 'So, what's he like? Just your type, I bet.'

She laughed. The ageing comedian-turned-actor's reputation in the village preceded him, much of it delivered by a fleet of late-night pantechnicons and daytime courier trucks. 'I don't know Kenny Kay personally.'

'I meant the horse, Pax.'

'You've seen the video.'

'Is he still not here?'

'He arrives next week,' Lester said briskly, 'Which leaves us ten days before Maumesby. Get a couple of runs in.'

Bay whistled, blue eyes darkening as he cast Pax an anxious look. 'That's tight. You're not riding him there, surely?'

'Of course. He's fit and ready. Mummy wants to aim him at Chatsworth if he goes well, so we've got to hit the ground running. Can't let the new owner down.'

'Mr Kay used to stand stallions with us years ago,' Lester told Bay, his creases tightening yet more. 'He is eager to reinvest in the stud.'

'As long as nobody shoots him this time,' Bay murmured, sounding as though he was quite tempted himself.

'Why would anyone shoot him?' Pax asked.

'Nobody's going to shoot anybody!' Lester blustered. 'We're very grateful to Mr Kay for stepping in to buy a stallion that will raise the profile and reputation of the stud while also providing him with a healthy return on his investment.' He'd read a lot of online articles about bloodstock economics while trying to syndicate shares. 'And if I may be so bold to say,' he cleared his throat uncomfortably, 'he is also doing it for old time's sake.'

'Whereas I'm just doing it for the love of it,' Bay said quietly, giving Pax that look.

She stared back, finding her eyes trapped with his, knowing the fireproof tin wasn't going to shut anymore.

With effort she dropped her gaze first and turned away to get Lottie ready to travel home, hearing Bay patting Lester on the shoulder with a regretful sigh. 'Sorry we missed out, old boy. Know you had your heart set on him.'

'Always wanted to own a Badminton winner,' Lester sighed. 'And if that horse doesn't do it, one of his progeny will. Mr Robertson knows how to spot them. He has the eye, just like Captain Percy did.'

Pax pulled the travel boots out of the tack locker, realizing Lester had been willing to invest his own money. For such a cautious man, it showed extraordinary faith. Bay must think so too.

'I tried talking Ronnie into cutting us back into the deal,' he was saying, 'but she was adamant Kenny has a 100 hundred per cent. Couldn't get hold of Blair at all. I even called the showjumper guy in Canada to see if we could negotiate something, the Flying Fig Leaf.'

'Maple Leaf,' Pax corrected, turning back in shock. 'He's the one selling the horse?'

'Bloody tricky character, hey Lester?'

'He can be quarrelsome,' Lester conceded.

Neither of them knew the truth about Luca's connection with the famously bullish Canadian rider, she realized. Why would they? It was his darkest secret. She tried to remember his face when he saw the video for the first time. Had the smile slipped? They'd watched it together, but she'd been far too wrapped up in her own self-absorbed traumas to realize. He'd told her he'd worked on the yard. But he hadn't wanted to scupper the deal, so he'd said nothing more, not even to her.

He messaged Meredith every day. Maple Leaf and his daughter could still ruin this deal, she realized. But much worse than that was what it could do to Luca.

25

Whenever Pax was away from the yard competing, Luca sensed the old Cotswold stud sinking back into museum-like complacency, the pace dropping, its past glories outweighing its future plans.

On a Saturday, it was better. He always found his mornings working with Carly a refreshing change from Ronnie's boundless bossy charm. She was a grafter who didn't talk much, lost to her playlists and horse love, and when she did speak, she spared no punches. His smiling song-and-dance routine and patter cut no ice with her. There was a flinty way she side-eyed him that reminded him of his Irish family, sometimes, wise to the blarney.

Today she was particularly testy. She usually brought her kids with her, but not this week, explaining over a late-morning tea break, 'They're at their Nan's. I know Ronnie's cool with them, but Sienna's playing up something rotten, and I don't think them shrieking round the place is good for the mares so close to foaling.'

Several of the home herd were very close now, a sense of anticipation building through the straw-lined enclosures. The oldest broodmare, Barbara, had been the first to paw at her bed and bag up, her milk starting to run, her labour close. Luca was checking her half-hourly, still cursing the yard's lack of digital monitoring.

'Sure, a few excited kids won't bother them,' he reassured her.

'Bothered me,' she sniffed, glancing at her phone screen to check the time. 'I'm not picking them up for an hour, so I'll skip the outside barn again before I go.'

'Stay longer and you might see the foal born.' He wanted to share this year's first Compton birth, but Pax and Lester were still out at a competition, and Ronnie had taken advantage to slope off to Kit Donne's cottage.

'Can't.' Carly pocketed her phone. 'Nana can only take so much of that little minx. She f-bombs non-stop right now.'

'My granny was just the same.'

She didn't smile. 'Don't even joke. Nana's been acting well-weird. Keeps saying she might go out for a walk.'

'How's that weird?'

'She's not left the house in twenty years.' She told him that Ash's mother, an agoraphobic who did nothing but watch TV, bake and mind the Turner kids, had announced out of the blue that she wanted a divorce from errant Nat. 'Of course, Sienna picks up on it and asks, "Is Grandpa Nat a fucking bastard like my dad says, Nana?" That girl is the bane of me. There's no filter with her and she's only three. Ash just thinks it's funny.'

'Sure, she'll grow out of it.'

'Like I fucking did?'

He laughed again and she gave him one of her stony looks, plugging her earphones back in and muttering, 'I can tell you've no kids.'

'Then you'd be wrong,' Luca muttered back, turning away to hook up the bridle he'd just wiped.

The earphones came back out. 'Seriously?'

'I've never got to know her,' he dismissed quickly, heading outside, grateful for a buzz in his back pocket as his phone found signal.

Carly followed him. 'How old is she?'

'This is great! The mare got placed on her first affiliated run,' he told her, reading the message as he walked. 'Pax is thrilled, so she is.'

'Baby, toddler, older?'

'Six.'

'You and her mum not speaking?'

'Something like that.' Messaging a lot. Needy, frightened, passionate messages. Meredith telling him she couldn't carry on like this, begging him to come back to Canada, pleading with him to forgive her for keeping Dizzy a secret so long.

Carly stepped in front of him. 'My dad didn't hang around. Same with Ash and his dad. It does things to your head. Always wanted to know him better. Worse when they leave before you can have a memory to hold onto.'

'That's not what happened.'

'It is to some round here. Look and learn, my lover. Act before it's too late. She deserves to know you, your daughter. You're quite nice as it goes.' The earphones went in again and she headed off to the side yard housing the half dozen visiting mares here to foal.

And Luca realized that, in those few sharp words, she had addressed his biggest dilemma more directly than weeks of skirting round the issue with Pax.

He'd never felt able to confide in Pax, even if they hadn't got into this messy no-ship collaboration of hard work and fast sex. Because the memories Pax held onto of her parents during her own childhood were fleeting, often unhappy. Her mother had faced exactly the same dilemma as Meredith. And the fallout from it had coloured her whole life.

Carly could also have been talking about Pax.

'Gosh, it feels so naughty doing this in the middle of the afternoon.' Ronnie pulled the silk throw up under her chin.

Beside her, Kit topped up their glasses and settled closer. 'But so very good.'

'Makes me want to take up smoking again – share a cigarette and talk about the best bits of the past hour.'

'Ah yes, definitely. I might have a packet somewhere.'

'No, let's not move for a bit. It's bliss not to have to queue for the lavs. I do love it that they have a proper interval like this.'

They were watching a streamed recording from the RSC archive, the late, great Anthony Sher as a bear-like King Lear, part of Kit's research for directing the play there.

'How many times have you seen this production again?' she asked.

'This will be my fourth recorded, twice live. But the play itself I've seen fifty times or more.'

Ronnie found it a tremendous turn-on when Kit said things like that. He'd witnessed many great stage actors in the role: from Michael Gambon to Anthony Hopkin, Tom Courtenay to Ian McKellen and Brian Cox, Pete Postlethwaite and Derek Jacobi. She'd seen one or two of them herself.

'Oh, I *have* missed theatre,' she sighed. When she'd been the mistress of her own late, great lion of a lover, married businessman Lionel, they had seen dozens of productions together, including Hermia's *Medea* which Kit had directed.

'I had no idea one could watch them at home like this,' she confessed. 'We could be completely naked here in the front row and nobody would know.'

'Quite.' He laughed awkwardly.

'Shall we?'

'It's much better live at the theatre of course,' he said, staring at the screen.

'We'd be arrested for it there.'

'It's starting,' he pointed out with relief as the house lights went down on screen.

Ronnie settled back and wondered how Blair was doing.

★

Pax returned to the stud on such a high from competing, and hoarse from singing nursery rhymes with Lester and Kes in the cab, it came as a relief that Luca was too preoccupied in the mare barn to come out to greet them. She needed to be somewhere quiet and alone together before mentioning that she knew their new stallion was in the Flying Maple Leaf's yard. There was always too much to do after a day out: washing off the mare and her kit, hosing out the lorry, cleaning tack, avoiding Luca, thinking about Bay.

She refused to let Lester help, sending him back to the house for tea and rest instead, worried how grey and exhausted he looked.

Within minutes Ronnie appeared, fresh from a long lunch with a friend and hurriedly pulling a waxed drover's coat over her smart weekend best to help empty the tack lockers, eager for blow-by-blow accounts of each phase. 'You must tell me everything! An eighth is marvellous.'

Rewarded instead with Kes butting in with a blow-by-blow account of his day's Minecraft gaming with Bram, Ronnie listened indulgently and then told him about the plot of the play she'd just watched. 'King Lear divides his kingdom between his two daughters who flatter him and banishes the third, who loves him plainly and honestly. She dies, then the other two reject him, and he goes mad and wanders through a storm.'

'Serves him right, don't you think, Gronny?' Kes offered.

'Absolutely. Ageing male egos can be jolly tricky to navigate. I'd have given the lot to Cordelia to look after if I was him, then buggered off on a cruise. You have charged Bay diesel for today, haven't you?' she asked Pax in a characteristic subject jump.

'I'll add it to the invoice,' she promised

'Good girl. This lorry won't plate itself. Got a VIP to transport soon.'

Pax felt an anxious tick starting in her temples. She had 'She'll Be Coming Round the Mountain' as an earworm.

'Why did you cut Bay and Lester out of the deal with the new stallion?'

Ronnie was rubber ball positive, 'The fact is we *have* a deal at last, the horse is on his way, and better still our new owner is happy for us to split the first season's stud fees.'

'How much do we even know about him?'

'Blair found him. Can't fault his breeding. Produced by pros. Flew through the ranks. His results in the US were terrific; he's fit and fertile and has passed all every vet check. He was imported to Canada by a tech billionaire as an expensive Christmas present for his wife, then the buyers changed their minds. Beware geeks bearing gifts, Kenny says.'

Pax didn't laugh, flipping the question Bay had asked her earlier. 'I meant how much do you know about Kenny Kay?'

Ronnie dialled down her bright-eyed smile. 'Enough to appreciate a bird in the hand.'

'As long as we don't shoot its fingers off.'

'That's not funny'

Pax had no idea why it should be, but her mother was still talking.

'We must put all that behind us and be grateful for a second chance. This horse is a little superstar. Maumesby will be his big British debut and there's bugger all prep time, so I think we need a top pro to take the ride. I've made some calls and—'

'I'm competing him.' If this was the horse Lester was prepared to blow his life savings on, and that Bay had personally pleaded with the Flying Maple Leaf to let them still syndicate, she wanted to hold their dream for the stud.

'That's very gutsy of you, Pax, but given you'll have so little time to get to know each other I do think—'

'I'm doing it!'

Ronnie's eyes glistened. 'You're too precious.'

'I'm *not* being precious!' She stomped off to gather Kes from the horsebox living, realizing too late that perhaps her mother had meant too precious to risk injury rather than precious and spoilt.

Either way, Pax was refused to lock horns with Ronnie on the subject, her day's high under threat. Then it occurred to her that Ronnie might simply be jealous. Did she still miss riding competitively, resent the buck stopping with her when she just wanted to be riding out the bucks?

Feeing all-too horribly precious now, she took Kes to thank Lottie for her bravery, rubbing the V star on her forehead with the heel of her palm while Kes reached up to feed her Polos.

'When I ride cross-country, Mummy, I'm going to be even faster than you!'

Her heart squeezed tight with pride and fear, already anticipating the strangulating, conflicted terror of watching him charging out of the start box on half a ton of horsepower with a brain the size of a walnut, as Bay had described eventing. Love made sport spectating tough.

Which was when she finally realized that must be how her mother felt.

Then it occurred to her that might be how Bay felt too.

Pax didn't see Luca until suppertime, a team effort with Kester and Ronnie helping him load huge home-made pizzas, as a 'treat for Mummy'. It had been Ronnie's idea, she discovered, which made her feel yet more awkward about being both definitions of precious.

Luca was quick to congratulate her on her place, high-fiving and hugging her because Kes was there and anything more than a back-slapping peck on the cheek was forbidden. A relief. 'Proud of you.' His eyes held hers to underline the point before melting away.

Despite the usual big easy smile, Pax sensed his disquiet mirrored hers. He avoided her gaze at the table, talking to

Ronnie in detail about the home broodmares, several of which were close to foaling.

'Barbara will be first – that'll be tonight,' he told them, bolting his food too fast so he could check again.

'You eat, I'll go this time,' Ronnie offered, having finished her usual tiny portion.

'Tell me how the mare went today,' he asked Pax, listening intently as she explained the dressage and showjumping errors that had been entirely her own, then took him jump by jump through her cross-country ride and the mare's extraordinary courage, getting more animated as she spoke, all the time fielding multiple interruptions from Lester complaining she'd set out too fast and Kes boasting he had a new friend. And all the time Luca's smile seemed to hide more secrets than ever.

'Bay was there,' she told him.

'Great.' He made no comment beyond that. Although his ambivalence had sometimes disquieted Pax more than her mother's invested emotion, it meant their passion was locked down, distilled into controlled explosions. They could walk away from this unharmed, surely?

'First one coming!' Ronnie rushed in. 'She waited for us all to be here, like a pro! Come on, Kes, you get to watch! And Lester must be there too – unless you're too tired?'

He was already on his feet, reaching for his crutches. 'Always has big foals, Barbara.'

Pax and Luca lingered, waiting for the others to hurry along the back lobby and out through the vestibule, excited voices trailing away.

'Were you ever going to tell me the new stallion is coming from Meredith's yard?'

'Forgive me, angel, I didn't know how to. I thought you'd figure it out.'

'Well, I got there eventually.'

He crossed over to her, cupping her face in his hands, 'I don't know what Blair was playing at. He knows my history there and he's no fan of the guy.'

He was so close, she didn't trust her reflexes, which were wired up to detonate. Yet anger seemed all wrong.

She craned her neck back until he let go. 'I guess he wouldn't have brokered it unless he thought the horse could be the making of this place.'

'He loves your mother,' he said simply, 'that's why he did it.'

'And you? Does Meredith's father know you're working here? Is that why the deal stalled?'

'No.' He raked his hair. 'It stalled because the money wasn't there. Blair's deposit is the only reason they waited this long. They knew his wife died, so...'

'Christ, Mummy even uses her lover's widowhood as leverage.' She chewed her lip, laughing at the awfulness of it.

'That's not fair. Your mother made the best of bad situation. Lester was in over his head, and Bay's a cash-flashing bighead.'

'Bay just wants to help!' she blasted.

He watched her for a long moment, tilting his head, more secrets crowding behind that big O'Brien smile. 'You know this auld comedian fella Ronnie's found to buy him is said to have some sort of local curse on his head?'

'A curse as well?' She laughed hollowly.

'Carly was talking about it earlier. He used to do a whole stand-up routine about it in the nineties. It's on YouTube, totally toxic, saying how he was driven away from the Cotswolds by a batshit crazy local travelling clan. It's obviously the Turners. But Carly says that none of the Turners have a grudge against him. They're all big fans. The family doesn't do curses, or tell fortunes, or any of that shit she says.'

Pax watched his smile, his eyes, his animation, sensing his affinity with Carly, the transferral of affection. It's what he does, she reminded herself. It intrigued as much as it hurt her, but the ache was still palpable.

They were standing in the shadow of the big chimney that

housed the range, its heat cloaking them. That shared nervous energy they'd always sparked off was catching alight, hot in her head. She wanted to talk to him about Meredith, to open that wound while she had the chance. She wanted to tell him, gently, that she knew he was drinking again. She wanted to hold onto their friendship and refuse to let it go. It was either that or...

He kissed her.

... that.

Just for a moment they kissed like war-torn lovers.

'Not here,' she said firmly. But he'd won his secrets.

'Let's see this foal born.'

Outside, a fox was barking just beyond the old walled garden. She liked to think it might be Lester's little friend Lawrence, released the night her heart had hardened, making sure she didn't lose control again. When she'd broken the news of its freedom, Lester had insisted Pax was right to let the young creature back into the wild: 'Too many of us been cooped up round here.' But she still felt responsible, that background mother ache of worry for the young.

In the mares' barn, Kes was beside himself with excitement as the big-kneed, wet-coated new creation wobbled to her feet and went in search of mum's milk, feather-duster tail flicking.

'Will she be a champion, Gronny?' he deferred to the expert.

'All Compton Magna horses can be champions, Kes,' Ronnie assured him. 'But it's people who *make* them champions. To do that, this stud needs someone passionate at the helm.' She turned round as Pax and Luca approached.

'Like you, Gronny?'

'After me, Kester.'

'*You* are quite old, Gronny,' he conceded. 'I could do it if you like?'

Pax put her arms around him and squeezed him tight. Beside her, Ronnie asked, 'Would you like to, Kester?'

His faced lit up. 'More than anything in the *world*! I love it here. It's my favouritest place ever, ever.'

Finding herself under her mother's intense, smiling scrutiny, Pax flashed a guarded smile in return. She craned round to catch Luca's eye, but he'd moved aside to check his phone.

Moments like this meant little to somebody who was just passing through, she realized. The stud's lifelong legacy would never stretch beyond her generation if she didn't let Kes dream.

'*Can* I do it, Gronny?' Kes was pleading. 'Can I please?'

'I have a feeling you might well.'

When Luca had the mares to himself again, his quiet muses, he took out his phone and typed carefully, wanting no ambiguity, to put it down plainly in black and white. It had been clear to him the moment he'd seen the first Compton foal, when Pax crouched down to wrap her arms around Kes, and Ronnie turned to smile at them. He'd known then exactly what it was he kept searching for wherever he went in the world, but he could never hold onto.

He went to look at the foal again. Big, as Lester had promised. Old-fashioned and well-timbered, built for power and heart, with a ridiculously pretty face. Like this place. And like all newborn foals, all new life, she was a miracle that made his heart soar.

He reread the message: *I want Dizzy to know who her father is. Promise me that and I'll cross any ocean to be with you both. Always.*

And then he typed *I love you. Only you.*

Because it was true.

PART FIVE

26

Kenny Kay had moved enough times to know the routine. As a child, all his worldly possessions had fitted into a single suitcase, dragged between the many cold-faced Birmingham homes in which he'd briefly lived, private houses shared with unfamiliar caretaker parents or staffed institutions in which he'd been cloistered with fellow strays detached from family by poverty, tragedy or neglect.

Those fellow strays had been more family than the pretend parents who went from Mr and Mrs to Mum and Dad and back again in the filling of a form. The trinity of Kenny, Peter and Tina. Their paths had crossed often. The other two were better at staying in placements, but not much. Peter used his fists when father figures laid down the rules. Tina fought back when they felt her up.

Kenny never lasted anywhere long. Too much lip, too much trouble, too hard to control.

Some would argue that this was still the case. Perhaps it's why he never settled. He'd owned more houses over the years than he'd owned cars. Kenny was fonder of cars than houses.

But he liked this house, and not just because it smelled like a new Rolls Royce, had more gadgetry than his Tesla and he knew it to be prettier than a Jaguar E-type. He'd waited for it to be fully specced, tuned up and run in before taking the wheel.

Kenny hired people to do the moving for him nowadays, transporting his worldly goods between residences, arranging the furniture, making them hospitable. It inevitably took a convoy to relocate the veteran showman, and a hotshot team of design professionals to set the scene before that. Other people packed his bags for him. They also drove his cars. In the early days, Kenny had hired and fired almost as many staff as he'd bought and sold houses. He valued them more highly these days.

When the doorbell rang – an unfamiliar artificial chime he'd have to get changed – he was already in his favourite winged-back chair, props in place, one of his few remaining foot soldiers rushing to answer it.

'If that's my new PA, show her through!' he shouted importantly.

'Hello, Mr Kay.'

'Kenny, please!'

She smelled good – a drift of something old-fashioned and familiar caught his memories straight away. Eternity. Ladylike.

The first thing she asked in that oh-so-creamy voice was whether he'd like to see her CV. 'I brought it up to date last night, and I thought it might help for you to take a look ahead of the job interview?'

'No, no, you already *have* the job, love. We did a phone interview, remember? This is day one.'

Years ago, when he'd first found fame, Kenny had met hellraising legend Oliver Reed on a chat show. Kenny had thought him a true gent. In the green room beforehand, he'd told Kenny about his beloved Broome Hall, a fifty-six bedroomed Surrey pile he'd bought 'because it had a field for Dougal my horse'. His staff were 'good chaps I met in the pub'. The anecdote had stuck, colouring Kenny's employment strategy ever since. He no longer went to the pub much – more's the pity – but he held true to employing on impulse.

'So you're the petite, flat-headed wrestler?' he chuckled.

'It'll be nice having a Dolly Parton lookalike round the house. Brighten the place up.'

There was an awkward pause. Then, 'Mr Kay, do you mind me asking – can you see me?'

'No, bab.'

'Would you like me to be petite and flat-headed?'

'For now.'

'Then I am. For now.'

'That's bostin' that is, bab. Now please tell me you're a wrestler, because I might well be in need of some serious personal protection shortly.'

27

'He's moved in at last, have you heard?' Ronnie told Kit once he'd lowered himself into the passenger seat of her little sports car with some effort.

'Have you been round to say hello yet?' He clung on as they sped along Church Lane and out of the village like bank robbers.

'I thought I'd let him settle in first.'

'Be sure to wear a large cross and carry Holy Water.'

'I'm not sure he's so devilish these days.' She swerved out onto the Chipping Hampden lane. 'He's rather evangelical when we speak on the phone. I sold him a horse.'

'You sell everyone a horse!' He laughed, feeling the g-force down the chestnut-lined hill.

'Where am I driving again?' she asked.

'Stratford. Lunch with friends. No hurry to get there.'

But Ronnie couldn't wait to get away. 'I need to be in the company of strangers who don't talk about semen and follicles, at least for a while.'

'You'll like them,' Kit promised. 'They're clever and naughty like you. Please don't try to sell them a horse.'

And she did like them. Actor Donald, a lugubrious raconteur who was to be Lear in Kit's forthcoming production, and his live-wire husband, theatrical agent Ferdi, along with two academics from the Shakespeare institute, one of whom turned out to be a keen dressage rider. Ronnie managed to stop herself trying to sell her a horse and found herself making a new friend instead. It was so rare for her to combine two of her favourite subjects, theatre and horsepower, and she delighted in all the backstage gossip, surprised how animated and irreverent Kit became in their company.

'I did enjoy that,' she told him afterwards. 'You're a marvellous storyteller.'

'You're a wonderful listener,' he said, sounding surprised.

'It's lovely to have people to listen *to*. Nobody at home talks much, apart from Kes, and he goes to bed at seven. Lester only talks about breeding and hunting. Pax and Luca exchange silences. I think they're having sex.'

'Good for them,' he said distractedly, as though she'd told him they'd both just read the latest Margaret Atwood.

'I used to think they were perfectly matched, but I'm not at all sure. He's far less laid-back and jolly than I remember, more aloof and changeable. And she's not like me at all.'

'Nobody is,' he said with meaning.

They stopped on the way back to walk her little dogs up to the six-arch windmill where the views took in the village, the stud and Eyngate. Sheltering from a spring shower, they kissed beneath it. It still felt rather wonderful, kissing Kit Donne.

They had kissed a lot since the first time, which Ronnie liked enormously. They'd talked even more. She'd never talked as much to a man she was attracted to without bed being involved. Even with bed involved. She was suddenly addicted to talking. And kissing.

And with Kenny in the village, it felt good to have an ally with whom to kiss and tell.

'You have to face him soon,' Kit pointed out. 'Especially now he's bought one of your horses.'

'The horse hasn't arrived yet.'

'And when it does?'

'I might just gallop off on it.'

'You're not thinking of bolting again?'

She didn't dare tell him how tempting that sounded.

'He's moved in, have you heard?' Gill asked the other two Bags eagerly. 'We spotted more lorries unloading yesterday and the pool pump was at full throttle when I took the dogs out last night.'

Mo said nothing as they hacked past the Manor, all up on their stirrups, their usual quartet down to three while Petra remained sequestered in her plotting shed trying to finish a first draft by Easter.

The manor's wall and gates were too tall to see over – at least on a low-slung cob like Pie – and she held her secret close a while longer. She knew what lay beyond Kenny's fortress walls. Her biometrics were programmed into both gate and door pads: fingerprints, iris and face all recognized as friend not foe.

'Remind me, how many houses he owns?' Bridge was still standing up in her stirrups to try to look. 'Imagine being that fecking loaded.'

'You'd think he'd chip in more to help save Church Meadow, hey Mo?' Gill chivvied as they rode past the maypole into Church Lane.

Mo gave a vague nod. It was her first Bags outing in six weeks, and a relief to be away from her parents and Jan for longer than half an hour. To have a secret mission.

She was Kenny Kay's spy in the village.

It should feel shameful and duplicitous, but it felt good. Everyone else had been talking about her. Now it was time to talk about them instead.

She would tell the Bags soon enough about her new job, but for now she was smuggling the tiny, rare jewel unseen. Besides, she'd signed a non-disclosure agreement which meant she couldn't say much. She must keep quiet on details of the amazing high-tech house, its finger-print and retinal scanner entry system, the huge man cave with full-sized bar, the vast gym suite and two lifts, and the air-purified, bulletproof 'panic room'. Most of all, she couldn't reveal what she knew about Kenny's sight and the reason he was rarely ever seen out these days.

And she could empathise with his need for privacy. Everyone talked about him as though he was public property – his marriages, his health, his wealth – and the Bags treated her much the same way these days.

This was the first time she had joined them on a hack since Barry's departure, and she'd told them up front she wouldn't talk about what was happening in her marriage. Her voice still just tightened up and disappeared when she tried, especially today. In recent weeks, Bridge had tried to draw her out when they were alone together with the horses, but Mo found it easiest to brush it off, say 'what will be will be', and get on for her sanity's sake, and for Grace. It was her way, she'd said, firmly enough to put a stop to it. But she still cried to the pigs.

And while absent Petra's supportive WhatsApp messages meant equally well – the power of late-night *Bake Off* gifs was surprising – it was only Gill who seemed to understand the depth of Mo's mortification, in the same way the vet understood pain in animals who had no voice to describe it. Her calm, firm reassurance was a much-needed buoyancy aid. 'Riding with old chums helps,' she'd repeated until Mo caved in. And she was right: riding helped.

The world always looked better from on top of a horse.

Bright spring sunshine was glinting off the scaffolding on the church spire ahead. She turned to look at the school as they passed by, sending an imaginary hug in to Grace whose behaviour there had changed, the teachers reported, her quietness a worry. Mo had been called in to speak with Mrs Bullock personally about what was happening at home, those small, painted eyes softening with sympathy as she'd reassured Mo that they would all rally around to help Grace through this, adding what a sensible and popular girl she was, and then suggesting a small part as a Greek villager in *Mamma Mia!* might help, which was kind.

Mo looked away to compose herself, cheeks burning. Thinking about Grace always made her well up. People being sympathetic had the same effect. Tears had no place out here.

An estate agent was coming to value the bungalow later. Barry said it was just a formality 'so we all know where we stand', but it felt far too fast. She was only grateful she wouldn't be home for it.

She pulled herself together. Spy, Mo. *Spy*!

'Mr Theatre over there's been seen out to lunch with Ronnie this week,' Bridge reported obligingly as they passed The Old Almshouse, the riders checking out the greenhouse. But Kit Donne wasn't out there, the curtains in the house's windows still drawn.

'Yes, I heard they're getting on *very* well,' Gill confirmed sadly, her SMC under siege. 'Their mutiny at the church roof meeting seems to have fanned a spark.'

Mo made a mental note. Mutiny. Investigate mutiny.

Riding ahead of her with Bridge, Gill had already moved on, now talking about the sale of the meadow they were about to ride into, its standing stones glinting beneath a milky sun. 'Petra told me they have to raise the best part of a hundred grand to stop it going to auction.'

'That much?' Mo took note again.

'I thought she resigned?' said Bridge. 'What with her being *so busy writing, darling*,' she did an impersonation of their friend's breathy Yorkshire voice. 'Or is it Bay Austen she can't resist, eh Mo?' She swung round to wink at her.

Mo forced a rueful smile, wishing she still harboured a Safe Married Crush, but all desire had deserted her. Perhaps not having a safe marriage disqualified her. That and the object of her crush being in jail.

'Petra *has* resigned,' Gill was saying. 'Says Bay has stopped flirting completely.'

'His wife *has* just left him,' Mo snapped, feeling his pain.

'I know why Bay isn't flirting with Petra,' Bridge insisted as they broke into a trot up the hill to the standing stone witches. 'This is strictly on the hush, but I heard he's given one of his ex-wife's horses to a certain redhead to play with.'

'Pax's producing a jolly nice mare of his,' Gill confirmed. 'And he's looking to buy her another to compete alongside.'

'Bet sexy Luca's fecked off about that.'

'And poor Monique!' Mo stood up for the Dutch ice queen.

'Deliberate brinkmanship,' Gill was tutting. 'Buying horses for another woman is far more hurtful than flowers to wives like us.'

'You might be right,' Mo panted behind them, not wanting to think how she'd feel if Barry bought Dog Tart a nice little cob.

'Hell, yes!' Bridge groaned. 'The day Aleš buys another woman a horse, I'll be on the dark web sorting out a contract on him faster than I can click and buy an Amazon gift voucher.'

'I'd do a *lot* worse than that if it was Paul,' Gill growled. Soon the Bags were trading the worst punishments they could enact for husbands who bought horses for other women, to which Mo eventually conceding that she would bury Barry in the muckheap and plant thistles over it. And she felt strangely cheered.

'That's the spirit!' Bridge tapped her crop against her hard hat, then dropped her voice to a gossipy whisper. 'But what would you do if he bought her a horse costing over a quarter of a million grand?'

'Did you say *a quarter of a million*?' Mo almost fell off.

'Cos that's what Bay Austen's up to.'

'Pax tell you this, did she?' Mo thought Bridge was being a bit disloyal spreading the details around.

'Flynn overheard her and Ronnie talking about it a week or two back,' said Bridge, who lived next door to the stud's gossipy farrier. 'They argue non-stop he says.' She dropped her voice. 'I swear, if I spoke to my mother the way Pax does, I'd never be allowed back in Belfast.'

'She always seems so gentle, Pax,' said Mo.

'She's a lot more rock and roll than she makes out, that chick. And she's a foul temper on her.'

'But why's Bay buying expensive horses?' Mo was struggling to keep up with both the conversation and trot.

'Because he wants to get in Pax's knickers, duh? Takes more than a bunch of service station flowers and a Ferrero Rocher triple pack to win a woman like that.'

'You are quite wrong, Bridget!' Gill held up her arm and they reined to a halt. 'Bay is *not* buying it! He doesn't have that sort of money. I know who is, and it's not Pax's underwear he wishes to inspect.'

Bridge snorted with laughter.

Gill ignored her, 'I looked over the American vet's reports and X-rays for the stud. The stallion's been bought by a Mr Kenneth Brian Kay of Compton Manor. Which means just one thing...'

There was a collective gasp.

'... Kenny Kay is *definitely* trying to woo Ronnie! I told you all along, didn't I, ladies? The suitors are lining up. There'll be pistol duels at dawn.'

Mo also noted this prediction, although she wasn't sure reporting it back would be wise.

They were at the highest point of Church Meadow, overlooking the village. Docks were sprouting up in the blackened circle where the travellers' fire had been.

Mo took her undercover work seriously, envisaging herself as the Donal MacIntyre of the Comptons. She sensed there was a vital piece of information missing. She'd seen the manor's security, after all. And Mum and Dad had told her enough about the Eyngate shooting accident to arouse her suspicions.

'You think Kenny's got any enemies round here?' she asked carefully. 'I heard he had a run in with Nat Turner?'

'There was a silly rumour about a curse,' Gill beckoned them all back into walk, 'but I think Kenny made that up himself to get a comedy routine out of it, like the finger story.'

'Oh yeah, someone posted that on Facebook!' Bridge guffawed.

'Are you sure he made it up?'

'If Kenny didn't, someone else did to give him the collywobbles,' Gill insisted.

'Nat Turner's pretty fecking scary, mind you,' Bridge blew out a breath. 'That man wouldn't have to curse me to give me the collywobbles, ladies.'

Mo rashly told them about her father's plan to hire Nat Turner to duff Barry up.

'I'll beat Barry up for you, queen,' Bridge offered.

'I'd give him a hand-bagging too,' Gill backed her up.

'I'll hold your coats,' Mo giggled, knowing it was probably a terrible thing to joke about it but it bucked her up no end. Laughing about Barry was far easier than talking about him.

'The Turners are all gathering for the King fight soon, aren't they?' asked Gill. 'It's usually around Easter.'

They'd all seen Ash Turner jogging around the village at dusk, shadow boxing like Rocky.

'That must mean Jed's getting out of prison.' Mo felt even cheerier. Perhaps she could still allow herself to harbour a fluttering weakness for tattooed mean boy Jed. She made a mental note to tell Kenny about the forthcoming fight.

'I don't fancy his chances against Ash,' whistled Bridge.

'I heard that Nat's been putting it about that he's coming back here to fight,' Gill told them.

'Nat Turner is fighting his *own son*?' Mo was shocked.

'I'm not sure who the fight is with,' said Gill.

'He'll fight anyone, that man,' said Bridge. 'Carly told me he's gone even more batshit crazy since Ash's mum asked him for a divorce.'

'Nana Turner wants a divorce?' Mo was taking so many mental notes now, she wished she'd brought a pad.

'One can hardly blame her,' Gill was saying. 'That man's barely been back for more than a couple of weeks at a time since Ash was born. The poor woman's agoraphobic, and all the Turners do is dump their kids on her.'

'Mum and Dad always said they was an odd couple,' Mo remembered. 'Him so wild and her so timid. I'm sure Mum said something about Nat stealing her from another gypsy king.'

'I know they lived on the road a long time,' said Gill. 'Nat hadn't been seen back here for years when he rolled up with his little family. I'd just started working at my father's practice, and I remember they had the most magnificent trio of Vanners tethered on Plum Run. Janine must have been two or three and Nana was pregnant with Ash. Then Nat took off with the horses in the middle of the night, leaving her high and dry here.'

'Bastard!' Mo growled.

The Bags growled supportively.

Remembering she had to report all this back to Kenny, she asked, 'Does he strike you as the vengeful sort at all, Nat?'

'Oh, quite definitely,' Gill didn't hesitate.

Mo hoped the boss was sitting down when she told him.

'He's moved into his big house, Nana, that comedian you like.' Carly told her mother-in-law.

Nana looked thrilled, although her eyes stayed glued to *Bargain Hunt* on her big TV. 'That'll cheer the place up. Always loved that man, I have.'

'Everyone's complaining on Facebook about his floodlights and his flagpole. They're more bothered about it than that old stand-up routine he did slagging off this family. That's just got a load of likes and shares.'

'If I bake him a gypsy tart, will you take it round?'

'Suppose so. You could take it round yourself, maybe? I'll walk with you if you like.'

'I might need a bit longer before I can do that, Carly love. I've only made it into the garden twice so far.'

'OK.'

They watched a set of orate fire irons sell at a backwater auction for two hundred pounds less than the contestants had paid for them in a touristy antique emporium, then Carly asked. 'Do you know why Kenny Kay believes our family is out to get him, Nana?'

'Because he thinks he was the one what shot Nat, I imagine.'

'And was he?'

'Shh, look, it's the Beswick shire horse!' Nana craned forward. 'I love a Beswick horse.'

'You don't say?' Carly eyed the large, well-dusted herd in Nana's dingy front room, many glued together after small sticky fingers had reached for them. Pride of place on her dresser were three Vanners she called Peter, Paul and Mary and which she said reminded her of her early days.

'Fifty quid!' she exclaimed when the hammer fell, looking round to count her herd with a chuckle. 'Fancy that. I could be rich.'

'Iago, meet my new Patti. Don't she look just like Kylie Minogue?'

Kenny's son was propping up the big new bar at the manor with his dad when Mo started her afternoon shift promptly at two, dressed in her best weddings-and-funerals suit and bearing a Lemon Drizzle cake.

'It's Maureen, Mr Kay,' she ventured, cheeks flaming, 'or Mo if you prefer.'

'I prefer Patti,' Kenny insisted.

Iago – a hefty, good-looking Ricky Martin type in a Pringle jumper – flashed very white teeth. 'Dad calls all his assistants Patti.'

Kenny's chesty cough rumbled approvingly. 'Because you're a PA who makes tea, Patti. I never want Gay the PA mentioned in this house again. Can I smell cake? Slice it up and debrief me, Patti. By which I mean, give me information, not take my briefs off, eh?!'

Mo shared a long-suffering smile with Iago, grateful her hourly rate was good.

Reporting everything she'd heard on her morning hack back to Kenny, she felt a flash of guilt at her hypocrisy – the mounted puritan turncoat – but she was hardly betraying any secrets, and she sensed he was more interested in her lemon drizzle cake and a bit of company than true village dirt. He already knew all about the village hall mutiny and the Church Meadow sale – 'never negotiate a land deal with a Christian, they've always got the higher ground, eh?!' – and was up to speed with all the latest at the stud: 'Cos I'm buying a stallion to stand there, bab. Like the old days. They tried to flog a leg of it to someone else, but I said who wants a three-legged horse, eh Patti?'

News that Mrs Ledwell was close to Mr Donne caught his attention. 'Still playing the field, is she? Good for her. Always was a flighty sort. Needs to marry again, that one.' He looked delighted at the thought. 'I'll invite her over.'

It was the mention of Nat Turner that made him splutter his second helping of cake.

'He is coming back to fight, he says,' Mo explained. 'The family thinks that means he's challenging one of their own for the King's Purse again – the bare-knuckle bout – but I just heard his wife wants a divorce and he's mad about it, so *I* think it could mean—'

The chesty cough exploded into panicked wheezing. 'I knew

it! I knew he'd come for me! Find out more, Patti! My life – and yours – depends on it! First, I need more cake!'

Iago followed her to the kitchens, a vast shiny cathedral of steel, black granite and German appliances. 'Don't mind Dad. He can be pretty paranoid and living in America made him a security nut. Even his stalker had stalkers for a while.'

'It's very safe round these parts,' she assured him. 'The Turners are fine once you get to know them.'

'Dad doesn't much like getting to know people anymore. He prefers a quiet life.'

'Do you mind me asking why he's come back to the village if he thinks there's a curse on him?'

'He's getting sentimental in old age. When he heard Tina had died, I think he just wanted to turn back time.'

'Like the Cher song?' Mo remembered the ashes the Bags had seen Kenny and Peter Sanson scattering all those weeks ago. She hadn't realized it was Kenny's poor first wife.

'Dad likes to joke that he's never given a tinker's curse about anyone or anything,' the white teeth flashed, 'not even a tinker's curse.'

'He's moved in, have you heard?' Luca told Pax as they undressed quickly in his attic room. 'That comedian fella.'

'Oh yes?' She was only half-listening, already zoning out into her sex-bot mode, sliding off softshell, base layer and sports bra in one. It was Kes's midweek night with his father, so they could afford private time together, although Pax never stayed long up here.

'I told your mother we should invite him over.' He watched her from the bed. He'd found a mountain of tartan blankets in the wardrobe and spread them over it like a Celtic roundhouse, but she still remained restless up here, never settled long enough to talk or relax.

'Mmm?' She went to choose some music from a selection

of vinyl they'd unearthed amid the clutter stored in the attic rooms, along with an ancient portable record player masking as a suitcase which must have once been a teenage Ronnie's.

'Invite him over to have a gang bang,' Luca said casually. 'But she says he doesn't like going out these days.'

She pulled her music choice from its sleeve. 'I'm sure he'll visit when the stallion arrives.'

'Are you listening to what I'm saying?'

'No.' A scratchy static started up as the needle fell on the seven-inch single.

He stared up at the ceiling, exasperated. 'Jesus! Is it just fucking to you, is that it?'

A scratchy static turned into the opening bass notes of the Police's 'Walking on the Moon'.

'It's sport, Luca.' She was dancing towards him.

'C'mere.'

The record player needle was bumping against the label for a long time while Luca and Pax were still bumping against each other.

'We're too good at this,' he said when they finally peeled apart.

She turned to smile into his shoulder. 'I'm still crazy about you.'

'I still adore you.'

'I know you do.' She got out of bed and headed to the record player. 'But you're in love with somebody else.'

He didn't deny it, watching her choose another record, 'Rapture' by Blondie, starting with its breathy descant and bells.

She turned back to him. 'Have you told her that you still love her?'

'Yeah, not long ago.'

She waited.

'She didn't get back to me.'

Blondie had started to rap about aliens from Mars making people into car-eating zombies.

He smiled as Pax swayed in time. 'Good choice.'

She went next door to the bathroom to clean herself up and he lay back on his tartan blankets. She'd be gone in no time, hurrying back downstairs to transform into a hardworking daughter.

Luca understood why she held herself back like this, the rapid role-switching, and that it was his bad habit not hers. Exciting at first, it smacked of déjà vu, of the affairs with unhappy wives that had become his calling card wherever he worked, all tied up with the drinking and denial, the constant need to move on. Except Pax had left her marriage before they'd met. And she'd made no secret of her desire to keep sex separate, or of her desire, which was often volcanic. He might get frustrated that she left friendship at the door for sex, but it kept it safe, somewhere else, in the same way love was made elsewhere. She'd never asked for more.

She was leaning against the bathroom door frame now, watching him as Blondie sent her alien back up into space, telling them it was unable to eat the world while the TV was playing music. The funky disco hip-hop played them out.

'Are you cold?' he asked.

She looked down at her nipples, upturned like hazel buds, then wrapped her arms around herself. 'You need more heaters.'

'You warm me up plenty.' He stood up, walking across to her. Sensing she was about to duck away, he swerved first and gathered up the fiddle from the top of the chest of drawers to play a few melancholy notes. 'Stay and talk.'

'It's my turn to check the mares.' She was already pulling her clothes back on.

'They're all fine. Your mother's on it.'

'Still, I'd better get back down.'

'Hey, I feel used and abused here.' He smiled to underline the joke. 'Stay and talk at least. We never just—'

'Another time.' She kissed him silent.

'Still crazy about me?'

'Still crazy.' She smiled quickly. 'Always crazy, me.'

'And I still—'

'Don't,' she interrupted. 'Let's not go there. Sex isn't sport, Luca. Sport is sport.'

'Meaning?'

'Be a good sport. Don't make me spell it out.'

He said nothing. They both sensed the end was close by. Luca could feel the countdown was in single days, hours maybe.

He held out his bow hand to indicate she should go ahead and leave. Then he played the Kesh jig, a family favourite. Faster and faster to blur his thoughts and cheer himself up.

When he came down later, his mood had darkened. He couldn't find a place for the easy-going smile on his face, all shared sexual connection with Pax washed away with a shower. He checked his phone every time he got signal, but Meredith still hadn't replied. It had been days.

Ronnie was sitting at the kitchen table, talking on the landline phone, all growling and giggling flirtation, glancing up at him quickly and managing a hand gesture that at once said the mares are fine, are you OK, I'm busy and go away.

He was grateful for Ronnie. Her transparency was a fertile little glasshouse compared to Pax's secretive laboratory.

Drawn to the dining room by the booming television, he found Pax watching a crime drama with Lester, who was reluctant to relinquish his temporary room digs, television, Wi-Fi and regular meal service. Neither of them noticed him come in. The killer was about to be revealed. The old man had a glass of plum gin on the go, not his first judging by the colour in his cheeks. Luca caught the familiar sweet scent, his tongue pressing into his teeth, longing for the slake of it.

He slipped back out, moving beside the coats to check messages again. Still nothing. Unable to stop himself he mistyped *Massage me.*

A scream from the dining room television made him jump and press send too soon.

He typed *Mess*—

'Skulking out here again, Luca?' It was Ronnie, about to head out on foal check, pausing beside him as she shrugged on her coat.

He'd pressed send again. 'Fuck! I mean fine! All good!'

She peered closer. 'Are you sure?'

'Yup.'

There was another bloodcurdling scream from the dining room.

Ronnie dropped her voice to an undertone. 'I am loathe to interfere, Luca, but I'm worried about you, and about Pax.'

'We're grand.' The last thing they needed was well-meaning motherly interference.

She tilted her head, rolling her lips beneath her teeth uncertainly.

'Tell me, do you know anything about these?' She swung one foot to the side as though dancing a rhumba, kicking a boot standing by the skirting. It clanked.

Luca looked down to see an empty bottle in it, and the one beside it, and the one beside that. 'No.'

'Come on, Luca!' She thought he was lying. He could see it in her face.

'I swear to God, I know nothing about them.'

Police car sirens started up in the dining room.

'Fine.' She picked up two of the bottles, slid them under her arm like a sergeant major's drill canes. 'Stop bloody drinking.'

She headed outside with them.

Luca was tempted to take after her to plead his case, but he couldn't leave his little Wi-Fi hotspot.

He tried again. *Message me. Please. I love you.*

Mo let Mum make her a fry-up, even though she still had no appetite. 'You're wasting away, Maureen, isn't she Sid?'

'Plenty of condition on her still.'

'Thanks, Dad.' She forked her bacon onto his plate.

He forked it across to Jan. 'They really tell Barry your bungalow is worth that much?'

'The agent says values have almost doubled round here since we bought it.'

'Cos all them London buyers are half-witted,' he huffed. 'What my dad paid for this place wouldn't buy a caravan nowadays. How much your new boss pay for the Manor?'

'Several million, I believe.'

'Lord alive!' Joan reached across to spear a tomato for Jan and help herself to the extra piece of bacon. 'To think, Kenny Kay came from nothing. He was ever so humble on that Piers Morgan interview.'

'Do you remember his wife?' Mo asked, detective hat on.

'Exotic. Brazilian maybe.' Sid offered too eagerly.

'That was his second wife, Dad, and she's Colombian. The first one was the one he bought all the showjumpers for.'

'Can't picture her.'

'They was always together, the three of them,' Joan's face scrunched up as she thought back. 'Him, her and Peter Sanson.'

'Rolling up swanky cars to drink in the Jug,' Sid's face scrunched too, 'Kenny always got all the attention, I remember that much.'

'We were none of us surprised when he strayed. He was always a one for the ladies.'

'Do you know what became of Tina after they got divorced?' asked Mo.

They both shrugged.

'I hope she kept the horses,' said Jan.

Mo ate a mushroom and felt sorry for poor Tina, traded in and forgotten. Except that Kenny hadn't forgotten her.

Just like Barry hadn't forgotten her.

He'd texted the news about the bungalow's value late last night. Surprisingly late last night. Lambing was over, so he must have just been wide awake at midnight, like her, unable to sleep. They'd exchanged quite a few messages. She asked him if he wanted to sell it and he said he wasn't sure. He said things were a bit tricky with Bev. Mo didn't like to pry, but he was quite forthcoming about it. Bev wanted to change him, he said. And she kept buying things. She'd bought him a rowing machine. And she'd put him on a diet. Then he'd messaged that he missed Mo, and that he was sorry he hurt her. Really sorry. And perhaps they could meet up somewhere neutral to talk about it sometime soon?

His spelling had got a lot better again, she noticed.

But she wasn't ready to drop her guard, so she'd told him she was too busy with her new job *working for Kenny Kay* right now and perhaps he'd like to treat Grace to a special day out instead, just the two of them?

Men who left their wives for younger women were bad enough, Mo felt, but the ones walking away from their kids that got her goat most.

'Do you remember Nat Turner abandoning his wife and kids to go back on the road?' she asked her parents.

'Never forget it,' Joan nodded. 'Poor little thing with a babe in arms and another on the way. Betty and Norm took her in and set her up on the estate. Betty used to say she was Mother Goose without Nat around. She just wanted her own little house full of children. She loves kids, does Tina Turner.'

Mo heard 'We Don't Need Another Hero' rasping in her head. Then the music stopped. 'That's really her name?'

28

'I hear you've moved in, Kenny! Welcome!'
Ronnie had climbed to the top coppice, from where she could just make out a flag snapping on the new pole beside the manor.

'Princess!'

'Your fabulous new horse arrives next Sunday. When would you like to come and meet him? We'll lay on a VIP tour.'

'That's very kind, bab, but they're all dangerous at both ends as far as I'm concerned. The first wife used to like all that patting and giving mints fandango, but I preferred the black-tie dinners and pretty Russian gymnasts dancing on horses' backs between classes if I'm honest.'

'He's an eventer not a showjumper, so it's a bit different,' Ronnie explained, 'but there's far more chance of royalty. Would you rather come for supper instead? I can rustle some locals for you to meet.' Please let Petra Gunn and her raffish husband be free; the senior Austens and Kit Donne would make for very dry company.

'Tell you what, why don't you just call by for a cuppa when you're passing? Patti makes a smashing cake. You were right about her.'

Vaguely wondering who Patti was, Ronnie asked, 'When did you have in mind?'

'No hurry, Princess, whenever you're free. I'm not going anywhere,' he chuckled and coughed, 'I'm Lord of the Manor now.'

She promised she'd pop by soon.

'He's not the party animal he was,' Ronnie grumbled to Kit later, having interrupted his writing on an evening dog walk to share an illicit glass of wine.

'You didn't invite him to a party, you invited him to meet his horse.' Kit was in a querulous mood, shirt on inside out, dark stubble, eye bags and a stifled yawns suggesting he'd not looked up from his play manuscript since their Stratford lunch. 'That's like complaining someone isn't an art lover because they don't want to bungee jump.'

'You really don't like horses, do you?'

He'd turned away to hide another yawn, spinning back crossly now. 'Do you blame me? One smashed up my wife's clever head.'

'It wasn't a horse that caused Hermia's accident, it was a motorist.' Uncomfortably aware that she might know who had been behind the wheel, she hurried on, 'And regardless of that, one horse is not all horses, just as one car driver is not all humans.'

'Spoken like a true philosopher.' His yawn was jaw-dislocating this time.

Ronnie might choose to ignore the intellectual sneer, but she couldn't ignore a third yawn, covering her still-full glass which he was trying to top up. 'Would you like to go to bed?'

'Not particularly. I am very grateful for your company, Ronnie, and I've enjoyed kissing very much but I don't think this should progress to a sexual level.'

'I meant you look tired,' she smiled. 'But I'm glad we've cleared that up.'

Luca knew Pax would want a quick getaway – galloping was her bad day default – so he waited until they were riding the three-mile point to talk to her. He was on Beck, she on Lester's cob.

It wasn't such a good idea in practice. Beck was acting up, picking up on his tension, wound up by the constant new arrivals on the yard, the heady density of mares, and the fact his corner stable was so visible to visitors, they all flocked to admire his beauty. Riding him was wall-of-death hair-raising enough without trying to tackle Pax about how difficult he was finding their relationship.

The grey stallion pogoed along beside the tough, fast trundling cob, his eyes white-rimmed, nostrils pink as peonies, veins in high relief.

He had to speak faster and louder than he would have liked because Beck was plunging and high breathing so much. 'I think we should cool it, Pax. There's too much going on. At the stud, in my head, in your head, in the fucking world. Sex isn't sport. I got that wrong. This isn't working, you and me.'

She rode bedside him in silence for so long he wondered if she'd heard. Beck snorted yet louder, pogoed higher.

At last, she cleared her throat. 'Yup. Absolutely. Point taken.'

He waited.

She didn't gallop off. Instead, she said, 'Didn't we already do this?'

'We did?'

'Sport is sport, be a sport, remember?'

'No, you've lost me.'

'In your room, after the Police walked on the moon last night, I told you that it had to stop.'

'You did? Then you were way too subtle for an Irish wrangler like me.'

'Luca, you have to stop drinking.'

'You sound like your mother.'

They rode on, Beck now performing airs above the ground like a carousel at full tilt while Luca eyed the horizon trying to work out what all the sport talk was about.

They crossed another headland in silence before he remembered to add. 'And I'm not drinking.'

'You expect me to believe that? I've smelled it on you.'

'Maybe I wobbled a couple of times at the start, like you did, but I haven't touched any since you and I... not for weeks.'

'You hide bottles in the boots like my father used to!'

Luca said nothing. He'd seen them being placed in there before Ronnie had pointed them out to him. A curious, private ritual. Only The Famous Grouse bottles, the really old ones used year after year for damson gin, some two or three decades old.

'Lester puts them there,' he said eventually.

There was a long pause, then she half-laughed. 'Nice try, but I'm not buying it.'

Now she galloped away, sending Beck into a tailspin panic.

Managing to anchor the eruption, Luca calmed the stallion enough to start jogging in the right direction again. Then his phone went off in his pocket, detonating a four-legged body swerve that deposited him underfoot.

Scrabbling up, he watched Beck trot off, his white tail high-flagging with anything but surrender, shrilling to the horizon for the cob, roaring for mares, then snake-curling his neck and eyeing freedom.

Last time he'd got loose, Beck had caused mayhem. Please not again.

He gave chase. His phone was still ringing in his pocket. He pulled it out. 'Luca O'Brien.'

'How...manytimeshave...I...told...you...toleavemydaugh–ter... a... lone, Luca?' It was the Flying Maple Leaf on a terrible line. He sounded as though he was going through a garden mulcher. 'How many... times, Luca?'

Luca was breathless from running. 'I've lost count, sir!'

Miraculously, Beck had abandoned the idea of catching up with his friend and was snacking nervously on a nearby hedge, eyes bulging, veins popping. Luca grabbed the reins. The stallion cast him a relieved *don't let go* look, deeply insecure beneath the bravado.

Luca knew plenty just like that.

Maple Leaf was still raging down the bad line. 'I'll... whipyourarse... if you... lay a... fingeronher... again!'

Luca found he could hear Pax in his head, that deep, calm voice dead-panning fear, finding laughter in adversity, telling him he loved Meredith.

He looked at Beck, who looked back, reminding him that he was addicted to loving the most difficult of creatures for a reason.

'Nice try,' he stole her line, telling Maple Leaf, 'but I'm not buying it.'

Pax let the cob thunder along the point, grateful for the rush of air roaring in her ears and drying a few stray tears, a burning sadness in her chest. She wasn't heartbroken; it wasn't that. And she wasn't particularly angry that Luca had completely failed to register they'd already had this endgame conversation, after sex and Blondie and him playing her out with a violin. Or at least she thought they had. She was still relieved it was over, but the thudding sense of failure chased her heels nonetheless, another demon. Even Luca's goodness hadn't been good enough to save her.

She felt she'd let him down badly. She was sure he was still drinking, the story about Lester typical blarney. He'd helped her stay off it, but she couldn't return the favour. And he had so much more at stake.

Luca the nomad was in love with somebody else's wife half a world away, his daughter not in his life. By contrast, Pax's son shared the fierce protection of both his parents. And as for her love – locked safely back in a tin she kept far from sight – it was right next door.

The cob's head shot up, small ears flicking sideways as he

spotted a tractor muck-spreading in the neighbouring field, the sour tang carrying in the air.

She was on Austen land, she realized, its headlands wide and well-tended, fat round hedges punctuated with hunt jumps, lambs bleating after ewes in the field ahead of her. Bay looked after his farmland conscientiously, letting pasture recover and maintaining wildlife habitats. His land was what old countrymen called 'in good heart', his long, wood-flanked shoots a haven for nature's family-rearing in this off season. The contrast between these lush, quilted surroundings and Sanson Holdings' industrially farmed thousand-acre crop desert on the horizon was all too visible. And then there was the stud's forgiving old turf, its grass tell-tale patchy on close inspection, hedging overgrown and fences broken, testament to years of genteel neglect. The stud needed good heart. Her own was ready to be kinder too.

She would make things better with Luca, Pax vowed. Help him stay sober. Unpack their friendship again. Be less fucked up together.

And she would behave like a grown-up with Bay. They were neighbours after all. With luck, their children would grow up alongside one another. She had liked the person she'd been when their childhoods had met across these fields, and she still remembered who she'd wanted to become. Who she had wanted to be with.

No sooner had she thought it than the urge to see Bay was burning around her head like a sparkler, refusing to go out.

The cob was back to a trot now, and Pax focussed on the rhythm of it, drumming away her wilfulness. It was wicked to want to rush straight to Bay the moment things came unravelled with Luca.

She rode determinedly past one of the back drives to Compton Farm. Then she stopped at the next field boundary to check her phone for signal. I was time to set things back on the right footing. She must put being a good neighbour and friend first. Safeguard the future for their two families.

Bay answered in two rings. 'What a coincidence! I was just thinking about you!'

'You were?'

'Given I can't stop thinking about you, it's nothing to get excited about.'

'Put that line back where you found it.'

'Not a line,' he said cheerfully. 'Is everything all right? How's my mare getting on?'

Talking to him was, she realized, surprisingly easy. Normal. A lot less stressful than hanging around by the coats messaging one emoji to say a thousand words. She brought him up to date on Lottie's latest progress, and told him about their first foal, and the anxious wait for more. Then she asked him for advice about how to put their land in good heart, and when he offered to fertilise it this year, they didn't even snigger. It was all gloriously, good-heartedly grown-up.

'Your new stallion arrived yet?' he asked.

'Flying in overnight on Saturday, and we pick him up the day after.'

'I was robbed of that leg.'

'Plenty more event horse legs out there.'

'In that case, you and I must discuss syndicated legs and soil improvement over coffee sometime. And that's not a line either.'

'Liar. You've used it before I can feel.'

'You're right. Always works.'

Laughing, she pictured her wall planner, its highlighted days like pixel art from next week, and before she had time to think it through, she was asking, 'Are you free on Saturday? If you have the children that day, maybe we get the boys together?'

'You're asking us out on a double date?' He sounded amused.

'I'm working the yard in the morning and Kes wants to ride, but we're free in the afternoon.' She pictured them at an historic castle, or a steam railway maybe? Woolly hats and colourful wellies, fresh air and laughing faces.

'Terrific! Tilly has some Pony Club sleepover thing, so I've promised Bram he can burn off a loaded gourmet burger in Broadbourne's finest ball-pit hellhole to make up for it. Join us.'

'*The Bounce Barn?*' Her heart sank. Mecca for weekend dads, the Cotswold soft play centre in the overpriced Shopping Village was a sensory overload, conveniently placed between a Joules outlet and The Entertainer.

'He's absolutely addicted to the place. Exhausts him completely. I'll buy you a coffee there and bore you about fertilisers while they hang off cargo nets.'

Her heart lifted back up, realizing Kes would love it too, and this this was exactly the sort of safe, friendly encounter she needed. 'We'd like that.'

'Good. Let's meet there. Message me when you're setting out. Lester's cob's looking good, by the way. Never seen him so fit. Or you, come to that.' He rang off.

She looked round, realizing his Land Rover was in the neighbouring sheep field, its sides coated in mud, two lambs in the back. An arm was raised out of the window before he drove on, turning onto a farm track and disappearing under the tree canopy.

From now on, Pax vowed to find good heart in everything: in herself, in her family's land, in the horses they bred, and in their neighbours.

Maybe some of Luca's goodness had rubbed off after all.

Walking around the foaling barns with Lester tested Ronnie's patience – he moved agonisingly slowly and spent a long time assessing each heavily pregnant mare – so she kept busy by skipping out the straw beds and filling troughs. She appreciated that his methodical, encyclopaedic knowledge was priceless. He knew many of the visiting mares from previous visits, his hands-on experience invaluable. 'She's had two breach, so we'll need to watch her closely; this one's last foal had contracted tendons and she tends to do too good by them with her milk; this old girl's had four here, all nice sorts – looks about ready, I'd say.'

'Pax is pH testing the milk,' Ronnie reminded him. 'She'll know which are likely to foal within forty-eight hours.'

'I always know when they're going to foal using these and this,' he huffed, pointing to his eyes then tapping his flat cap.

'Yes, but we can't carry you around like a test kit, can we Lester? And you can't do overnight watch anymore. Eight hours sleep on doctor's orders, remember?'

He needed a little sit down on a straw bale before they looked over the home mares. 'I'll be right in a minute. Not ready to be pensioned off just yet.'

'Who said anything about pensioning you off?' She perched beside him. 'Although I did hear a rumour you might be tempted to visit New Zealand?'

His old face brightened. 'Nice to be asked, but I think I'll stay here thank you. If I'm wanted, that is.'

'Of course you're wanted, Lester, and needed. Pax will need you,' she added, watching his face.

He nodded, half smiled to himself, looked away. 'Our little Master Imp thoroughbred will be here in two days.'

'You worked hard to get him here,' she acknowledged.

'Mr Robertson said to. He said not to let this one go under any circumstances. That you need it.'

'Good to know he cares.' There had been no further contact from Blair. In quieter moments, she played Bunny's warning that he might go back to Australia back and forth like a tongue across a broken tooth, but she knew better than to break their silence. His grief deserved more loyalty than that.

'I should have thanked you properly for approaching Kenny Kay about him,' she told Lester. 'I wouldn't have been so bold. I was always rather fond of Kenny, but I know Daddy hated him by the end.'

'No, he didn't,' said Lester.

'Oh, come on Lester. He told him never to darken our door again. He was terribly angry with him for welshing on their deal. He even took a shot at him, if Kenny's version is to be believed.'

'That's not what happened,' Lester muttered. 'I was there.'

'Tell me what did happen then.'

He propped his crutches against the straw bale, fussing with them to give himself time to think.

'Mr Kay had drunk too much at the shoot lunch, as I recall,' he said eventually. 'Nobody held back in those days. He became rather offensive afterwards, shouting the odds in the gun bus. He seemed to want to annoy Mr Sanson. They had a somewhat unusual arrangement, if you recall, involving Mrs Kay.'

'Kenny's wife moving in with Peter after the marriage ended, you mean?'

'That's right.' Lester reached down to scratch Stubbs who was lying stiffly underfoot. 'Mr Kay seemed very vexed about it. He suggested Mr Sanson couldn't give her what she wanted because he was,' he paused then said over-quickly, 'because he was secretly a homosexual.'

Ronnie waited for Lester to regather the creases of his face, aware how hard he still found it to talk openly on the subject. 'Then Mr Kay drew your father into it, telling him that Mr Sanson and Johnny – saying they were...' He stared fixedly at a partition hurdle. 'Saying things.'

'Peter and *Johnny*?'

'That's what he said. Mr Kay claimed he'd caught them together at a party here at the stud.'

'Was there any truth in that?'

'A brief liaison, no more. Johnny had other – acquaintances.'

'But he loved you above all others, Lester.'

'If you say so,' he mumbled, clearing his throat and patting Stubbs again, hugely uncomfortable.

Ronnie let out a long breath, finally starting to make sense of it all. If it was true, it could be why Peter never laid a finger on Hermia. Her friend had been right, it was all for show. Like the models he used to hire by the limo-full to party with. And Kenny would be bound to know his secret. They'd been best friends since infancy, after all, they had each other's backs. 'But what possessed him to out Peter as gay at a shoot, in front of others?' she said aloud. 'And Johnny too? No wonder Daddy was livid. *I'd* have shot him.'

'Your father never shot Mr Kay,' Lester said quickly. 'I did.'

Ronnie turned to him in shock.

'I was loading the second gun for your father. It went off.' He paused. 'Accidentally.'

Ronnie remembered Lester had been an absolute stickler for safety protocol, but she wasn't about to question this.

'Terrible, it was,' he went on. 'The flags went up and the warning whistles to stop the drive, but a lot of the guns were total novices, so there was a fair degree of chaos and loose shots. Which was when we heard screaming from the woods and found Nat Turner had been injured.'

'My God, did you shoot him too? Two birds with one Beretta?'

'The guns were Holland and Hollands, Mrs Led— I mean, Ronnie. And no, I didn't shoot Nat. He was out of position, a long way from the other beaters, stopping birds running from the woods. Peppered with shot in his neck and shoulder, he was. Terrible mess. Nobody took responsibility. There were a lot of low birds that day and the guns had enjoyed a very good lunch, as I say.

'Nat Turner was paid a large sum of money for his silence afterwards. I don't know how the rumours started that it was Mr Kay who shot him. Same way all this nonsense about a curse caught hold, I imagine. But I do know it couldn't possibly have been Mr Kay, whose gun was still loaded with two unspent cartridges.'

'Too busy shooting his mouth off to shoot a beater.' Ronnie could imagine her father's outrage and Lester's quiet fury. 'Goodness, what a day you all had!'

'Your father insisted on taking the blame for my actions. A gentleman's agreement, he said. We never spoke of it again, nor what was said about Johnny that day.'

'But Daddy knew about your relationship?'

'Oh yes, he knew. He was very kind when Johnny died. Very understanding.'

'You must have been so heartbroken.'

He sniffed, keeping his voice deliberately no-nonsense. 'I don't mind saying, I miss him every day. Especially when the foals are close.' He looked up at the mares shifting through their straw, their bellies low with readiness. 'Johnny loved the foals coming. Out here night and day, he was.'

She remembered.

'Used to keep his whisky bottles in the boots in the back hall – swig on the way out, swig on the way back in, not a drop between. Only time he could control his drinking, foaling.'

Ronnie would argue Johnny could never really control it but stayed quiet because Lester was still staring at the mares, misty eyed with nostalgia and love. 'I put a bottle there myself sometimes, just to remember him.'

'You do?'

'Makes me think he's still around when I catch sight of it. That he's just gone outside to check the mares, you know?'

Ronnie had accused Luca of hiding them there, she remembered guiltily. As if such a thing would even occur to the Irish rider. It was Lester's memento mori.

She covered his hand with hers for a moment. 'Which makes even more extraordinary that you suggested Kenny stand a horse here again.'

'Not at all. The least the man can do is help this place back on its feet.'

They could hear hooves clattering into the yard.

Ronnie glanced round. 'That'll be Pax and Luca. They can talk to you about pH testing milk.'

'She's very like him, I've always thought.'

'Like Johnny?' She found herself double-checking.

'The most like her father of the three, by far. See Johnny in her all the time.'

'Yes, so do I.' She smiled.

The klaxon was ringing out. She checked her watch. 'That might be the yard in Canada about the stallion. I'll be back to look over the rest of the mares with you in a minute.'

Pax had returned alone and beaming beneath her helmet peak.

'Good ride?' Ronnie hurried past. 'Where's Luca?'

'We had a disagreement.' She jumped off.

'Not about anything important I hope?'

'Just sex,' she ran up her stirrups, 'and his drinking.'

Almost at the tack room door, Ronnie turned back. 'I was wrong about that.'

Pax turned away, her forehead resting against the cob's shoulder for a moment. 'It doesn't matter. It's better this way.'

Ronnie could guess the rest. Whatever they'd had was over. She'd always feared it might crash early like this, because no matter how compatible two people were, being hopelessly in love with someone else inevitably blew the tyres of the getaway car. She should know.

The phone was ringing still.

'I must get this,' she said. 'Let's talk later.'

The yard extension was horribly crackly, its wires held together with bandage tape. But there was no mistaking that deep, rumbling bass.

'Hi Ron.'

She let out a silent cry of relief, leaning back against the wall. 'Hey you.'

'Sorry I've been quiet. Funeral was a crock of shit, wasn't it?'

She swallowed a smile. 'How've you been?'

'Oh, y'know. Lonely. Just want to see her.'

She thought of Lester putting bottles in boots to conjure Johnny being outside checking the mares, even though he'd died twenty years ago. 'I'm not sure that goes away.'

'Good. Means I get to keep her with me. Carrying quite a weight here, what with you still sitting on my shoulder.'

'Am I?'

'I miss you, Ron.'

'Same.'

There was a long pause, filled with the bone-deep relief of being back in touch.

'I wasn't going to call just yet,' he admitted. 'Don't want you dragged into everything going on here.'

'Is it that bad?'

'Had easier months.'

'I heard the Verneys wasted no time circling.'

'They were always going to jump on my neck. I can tough that one out. Thing is, Ron, I need your help. I've landed us both in some hot water. I'm sorry. And I'm going to have to ask you to let me have something I know you want to keep.'

Ronnie watched her dogs curling into patient little doughnuts at her feet.

'Not Cruisoe's yearling?' Blair had been after the dun buckskin from the start.

The laugh started so quietly it was barely a vibration over the crackling phone line. Then it built, roaring closer and louder like a great surf-topped wave rolling in. How she'd missed that laugh.

'Only you would think I'm after a horse.'

'You're not?'

'My kingdom for a little more trust, Ron.'

A long pause followed, loaded with thirty years of love and understanding.

Then Ronnie started to laugh too, knowing him far too well.

'It's a horse.'

★

Lester had given up waiting for Ronnie to return to the foaling barn. Out on the yard, Luca had just ridden in, muddy-breeched and pale-faced, the grey stallion dancing on hot coals.

'What happened?' Lester made his way slowly across to them. 'Not like you to fall off.'

'Just a bit of a green moment. Irish riding!'

That infernal smile of his infuriated Lester. The lad was plainly a brilliant horseman, handled the stallions well – especially this one – was a more than passable stud groom and charmed the clients, but the ever-present smile was far too dazzling. The Captain would never have stood for it.

Ronnie was shouting from the tack room. 'Luca! Can you come in here and take over this call?'

'Hold him, will you?' the smile demanded.

Finding himself clutching the reins of his *bête noire*, Beck, Lester gripped his crutch in the other hand and prayed quietly. The *bête noire* glared at him. He glared back. They'd never got on.

Slowly, he eased his sweating fingers from the crutch handle and propped it against his side to feel in his pocket for a mint.

The *bête noire* snorted and eyed him closer.

He offered a medley of Extra Strong, Polo and Fox's Glacier.

The *bête noir* whispered them into his mouth with the lightest of flicks from his pink-tinged muzzle then looked at him with murder in his eyes.

Ronnie broke up the duel, striding across the yard to take the reins and lead the horse away. 'How fit are you feeling, Lester?'

'Greatly improved Mrs Led— Ronnie.'

'Excellent! Because we're about to ring in some big changes around here.'

Lester hadn't seen her this effervescent in months. This was the Ronnie he knew of old, marching off, tiny and indominable, the big grey horse at her side putting on a great plunging power show of dominance and aggression that didn't faze her for a moment, although Lester personally thought her lucky to survive in one piece when they passed Cruisoe's stable and the two stallions reared up, roaring like male elephant seals.

'Stop that at once!' she snapped, much as she'd tell off Kes for putting his fingers in the butter.

Lester let out a breath of relief when she got the horse into his stable.

He started after her, crutches squeaking. 'He doesn't belong here, he's not safe. Pax can't handle him, for a start. We don't want to see her hurt.'

'I'm sure she's perfectly capable of handling him, but you're quite right. He doesn't belong on this yard. He only came here to get away from somebody who was quite hopelessly in love with him and couldn't give him what he needed.'

He cleared his throat awkwardly. 'Are you talking about the stallion, Mrs Ledwell?'

She carried his tack out of the stable, shutting the door quickly before Beck could plunge out too. 'What do you think?'

29

'**D**idn't he do terrifically? Lovely sight to see!' Ronnie's voice rang out as she led the pony across the little training paddock where Kes had been enjoying his Saturday morning riding lesson.

Reaching for the gate, Pax wondered whether her mother was talking about her grandson or Lester, who – resplendent in head-to-toe moleskin – had stood without his crutch or stick for his longest stretch so far to teach his third generation of Percy children to ride. Refusing to be seated, he'd leant against the rails of the small schooling paddock while Ronnie towed her grandson around for twenty minutes on their borrowed Shetland, both repeatedly barking a 'chin up!' or 'kick on!' like something out of the Raj.

Not that Kes seemed to mind, chattering excitedly at the end of a lead rope, the joy of a child on a pony no different if his instructor was modern and holistic or an old school boot-thumper.

'Can I keep riding?' he asked when Pax took over the lead rope from her mother, dark eyes luminous beneath the low helmet peak. 'We can go round the village green like we did last time? Please, Mum, *please!*'

He'd dropped the tail-end 'my' from 'Mum' since starting at the village school, she'd noticed. While Pax was happy to adapt, Ronnie would only answer to 'Gronny', waving them through the gate now with a pointed, 'What do you say, *Mummy*? Quick trot round the block? I'll bring old Dickon along for a spin.'

'Can't I'm afraid, we're going into Broadbourne.' She'd kept the plan to meet Bay and Bram secret, hugging it to herself, a surprise for Kes whose weekends with her were usually far duller and more practical than his father's.

'I want to keep riding!' Kes howled in protest. When Pax promised him there was a special treat in store, he looked doubtful. 'Last time you said that it was the dentist, Mum.'

'Followed by a Happy Meal.'

'The time before that it was a haircut.'

'Followed by a Pixar movie. Popcorn. Strawberry laces. Rotten teeth.'

He still looked sceptical, a small scowling cowboy. 'I like riding Coll best.'

'Then I promise I'll take you around the village tomorrow,' offered Ronnie, taking a photo of him on her phone. 'Back in the day, I used to take Aunt Alice and Uncle Tim hacking with me, leading one each side.'

Not for the first time, Pax sensed her mother reliving the past through Kes, hoping for a different outcome. This morning's trip down memory lane being a prime example. Pax also sensed she was deliberately making memories for them all.

Although Pax had been a toddler when Ronnie had abandoned her family – had barely started walking in fact – she'd already been in the saddle. There was a photograph somewhere of her being held in a Shetland's basket seat by a smiling, red-cheeked nanny at a hunt meet alongside an immaculately booted Ronnie, her mother's merry blue eyes drifting off camera, doubtless seeking out the handsome jump jockey she'd later run off with.

Pax had no memory of the day, but the photograph had planted one, an image she'd clung to for years. Amongst the

blurred figures in the background had been the Austens: Viv
and Sandy looking very Charles and Camilla with their blue
hunt collars, their children all in ratcatchers and mounted on
hairy ponies. One of them was Bay, then about the same age
as Kes, grinning mischievously straight at the camera. The
naughty boy next door.

Ronnie was still reminiscing about her days leading her older
children on ponies. 'D'you remember the picnic rides we did,
Lester? Up to the windmill, with the children all mounted?'

'Quite the sight.' The old man nodded. He was stony faced,
creases deep furrowed, a sure sign that he was in pain again, his
exertions over-stretching him.

'You need a rest.' Ronnie took his arm to help him back to
the house, ignoring his protests. 'Big day tomorrow.'

The new stallion was arriving at last. The lorry had been
pressure-hosed especially, already brim-full of fuel and water,
and loaded up with bulging haynets and their best travel gear.
As skittish with excitement as any of the mares, Ronnie was
bossier than ever, an alpha exerting her authority. Messages
had been hurtling back and forth across the Atlantic all week,
Mostly forth.

'The time difference is infuriating,' she was telling Lester, 'I
appreciate they're all asleep in Canada right now, but nobody
replied to my messages or calls yesterday, not Maple Leaf
or Kenny. I think I should be in the loop, don't you? By my
calculation, it'll be two in the morning UK time when they load
him on the cargo flight.'

'Easier when they came over on a ferry from Ireland,' Lester
remembered.

'Weren't those the days! A clutch of Imperious and Chair
Lift yearlings for a few hundred guineas.'

Watching them walk away, the house beyond them a vast,
honeyed mausoleum of old bloodlines and family secrets, Pax
felt the weight of the past on her shoulders, the repressed
formality of her grandparents still overshadowing them, their

customary resistance to change, their utter refusal to tackle emotions. Misogyny was a running Percy theme. Her mother's wildness had never found comfort here, nor her own. Both had run away. Pax could see the irony in this opportunity to rebuild it together, two strong Percy women at the helm.

Perhaps Ronnie was right. They must make new memories. But not by replicating the past. The snobbery and feuds belonged to another era. They must modernise, adapt, build new alliances and find a relationship which allowed them to live and work more easily together. Unaccustomed to close proximity, or a maternal bond, they created constant invisible static. Picking up on it inevitably made Kes even more hyper.

'Don't want to go out shopping!' he complained again now.

'It won't take long.'

'Want to see Dad!'

'You'll talk to him on the phone later.'

'Want to say *here*!'

'That's not possible Kes.'

'Luca promised me to ride on the tractor.'

'It's his day off, Kes. He's not here.'

Luca had vanished at first light, borrowing the yard's elderly Subaru, leaving Ronnie to relate an over-complicated explanation about arranging for him to visit her friend Bunny near Chippenham. Pax understood that he was maintaining a diplomatic distance; the awkwardness between them would take time to pass. But her mother's bossy involvement in it irritated her, just as it has in Kes's riding lesson, leaving her unchecked in her mounting desire to overturn tables, or to snatch up the ever-klaxoning phone and tell callers to bugger off.

Dumping the pony's saddle in the tack room, she took the latest call, trying to be jaw-aching polite to an owner who wanted to drop a maiden mare off today instead of next week. 'Taking one we've just sold off at Moreton Morrell later so we thought we might as well throw her on the lorry too and save on diesel. And the goat.'

'A goat?'

'Companion. Nippy. Can't tolerate straw. Put a shavings down for them both, will you?'

'Is the mare about to come into season?'

'Shouldn't be too long. Captain P never minded taking them a couple of weeks early. You'll be doing me a favour, darling. There's a bottle of good malt in it.'

'I'm afraid we simply can't take them today.' She tried to inject some of her mother's firm jollity into her voice, looking round and realizing Kes had sloped off to dinosaur hunt with Ellis Turner again.

'You the daughter?' he barked.

'Granddaughter.'

'Word of advice, darling: be less of a two-star fucking motel receptionist.' He rang off.

'Bastard.'

'Not Mack again?' Ronnie hurried in to grab Dickon's tack.

'A client. Oh God, I think I was too officious. Perhaps I should call him back? He could drop his mare off today, couldn't he? You're here.'

'Is she ready to cover?'

'No.'

'Let him wait,' Ronnie stood beside her, saddle in hand. 'Visiting mares eat profit and man-hours.'

'I do know.'

'Of course you do. You're far more clued up about how this place runs nowadays than I am.'

Pax knew that wasn't strictly true, but her mother said it so often and with such assurance that she was grateful for the faith in her.

'Now you're sure none of our girls are about to foal today?'

'I tested those closest to foaling first thing. Nothing imminent.'

'Just what I thought looking at them, although Lester's convinced Nancy and Maggie have got a bet on who'll be first.

He's just having a nap then he'll be checking again. You and Kes stay out as long as you like. I'm hacking, then I'll take over after Carly goes. Could you let her know?'

She shot off, which Pax realized meant the petty cash must be too low to pay wages.

Carly was in the bachelor barn, currently empty while the little herd was turned out for the day, Ellis and Kes trampling through the bedding nearby in search of pterodactyl eggs.

She reluctantly removed an earphone while Pax approached.

'I'm only here till one, remember,' she said when told she'd be on her own for a while.

Pax called for Kes, who ignored her, charging off with Ellis to clamber on the round-bale feeder that Ronnie had bent so much with the tractor forks they were pretending it was a cage recently vacated by an escaped Tyrannosaurus rex.

'ELLIS!' Carly bellowed.

He came straight away, cheeks blazing pink with excitement. 'We're going to breed Iguanodons!'

'And a Stegosaurus!' Kes panted up behind.

As they made their way back to the yard all together, Pax asked if Carly would like Ellis to try out a riding lesson with Kes. 'We could make it a regular Saturday thing if he likes it?'

She was quick to dismiss the offer. 'We're good. thanks. Petra let him sit on one of their other ponies a while back, but Ellis wasn't keen. He wants to be a boxer like his granddad.'

Pax watched the boys bounding side by side. 'How is Ellis's grandfather?'

'Gathering an army, Uncle Norm reckons.'

'Where's the war?'

'In his head, most likely. He's a Turner man, don't forget.' They watched Ellis and Kes gunning down imaginary T-rexes. 'One minute they're playing at dinosaurs, the next they are one.'

'Not just Turner men.'

'Luca mucking you round, is he?'

Pax looked at her sharply, wondering how much she knew.

'He's not so modern as he likes to think, that one. Classic Ross and Rachel situation.'

'From *Friends?*'

'Me and Nana love watching it. You're Emily, the posh British one Ross accidentally calls "Rachel" at the alter on their wedding day.'

'Flattering.' She checked the boys were out of earshot. 'But I turned down Luca's marriage proposal, so no risk of that.'

'He's asked you to…?' Carly stopped, laughed. 'Ha! Right. Funny.'

They'd reached the stable yards now, Ellis circling obediently back, Kes ducking away when Pax tried to catch him, yelling that he didn't want to change his clothes to go out. In the end she had to gather him up into a grumbling growling fireman's lift.

The klaxon was sounding out again.

'I'll get it,' Carly offered, heading towards the tack room with Ellis at heel.

'If it's an owner saying he wants to bring a mare and a goat today, the answer's still no!' Pax set off for towards the cottage, carrying Kes, grateful that his groans were turning into giggles.

When they came back out five minutes later, Ellis was waiting by the step on dinosaur watch, the sound of Carly's brush on the cobbles just out of sight beyond the archway. 'Mum says to tell you the phone caller said they are coming with the horse today, and that your mum's just gone out without paying her again.'

'Great,' Pax groaned, finding some cash to give to him for Carly before hurrying to the car.

She'd call her mother to let her know about the mare arriving as soon as they had a decent signal. Strapping Kes into his booster seat beside her and handing him her phone, she remembered as she did so she was also supposed to be messaging Bay to say they'd set off.

'Can I play Crazy Gears, Mum?'

'Don't use the battery up,' she warned him, always astonished how quickly he could crack through her security lock and open his favourite game.

'It's got 100 per cent!' Kes reported.

It was only later that Pax would realize her son still couldn't tell the difference between the numbers 10 and 100.

The day might have worked out very differently if he had.

30

R onnie rode Dickon around the big new tree trunk that had been placed in the Church Meadow gateway. There was a local surveyor's FOR SALE BY PUBLIC AUCTION sign by the entrance, on which somebody had circled the tiny Unless Sold Prior line in fat marker pen and written *BOMB says it's a con!* She suspected Petra's hand.

She trotted up to the standing stones. The gypsy chalk marks had been back over a week, bolder this time. It cheered her to see them, grateful the meadow's visiting custodians were undaunted.

She took out her phone, reading the one line sent from Blair's number late last night: *Run away with me.*

It was an old, shared joke, but it made her heart fly to read it each time. At least, she hoped it was a joke. There was far too much going on to run away right now. So much pivoted on today, and Luca.

Pax wouldn't talk about what was happening between them. She'd always been fiercely private, and any confiding went on far from her mother's ears. Luca was equally reticent behind the smile. But Ronnie sensed two kestrels edging to the furthest ends of their branches ready to take flight.

Run away with me. She read it again. Oh, to flap these wings and soar high above it all.

She just hoped the new stallion was all Blair promised. Its registered name was a bit of a worry. She hadn't broken it to Kenny that he couldn't rechristen this one as he had his showjumping stallions back in the glory days. The rules were different for thoroughbred and event horses, meaning they were stuck with it.

From up here she could clearly see Kenny Kay's St George's cross flapping on its new flagpole, cause of much village consternation. She must visit him. She couldn't keep putting it off.

Her conversation with Lester had left her deeply uneasy, old secrets playing on her conscience. It had come as a shock to find that Kenny had known the truth about Johnny. She wasn't surprised to learn her father hadn't pointed a gun at the comedian at all. It was Lester who had inflicted the injury which became Kenny's celebrity trademark. Whether by accident or to protect Johnny's and his own reputation hardly mattered now. But who had shot Nat Turner, and why?

Sir Peter Sanson's name kept running around in her head, questions about him unanswered. Eyngate Hall was the one property he'd never developed despite decades of rumours about a hotel and golf course. Then there was the land he'd bought wholesale from her father, and the high-handed way he'd treated Hermia. Perhaps she was being as paranoid as conspiracy theorist Kenny imagining he might also know more about Hermia's accident, and yet she couldn't shake the feeling she was missing a connection. She knew Peter had stopped visiting the village afterwards, and the land deals with her father had stopped too.

Turning to look the other way, Ronnie took in the last vestiges of the rampike that had once been a grand cedar known as the Percy Family Tree, set on land she'd reluctantly seen sold to the Austens last year to settle her father's inheritance tax. That the tree had been struck by lightning afterwards was surely a sign she should have held onto it.

From the highest point of Church Meadow, it was easy to see how little land the stud had left, its boundary half a mile closer to the yard and stables than it had been when Ronnie was born. No wonder her father had been so delighted when Pax and Bay started going out together, eager to marry them off and combine the two dominions like a medieval betrothal, finally healing the feud between the Percys and Austens.

Ronnie still suspected Bay might be behind the private bid on the land currently beneath Dickon's metal shoes. It was no longer Peter Sanson trying to buy up the village, she feared. It was Bay Austen, fresh from making a mint diversifying his parents' farm, now eyeing new territory like a warlord.

'*And* he's after my daughter,' she told the witches.

Something caught her eye on the far side of Lord's Brook, under the skirt of the trees shielding the Austens' game drives.

A man on a horse. Its mane had drawn her attention, pure white and almost down to its knees, its coat jet black by contrast, blending in with the dark woods. The rider was bareback, a battered leather fedora low over his face, dressed in jeans and waistcoat, red neckerchief tied above a plaid shirt. Loose-limbed, unhurried, riding one-reined, he was a natural horseman. In his other hand was the wooden stock of a shotgun, its barrels resting against his shoulder.

It was years since Ronnie had seen Nat Turner. He'd been wild and handsome back then, with a crown of black curl, palest silver eyes and too many teeth. And he'd ridden better than most of her eventing teammates. He'd ridden just like this.

Her first thought was that he must be poaching, although to do so in broad daylight on horseback was unconventional in the extreme. For a law unto himself like Nat, less so.

Dickon had started to dance beneath her.

The track Nat was on led north from the trout farm alongside the brook, a popular bridleway that then crossed over a grass-topped stone bridge to the village side where it cut through Church Meadow, past the tennis club to Church Lane.

Dickon was throwing up his head, snorting and whickering in the direction of the chestnut avenue.

Ronnie battled to stop him turning to face the lane, still watching the rider who carried on past the bridge, sticking to the opposite bank of the brook. The track he was on led eventually to a small lake at the confluence of the mill chase and another tributary. Although now overgrown and reabsorbed into the surrounding farmland, the lake had once been a decorative feature in Compton Manor's grand gardens, complete with an ornamental island and swan-shaped peddle boats. Another crossing point modelled on the Chinese Bridge at Croome led across the brook to a set-aside field by the cricket pitch, beyond which the lay manor's topiary hedges and formal gardens.

Ronnie realized that's where the rider must be heading.

With a gun.

Still staring at the road, Dickon let out a full-body whinny. The rider by the brook didn't look back, nor his horse, but a shrill reply came from the distance where the old horse was looking. Then another.

Dickon tossed his head and shot round to face them. He was as brave as a war horse, wise to the world after their long, joyful eventing campaigns. Together, they'd just missed out on the sport's top rung, his phlegmatic personality a little too laidback for the big tracks. Nothing fazed him, yet his ears were twitching all over the place, his rheumy eyes gazing brightly past the ancient chestnut avenue that led down to the Fosse Way.

He'd sensed them coming, but now Ronnie saw them. A great caravan of travellers making their way up from the Fosse Way.

And far ahead of them, moving stealthily towards the Manor with a gun, was Nat Turner.

She had to do something.

*

Carly took her cup of tea to the top field where the young bachelor herd were turned out, Spirit her favourite amongst them, golden-coated and black-legged, barging for attention. She was keeping an eye out for Ronnie, who had taken her old horse Dickon out for a hack almost an hour ago and not yet returned. She didn't like to leave the yard without anybody there, especially with a horse due to arrive. The caller who was bringing the horse today had sounded pretty pressed, especially when Carly had asked about the goat. There *was* no goddamned goat, they'd said, sounding more *Schitt's Creek* than horsey clique.

Ellis trailed behind her, tired and bad-tempered because his friend had been taken from him. His 'Splorer Stick – part transitional object, part feather duster, part light sabre – rested on his shoulder like a soldier's rifle.

'Here, see how your dragon hatchlings are doing.' Carly let him play with her phone. The sun had come out, fierce as stadium lights.

'Can we have Kes round to ours for tea sometime?' Ellis demanded.

'If his mum agrees, then maybe.' Carly didn't want to like Pax, who had been born to such privilege and beauty yet treated it like an embarrassing birthmark. But there was a nonconformity and warmth about her which meant Carly had formed a begrudging admiration. And she rode as though she'd been born on a horse.

'She will,' Ellis predicted confidently. 'She likes me. I'm going to come and work for her here one day, like you.'

'So you do want learn to ride horses after all?' she asked.

'Nah, just dragons. Dinosaurs too, maybe.'

In his hands, her phone rang and Ellis looked at the caller's picture. 'It's Auntie Janine.'

'Answer it, then.'

Swiping green, he said hello in his best phone call voice then held it away from his ear and pulled a face, handing it up to Carly. 'She's shouting.'

'Dad's called!' her sister-in-law squawked. 'He's in the village now and he says the fight's on!'

'Nat's here *now?*'

'Along with a hundred or more headed for the meadow. He wants us all there. Ash is still at the gym. Mum's locked herself in the bathroom and refuses to come out, so I've got your kids with me, and now Uncle Norm's oxygen's run out! I need you here!'

'I'm working. I can't go till the boss gets back.' Carly scanned the horizon for Ronnie. There was no sign, but now she looked, she could make out a battered transit van towing a caravan making its way very slowly along the straight lane from the Fosse Way at the head of a procession of other battered vans and caravans, trailers, pickups, vardos, flatbeds loaded with diggers and a horse-drawn cart with several black-and-white Vanners tied to the back.

'What's happening?' Ellis clambered on the fence to get a better look while Spirit charged off to whinny at the advancing army.

'Your granddad.' Carly sighed. 'That's what's happening'

Kit looked up from his greenhouse writing desk to see a horse on his drive, a moment of déjà vu quickening his blood as its blonde rider waving to him reminded him of Hermia, only to realize it was Ronnie, looking hurried and determined.

'It's time you made friends with one of these things!' she told him when he ventured out of the safety and warmth.

'That the beast that destroyed my last greenhouse?' Kit eyed it warily.

'Yes. Dickon, meet Kit.' She jumped off and quickly whispered in its ear. 'I rather like him, but I'd like him more if he forgave your species.'

The horse eyed Kit's greenhouse with interest.

'I'm afraid I'm in a hurry otherwise you'd get more of these,'

Ronnie said and gave Kit a kiss which he drew on like a rare toke on a spliff. He adored her energy, its effervescent echo of his wife.

The horse was a less welcome reminder.

Kit bestowed a stiff pat on its neck.

'You'll have to try harder than that.' She glanced over her shoulder towards the lane, speaking too fast. 'How can you truly understand Sassoon – or Sherston – if you don't like horses?'

They'd talked about this before. He was adamant they weren't his thing and he'd pointedly avoided going anywhere near the stud so far. Ronnie was just as adamant that he must if he was to nail his play. Or nail her. He had an uncomfortable feeling that Ronnie saw his failure to do either as a sign of weakness, along with his aversion to horses.

'Can you hold him for me?' she asked, clearly deciding more direct action was needed, handing across the reins. 'You just need to grit your teeth and be brave and you'll find he's an awful lot less scary and dangerous than you remember. I'm hoping the same might apply to my own situation. Think of him as Harkaway.' It was the name of George Sherston's first hunter. She turned to hurry back down the drive. 'I'll be back before you know it.'

'Absolutely no—'

She was gone.

'You OK, Kenny love?' a voice said over-loudly by his ear to penetrate Bose's noise-cancelling technology.

Sarah the Carer had come to check on him. Or was it Patti the PA?

'Don't fuss!' he snapped, lifting his headphones a fraction. 'What time is it?'

'Almost lunchtime, Kenny.'

That was Patti the PA's creamy tones. He liked her best.

He'd been parked up all morning in the office where they'd fixed him up with a recliner chair by the radiator, noise-cancelling headphones and the recorder on which to dictate more audio notes for *So Kay*.

He could hear industrial vacuums in the next room so there was no point recording more. 'They nearly finished?'

'I hope so – there's dust everywhere in here.' Cool air caught Kenny's face in as she opened a window. 'I can't believe it fell down like that. Could have killed somebody.'

'I'm cursed, bab, like I told you.'

'With workmen, maybe. You should never have put a light that heavy on an old beam. Asking for trouble. Even my Barry would know that.'

Last night, when the thirty-six light, ninety kilo crystal chandelier had come crashing down onto the five hundred hand-cut Bath flagstones in his galleried hallway, Kenny had thought his hour had come. A day before that, his new lift had failed spectacularly, leaving him trapped in it for two hours.

Tina – who had been a superstitious sort – had always said things happened in threes, so Kenny was bracing himself.

'That window you just opened have grills on?'

'It's stuffy in here, and the sun's out. Lovely spring day.'

'I need a drink.'

'I'll make you a cuppa.'

'You'll fix me a drink.' He closed his eyes as her footsteps moved away, a clanging ring coming from the entrance gate bell. 'And tell whoever that is I'm not accepting callers – unless it's a beautiful woman!'

He groped for his recorder, telling it, 'I met the fifth Mrs Kay while trapped in a downward dog in palm Springs. Within two weeks of taking her number, she'd taken over my life.'

He started and turned as he smelled the acrid tang of rolling tobacco. There was somebody at the window.

'Hello, Mr Ken, sir. Heard you were back.'

For a moment, Kenny went motionless, senses on high alert.

Then he flailed around wildly for something to grab to protect himself, finding himself clutching his recording device and a tin of throat sweets. 'Patti!'

'Been a long time, Mr Ken, sir.'

It had to be Nat Turner. That tobacco smell, the strimmer whine voice.

'How the hell did you get in?' The gates were kept locked. The garden walls were eight feet high. The guard dogs were loose. He'd been assured the topiary was practically impenetrable.

'Through the fields. Nice topiary. Tied my horse up to a tree shaped like a lollypop. Love these beautiful dogs of yours, they Leonbergers, are they? Cushty.'

Kenny groaned, deciding the best ploy was to play for time by pretending to be old and mad. 'Do I know you? Jog my proverbial.'

Nobody forgot Nat Turner after meeting him, even blind drunk, even blind. That looping laugh, the sing-song voice, turbulent enthusiasm and sudden bouts of extreme violence. He'd been a regular drinker in the Jug before Peter recruited him as an extra hand at Eyngate, a poacher turned gamekeeper – or at least, poacher turned occasional driver and hired heavy, there to stop the other Turners nicking stuff. Peter liked to have a pet thug around. Nat and Kenny had got on famously, largely because Nat was so excited Kenny was famous, he'd given him no choice.

Nat wasn't falling for the mad act. 'Told you I'd come calling if you ever showed your face round here again, Mr Ken sir.'

'I have no memory of any of this, son. Dementia, you see. Or is it amnesia? Possibly both. Patti!'

'You recall *her* name!'

'That's not her name.'

'C'mon, you know who I am, Mr Ken, sir.'

'Well, *I* certainly do!' a woman's voice cried from the opposite side of the room, clear-cut and fearless. 'Where's your gun, Nathaniel Turner?'

Kenny swung round, demanding, 'Who's that?' Then, '*What gun!*'

'I'm not here to shoot nobody.' Nat sounded offended. 'I left it by the horse.'

'Mr Kay,' his PA interjected, trying to sound calm, but she was tell-tale breathless, 'Mrs Ledwell from the stud is here to see you, only this gentleman appears to be outside the window. Shall I have him seen off the premises?'

'You know who I am, Maureen Stokes!' Nat complained. 'And me and Mr Ken are reminiscing! I have a few things I need to get off my chest here.'

'Perhaps I can help,' cried the voice that had hardly changed in its husky intensity in forty years. 'I can't stay long – like Nat, I've left a horse parked on a meter – so I'll get straight to the point: I have it on *very* good authority that Kenny cannot have shot you, Nat.'

'I didn't shoot you. Nat!' Kenny squeaked. 'I sweat I never shot you, son.'

'Oh, I know *that*, Mr Ken, sir.'

'You do?'

'That was just something Mr Sanson wanted you to you think.'

Slowly, Kenny put down the throat lozenges tin, although he kept hold of the recorder, his finger still pressed on its record switch. 'Pete wanted me to think I shot you?'

'That's right. But I know you couldn't have.'

'As do I.' Ronnie's voice moved closer as she crossed the room.

'So who *did* shoot you?' asked Kenny.

'Nobody. I fell out of a tree.'

Kenny felt a sudden tightness in his chest, for a moment fearing the worst, before the laugh took familiar hold and his shoulders started to shake. 'You fell *out of a tree*?'

'Yeah. Bad fall, as it goes.'

Kenny tried to get a grip of the hilarity. 'But I saw the

damage. We were in the same ambulance. You almost lost an eye. You had a bloody great hole in your shoulder, had lead pellets in your face and neck.'

'Blackthorns and splinters. Big bloody ones. It was bad fall, like I say. Landed on an old park fence hidden in the sloe bushes and spiked myself. You kept fainting in the ambulance at the sight of all the blood. Mr Sanson paid for private hospital treatment afterwards. I needed an operation, see. Lovely it was there. Loads of drugs, fantastic grub.'

Kenny half-expected Ant and Dec to jump out of the shrubbery with a camera crew explaining this was all a wind-up. Except that this was something he'd suffered nightmares about for years. 'What about the gypsy curse your family put on me?'

'Mr Sanson made that up too, Ken, sir.'

'Why would he do that?'

'You said some defamatory things that day, Kenny,' Ronnie pointed out sharply.

'Everyone heard you call him a poofter,' Nat confirmed.

'He'd nicked my missus!'

'I'd never curse you, Mr Ken, sir. Big fan.' Nat had lit up a fresh roll-up, tobacco trailing in alongside his nasal, Jagger-like voice, falsetto-high with feeling. 'That's why I'm here. Want to make it up to you, sir. Want to explain about Tina.'

'Don't tell me it was *Tina* you cursed?'

'No, Mr Ken sir. I married her.'

'Patti! PATTI! Get Pete Sanson on the phone NOW!'

31

L ester had felt the chill coming on all week but had been
loath to miss out on his horsebox outings with Pax or
instructing young Kes. Now he couldn't get warm. He'd added
as many layers as he could and turned on the electric heater
by his chair, but his teeth still chattered and his bones ached.
He'd mixed a hot toddy, put extra mustard in his lunchtime
ham sandwich and endeavoured to keep himself distracted
watching the racing, but he just felt worse. And cold to his
bones.

More achy and shivery by the minute, he lit the open fire
which had been a merry comfort throughout the colder months.
The chimney smoked like billyo when damp, but it would soon
catch an updraft and draw heat. Stubbs was already curling up
stiffly and gratefully in front of it and the first hurdle race from
Newbury was about to start. He'd check the foaling barn as
soon as it was over and he'd warmed up.

He settled back to watch it through the smog of cataracts
and woodsmoke.

Ronnie watched Nat stoop down and climb in through the
full-length Georgian sash window, removing his hat to reveal a
tanned, bald head. What was left of his curly mane was scraped

into a ponytail, and what was left of his teeth beamed a wide smile as he thrust out a ringed hand to shake. 'Don't I know you?'

Before she could introduce herself, Kenny boomed, 'LISTEN UP!'

He'd stopped barking into a phone at the other end of the room and turned to bark at them, adopting the familiar role of gravelly gangland dad he'd played in multiple Hollywood bit parts. 'Pete's on his way from London to sort this out. Forty minutes tops by helicopter, he says. You two stay where you are until he gets here. I want answers.'

'I really can't stay,' Ronnie checked her watch.

'And I'm out of here if that bastard's coming.' Nat headed for the window.

'STAY!' Kenny ordered. 'Patti's making tea. There's pikelets and jam roly-poly. Sit down.'

Ronnie found it secretively very impressive that Kenny had convinced Peter Sanson to drop everything and leap in his helicopter. She pictured it sitting on top of a glittering mirrored-glass office block, the pilot powering up the engine.

Except it was a Saturday, so it was more likely he was shouting at his driver to avoid Wandsworth Bridge traffic on the way to Battersea heliport.

But how lovely to be able to just take off and fly wherever you wanted in minutes.

She imagined swooping down on Blair's hilltop. *Run away with me.*

Then she thought guiltily about poor Kit holding Dickon, and Carly and Lester holding the fort at the stud, and the fact none of them knew where she was. But Kenny was now their biggest owner, she reminded herself, and she wanted to hear answers too.

He'd slumped back in his chair, coughing and wheezing from his exertions to quiz Nat. 'You're saying you wed my Tina?'

He looked terribly old beneath the tan, Ronnie thought, plainly unable to see much at all, and terrified of Nat Turner, which struck her as nonsensical because Nat – for all he could swing a punch at a fly when drunk – was an old-school traveller who lived for the moment, and was obviously still a huge Kenny fan.

'That's right, Mr Ken, sir.' Nat was perching on the edge of his chair, elbows on his knee, moving the leather fedora from hand to hand, a ring and a tattoo on every finger. Ronnie admired his cowboy boots.

She accepted a cup of tea gratefully from Mo Dawkins, who had placed a written note in the saucer saying: *POLICE AWARE OF SITUATION. WE HAVE CONFISCATED NAT'S SHOTGUN. (HIS HORSE IS LOVELY!).*

Ronnie smiled up at her gratefully. Having forgotten that she'd been the one to recommend Kenny employ Mo in the first place, she'd been surprised to find her here at the manor, more still to hear Kenny introduce her by a different name entirely, but now wasn't the time to ask questions. Unless you were Kenny, of course; Kenny was asking a *lot* of questions.

'How come you fell for each other? And Peter had no idea? He never told me this. You two wed? How did that come about?'

'She visited me in hospital, Mr Ken, sir. She felt bad I'd been hurt that day. Ever so kind she was. Brought me home-made biscuits and tarts. We got on so well, she came back. Visited me a lot after that. Talked about horses.'

'Always crazy about horses, Tina.'

'After I recovered, I started working for Mr Sanson again, driving Tina around. He wasn't there much, always away cutting deals. She was scared alone in the big house. Said Mr Sanson bought it for her, but that she didn't feel about him the same way she'd felt about you.'

'They were like brother and sister.'

'That's what she said. Tina called him her astral twin. He wanted them to get married, but she said it was like another one of his business arrangements. She was sad because you'd just become a dad.'

'Iago. Golf pro. Very proud of him. Got two daughters, too.'

'Cushty.'

They took a moment to silently honour Kenny's fatherly cushtiness.

Which was when it struck Ronnie how alike they looked in middle age – the leathery tanned skin, iron grey curls snaking from the same receding hairlines, skinny legs and pot bellies. They could be brothers. Both were born entertainers. No wonder Tina had fallen for Nat, although more surprising, perhaps, that the notoriously polyamorous Nat had married such a quiet mouse.

'How did you and Tina finally get together?' she asked him.

Ronnie found the daddy of all silver eyes on her, fierce with self-dramatization. The hat was flying back and forth between the ringed fingers. 'We eloped!'

Kenny harrumphed.

'Mr Sanson had hired her the best lawyers so she could divorce you and wed him quickly. Some tax dodge to do with the house being in her name, she said. He was going to turn it into a luxury hotel or something. She hated the idea.'

'Of marrying Peter or Eyngate being a hotel?'

'She just wanted a quiet life, a little family of her own. She loved it when I told her all about growing up on the road, of our home travelling with us, and nobody from outside bothering us cos we never stayed anywhere long enough for them to find us. Easier back in those days, before social services went digital. The day her divorce came through, we ran away together.' He flashed his gappy teeth at the memory. 'Middle of the night, like a pair of thieves.'

'I remember that feeling,' Ronnie sighed.

'In a vardo.'

'Sports car.'

'Cushty.'

The hat slowed between his hands and he let out a long, deep sigh. 'Only it turned out Tina didn't like life on the road overmuch. Too much boozing and fighting and getting moved on by the law. She found the old ways hard to understand, especially being called *marime* when she was expecting the babby.'

'You had children together?' asked Kenny, nonplussed.

Nat rose to his feet, cowboy boot heels tapping together. 'Girl and a boy.'

'She always wanted kids.' Kenny sounded shell-shocked. 'Bet she was a great mum. Loved kids, did Tina.'

'Grandkids too, now.'

Kenny harrumphed again, this time more wistfully.

Ronnie distinctly recalled Carly saying Ash's dad had barely met his grandchildren. She got the impression Nat hadn't featured much in Ash and his sister's childhoods either, their grandparents Norm and Betty looking after them along with all the Turner family members who had settled in the village.

Absent for much of their lives, Nat had reputedly fathered many more offspring on his travels. His charm was all firework show: short-lived and best staged outdoors, currently going off in Kenny's gold-and-teak designer study.

'Can't tell you how made up I was to hear you're moving in here, Mr Ken, sir.' He was looking round the room in wonder, checking out framed photographs of the comedian with fellow celebrities. 'You are a legend, sir. Been trying to make it back all month, but I got waylaid, you know how it is. Bit of a tribe situation going on. Circling wagons. Now I'm back here to fight.'

'Fight me?' Kenny yelped.

'No, sir! Although we'd certainly appreciate your help. There's an old Roma saying, see: *Kon del tut o nai shai dela tut wi o vast*. He who willingly gives you his finger will also give you the whole hand.'

Kenny covered the stump of his shortened finger with the other hand. 'I'm not losing any more fingers, son.'

'Of course not, Mr Ken, sir.' Nat paced by the window he'd

first appeared at, leather hat moving faster between his hands. 'Will Mr Sanson be long?'

'It's Sir Peter now, son.' Kenny rubbed his face tiredly. 'And I'm just plain Mr Ken, I mean, Mr Kay. Just you wait till he gets here! Pete never told me none of this when we—' Voice cracking, he looked away to gather his composure, and then sighed, half-smiling. 'I kept her heart, you know?'

'I can't argue with that,' Nat nodded.

'I should have never let her go.' Kenny pressed his foreshortened fingertip to his nose, and then pointed it at the wall three feet to the left of Ronnie. 'I blame *her* dad for taking a pop at me that day.'

'Knew I recognized you!' Nat cocked his head to look at her again. 'You're the Percy girl what ran off with the jockey – the Bardswold Bolter, they called you.'

'Good to be remembered,' Ronnie said crossly, then told Kenny, 'Daddy didn't shoot you.'

'Well, *I* didn't fall out of a bloody tree,' he said, coughing and laughing. 'But you're all right, bab. This missing finger is my trademark. I bear the man no ill will, God rest him.'

Remembering what Lester had told her about Kenny's drunken invective that day, she thought it best left there.

'Besides which, that's not the sort of pop I'm talking about, bab. He gave me a right telling-off, did Captain Percy. He told me I had no moral protractor, that I should do the decent thing by my unborn child. I had a lot of time for the Captain. He was a good man. Upstanding. He made me see I was wrong to have promised I'd try and buy my Tina the stud. He told me it was more than a home, it was family: every stone, every clod of earth, every horse. Percy family.'

Imagining her father saying it in his booming patrician voice, Ronnie felt as though those stones and clods of earth was in her throat.

Kenny was still talking, his tone confessional now, its contrition hoarse. 'So after he shot me – or didn't – and I found that all I'd lost was my finger, I took it as a sign to clear out of town and clean up my act.'

'Nothing to do with being framed for shooting Nat and believing you had a gypsy curse on you?'

'Contributing factors, granted, but I knew I wasn't wanted around these parts no more. Shame, cos I loved it here. And I knew Tina would be better off without me,' he went on, 'that Pete would look after her, because she was family to him. I didn't want to hang around and see them living in that big house of his.'

'Hers,' Nat corrected.

'Hers,' Kenny nodded. Then he paused for a long time. Eventually, he cleared his throat. 'Did you say something about Pete putting Eyngate in her name?'

'That's right, Mr Ken, sir. Some sort of tax dodge, she said. She got the deeds out of the safe and brought them with her when we ran away.'

Kenny started to chuckle again, soon coughing so much he couldn't speak for laughter and hacking.

'Top up, Mrs Ledwell?' Mo took Ronnie's cup.

Another note appeared in the saucer. TINA IS STILL ALIVE.

She looked up in shock. Mo's eyes were huge.

Looking down again, Ronnie realized she'd missed another line: AND LIVING IN THE VILLAGE!

32

As Pax sat in the Bounce Barn, one eye on Kes and one on the door hoping for signs of Bay, her attention was drawn to a vaguely familiar blonde at the next table, absorbed by her phone, scrolling and tapping furiously.

Her own phone had no battery left, Kes's number miscalculation and a vigorous game of Crazy Gears draining its last 10 per cent long before they'd pulled into the car park. Now feeling foolish coming out without a power bank, or even a charging cable, Pax had no way of contacting Bay to let him know she was here, or her mother to warn her an owner would be dropping off a mare and goat after all. Nor could she take a photograph of Kes who had started waving at her frantically from the third level up. 'Mummy, Mummy, Mummy, look at meeeeeeeeee!'

A boy standing beside Kes was shouting the same thing. They had their arms around each other's shoulders like a rowing pair.

The blonde looked up and took a photograph.

Pax glanced across at her again, feeling a heat rash spreading at speed down from her scalp.

It was Bay's wife, Monique.

On the giant, multi-coloured indoor play scaffolding of padded passages and cargo nets in front of her, she realized Kes was now thundering round with Bram Austen.

Pax pulled up her hoody, mind racing.

Bay must have messaged at the last minute saying there had been a change of plan, which of course she wouldn't have seen. Did Monique know she would be here with Kes? Had Bay said anything? Was she perhaps here to warn Pax off?

Pax had only encountered Bay's ice-cool Dutch wife a handful of times, most unforgettably and recently at her one visit to a local AA meeting with Luca, at which Monique had talked openly of her own struggles with alcohol addiction. She still didn't know if Monique had recognized her there. Or here.

'Mummmmeeeee!' Kes was on the top level now, jumping up and down.

Pax raised a hand and peered out of the side of her hoodie, embarrassed by her cowardice. Monique was no longer sitting at the next table. Phew.

A tough, outspoken former professional dressage rider, Monique Austen was well known for mowing down the opposition in the warm-up arena, hypnotising judges with a single laser-beam stare and making grooms cry. Her diamond cool and lithe athleticism – not to mention the well-rumoured bisexuality – had thrilled Bay at first, keeping him firmly on best behaviour, but their marriage had eventually become toxic, a cat-and-dog mismatch that had driven her to drink and both to play away.

'Mummmmeeeeeeee, looook!' Kes was flying down a slide into a ball pit, Bram right behind him.

'Stop pretending you haven't seen me.' Monique placed two coffees and muffins on the table in front of Pax and plonked herself beside her. 'You can take the cowl off. I got you a skinny latte, although coffees in this dump taste the same, OK.'

Pax lowered her hood reluctantly. 'Wow, thanks! How are you?'

'So-so. You?'

'Same.'

'You bring Bram here often?' Pax found herself asking, then realized it sounded like a bad pickup line.

'Not if I can help it, but his daddy promised him this today.'

Pax looked round the other parents, wondering if Bay was here too after all.

'He is driving Tilly and her friends to a Pony Club thing,' Monique went on, picking the blueberries from her muffin. 'The other mother had to work so I offered Bay's services instead. He was *very* bad-tempered about it, but I can't do it, worst luck.'

Pax remembered Monique had lost her licence. It terrified her how close she could have come to the same thing happening herself when her drinking had been at its worse. She felt an unexpected affinity that went beyond being two thirty-something rural mothers going through divorces.

'Bram loves it here and a promise is a promise,' Monique sighed wearily. '*I* hate this place.'

'Kes too and me too.'

'But here we are. It is kismet, I think?'

'Isn't it?' Pax braced.

'I've been wanting to talk to you for a while.'

'Oh, yes?' Here we go.

'I hear you're riding our young event horse.' Monique drew her coffee through her teeth to cool it.

'That's right.'

'I didn't like her. My groom was keen, OK, but I think she's not got the mind for big pressure. Too neurotic.'

'I love riding her.'

'I see...' Sipping more coffee, Monique watched their sons flying back down the red slide. 'And do you love riding my husband also?'

Pax turned in shock, whispering, 'What sort of a question is that?'

Monique's eyes were the palest, see-through blue, her voice a steely bullet. 'An honest one. He's like a dog with two tails around you, giving you horses to ride. I remember him like that.'

Pax dropped her voice even lower. 'I am *not* riding Bay,'

'OK, let's take the riding out of it. Do you still love him?'

Pax looked down at her hands. 'That was a very long time ago.'

'Still...' Monique shrugged, looking away. 'You were childhood sweethearts. That's a very addictive love, and you are an addict.'

Cheeks burning, Pax glanced at the families crammed around nearby tables, disconcerted to be confronted here, amid the shouting and bawling and tear-mopping.

Beside her, Monique had picked up her phone again and was reading a message.

Pax glared straight ahead in silence, and Monique laughed. 'Oh, drink your coffee, you uptight bitch, and let's talk horse. We must learn to get on, you and I, because that,' she nodded at the two boys charging around the play frame, 'is the start of something beautiful. I think they would be good stepbrothers, don't you?'

Pax put her cup back down. 'Are you seriously trying to pimp your husband?'

'Not mine for much longer.' She raised a thin, immaculately plucked eyebrow. 'I'd like him to go to a good local home. Experienced owners only; needs plenty of work; not novice ride. Bombproof, but not vice-free.'

Pax looked away, laughing despite herself. 'I'm way too rusty.'

'Hasn't the Horsemaker broken you back in yet?'

She turned back, shocked afresh.

Monique's pale eyes glowed with secrets. 'Luca has such a naughty reputation. Heartbroken men so often do, I find.'

Pax wondered how much Monique knew of Luca's past. She was supremely well-connected, a frequent visitor to the European studs where he worked.

'We're horse people, Pax,' she said now. 'We all break something.'

'What have you broken lately?'

'My marriage vows.' She sighed, leaning back to photograph the boys climbing to the top level of the big frame. 'And now my silence. I think you and Bay are very well-suited.'

'Have you told him this?'

Monique swung round turned to take a photo of Pax, eyed it critically, edited it swiftly, added a caption and smiled. 'I have now.'

33

'Appreciate you coming over here at short notice, mate.'
Blair thrust a steaming coffee at Luca made in the
elaborate Italian machine kept in his office.

Luca took it. He hadn't been asked if he wanted one.

Nor did the Australian ask if he wanted a tour of his yard, but
he gave him one now, at speed, names and expletives dropping
at will, hollering regularly for his errant pointer, George, who
was trying to slope off for nookie with his groom's miniature
dachshund. 'COME *HERE* GEORGE! She's too small for you,
you pervert. The Verney family want to focus on rearing and
breaking here now,' he explained to Luca in the same breath,
'plus breeding a few ourselves. And they're right. GEORGE! It
was Vee's passion. It's what we were planning before she got
ill. Vee was the one that found Beck. Always had an eye. She
bloody loved that stallion, so it's right he should come back
here. *GEORGE!*'

Luca, who bloody loved the stallion too, was confused. 'I
thought he was going back to Germany?'

Blair shook his head with a sardonic laugh. 'I'm accountable
now, mate. Plans change. He was only ever on loan, like I was.'

'And Ronnie's OK with this?'

'Yeah, we thrashed out a deal with a couple of added
conditions. She'll still get her dynasty from him.'

Blair strode on ahead, pointing out a state-of-the-art horse walker, behind which a covered barn housed a treadmill and solarium. Modern, immaculate and run with supreme efficiency, the yard was the complete opposite of beautiful, archaic Compton Magna. It was absolutely Luca's cup of tea, unlike the bitumen-strong coffee.

Having spent the morning with Ronnie's friend Bunny on his even more antiquated and grandiose crumbling country estate – host to one of England's most beloved three-day horse trials – he was in heaven to be back in the twenty-first century.

'Did Bunny offer you a job?' Blair shouted back as he led the way through a purpose-built foaling station.

'Does he always do that?' Luca's visit there had also included a breakneck tour of the cross-country course by Mini Moke, a kedgeree brunch and a likeably shy, bumbling attempt at flirtation while watching vintage footage of the trials since the seventies.

'Only for friends of Ronnie. GEORGE! The staff cottage there is bonza, and you'd hardly have to lift a finger.'

'I prefer hard work,' Luca explained, 'it's why Ronnie's place suits me. They need at least one more permanent yard hand and more part-timers, plus Lester back, ideally twenty years younger. The place only needs one Pax, mind you.'

'Yeah, I heard she can be tricky.'

'No, she's brilliant. She's on top of everything. Perfectionist, but in a good way.' He tested the new broken glass under his emotional heel, longing for it to soften to friendship's sand. She'd love seeing round this place. They would find their way back to equilibrium eventually.

'Then I could do with her here!' Blair laughed, walking him through a wide aisle with rubber matting underfoot, big airy stalls to either side. 'This is the stallion barn where Beck will live. It's not normally so quiet here.' He explained his Head Groom had taken the big six-horse lorry loaded with his younger string to an unaffiliated event.

Two stablehands in matching sponsor-logoed fleeces were nonetheless far busier than Ronnie's unruly team as they swept, lunged and tail-pulled in this wood-fringed, hilltop horse haven.

Perched high on well-drained chalk downs on Verney land, and built as Verity's divorce settlement, it boasted two hangar-like, climate-controlled American barns crowned with solar panels, indoor and outdoor schools, an all-weather gallop and an ugly red-brick low-carbon farmhouse and staff bungalow. It was all about the horse, not the history or status.

And what horses! Even a third full, the yard boasted some of the smartest eventing youngstock Luca had seen in years, many of them Percy-bred.

'I still have eight of Ronnie's unbroken hooligans out there, ready to start work.' Blair pointed towards a field dotted with four-legged juveniles. 'Vee loved her babies, so we bought a lot to keep her happy. *GEORGE!*'

The naughty-eyed English pointer came curling back from flirting with the dachshund to quiver waggily at his master's ankle as he marched back into the office to hiss, spit and steam more unwanted coffee in Luca's direction.

Unaccustomed to caffeine, Luca was jangling, headache clamping tighter.

There was an impatient brutality to Blair, that dark side of grief in its fourth stage. He had a split eyebrow and swelling above one cheekbone – no doubt from a horse fall – and he hadn't shaved. He wasn't to be messed with.

Ronnie had been the one who had pushed Luca to come today, and he'd accepted the last-minute invitation without questioning its reasons too deeply, relieved to get away from the whispering-walls atmosphere at the stud. Mr Sit Tight was a legend; to be shown around his barn was a rare privilege.

To be offered a job, however, came as a total shock.

'Three-month contract initially, no guarantees. You can start as soon as you like,' Blair told him matter-of-factly. 'Stud work and breaking. Accommodation on site. *GEORGE*! And don't say you're contracted to Ronnie because I know she never gave you a contract. She doesn't believe in them.'

Luca could point out that he had work lined up until next year but instinct told him to stay behind the smile longer. Two work offers in one day was no coincidence. 'Has Ronnie put you up to this?'

He shrugged. 'Not exactly, but we agree it makes sense having you come here with the stallion, and you and I both know that you're never going to work for Bunny. We've taken enough horses out from under each other over the years, and a few owners, me and Ron. Why not a Horsemaker?'

Luca glanced round at the pictures decking the walls: Blair winning his first Olympic medal, first Badminton trophy, first Burghley and Kentucky. Blair with royalty, with sporting legends, with his Australian teammates, and most of all photographed with a dusky-eyed older brunette in possession of a smile that lit up the clustered frames like small, dazzling constellations.

'Vee would have liked you I reckon.' Blair followed his gaze, deep voice cracking with sadness. 'She always saw the best in people – and horses – whereas I don't trust anyone except myself, and that's being generous. GEORGE, get *BACK* here, you bastard!'

Luca's eyes were drawn to an old, faded shot of a young Blair posing between a married couple he knew well. He'd seen the same picture framed on the walls of the big lodge house in their Canadian barn. The legendary showjumper turned trainer and dealer had been with his tiny dynamo of a wife on and off since their early teens. Although both had longed to raise a huge jumping dynasty, the big baby bump in the photograph had been their only precious child, combining her mother's petite frame and boundless energy with her father's gift. And temper.

Meredith.

Prenatal Meredith.

With Blair Robertson?

Surely not!

His gaze switched between the Flying Maple Leaf, a sandy-haired freckled giant, to Blair, olive-skinned and wiry, and back again to Meredith's mother.

Then he dismissed the idea.

'*GEORGE*, you bastard! Lay off that poor bitch!'

Luca was reminded of his old Canadian boss shouting for his little Duck Toller dogs. The two men weren't so different – brusque, old-school horsemen with matching superhuman talent and short fuses. Like Luca, Blair had worked for the Flying Maple Leaf when he was first starting out, a talented tyro spotted by the great man and taught more than he'd learn at any college course in exchange for backbreaking hard work. Although there was no love lost between them all these years later, it apparently hadn't stopped them cutting deals.

Luca downed the coffee with an apologetic grimace, knowing he couldn't trust Blair while he was still in cahoots with the Flying Maple Leaf. 'I've got work lined up in Holland over the summer, Italy after that.'

'They'll find someone else,' Blair dismissed. 'You're too good to be moving on from gig to gig every few months, mate. You outgrew that years ago.'

Luca couldn't deny it.

'Don't tell me this place isn't your dream.' He stooped to praise the now heel-hugging George who flipped on his back and wriggled ecstatically, forgiven at last. 'You'd slot straight in here.'

Luca couldn't deny that either, but there had to be a mountainous catch. 'You want to hire me to nanny Beck?'

'I want you to oversee this place. And to nanny Beck.'

'I couldn't do it to Ronnie.'

'She's the first to admit she can't afford to fucking pay you!' Blair laughed unapologetically, that bulldozer directness for which he was legend, his career built on grit, along with split-second decision-making that had brought glory to his owners and country. 'We both know Beck's too risky covering mares without someone like you around. Why d'you think I found her another stallion?'

'That American horse was originally meant for you to compete.' Luca called his bluff.

Blair laughed again, a short bark acknowledging the truth. Then his jaw tightened and he squinted at a photograph of himself on a World Championship podium twenty years earlier. 'Yeah, well I'm not competing at all this year.'

It had already struck Luca that Blair was winding his yard down, simplifying it, making space to grieve. But the speed of change was now laid clear, that bloody-minded Robertson resolve in full force.

'The decision was made before Vee died, when I could see just how ill she was getting. I started ringing round, moving horses, told old Lester about the American stallion cos I knew it would suit Ronnie's outfit, and he said he had a buyer waiting.' He let out a puff of breath and rolled his eyes, more enlightened now.

'My advanced horses have other riders deputising this season,' he went on. 'Their owners understand I'm taking a sabbatical. My eye's not on it nor my heart in it, plus there's legal stuff going on. But the little American fella was too special to let go. Besides, I'd already paid that Canadian bastard a fat deposit I knew I'd never get back. That's when I thought of Ronnie.'

Luca took a slow breath in, aware he was in a minefield, saying carefully, 'So you knew all along he was with the Flying Maple Leaf?'

'Of course I bloody knew! That's how come I got the heads-up in the first place. He doesn't sell a lot of event horses. He hasn't got my contacts.'

'I thought you two hated each other?'

'*He* wasn't the one who tipped me off about the horse, mate.'

The been-there done-that gunmetal eyes slid in direct line with his.

Luca played this through. 'So who did?'

But he already knew.

They both looked at the old photograph, at Blair standing between the couple, and Luca realized his suspicions weren't so wild after all. There wasn't just one small, fierce female dynamo on the yard, not just the girl he'd loved so long. There was her mother.

'You're not the only one who's got snowed up in Ontario and lost his heart, Luca mate,' Blair said softly. 'Or his sobriety come to that.'

Now it made sense why Blair had kept up the contact. Years ago, he'd fallen for the Flying Maple Leaf's wife and they'd stayed in touch. Luca really had walked in his footsteps.

'Is Meredith yours?'

'No idea, mate. We don't go there. Me and Maple Leaf trade insults and occasionally horses. Sometimes blows.' He touched his swollen cheekbone and winced.

'So he's aware you're involved in this deal?'

'Of course he's bloody aware. We both know he'd sell the devil a horse if the offer was right. Don't worry, we kept your name out of it.' Blair turned away to make himself another coffee. 'I didn't want Ronnie getting the sharp end of any of this. Only now I hear you've fucked the whole thing up.'

'Not so. He's on a flight here tonight,' Luca assured him. 'I collect him tomorrow.'

'That's what Ronnie told me when we spoke.'

Luca felt the caffeine spike, the room tilt. 'Are you saying he's not coming?'

'Not on that flight, mate. He disappeared two days ago, along with a pickup truck, a float and—'

'Meredith?' Luca closed his eyes.

'Maple Leaf's spent the last forty-eight hours uprooting half of North America trying to find them. Thinks they're headed to Compton Magna, like Bonnie and Clyde.'

'When did you find out?'

'Late last night. I had our mutual Canadian friend on the phone threatening to kill us both.'

'Thank God he's in Canada.'

'He was calling from Toronto's international departure lounge.' Blair sucked his teeth and grimaced. 'Arrived in Heathrow at seven thirty this morning.'

'He'll be heading for the stud!' Luca clamped his hand to his forehead. 'And I'm standing *here* talking about a job?'

'Yes.' Blair turned back to the machine. 'More coffee?'

'Christ alive, I have to go!'

'Stay where you are.' Blair didn't look round. 'I haven't finished talking.'

'And I haven't started,' snarled a voice guaranteed to make Luca's arteries turn to glacier flows. 'I'll have three espresso shots, Blair.'

The Flying Maple Leaf was framed in the doorway, a greying man-mountain of jet-lagged fury. Like Blair, he hadn't shaved in a while. He was also sporting a swollen, blackening eye, bloodied nose and split lip.

He glared at Luca. '*What* have you got her doing this time, you bog-trotting little weasel?'

Luca glared back, wishing he knew.

'I might have guessed you'd be in league with this wily kangaroo bastard!' He never minced his national insults.

Blair laughed, sounding almost affable. There seemed to be grudging peace fire going on between the two veteran Olympians, although Luca suspected they'd come to blows, and not for the first time.

'I met this fella at the airport.' Blair took the coffee across to him. 'We didn't exactly hug.'

'I've just been on the phone home,' Maple Leaf knocked it

back in one. 'It's been confirmed that the horse flew to Liège with the World Cup showjumping squad two days ago, and he's been on the road ever since.'

'How in hell did that happen?' Luca was in shock.

'Because the woman who caught a passenger flight to Belgium at the same time can make things happen,' the Canadian fumed, 'and you know that better than anyone, Luca. Don't tell me you don't know about all this. You probably helped her hire the horsebox to drive the horse through Europe. And you're the reason she's got a six-year-old girl in there with her.'

'Dizzy's with her?' Luca breathed in shock. Meredith had done exactly as he'd asked of her, he realized. He couldn't love her more right now.

'How soon d'you think they'll get to the UK?' asked Blair.

'Allowing for rest stops and the wait for a ferry crossing, I'd say tomorrow.' Maple Leaf predicted.

'She'll be here sooner,' Luca told them.

34

K it quoted King Lear's words to Dickon the horse:
'*My wits begin to turn.— / Come on, my boy. How
dost, my boy? Art cold? / I am cold myself.—*'

Dickon looked at him wearily, unimpressed to be played
for a fool. Bottom lip drooping, one hind hoof propped up on
its rim, he'd stopped trying to drag Kit closer to the garden's
edible plants or swing his head around to listen to the clatters,
shouts and whinnies coming from distant Church Meadow,
and he was starting to doze.

Kit now realized that this hold was some sort of misguided
aversion therapy on Ronnie's part. And Dickon was certainly
quite genial as horses went. Kit had chatted to him about the
Sherston Trilogy, recited Sassoon's 'Nimrod in September', and
patted him some more. They'd shared the last two dusty mints
in his pockets and he'd even told him he was very handsome,
and that Hermia would have loved him.

Eyes drooping, the old horse shifted his weight, lowering
the propped hoof and leaning companionably against Kit,
solid and warm. And that's when another cog in his elusive
connection to Sassoon clicked into place from nowhere, the
passionate horseman who had pressed his shoulder into the heft
of a hunter so often to reach for a stirrup, or pull up a girth

strap, his bucolic passions at odds with the battlefield's relentless mud and death. Like Nimrod, *In mulberry coat he rides and makes, / Huge clamour in the sultry brakes.*

Kit knew he had to try harder to capture that contrast between old-fashioned warfare and blood sport in his play, both romanticised yet brutal pursuits writer Sassoon couldn't conflate, giving the lie to the nobility of man and horse.

But first this fellow writer must get rid of the horse he was holding. Ronnie had been gone over half an hour. If this was a test, Kit was getting extremely annoyed about it. He wasn't a chest-beating Crocodile Dundee-type like her last dalliance; he was cerebral and cautious and needed to write something down. He was going to have to lead the horse back through the village to the stud.

Not easy in slippers, but he couldn't risk going back into the house to change them given this was the beast that had destroyed his last greenhouse. His phone must be in there too.

He tugged at its reins. '*Where is this straw, my fellow?*'

Depositing a pile of droppings with a groan of effort, Dickon reluctantly shuffled round to be led back down the drive.

'*Come, your hovel— / Poor Fool and knave, I have one part in my heart / That's sorry yet for thee.*'

On Church Lane, Dickon threw up his head and walked faster, dragging Kit along, excited by the cavalcade of travellers who were setting up their temporary home on Church Meadow.

'You just found that, mate?' one of them yelled as Kit led the old horse past. 'Not one of ours, but I'll give you twenty for it!'

Hearing this, Brian Hicks – who was videoing them on his phone from the edge of The Green – hurried across to Kit. 'That's Mrs Ledwell's horse, isn't it? She must have come off. I'll put the word out.'

'Mrs Ledwell may be a fallen woman but trust me, she has

both feet firmly on the ground,' Kit said theatrically. 'And if you see her, please tell her I've posted her bloody horse back.'

'Right you are.' Brian stepped aside nervously.

Kit marched on up the driveway to the stud's cobbled turning circle. Ronnie's battered little sports car was the only car parked there. Surely somebody must be here?

'Hello? Service!'

He trailed the horse around the two large, cobbled yards, attracting the attention of multiple long faces and pricked ears.

Uncertain which stable to use – and reluctant to share a dark, confined space with the animal – he decided to put him in a field, selecting one of the lush, high-hedged ones at the front, which Dickon seemed delighted about. Remembering how to take the tack off was a challenge, a warm, horse-smelling heat rising when he reached under the flap for the girth buckles, giving him another Sherston fix. After much unbuckling, the bridle came off in several spiderly leather pieces with help from Dickon, who shook the bit out of his mouth before gambolling off to sink down and roll.

The sight made Kit feel unexpectedly cheerful. Maybe Ronnie was onto something. He'd survived his heroic test and he felt triumphant.

A horsebox was making its way up the drive and he hurried to greet it, expecting Ronnie's redhead daughter at the wheel. Instead, a small blonde woman in a baseball hat jumped out. 'Gotta horse for you!'

'I've just put one out, thanks,' he joked.

She frowned. 'Can you tell me where Luca is?'

'I don't think anybody's here right now.'

'Jeezus!' She crossed her arms.

Dark-eyed and pretty, she had a hint of the damsel in distress that made newly heroic Kit square his shoulders. 'Have you come far?'

'Canada. Fucking Canada!'

On closer inspection, she looked both fierce and tearful beneath her cap peak, a combination Kit was less keen to investigate, sensing an explosion of emotion building beneath the red fleece and skinny jeans that might shoot her straight out of her gaucho boots any second.

'I don't work here,' he explained apologetically. 'And if you'll excuse me, I really must be go—'

'Just walk off, why don't you? What am I supposed to do here?'

'Mom? Is this the place?'

Kit realized there was a child in the cab.

'Let me see if anyone's in the house,' he offered, hurrying up the steps.

Which was when he smelled the smoke.

'Kenny says his first wife died last year,' Mo whispered urgently to Ronnie, 'and I saw him and Sir Peter scatter her ashes with my own eyes. But Nana Turner is Ash and Janine's mum, and she is totally alive on the Orchard estate. And she's called Tina.'

The two women were huddled together in a state-of-the-art downstairs loo, which boasted a high-tech Japanese toilet, mirror television, mood lighting and copies of memoirs *Oh, Kay* and *Doh, Kay* in eight different languages on a marble shelf.

Having excused herself to the lavatory so that they could talk, Ronnie found she did need to use it quite badly, but Mo was eager to impart everything she knew and seek Ronnie's advice.

'Kenny asked me to keep my eyes and ears peeled in the village, but I didn't expect to find out anything like this. I can't tell him until I know for certain, can I? He's so upset about his Tina dying, what if they're not the same woman? Nat's a complete fantasist. He could have made all that up. He used to boast he once won the Mongol Derby. And he tells people he taught Tyson Fury to box. Just cos his wife's called Tina, it doesn't mean she's the same woman.'

'Have you asked her?' Ronnie was jigging slightly to keep her full bladder at bay. 'Or can we get Tina Turner to come here?'

The name made them look at each other for a moment, eyes bright. Mo made a strange humming noise, which could have been 'Simply the Best' or just a nervous excitement.

Ronnie jigged from foot to foot some more.

Mo started jigging too, out of misplaced politeness. 'She don't ever leave the house. I was going to call round there next week, but now all this has kicked'off, and Sir Peter's on his way here.' Her kind, round face glowed pinkly. 'That man scares me a bit. More than Nat, if I'm honest.'

'Leave him to me.' Ronnie patted her arm, crossing her legs and jogging quite vigorously now.

'You hear it in your head too, don't you?' Mo moved her arms back and forth and swung her hips. '"Nut Bush City Limits", am I right?'

'No, I just need to pee.'

'Of course!' Mo went even redder, hurrying out.

Sitting on the loo, Ronnie took out her phone to read Blair's message again: *Run away with me.*

Whenever you're ready she replied with a wink.

Before she could check any of the new messages, she heard a cry from the main house.

Hurrying out, she found Mo standing by the open window in Kenny's office. Nat was no longer with them.

'He's taken his gun!'

Kenny was groping around him. 'And he's swiped my recording device! That's my new memoirs, that is!'

'Along with any proof he just told us what he did,' Ronnie muttered.

'I think he might have swiped that signed picture of Tommy Cooper as well, Kenny love,' Mo said, eyeing the wall above the mantelpiece.

Outside, the sound of fast-retreating hoofbeats was drowned out by the unmistakeable whirring of approaching helicopter blades.

Carly had searched in vain for Nat amid the Church Meadow travellers, messaged Ash multiple times, fielded Janine's many calls and given Brian Hicks's ever-videoing phone camera the finger more than once, but her father-in-law was lying low.

'Haven't seen him,' was the standard answer from his big, cheery caravan. But there was no doubting who had organized a gathering intended to disrupt the church's plans to sell somewhere the travellers saw as ancient common land.

Ellis had found a group of kids to kick a ball about with. They all looked up as a helicopter swept past overhead, absurdly low.

That's when Carly noticed how much smoke was coming from one of the stud house's huge chimneys. It struck her as a bit odd, but she was too distracted by the helicopter circling overhead to give it much thought, the Vanner horses throwing up their heads and starting to panic and Ash's name lighting up her phone at last.

'I think you'd better come to Mum's,' he said.

'Is it the kids?'

'They're fine. But Dad's here. Rode here like the Lone Ranger a few minutes ago. He just told us something I can't get my head round. Janine's gone apeshit, Norm's having one of his turns and Mum says she's been living a lie and still wants a divorce.'

Peter had been on a Peloton watching an old western when Kenny called. He always stayed in his flagship London hotel when in the UK, a big slab of Kensington Wren Baroque. The weekend invitations inevitably started once word got out that he was in the country, all valuing his wealth above his company: the sporting and charity events, the country house parties at which impoverished aristos danced attendance on Russians, Arabs and new money like Peter. He rarely accepted. Long-term partner Eduardo, who only openly accompanied him amongst their small social set, remained in the Virgin Islands and Peter was tired of hiring glamorous walkers and models by the kilo. He found these events boring. He preferred a bike, a beer and wide-open plains, even if he had to savour those on a QLED screen in the privacy of his penthouse suite.

His lawyers had been working all month to put Sanson Holdings in a strong enough position to push ahead with drawing up a commercial proposal for Eyngate, but the old house was fossilised in forty-year-old contractual covenants, cast adrift by missing paperwork and steel-armoured in Historic England listing restrictions. Determined to see this through at long last, Peter had stayed in the UK, pushing personal, political and planning advantage to no avail.

Then Kenny had called out of the blue, his voice hoarse as a football rattle, declaring a life-or-death situation, wheezing and coughing so much he made no sense. Telling him he was on his way, Peter had showered so fast he still had soap in his ears.

Having guessed that if he sat tight long enough something would give, he was appalled to think it might be his old friend's health. What if Kenny was dying?

Down his helicopter swept, lowering its skis onto the H by the manor. It was a good-looking house, he acknowledged. A true gentleman's residence. Not that anybody could call Kenny a gentleman.

A small blonde woman in riding breeches came out to greet him, hair blown sideways, the searing blue eyes familiar even after all these years. She thrust out her hand and shook his, forthright and businesslike. 'Sir Peter! You'd better come in. He's expecting you.'

She marched ahead, so full-scale Pussy Galore that Peter felt obliged to pull at his cuffs and straighten his hair before following.

Kenny was lounging in a recliner seat in a designer tracksuit and dark glasses like a pound-shop Goldfinger. 'Pete, welcome! Bostin' place this, isn't it?'

'You're not dying?'

'For a drink, maybe. What's your poison?

'Just water for me.'

'Bollocks. Get us both a beer, Patti love... Patti...? PATTI!'

'Maureen Dawkins has gone to out on an errand, Kenny,' Pussy Galore informed him, discreetly glancing at her watch.

'Is Geoff the Chef here, bab? He mixes a mean Old Fashioned.'

She crossed her arms impatiently. 'It's the weekend, Kenny. I believe your staff are off duty.'

'Then can you fetch us a beer, Princess? It's on tap in the bar.'

'Hurry up and tell him why he's here.' She stalked out.

'*She's* not changed a bit.' Peter settled on a low settee opposite Kenny, trying to get a handle on the situation. 'You always were a quick worker, Kenny.'

'A purely professional relationship, Pete. Just bought a horse off her. Not sure what flavour, but if she says it's good, that'll do for me. The Captain used to say, "buy enough nags, Kenneth, and you'll own this stud".'

'He only said that so you'd buy more horses off him, Ken.'

'You might have a point there!' He chortled, taking off his shades to rub his near-blind eyes and leaning forwards, elbows on his knees. 'Not that Tina ever minded having more neddies. Tell me,' he peered in the general direction Peter was sitting, 'whose ashes did we scatter last month?'

Peter cleared his throat. 'When you two split, she made me her next of kin, Kenny. It's my legal responsibility to deal with her death.'

'She really is dead?' He looked devastated, the jowls drooping. 'So she didn't run off with Nat Turner after all?'

At the mention of Nat's name, Peter took a moment to regroup. 'She was in a terrible state after your marriage ended, Ken. Mentally very unstable, you know? I tried to protect her, but he took advantage. Briefly.'

'Did she come back to you then?'

'I had a very good team on it, Pete. They couldn't find her. She just vanished. No paper trail, no social track record. It's our belief that she may have taken her own life shortly afterwards.'

Kenny's rheumy eyes looked even more lost.

'Up till a few years ago,' Pete hurried on, 'when somebody went missing like that, there wasn't much you could do about it. Take Lord Lucan. The Presumption of Death Act changed that. When my team failed to find any evidence of her being alive for seven years, we applied for a death certificate.'

'Nat says he married her, had babbies?'

'There's no record of it, Kenny.' Peter sighed. 'We both know Nat Turner would say anything for a fat roll of cash. She was a wealthy woman after your settlement and she never touched any of it. He probably wants a slice. But Tina Kay is legally dead, Kenny. She's gone.'

'Tell that to Tina Turner!' Pussy Galore carried in two brimming pint glasses.

'Now is not the time for musical jokes, Princess,' Kenny said in a choked voice, wiping his eyes again.

'Let's drink to Tina, shall we?' Peter suggested, leaping up and grabbing a beer.

'To Tina!' The two men raised their pints.

'Always alive in our hearts!' Peter eyed Pussy Galore who eyed him back, undaunted. 'Let's get drunk, Kenny! Like the old days.'

'Thought you'd never ask!'

★

A phone was ringing deep in the house as Kit found his way in through the back entrance, smoke billowing towards him along with a pack of dogs – one all hairy pipe-cleaner on legs, two small black-and-tan bullets and a lame terrier yapping its head off.

While the first three shot outside, the terrier turned and disappeared back into the smoke.

'Wait!'

Eyes already smarting and lungs roaring from the toxic assault, Kit pulled his jumper up over his nose and ventured inside.

'Is anyone in here? Lester, are you here? Can anyone hear me?"

He didn't know the house layout, but he could hear the little dog bark and followed it, the smoke thickening until he was barely able to see. He could hear a voice too now, which he realized was a TV commentator going through runners and riders for an upcoming horse race.

He whistled. 'Here, boy! Where are you?'

Another bark led him to the far end of the corridor, a narrow gloomy space with doors off in every direction. One was partly open up some steps to the right, the racing commentary booming behind it. As Kit stepped up to reach for the handle, it swung open at speed, pushed from the other side, thwacking him on the temple, propelling him off the steps and slamming the other side of his head against the wall hung with coats. For a moment, he saw stars. He'd swallowed part of his chunky fisherman's jumper collar, a decorative toggle almost choking him.

'Quick, lad!' called a hoarse voice through the muffle of something held over his mouth to mask the smoke. 'Follow me!' The footsteps limped away. 'Come on!'

Kit tried to call out and explain that he was feeling a bit too faint to follow, but his own mouth was full of woolly jumper and toggle, its stitching trapped between his teeth like floss.

He wrenched it out.

The voice, more distant now, said, 'Good lad! This way! Atta boy!' and Kit realized it was talking to the dog.

'Wait!' He started after them, but his sense of direction was all wrong because he found himself in the kitchen, also thick with smoke. Trying to retrace his steps, he walked into a larder instead, sending a row of cans crashing onto his feet. 'Ow!' He backed out, treading on one and tripping, bringing him crashing down with a crunch of coccyx against flagstone.

He lay for a moment to let the tears of pain dry and regain his breath, the smoke thinner down here.

The phone was ringing again, somewhere just across the room.

He crawled towards it, realizing he could alert whoever it was to his plight.

'Get help! There's a fire. I have a head injury!'

'I am calling from Windows about a problem with your computer,' announced a thick foreign accent.

No sooner had he hung up than it rang again.

'Ron?' a deep Aussie voice shouted over a lot on engine noise. 'Pack your bags. I'm on my way. We're going walkabout.'

35

There was a horse tied up outside Nan Turner's maisonette, of such extraordinary beauty it had drawn quite a crowd. A piebald with an outrageously long, crimped white mane and tail and almost entirely black body, it was being fussed over and fed carrots by the youngest members of the family not at Church Meadow helping set up the camp. Ellis rushed to join them, boasting, 'This is Grandpa Nat's horse!'

Inside, Carly had found her younger kids glued to *Peppa Pig* on the huge TV while Ash paced round punching one fist into the other palm. Sister-in-law Janine sat, shell-shocked and tearful, on the settee, make-up sliding. Somebody – presumably Nat – was thumping around upstairs.

'What is going on?'

'He's looking for something,' Ash hissed. 'Won't say what and Mum's locked in the bathroom again.'

'Mum has a secret past, Carl!' Janine wailed.

'What secret past?' Carly perched beside her, reaching for a tissue from the box on the coffee table, kept there for Nan when sobbing through her soaps.

When she heard who Nana claimed she'd once been married to, Carly thought it was a wind up. 'I know she's a big fan of his, Janine love, but she's been acting a bit confused lately. Are you sure she's not fantasizing?'

More thumping came from upstairs, the sound of drawers being opened and closed. The doorbell rang.

Mo Dawkins was on the doorstep looking very pink and strangely formal in a navy suit and silk shirt. 'Sorry to bother. I wonder if I might have a word with Tina? It's very important.'

'You can try,' Carly waved her in and pointed towards the stairs, 'she's up there.'

Mo hesitated, hearing the banging and thumping of cupboards and drawers, along with Nat's distinctive shout of 'Where the bastard hell is it, Tina?'

She cleared her throat anxiously. 'Has he got the gun up there?'

'What gun?' Carly felt her blood drain.

'It's in the kitchen,' Ash muttered. 'It's fake. He nicked it out of a countryside museum near Cirencester. It's even got This Is Not A Weapon stamped on the stock.'

'Is this about Kenny Kay?' Carly asked Mo, who she'd heard was working for the comedian.

'It's rather personal.'

Her father-in-law's voice boomed from upstairs: 'You kept them deeds to Eyngate Hall in the vardo, Tina, I know you did! You brought them and your divorce papers from Kenny so we could wed.'

Mo smiled at Carly and Ash kindly. 'That sort of answers my question, I suppose.'

'Well, I ain't got any of it now!' came a shout from the bathroom. 'Just some stupid piece of paper saying I've a no-good lump of a husband! And that's not even legal, our Carly reckons!'

'I saved you, Rapunzel! I rescued you!'

'You turned me into a skivvy who had to pee in the bushes!'

'Hold your tongue, woman!'

Carly went to fetch Nana's sewing bag and pulled out the decorative patterns folder, bulging and battered with age, its *Prima* pull-outs crammed between the concertina sections.

At the back, where she'd put back Nana and Nat's strange New Age marriage certificate, was a very thick, tattered brown envelope.

Inside were a lot of old, legal-looking documents, some gossamer thin. One – double-folded, yellow with age, edged with official-looking red stamps and bound with green ribbon – was by far the oldest and thickest. At its head, in large curly black writing surrounded by swirls, was written *This Conveyance*.

It was snatched out of her hands. 'That's my girl! Cushty!'

Fast as a cat, Nat hurried for the door

Ash was quicker, fiercer and trained for this, barring his father's way out and putting him in an armlock that made Nat howl in pain.

'Not in front of the kids!' Carly wailed.

Ash's momentary distraction was enough for his father to break loose, diving through the kitchen to the back door. Snatching his fake gun from the draining board, Nat was gone in an instant.

They all stood in shock for a moment, the kids still watching *Peppa Pig* beside Janine, who was gazing, panda-eyed, over the back of the sofa. 'What was that all about?'

'Were those the deeds for Eyngate Hall?' Mo asked in a small voice.

'Why d'you get them out?' wailed Ash.

'I didn't know they'd actually *be* in there.'

'Let him have it!' Nana appeared back down the stairs. 'Horrible place.'

Mo shook her head. 'If his name's not on those papers, it's no use to him,' she explained. 'It's your deed. Peter put it in your name.'

'A friend indeed,' Nana chuckled, sitting back down in her chair. 'Poor Peter. He meant well by me, but I didn't want us to wed. He's my astral twin so that would be ever so weird. And he was so nasty to Kenny, I couldn't forgive him that.'

'Would you like to see him?' Mo offered. 'He's never stopped loving you, you know.'

'Don't be daft. Peter likes other men. Always has.'

'I meant Kenny, Tina.'

'Oh, I don't think so dear. Kenny can have any woman he wants.'

'He only wants you.'

'That's very sweet of you to say.'

'He'll tell you himself if you let him. He only lives up the road.'

'I don't travel that far.'

'What if I bring him here?'

'Have I got time to bake him a treacle tart?'

When Lester hobbled and spluttered around the side of the house, Stubbs limping and sneezing at his side, both their eyes were streaming too much to see clearly.

He listened hopefully for a siren approaching, but only heard a cacophony of barking as Ronnie's dogs raced to meet them.

'Confounded birds nesting in the chimney again!' he told them, wiping his eyes and moving far enough away from the house to blink and squint up at the sparks and flames visible at the cowl of one of the east chimneys, a mini volcano plume rising over the roof.

Having lived through half a century of chimney fires here, he tried not to panic that it might spread. Nevertheless, the fire brigade would have to be summoned urgently.

Turning to hurry to the yard to dial 999 from the tack room phone, he found an unfamiliar horsebox was parked in the way with its ramp down. 'When did that get here?'

As he limped around it, he spotted Belgian plates.

A tiny figure made her way towards him through the arch, a blazing sun of smiles. 'Hey there, hi! Luca said this place was pretty shambolic, but I had no idea how bad! Where is he, by the way? I can't believe you guys have no phone reception here! I'm Meredith. I brought you a horse from Canada. Jeez, is your house *on fire?*'

A small blonde-haired girl dashed through the arch behind her. 'The little pony is *soooo cute*! Look, Mom, a fire!'

Lester looked from one to the other, baffled. He coughed to clear his throat, his voice a hoarse crackle. 'Madam, forgive me, I have no idea who you are, and right now I need to call the fire brigade.'

The woman was staring at the house. 'Where's the other guy? The one who went inside?'

Pax had bought a phone charging cable from the gadget store in the over-priced Shopping Village and plugged it into her car's socket. Her battery was on 1 per cent with a *Charging Slowly* warning flashing. It stubbornly refused to turn on.

She and Kes had just waved Monique and Bram away on bicycles along the byway that led down to the valley in which they now lived, the picture of mother and son healthy living.

In the passenger seat, Kes was guzzling sweets from the Pic 'n' Mix, pink-faced with sensory-overload happiness.

'Did you enjoy that?' she asked him as they set off at a crawl on the less bucolic Broadbourne ring road, stuck behind a slow-moving caterpillar of cars.

'Lots and lots, but I like still riding Coll more.'

'Right answer,' she laughed, trying her phone again. Still off.

At the head of the caterpillar was the arched, open-topped rear of a pony trailer. It made her think of Bay and wonder where the Pony Club event was. Her sister Alice, a loyal Fosse and Wolds volunteer, was probably there too.

'Bram's mummy is really pretty,' Kes said. 'Like a movie star.'

'Isn't she?' she said brightly.

'But *I* think you're prettier, Mummy.'

'Also the right answer.'

'Bram says his mummy is the best rider in the world and the best cook and the best dancer and *brilliant* at giving tickles.'

'Loyal of him.' She waited for the positive comeback, but he was yawning widely. A moment later he'd nodded off.

Driving in the slow-moving crawl, Pax tried not to obsess about what Monique had written in her message to Bay or how hideous the photo had been. She'd made an extra effort getting ready today, thinking she was going to see him, so the hair was at least washed and springy, the eyes kholed, earrings matching. Not a movie star, maybe, but both X chromosomes were on show. And her teeth and nose in twelve-megapixel close-up. She checked them in the rear-view mirror.

Stop it! Pax chastised herself. Monique was still his wife. She'd probably added a vampire filter.

Give it time, Pax. Let their separate lives all fit into their grooves. Find some more distance from Mack. Don't make the mistake you did with Luca, thinking you could rush at it and separate it all like a food obsessive. Love, friendship, recovery; they needed to be cooked slowly together and seasoned. The Bounce Barn was hardly a recipe for romance.

She'd work towards that steam railway get-together, she vowed – the boys could share Harry Potter imaginary play while she and Bay shared a stolen glances and clipped vowels over a cup of coffee. *It's only something in my eye...*

She pulled into the petrol station on the far side of Broadbourne, checking the phone again. Up at 3 per cent. It turned on!

Leaving it waking up and Kes sleeping, she jumped out to fill up, glancing at the pumps beyond hers, noticing a Land Rover already parked at the far one, the traffic-slowing pony trailer hitched behind it, a familiar figure just visible turning away to slot the nozzle back in its cradle. Then he turned back and saw her too.

It wasn't a railway waiting room. It wasn't even the Bounce Barn. They were gazing at each other over a display of bagged kindling and the roof of a Honda Jazz, but she could hear the guard's whistle and the steam puffing and blowing.

Good local home wanted. Not novice ride. Bombproof.

Waving, he made his way into the payment shop behind him.

Why had she pressed Pay at the Pump? She couldn't think of a reason to go in. Chewing gum? Then she'd have to leave Kes.

She spent so long deliberating he came back out, crossing over to speak with her, ignoring an angry toot for the car waiting for his pump.

'You had fun? Sorry I missed out. You got my message?'

'Dead phone, but Monique explained you had to drive Tilly and friends.'

'I've just dropped them all off. *Very* excited.'

'The boys had fun.'

'I saw.'

'Monique sent you pictures, then?'

'Yes.' He looked away, smiling down at this feet, which was quite unlike him.

The car behind his tooted again.

Pax waited.

He smiled at his feet some more.

The car tooted.

'OK, *what* did her message say? I know she sent you one about me. And a picture, which I wasn't ready for by the way so I probably have a hideous—'

'She said,' he looked up, 'that if I don't make a move on you, she will.'

'No! She didn't? Really?'

'Of course not,' he laughed. 'Monique didn't mention you. Or send a picture. Just the kids'

'That's good.' She scrabbled to replace her fuel cap. It wouldn't go on.

He covered her hand in his and helped her turn it. 'Let's not talk about Monique.'

The waves of heat rushing up her arm were extraordinary. She half expected the whole tank to explode.

'Listen, mate!' The furious motorist behind the pony trailer had got out of his car to stomp across the forecourt. 'I can see you're trying to chat the lady up, but frankly, unless you're fucking proposing, can you move your fucking wagon?'

'You're quite right – and why not?' Bay beamed at him and nodded. 'First of many, I suspect. Here goes.'

He got down on one knee.

'Stop it!' Pax growled, suddenly alarmed, glancing into the car where Kes was still sparko.

'Patricia Claire Johanna Forsythe née Ledwell. My darling, darling Pax. One day, even if it's when we are old and wizened and far too decrepit to make love, will you do me the very great honour of being my wife?'

She laughed, then jumped as a small cheer went out around them and she realized other motorists and garage users had gathered to watch, taking this seriously. The server had come out of his shop, Somebody was videoing it on their phone.

'I— that is— gosh—'

Her own phone started ringing in the car, a sleepy Kes answering it in his phone voice. Then. 'Mummmeeeee. Mumeeeeeeee!'

'One moment.' She opened the door. 'What is it, Kes?'

'Lester says the stud is on fire!'

'No!'

Bay was already on his feet, a reassuring hand on her shoulder. 'You go ahead, I'll follow right behind. Will you be OK?'

'Yes. Of course.'

He started sprinting towards his Land Rover, and then spun around to tell their audience. 'She said yes!'

36

Mo had driven her parents' ancient Isuzu Trooper to the manor to pick up Kenny. He had several lovely cars, but driver Ivor was visiting family and she was sure she wasn't insured to drive them. Or knew how to without accidentally propelling her passenger out of the sunroof by ejector seat.

No sooner had she touched her fingerprint to the sensor pad and the huge gates started to open than Ronnie shot out of the house. 'I think you'll have to take Peter too. They're inseparable.'

'But he's the one that told Kenny Tina was dead!'

'I'm pretty sure he thinks she *is* dead.'

Mo had heard enough bad stories about Peter Sanson from her parents for this to cut little ice. 'He let Kenny think she was living in the South of France for years. And it was him what made up all that nonsense about a gypsy curse. He just wants his house back, I reckon. Dad said he used to come here with his shooting parties, acting like lord and master, taking over the pub, careering round the lanes in their Range Rovers.'

Ronnie glanced over her shoulder, lowering her voice. 'Do you remember the day of Hermia Austen's accident, Mo?'

'Long time ago, that was. I was living at Mum and Dad's farm. It was an awful day.'

'Did anyone see the car?'

'Not that I recall. I think there was some talk of it being a big, shiny thing. Blacked-out windows...' She gasped as she realized what Ronnie might be saying. 'You don't think...?'

She shook her head quickly. 'Forget I asked. It was summer. They weren't shooting.'

Mo swallowed uncomfortably. 'Peter Sanson and his hangers-on used to come in summer too. They had an outdoor concert thing over there every July, raising money to help rhinos or some such.'

'It was a long time ago as you say,' Ronnie dismissed cheerfully. 'And it won't bring dear Hermia back to life whereas we *can* bring Tina back. You're absolutely sure it's her?'

'Totally. They're all waiting in Medlar Avenue. But I don't think she could take seeing Peter as well, not today.' She explained about Nat making off with the deeds to Eyngate.

'She really did have them?'

'Along with deeds for a house in Selly Oak and a lot of old share certificates.'

Ronnie's face brightened. 'I wonder if she wants to buy a horse?'

Mo could hear singing from inside. Kenny and Peter had moved into to the purpose-built bar, now alternating pints with shots and reliving their Jugged Hare days. They were singing 'Hi Ho Silver Living'.

'You keep Peter talking,' Mo whispered to Ronnie, 'I'll get Kenny outside while he's distracted.'

The two women regarded the drunken sixty-somethings hopelessly. Superglued to barstools, arms around one another's shoulders, they moved on to 'The Boys Are Back In Town'.

Serendipity struck when Peter announced he was going for a slash and lurched off to the high-tech Japanese loo.

Finding himself bundled into the back of a twenty-year-old Isuzu that smelled of pig pellets and creosote, Kenny started coughing and giggling, asking, 'Am I being kidnapped, babs?'

'By love, Kenny, just by love. Now hold on tight and enjoy the ride.'

★

The ancient Fosse Way, built during the conquering occupation of Emperor Claudius in the first century, drew an almost die-straight line from Exeter to Lincoln, cutting through some of England's most picturesque countryside, and passing within a few miles of Blair's Wiltshire base and Ronnie's Warwickshire one. As Roman Roads went, it was the widescreen, big-budget road movie.

Like Maximus and Commodus forced to share a chariot, Luca and the Flying Maple Leaf charged along it as fast as the elderly Subaru and a cautious Irish driver could go, arguing all the way.

'Sir, you have to give me this chance, *us* this chance. She's come all this way. Blair's offering us an amazing break.'

'NO!' The Flying Maple Leaf was not enjoying his ride at all. Sitting on the side of the car where he expected a steering wheel to be, finding the roads alarmingly narrow, he was being subjected to a constant earache and an over-vigilant respect for the national speed limit. 'Can't this thing go any faster?'

'Why d'you always hate me?'

'I don't hate you! But you could be so good, Luca, and I've watched you pissing your life away! You might drive like a pensioner, but you can't stay still. And her life's in Canada. She has a husband and three young kids in Canada.'

'One of those kids is mine.'

To his surprise, Maple Leaf didn't deny it.

'We'll make it work,' Luca vowed. 'Somehow, we'll make it work. I swear I'll stay still.'

'Right now, I want you to drive faster! That horse she stole is valuable.'

'She didn't steal it, she's transporting it! And she did it to show me how much she loves me!'

'Get over yourself. Quick, overtake this lot!'

And they would have kept fighting and shouting all the way

were it not for the fact that moments later, climbing out of
the deep combe where the Fosse Way crosses the River Colne,
taking advantage of a stretch of overtaking lane to cruise
past slow-moving traffic, they heard a loud bang up ahead.
Screeching wheels. Horns and hazards. Burnt rubber and hot
metal. An accident just out of sight.

Luca pumped the Subaru's old brakes frantically and it
juddered to a halt with a safe stretch of clear tarmac ahead.

Only suddenly it wasn't clear. A truck was barrelling side-on
towards them, a high-sided tsunami of steel and rubber and
glass and aluminium moving way too fast to avoid, engulfing
them in shadow, giving them only the briefest moment of
profound sadness and regret in preparation for tragedy.

And yet somehow it missed them, clipping another car and
spinning away into the far verge to nose-dive into a ditch,
leaving the Subaru rocking and the two men shaking, half
believing they might be dead already.

The Flying Maple Leaf put his head in his hands and took
a long, deep breath of life-affirming, second-chance air.

Putting his arm around him, Luca knew before he said a
word that he would get his chance.

Not long after Peter Sanson had lurched into the Manor's
high-tech washroom, Ronnie realized she'd left her phone by
the basin in there.

When he failed to come out after ten minutes, she half suspected
him of hacking into it to read her messages. Soundproofing
being a part of all the high tech, it was impossible to tell.

She paced around the hallway close to its door, trying not to
look at her watch. Kit would be apoplectic, left with Dickon
this long, although perhaps that wasn't a bad thing. She'd been
looking for an excuse to switch course since they got stuck
at kissing, and now that she and Blair were back in contact –
she glanced at the washroom door, longingly envisaging *run*

away with me – she would have to rein it back to friendship. Something told her he'd be just as relieved.

She was more worried about abandoning Lester alone at the stud. What if he was right and more foals were imminent? Hadn't Pax mentioned something about a mare arriving? While well-accustomed to sole charge, he was still massively underpowered.

'Everything all right in there?' She tried to penetrate the soundproofing, banging sharply on the door.

She heard a faint, surprised sound.

Shortly afterwards, Peter reappeared looking sheepish.

'Were you asleep?'

'No! I was reading this book. Might get Ken to sign it.' He was carrying a copy of *Oh, Kay*, she realized.

'Where *is* Kenny?' Peter headed through to the bar, listing slightly.

'Being reunited with Tina.'

One eyebrow lifting, he poured himself a Lagavulin, holding up the bottle to offer her one.

She shook her head, glancing at her watch again.

'You don't believe all that nonsense about her being alive, do you?'

'Yes, I do. So do you.' She looked up. 'You knew all along.'

Although Peter had never possessed his friend Kenny's beddable good looks, he'd invested in ageing better. The bulldog face was expensively smooth, the teeth as straight and white as money could buy, and his neatly cut sisal helmet hinted at high-end hair transplants. He was trim and tanned, lean and mean, well dressed and no less chippy than thirty years ago.

'You always did have a sense of your own importance, just like your father,' he said eventually. 'Just as easily bought, I'll wager.'

Ronnie smarted. There was no point raking over the past here, taking him to task about the pieces of Percy land he'd acquired. He'd paid more than a fair price, after all. It was the reason the stud was still running.

But there was something she couldn't let rest. 'You preferred my friend Hermia, didn't you?'

He took a big gulp of the malt, wincing as it burned. 'Nice girl.'

'Charming, funny, kind, talented. Always saw the best in people. Saw the best in you.'

'Like I say, nice girl.'

'You nearly killed her once, do you remember? Driving a car too fast. She was riding a horse. She wrote to me about it afterwards, I still have the letter somewhere.'

He stared at her for a long time.

Ronnie knew he might be thinking back to the day he'd bought Eyngate and got drunk with his friends in the pub before driving back across the fields, pranging his car into a tree. The day Hermia had shouted at him and he'd decided to try to woo her again. That day. That was the day Hermia had written to her friend about.

But there was just a chance he was thinking about another day entirely. The day many years later when she'd been hacking a horse along a quiet lane and a car had driven past wildly fast, crazily close. And even if the driver hadn't seen horse and rider coming down onto the tarmac behind them, how could they have missed the news headlines afterwards, and yellow roadside boards appealing for witnesses and the outpouring of shock and grief in the village and through theatreland?

'You never came back here after Hermia's accident, did you?' she asked Peter lightly to test it. 'Not once.'

'Put that in her letter too, did she?' He poured himself another whisky.

She said nothing. Hermia had never written to her about the circumstances of her head injury. Learning to write again had taken her over a year. She had never recovered her memory of the day at all.

'What do you want?' he asked quietly.

She thought about this, tried to imagine what Hermia would want. Nothing would bring her back. Screaming *Kit wants his wife, his children want their mother, I want my friend* was as futile as wishing for the stud's long-lost gallops and hayfields, its ploughed-away streams and coppices. What would Hermia ask of him?

'Don't buy Church Meadow.'

He looked at her disbelievingly. 'Is that it?'

'Yes.'

He raised his glass. Then he drained it with a satisfied sigh, picked up his copy of *Oh, Kay* and headed for the door. 'Tell Ken I said goodbye and I'll be in touch.'

'I'll pass it on.'

She watched him go, then hurried to fetch her phone from the high-tech loo.

The helicopter blades were starting up outside again as she read her messages and let out a cry of horror.

Pax found herself speeding up the stud drive behind the wailing, blue-flashing fire engine, her heart in her mouth. Bay was right behind them.

Beside her in the passenger seat, Kes was in ecstasy at the prospect of starring in his very own *Paw Patrol* episode. 'Is Marshall going to put the fire out? Look at the flames coming out of the chimney, Mummy! Will they use their hosepipe?'

She could see Lester limping towards the fire truck to greet it.

Parking a safe distance away and telling Kes to wait in the car, she hurried towards them, Bay hot on her heels.

'Doesn't look too bad,' he said, looking up at the pluming chimney as they ran.

'What do you mean, not too bad? It's *on fire!*'

The chief fire officer agreed with Bay. As his crew jumped out and got to work, he reassured Pax and Lester that the Micklecote retained fire squad had the procedure off pat. 'The lads will proceed to place an exploding extinguisher up your chimney. Basically, it's like a distress flare. We pop it up your flue and it deoxygenates with a zinc powder and sulphur combination. Common procedure. Known in the business as a Quickie.' He left a practised pause. 'I take it there's nobody currently in the building?'

'We think there might be,' Lester said between coughs. 'A witness saw somebody go in.'

'Who's in there?' Pax asked in shock.

'I saw him. Hi!' offered a breathless voice.

Pax realized a small, smiling figure in a baseball cap was standing alongside.

She knew it was Meredith straight away, and not just because her jealous early Google image searches had mosaiced that high-cheeked face, its upturned nose and bold, dark gaze. Nor was it the Canadian accent. It was because there was a force to her, an energy, that was pure Luca.

'So, the dude I saw go in is fifties, sixties maybe,' she was telling the fireman, 'about six one, one eighty pounds, kinda like Harrison Ford in *The Fugitive* before the beard, only less ripped.'

Telling her that was very helpful, the fire chief hurried off to brief his team with the description.

'You forgot to tell them he was wearing slippers, Mom!' trilled a high voice at hip height.

And Pax found her next breath missing because she was staring down at the tight white-blonde corkscrews, the green eyes, the Luca-ness of his daughter.

Not for the first time that day, she drew on her Percy upbringing, with a polite fanfare of charm and apology. Pax the peacemaker. 'Goodness, what strange welcome you've had! I do hope you're both all right?'

'Hi, ohmygod, you must be Pax!' Meredith beamed even brighter, thrusting out a hand to shake. 'You're *way* taller than I thought! I'm Meredith. This is Dizzy.'

'You have beautiful hair,' she told the little girl, still mesmerized by her similarity to Luca.

Dizzy pulled a face. 'Everyone says that.'

And Pax laughed, because everyone always told her that too, especially at six.

After which she found her arms almost shaken off by handshakes with first mother then daughter, who both repeatedly said 'Hi!' in the same bright voice and had the same thousand-watt smile, only Dizzy's had two front teeth missing.

They were so unexpectedly positive, Pax could feel her jaws aching, running out of room for the wideness of her own smile. 'How wonderful you're here!'

She tried not to let the shock of it knock her off course, but it was like an internal injury that was bleeding so fast through her system she couldn't gauge how much it hurt. And all the time she was glancing at Lester coughing, and the firefighters talking about somebody inside the house, and the chimney burning, and the noddy car with Kes in it, and Meredith and Dizzy, and she felt too light-headed to keep Pax peacekeeping.

A warm hand was placed on her shoulder. 'I'll take the smoke if you take the fire.'

Reaching up to cover it with her own, she ran her fingers around the familiar signet ring, sensing the world starting to turn the right way up again.

Bay leant into her ear. 'Let me deal with the Quickie, Lester and the search for Harrison Ford. You and Kes take your guests to the yard to meet the new horse.'

It was the first time it occurred to Pax that the American stallion had arrived.

'Do you think we should check on them again?' Janine asked Mo, lifting a net curtain to peer along the road. 'Should I go back round there?'

'I'm sure they're fine, love,' she reassured her, although quite why Mo was the authority on reuniting long-lost lovers, she wasn't sure, given her recent romantic track record. If today had restored her faith in love, she wasn't letting on just yet. That said, it had been a truly tear-jerking moment witnessing all the shock and weeping and laughter and tenderness when Kenny and Tina were brought back together. There had also been a fair bit of swearing and a wail that the tart needed to come out of the oven.

The other Turners and Mo had now relocated across the road to Social Norm's house to give the first Mr and Mrs Kay some privacy. Just back from Church Meadow on his mobility scooter, Norm was far too preoccupied by the fact that Nat was laying siege there to reclaim it for his forefathers than his daughter-in-law's shenanigans. '*That's* the fight my boy was talking about, don't you see?' he kept proclaiming between toots at his oxygen mask. 'The fight for old gypsy land!'

Mo noticed Carly looked particularly relieved at this. 'No need to fight for the King's Purse just yet then, is there, Ash?'

When he didn't answer, she recited:

'*Star light, star bright*
First star I see tonight
I wish I may, I wish I might
Have the wish I wish tonight.'

Mo had said it to Grace so many times, she joined in without thinking, catching Carly's eye and making a small wish of her own that Barry would soon come to his senses with minimal shock and weeping, and much laughter and tenderness.

Ash was now at the window, peering out beside Janine, who asked her brother, 'How do you feel about having Kenny Kay as a stepdad?'

'Might get Mum out of the house'

'I'm going to check on them again.' Janine hurried to the door, grabbing her coat.

Five minutes later she was back, panda eyes running again.

'What are they doing?' asked Mo.

'Watching telly together and holding hands.'

37

A figure was being helped from the house when Ronnie arrived back at the stud, the fire team calling for an ambulance: 'Possible mild concussion and smoke inhalation according to the patient, complaining of pain in his coccyx and lower spine.'

'No, I said a pain in the *arse*!' Kit raged. 'What I specifically said is "that woman is a pain in the arse". *That* woman!' He spotted Ronnie hurrying up.

'Is he OK?' she asked the fireman.

'*He* is absolutely fine,' Kit fumed. '*He* made it into some sort of office which the smoke hadn't reached and awaited rescue. *He* never wants to see you or your bloody animals again, especially *that* beast.' He pointed behind her.

Still breathless from running, she turned to see Dickon in the high-hedged front paddock which had been rested all winter, belly already gorged like one of the pregnant mares.

'You turned him out on all that spring grass?' she gasped. 'He's laminitic! It could kill him.'

'That fire could have killed me!'

'Thankfully it just was a minor chimney obstruction,' one of the firefighters told him. 'Probably stood by smokier Guy Fawkes bonfires. This gentleman faced the brunt of it,' he turned to a figure standing ramrod straight behind them, 'but he insists he's all right. I can tell you were military, sir.'

For the first time, Ronnie realized Lester was standing with them, his old face positively animated from all the drama.

'Had plenty of chimney fires here over the years,' he said gallantly. 'As Mr Austen will vouch, we're not ones to panic.'

Bay was here too, Ronnie realized, feeling inexplicably grateful for it.

He'd put a proud hand on Lester's back, telling the fire crew, 'This man's witnessed more smoke and mirrors than most in the village. Is it safe to go in, now?'

'Absolutely sir. There's very little damage as you'll see, although it will smell for a while. We're just awaiting an ETA on the paramedics and then we'll be out of your hair.'

Clearing his throat, Kit straightened his sweater neck and pulled at the toggle to tighten it. 'I don't think I do require an ambulance after all. I'd rather like to just go home. Thanks very much for your help.'

'Anytime, sir.' The fireman turned away to call a colleague and cancel the shout, and Kit caught Ronnie's eye. The anger and indignation had gone, replaced by a rueful gleam.

'I really am terribly sorry, Kit.' She walked towards the drive with him, trying not to let her attention drift anxiously onto greedy Dickon in the field beside them. 'I had no idea all this was going on. I never meant to leave you that long – the thing is, I—' He must never know about her conversation with Peter Sanson, she realized. It would only hurt him. There was no proof. 'I behaved very selfishly and I apologize.'

'It worked,' he smiled. 'And while I could have done without being smoked like a haddock afterwards, I've had worse days. I can't wait to get back to writing. You've inspired me.'

Ronnie felt immensely cheered. 'I'm glad.'

They'd reached at the top of the long drive. He halted and coughed, gazing down, over its two rows of pollarded poplars to the bustling Church Meadow. 'Hermia was quite right about Percys and Austens.'

'What did she say?'

'That you love to hate each other but that really, you're a perfect match.' He threw a glance over his shoulder back towards Bay, still talking to the firefighters. 'For what it's worth, I think she'd want you to give him another chance.'

It was Ronnie's turn to smile to herself. 'Hermia was always more forgiving than me, and an unfaltering romantic. A far gentler, sweeter person all round, in fact.'

He didn't deny it. Neither of them spoke, because just for a short moment, it felt as though Hermia was there, standing right with them, her arms slotted through theirs, insisting they must stay friends, but do please stop kissing.

'Thank you for making her so real again,' Kit said eventually. 'I think I'd like her memory to myself for a bit now, if that's OK.'

'Of course.'

He started off down the drive and then stopped again to hold his hand up. 'Almost forgot. Your Australian friend phoned while I was in the house. Something a walkabout?' He set off once more. He was wearing slippers, Ronnie noticed.

Heart skipping guiltily, she ran to the front field to catch Dickon.

His tack was abandoned on the gate, the bridle in three separate sections. Grabbing these as she let herself in, she started buckling it together and walked towards him. 'You've had your fun, my darling, but this is really not good for you.'

Dickon gave her an old-fashioned look and gambolled off.

'*That's* the new stallion?' Pax looked at it incredulously.

Meredith had found the right stable to put the new arrival in. The only problem was it looked like the wrong horse.

Smaller than he'd appeared on the video, with a short bullish neck, narrow thoroughbred chest, thin tail and a coat that was more dry husk than polished walnut, he was astonishingly ordinary. Tiny, tired, tucked-up and temperamental, he flattened his ears and turned away.

'He looks dull as fuck,' Meredith told her, 'but he's sweet as treacle to handle and motors like a Ferrari. Where d'you say Luca is again?' She was looking increasingly wired.

'Seeing friend of Mummy's in Wiltshire,' Pax remembered.

'I fucking love it!' she raged. 'We come halfway across the planet to surprise the guy and he's out!'

'We weren't expecting the horse until tomorrow.'

'We switched his flight last minute, so me and Dizzy could have a girls' adventure. I messaged the buyer. Kenny, is it? He sent a thumbs up.' She spoke in breathless, urgent bursts, as tense and overtired as the horse. 'And I rang here when we got to the UK, but whoever I spoke to seemed to think I was bringing a goat? Was that you? Say, has my dad called?'

'Not to my knowledge.' Pax's smile was being held up by willpower, an unstoppable, wide-eyed manic nod greeting much of what Meredith said.

'Dad will be super pissed.' She sounded even more hyped. 'My bones are so fucking broken over this!'

'Gosh, sounds tough. Painful.' Pax nodded some more, trying to remember to blink.

They couldn't be more different. Brash, vivacious and outspoken, Meredith was a gusher and a sharer who swore a lot and laughed a lot. She was also tiny – barely more than five feet – and curvy, with generous brown eyes like a cartoon mother deer and golden skin, an inch of dark root creeping into her blonde hair.

'Those two get on – look!' She laughed at the sight of Kes introducing Dizzy to Coll the Shetland. 'He's one handsome kid, your boy.'

'And Dizzy is gorgeous,' she said, nodding too much.

'Luca told you about her, yeah?' The dark eyes watched her anxiously.

'Of course!'

'I did what he asked and he's not even here. Talk about shit timing.' She turned back to the stallion. 'This is a good fucking horse, trust me.'

'What's he called?'

'Devil's Bay. Everyone just calls him Bay.'

Pax took a moment with this information. 'We'll probably call him Dev,' she said eventually, looking over her shoulder as the original Bay came striding under the first arch, longing kneading her stomach.

'Lester must have his cottage back! His quarters stink like a bacon smoking shed. Hello, I'm Bay Austen,' he thrust out a hand to Meredith, who stopped eyeing him approvingly and started laughing so much she couldn't speak. Bay looked amused. 'What did I say?'

'You share the same name.' Pax nodded at the horse.

'Hello, Austen.' He peered into the stable, where the little horse gave him a withering look.

Lester had following behind at a sprightly limp with Stubbs, waving Pax's concerns away when she hurried to check he all right. He was remarkably bright-eyed. 'I am perfectly well, thank you. The fire brigade is just leaving. Your mother will be with us shortly. I've just explained to her that the young lady has brought the stallion here in person.'

'God, you're marvellous, Lester. I can't thank you enough. Do you need your cottage back tonight?' She was horribly aware that she had nowhere to go. The old Stables Flat beneath the clock tower was an unheated rat run. There was no way she was shacking up in the house beneath the Luca and Meredith reunion, nor did she fancy sharing close quarters with her mother.

Lester looked long-suffering, 'I suppose I might be able to find a temporary alternative.'

'Is your barn conversion still free,' she asked Bay, 'just short term?'

'Afraid not,' he grimaced. 'Got snapped up by a power-walking opera singer my mother is trying to recruit to the Parish Council. But the au pair went back last week, so the old nanny flat in the bakehouse is empty. Rather charming. Doors straight through to my place...' He gave her long look which she found far too horribly tempting. But they both knew it was way, way too soon for anything like that. Holding hands at a steam railway first, Pax reminded herself.

'Did you hear that, Lester?' She turned to him cheerfully. 'Bay's just offered you his nanny flat.'

Bay opened his mouth to protest, and then closed it again, blue eyes glittering with reproachful amusement. His family all adored Lester.

'What's your Internet like?' Lester demanded beadily.

'Ultra-fast fibre.'

'I'll give it one night and see.'

Bay cast Pax another rueful look then added a ghost of a wink before telling Lester, 'It will be an honour.'

Lester bowed his head modestly, quick to mutter, 'And isn't our new stallion a fine stamp?'

'Mummy will love him,' Pax predicted. He was just her type, like a younger, fiercer Dickon. 'Where is she?'

Lester cupped a hand to his ear indicating for her to listen. They could hear faint shouts of *'you bloody bastard!'* coming from the direction of the driveway and front paddocks.

'Is she still with Kit Donne?' she asked before realizing her mother was trying to catch the older, more gluttonous Dillon.

'He's remarkably chilled.' Bay had moved closer beside her to watch the new arrival over his half-door, grumbling. 'Now I know he's my namesake, I'm furious Ronnie wouldn't let me buy a whisker.'

Unimpressed with his admiring audience or new surroundings, Bay the horse was ignoring the challenging roars from Beck a yard away along with Cruisoe's authoritative bellows, and the mares shrilling. He closed his eyes disdainfully on them all to take a doze.

'Jet lag.' Meredith yawned sympathetically on Pax's other side, then grinned. 'Give him time. I love how *old* this place is.' She spun back to gaze round. 'How many stallions do you have standing here?'

'Three now,' Lester informed her proudly. 'Irish Sports, German Warmblood and now Thoroughbred. And a near-full book of visiting mares thanks to this new fellow's pedigree.'

'Great, cos he could *really* use some sex,' she beamed over her shoulder, then her eyes lit up. 'Now *that's* my kind of horse!' She strode across the cobbles to admire Beck, Lester hurrying after her.

'How does she fit in?' Bay asked lightly, moving yet closer to Pax, his warmth up against hers.

'Love of Luca's life,' she whispered back. 'Wasn't that always part of the masterplan behind buying this horse?'

'Darling Pax, you always did credit me with far more guile and intelligence than I possess.' He looked over his shoulder at the little thoroughbred, and then at her. 'But that's why I adore you,' he dropped his voice lower, 'love of *my* life.'

'You promised you wouldn't ever say that again.' She watched Lester telling Meredith all about Beck's illustrious pedigree.

'Thinking aloud, sorry.' His hand found hers and squeezed it.

'Forgiven.' She squeezed back, wondering how soon she could legitimately do a U-turn on the *I love you* ban without getting burned.

'Horseboy's ex came all the way here, eh?' Bay was also watching Meredith chatting animatedly to Lester. 'Mind you, I've heard he has a lot of them.'

'Touché, lover boy. But this one is up there, out there, forever special. And they have a...' She glanced at corkscrew-blonde, green-eyed Dizzy, now receiving a guided tour of the stud from a smitten Kes.

'Bloody hell,' he chuckled, eyes softening. 'He certainly stamps his stock, as Sid Stokes would say.'

Their shoulders leant tighter together, sharing the private joke. I want to be loved by him again, Pax realized. I want him to tell me he loves me every day for ever and ever.

'The proposal still stands, by the way,' Bay said ultra-casually.

'Thanks, I'll think it over.' And I want to love him back.

'Take as long as you like.'

'I will. I love you too.'

He stared at her in shock, blue eyes pooling darker.

'Thinking aloud, sorry.'

He kept looking at her for a long time, finally murmuring, 'You read my mind.'

There were excited shrieks as Kes and Dizzy came charging out of the foaling barn. 'There's babies coming out of two horses' bottom and they're both stuck!'

'Two?' Pax wailed, hurrying towards the barn. 'Jesus, we need Luca here.'

'You have *me*.' Lester gave chase lamely.

'And me.' Bay was right behind them.

'Count me in.' Meredith caught up.

There was a clatter of hooves as Ronnie led Dickon onto the yard behind them, both out of breath. 'I'm right behind you!'

38

Luca parked the old Subaru in the lane below the stud, taking a moment to gather his wits. Beside him, the Flying Maple Leaf was snoring, brow low, chin high, mouth open, a sleeping dragon. For now.

The accident had delayed them badly, yet it had also fast-tracked a friendship that had taken a decade to find a crack of an opening, And what an opening, a treasure trove of shared thoughts. They'd talked non-stop for two hours, until the emotionally exhausted, jet-lagged Maple Leaf had dropped off mid-sentence. But they already had a plan. *If she says yes, I say yes.*

There were travellers camped on Church Meadow, a higgledy-piggledy assortment of modern white caravans and old vardos, sheep trailers and vans. Horses were tethered on the best grazing. Wood carvings were already lined up close to the lane. The AUCTION sign had a horse rug over it. Several figures were sitting around a campfire, one playing on a mouth organ. Luca's fingers itched to fetch his fiddle. But they itched more to pack his things.

No more travelling aimlessly from yard to yard, horse to horse, woman to woman, bottle to bottle. He was going to go to work somewhere he could never have dreamt of being offered the charge of without Ronnie, without being in this place at this time.

Pure happenstance had presented him with a unique opportunity, the perfect sanctuary. The horse world was often like that, and Luca knew better than to screw this up. With kismet still on side, he had enough time to explain to Pax, to apologize to Ronnie, to ready himself for Meredith. He was going to talk this thing out properly for once.

But when he drove into the arrivals yard and saw the Belgian horsebox, he realized kismet had done a bunk and his extraordinary, fearless, can-do action-woman had powered in. Meredith had left everything she knew and loved behind to come halfway around the world to join him. He was taking this.

He woke Maple Leaf. 'She's here already!'

He spluttered awake, squinting out at a low-lit spring dusk spilling over the old Cotswold house and stable yards. 'You're fucking with me, right? You want to leave all this for that little hilltop horse hangar?'

'As soon as we can. Tonight.'

Maple Leaf raked his short, bristly grey hair. 'If she says yes, I say yes. If she hesitates, even for a moment, you never see us again.'

It was a tough deal. He expected no less.

They were all in the foaling barn, new lives on their feet for the first time ever, quivering hungrily for mother love. Nancy's filly foal – golden dun like father Cruisoe and full brother Spirit – was as exquisite and fine as blown glass. And from Maggie, a strapping bright bay colt already looking around with bold eyes, working it all out.

Luca heard Meredith's laughter first, his mission bell.

The moment he saw her, he knew he had to stop running because love always caught him up.

Then he saw the blonde head and his heart windmilled.

Sometimes the most joyful meals were shared with unexpected

company, Ronnie reflected later as she took her phone outside to find enough signal to call Blair.

Although the house smelled of acrid woodsmoke and the dining room was out of bounds until it had been thoroughly scrubbed, the kitchen had been back at its glory days of warmth, noise and crammed-together chairs, its big, scrubbed table playing host to an unlikely band of horsemen and women and two pony-mad children. With a great mountain of Luca's pasta and endless pots of tea, they had somehow forged an alliance that felt lucky, toasting Devil's Bay and Compton Magna stud with chipped mugs and great cheer.

She paused in the arrival's yard to repeat farewells to unlikely new housemates Bay and Lester, who were climbing into the Land Rover with Meredith's father, who they would drop off at the luxurious Le Mill hotel where he'd booked himself a room.

'Thank you again for your hospitality.' The Flying Maple Leaf shook her hand and kissed her cheek, no less magnetic now than he had been when they'd met in Vechta, a giant powerhouse of a man who had to be boss. 'I appreciate you putting them up. We'll sort everything out tomorrow.'

Meredith and Dizzy were staying in the house, mother and daughter falling exhausted into twin beds already.

Across the arrivals' yard, the lights glowed in the cottage where Pax was putting Kes to bed. Beyond it, the working lights beamed brightly, Luca checking around the new arrivals, old and young.

Waving Bay's car away, Ronnie went to stand on the front wall where she could get two signal bars.

It was a clear night, the stars on show. She could see curls of village chimney smoke above the treetops, hear laughter and music from Church Meadow.

Her little screen glowed, Blair's most recent message beside his name: *I need an answer tonight.*

She heard Beck's distinctive bellowing call on the yard,

neurotic and needy, sensing his great champion Luca close by, the one he felt safest with in the world.

Hers was Blair.

'About time,' he picked up her call. She could hear music – Bowie, of course – and a loud background hum.

'You know I can't run away,' she sighed. 'We have foals due, mares to cover, horses to sell. You're already taking my wildcard stallion *and* poaching my manager.' Taking on Luca had been partly her suggestion, but she had no idea he'd act on it so fast.

'And his child and girlfriend!' His familiar deep laugh rang out. 'Looks like I'll get the father-in-law too for a while. They're planning to make it a family affair. Good job I'm moving out.'

'Where will you go?'

'That's kind of up to you, Ron.'

'I must see this thing through, Blair. I'm needed here.'

'I appreciate that.'

'Believe me, I'd go walkabout with you if I could. Our timing's all wrong. In six months maybe, a year.'

'You know your problem? You're bloody short-staffed.'

She listened to the rumbling at his end, recognized the opening bars of a favourite Bowie song. 'Are you in your lorry?'

'Got a horse to collect. Thought I'd drive there so I can make an early start tomorrow. Something I want to ask a friend of mine.' He turned up the volume and she recognized 'Heroes'.

Ronnie laughed. They'd listened to it together so often, recognizing that they were the couple who nothing could keep apart, even if it was just for one day. They'd never called it their song, but now perhaps it was.

She could hear a big engine climb up the chestnut avenue, branches hitting the roof of a high vehicle. Then she saw the lorry's marker lights emerge through the trees and she whooped, leaping off the wall to run and greet it at the top of the drive.

Leaping out, Blair scooped her up, swinging her round and

kissing her. 'While we're waiting to run away, I thought you might use some help. I've got someone looking after my place for a bit, you see.'

'Handy.'

'Someone I love has just let me poach her manager.'

'Kind of them.'

'Bloody good horseman, knows his breeding.'

'I could use one of those.'

'I hoped you might. I can only do part-time, but I'm cheaper and have more experience. Although I should warn you, I will want to sleep with the boss.'

'I don't think one's allowed to say things like that anymore.'

His deep, undomesticated laugh rolled over them both. 'What *should* I say?'

'I'll say it.' She kissed him. 'Let's go to bed.'

PART SIX

39

The stud's foals soon started arriving in quick succession, which, as Ronnie had predicted, made everyone feel better.

Born mostly in the early hours, often watched over by just Pax and Ronnie, these quiet moments of new life deepened the mother and daughter bond they'd struggled to hold steady. Now it finally settled into a deeper cup, the foals gifting the stud its *élan vital*.

From trembling up onto unfeasibly long legs in search of milk and safety, to bounding out onto pasture for the first time, they filled up and filled out, soon charging around amid the family herd in the nursery paddocks, skipping and nipping and squealing and kicking, before flopping down beside their mums for tail-twitching naps. They were a robust, magnificent bunch seen into the world by two women – with occasional help from an opinionated elderly man and excited five-year-old – who had learnt the old-fashioned way that mares knew better than any gadget when the time is right.

Sometimes Blair joined them overnight, commuting between the North Cotswolds and Wiltshire, where Beck had fast established himself as the ninth magical white horse of the Wessex Downs, far better suited to a modern, regimented yard and AI duties.

Luca was proving sober and indefatigable, determined to show the Flying Maple Leaf he would do whatever it takes to prove his maturity and dependability. Having flown back to Canada with her father to appease her family and negotiate the long-distance separation, Meredith returned a week later with Dizzy, her two younger children and both parents. 'I'm worried they'll bring the horses next time,' Blair joked drily.

In between shouting for errant pointer George and making impossibly strong coffee, Blair was invaluable helping Ronnie deal with the Compton Magna stallions' stud duties, especially now Pax had so many to ride. When she wasn't up late foaling, Pax was never out of the saddle, both at home and out training and competing. She was on a fast track to get to know tough, missile-quick Devil's Bay, whose owner had yet to visit.

Lottie's owner, by contrast, was around a lot these days, dropping Lester in and then staying on to help. Even on the days Lester whizzed back and forth along the lane on his electric bike, Bay would find an excuse to drive up, ride past or walk in.

Lester had bedded straight in at Compton Magna Farm, delighting in the better heating and meat-based diet, particularly when home-cooked by Viv. He was proving to be a big hit with the senior Austens. 'He's tracing Dad's Dexter herd lineage back ten generations,' Bay reported, 'and he's a terrific racing tipster.'

When Kes was staying overnight with his father and his own children were with their mother, Bay took Pax out for old-fashioned dinner dates and big-screen movies, although her early starts and competitive ambitions ruled out late nights. Ronnie sensed her daughter's cautious excitement, her old spirit returning, and while she still found it hard to trust Bay, she could also see just how hard he was trying.

They also needed him. He was practical, generous and happy to be constantly on call, helping out on the tractor or lending a hand on the yard, one day sending one of his farm labourers over to mend their fencing, or another arranging for contractor Barry to fertilise the stud's fields because 'there was some going spare after we'd done ours'.

Most importantly of all, he kept Pax cheerful.

A fortnight into her partnership with the new stallion, she was still struggling to gel with him.

Bay's equine namesake – known as Bay Horse for differentiation purposes – was the polar-opposite of scopey, spooky ground-eater Lottie. Economic, lightning fast and unfazed by the big occasion, the cool-headed little dynamo wasn't a natural match for Pax, whose legs seemed to stretch down to his knees, and whose careful nannying irritated him.

'You do know I put him your way because I thought he'd suit you?' Blair told Ronnie on one of the nights he stayed over.

They were sharing a bath and a bottle of wine, listening to unapologetically loud eighties music.

'Of course I knew that, but Pax needs this more.'

'You sure about that?'

'I've hung up my competitive boots.'

'C'mon, Ron, we both know that's never going to happen.' He topped up her glass.

She raised it, conceding with a 'for now'.

To the consternation of some Compton locals, the travellers remained camped on Church Meadow over Easter and into April, fire smoke curling up into ever-later sunsets. Only Nat came and went like a village weekender, disappearing without warning for the night, sometimes two. He boasted to the Turners and to his caravan that he was busy making enough money to buy them the land at the auction. They all knew that the call of the road was simply too strong.

The day soon came when he packed up his vardo for a longer trip. Taking his favourite Vanner and second favourite girlfriend, he tasked son Ash to challenge his cousin Jed for the King's Purse. 'When the mean little bastard gets out. But if you're not up for it, son, get a message to me. I know enough to get another two years on his sentence. Cushty.'

'So much for being a fighter,' Ash grumbled after he'd gone.

'He's a lover, not a fighter these days,' Carly told him. 'You could learn a lot from that.'

'This is Nat Turner you're talking about. We'll be lucky to see him again this side of next year.'

'Dad will be back for the auction,' Janine boasted. 'He's going to sell them Eyngate deeds and buy Church Meadow for the Turners, I reckon.'

But the morning after Nat's departure, Mo Dawkins unlocked Compton Manor's letter box and found the Eyngate deeds in it, along with signed photograph of Tommy Cooper and a four-leafed clover. While Kenny Kay appeared far more excited by the return of his showbiz keepsake than his first wife was by her legal documents, Tina nonetheless took it as her cue to make a surprise announcement to the Turner family.

'Kenny's asked me to move in with him,' she told them, 'and there's no point hanging around at our age, so I said yes, as long as the kiddies can all still come round to ours when you need them minding.'

Overjoyed that she'd agreed, Kenny asked Mo to order the mother ship of all climbing frames before sending her off to Smyths toy shop with an unlimited budget. Then he told her he was promoting her from PA Patti to Mo the Pro ('it's that or Commando, bab'), along with a pay rise that meant she could afford to hire some part-time help on Mum and Dad's farm. Kenny also loaned them Sarah the Carer several mornings a week to assist Jan because, 'I feel young and carefree now my Tina's back.'

When Barry sloped back to the bungalow at Spinney End after one too many rows with the Bev, complaining his back hurt and he couldn't take another full body wax, Grace was so ecstatic to find her dad there after school that Mo didn't have the heart to show him the door. The Bags told her that he didn't deserve her forgiveness, but she was secretly pleased to have her husband home where he belonged, especially this contrite. His toolkit was seldom out of his hands. He got the bathroom finished in no time and started on the disability ramps. Mum, Dad and Jan were so impressed when they came to admire all the changes at Greenways over a Sunday roast, negotiations had reopened on a retirement house-swap.

But Mo was in no hurry to take over the farm. She loved her new job and the freedom it afforded.

She was also revelling in her first theatrical role since playing Rizzo in her school's sixth form production of *Grease*. Cast as Rosie in *Mamma Mia!*, alongside Gill as a very posh church choir Tania, both had been utterly intimidated to find their Donna was the glamorous opera singer who had moved into one of Bay's barn conversions. To their delight, it turned out she was a terrific giggle and owned an ex-racehorse, so a fresh Saddle Bag had been recruited.

As soon as word got out that Peter Sanson had withdrawn his offer to buy Church Meadow prior to auction, the BOMB campaign had gained momentum. While the search for generous private donors was seen as the real banker, staging *Mamma Mia!* outdoors in the meadow itself would make for terrific publicity, everyone agreed.

Director Auriol was the self-styled Phyllida Lloyd of Compton Magna. Casting her production with single-minded determination, much bribery and more than a few veiled threats, the village school head had also press-ganged Bay into playing one of the three dads, alongside the dishy Well Cottage husband and, controversially, Mack Forsyth 'for his strident tenor and windswept good looks'. She flirted mercilessly with all three at rehearsals. Fierce stage manager Bridge made sure nobody missed any of those. Petra was lured out of her plotting shed to orchestrate PR and a concerted campaign was kicking off to promote ticket sales. The race was on for big headlines and big patrons.

Even Kit Donne had sloped back from sulking in London to help, enlisting a terrific feather in their crown with a knighted RSC alumni who agreed to make a guest appearance as Father Alexandrios. Once word got out – and Petra's *I do I do I do* Professor Lockhart gif went viral – ticket sales flew.

After his first rehearsal with the local cast, however, Kit Donne put his head in his hands and complained that his career would be in flames after this.

'Your problem,' Auriol told him grandly, 'is that you are a curmudgeon. You must try wearing bright colours and write a Gratitude List. Now, does anyone know where we can borrow a donkey?'

40

Ronnie wished she felt more ebullient after Maumesby Park International, but a worry that Pax was taking on too much too soon kept retying the knot in her stomach.

Pax had only sat on Bay Horse a handful of times and managed one competitive run beforehand, so eventing's big international opener was bound to be a learning curve. They'd made it round, at least. Pep talked by Ronnie, she'd let herself trust this rubber ball of energy, and he'd believed her precision-point steering, a shared fearlessness that just about paid off. In Lester's words, it 'got the job done'. They came back with a good placing and the event won Devil's Bay a lot of new admirers, but Ronnie sensed the match was still far from gelling.

Next time out was even less pretty. Their dressage was crabby and tense, after which they disagreed over when and how to leave the ground. Misinterpreting his snatchy, bullish way of going as hesitation, Pax took him out of his natural rhythm by over-riding him at fences, hitting coloured poles then wasting time cross-country. They scrambled round to finish mid-rank in their section, giving neither much confidence in one another. It was still early days, the home team sympathised, building a bond took time. But they all knew a horse of the stallion's calibre and experience should have beaten the opposition hands down.

'Burghley on the cards this autumn, eh, Ronnie?' Bay, who was endlessly cheery, championed Pax at every outing he could get to, a bottomless source of picnics, and partisan enthusiasm.

Ronnie was privately less confident, aware that this tough little campaigner wasn't as forgiving as wide-eyed, adventurous Lottie, with whom her daughter had now won two classes on the trot. She'd ridden the stallion a few times herself – stole the ride at home as often as possible in fact – and loved the feel of him but understood why Pax's analytical, sensitive way of riding might not get the best tune out of him. He was a point-and-shoot power pack, immensely neat and quick-thinking, rhythmic and disciplined. He needed an old-fashioned bomber pilot, not a clever modern navigator.

As a sire, his previous track record and breeding were at least still proving to be the catmint Blair had predicted they would be. The stud's AI bookings for him this season had already doubled. Now just one advanced run away from a five-star qualification, their son of Master Imp was being talked about in lorry parks everywhere.

Thankfully sex suited him, as Meredith had promised. Two natural coverings and half a dozen excited humps on the dummy mare for AI collection later, and Devil's Bay was back on the lorry to compete again, dropping down a level to get a confidence-booster in while he and Pax sweated it out on a waitlist for high-profile Chatsworth and the opportunity to step up a level.

But eight hours later when Ronnie welcomed the lorry home with news that their Chatsworth entry had at last come through, anxious faces greeted her. The pair had been like bad-tempered Sunday motorists, arguing over the map cross-country, Pax explained, eliminated early on the course at a tricky combination. 'He locked onto the wrong element; I had no steering whatsoever.'

It didn't help that she'd also competed Lottie in a Novice class that day and Bay had brought a bunch of friends to big it up in the sponsor's and owner's tent, bragging loudly that his home-bred Compton mare – who made it a hat-trick by winning her section – had cost a twentieth that of the tricky, trappy American horse.

Ronnie was furious, collaring him alone later. 'Much as I appreciate you pointing out how good Compton-bred horses are, you are *not* helping her confidence.'

'And you *are*?' Bay's quick, quiet anger surprised her. 'I don't think Pax should ride that horse at Chatsworth. They're too new together, too unproven. It's getting dangerous.'

'You're not the owner,' she reminded him.

Awkwardly, that owner was finally taking an interest, or rather his lady friend was.

When Kenny brought Tina to the stud to meet Devil's Bay, the horse had to be led to their chauffeur-driven car to meet her. She fed him carrots through the rear window and told him he was beautiful while Kenny told Ronnie how they were tackling her agoraphobia. 'She's quite happy inside the car, which helps. Getting her back out's trickier. We've only managed five minutes walking around a garden centre so far, but she's very determined.'

As soon as he learnt the stallion was going to be competing at Chatsworth, Kenny insisted they would be there too. 'Bet they lay on a good spread, somewhere grand like that! It's what ownership's all about, isn't it? My horse better win, Princess, or I'll want my money back!'

Ronnie knew he was joking, but still...

As the trials approached, she forced the thought from her mind that Devil's Bay was simply never going to be Pax's type of horse. Instead, she tried building her daughter's confidence with more bolstering pep talks, assuring her how brilliant the horse would be if he was just allowed to get on with his job.

But this just seemed to make Pax less certain. 'Perhaps

you should take him round and let him get on with his job, Mummy? You still have the rider rank.'

'Withdraw the horse and aim him at something later this season,' was Bay's opinion.

Even Lester ventured that it might be wise to ask another professional rider to deputise.

'*You* should take on the bloody ride,' Blair told Ronnie in a shared bath while Bowie and Freddie Mercury sang 'Under Pressure'. 'You can show them all how them how good he is.'

'I want them to see how good Pax is too. She's the face of this place, its future.'

'Not on that horse. You and I both know it's like human relationships, Ron. Some just aren't meant to be. Others, like you and me...'

A lot of bubbles flew onto on the wall and bathroom floor while he tried to convince Ronnie she could still ride with the best of them.

Just a few days before Chatsworth, the decision was made for them when Pax fractured her wrist falling off the Austens' trampoline on a playdate. 'I know, idiotic. I do a high-risk sport, and this happens instead!' She looked suspiciously elated, as did Bay; Lester and Blair were unsympathetically euphoric too; Kes was most excited of all because he got to write his name and draw an NHS rainbow on his mother's plaster cast.

It was ridiculously late to ring around other riders trying to get a replacement jockey. Nobody else had sat on Devil's Bay in the UK except Pax and Ronnie. This was down to her. The others all told her she should take on the ride. 'Just do the dressage, Mummy, see how it feels.' 'You can do it Gronny!' 'The Captain would be very proud.' Even the horse's owner was behind the idea. 'Always liked you on top, Princess.'

Ronnie knew she'd been well and truly skewered, but somehow that didn't matter. Because the stud team had pulled together. They were a team at last

The entries secretary and British Eventing were satisfied that

Ronnie's accreditation still stood from the previous year. If she wanted to deputise for Pax, she just had to declare the change of rider in time, they told her.

But Ronnie's nerve was not what it had been. Although she'd competed for longer and more recently than her daughter – regularly campaigning two horses when she'd run the estate office for Bunny in Wiltshire – she'd long ago given up any top-level ambitions. Retired old Dickon had been the last horse she'd ridden at this level.

'Maybe I *should* ask somebody else?' she confided in Blair in the bath while Peter Gabriel sang 'Sledgehammer'.

'No bloody way,' he insisted. 'I've told you enough times that this horse was always meant for you.'

'But I've never even competed him. If he was tense at events with Pax, imagine what he'll be like with me?'

'Plenty of sex beforehand will help relax those nerves.'

'He's got no mares booked in.'

'I wasn't talking about the horse.'

Laughing, she slid beneath the bubbles.

In bed, later, she reminded Blair that he shouldn't be seen supporting her at Chatsworth. Only a few close friends knew how often he was here helping her out here; they'd kept it extremely quiet. 'It's too soon after Vee,' she said. 'We know how everyone talks.'

But Blair was adamant. 'I don't care what anyone else thinks any more. I know Vee wouldn't mind, and that's what counts. She liked you, Ron. And she bloody loved me, like I bloody loved her. Life's for living. And loving. You're a long time dead.'

Dying was something Ronnie feared might be a very real possibility if she tried to ride the American stallion around a course as big as Chatsworth's with so little preparation, but she knew she couldn't say that.

Instead, she said, 'I think I might need my nerves relaxing a bit more.'

★

'I can't believe they fell for it,' Bay said, admiring the much-graffitied cast on Pax's wrist when he called on the stables cottage with a box of farm shop goodies to aid her recovery.

'I have X-ray proof!'

'Hairline? Buckle?' he teased, taking a closer look at the artwork, now embellished by his son Bram and by Ellis Turner. 'They usually splint and brace bad breaks, don't they?'

'I *did* actually fracture it!' she pointed out. Then, 'Twenty years ago, maybe.'

It was true Pax had fallen off the Austens' trampoline and it had hurt so much, she'd reluctantly let Bay take her to the local small injuries unit, where they'd advised them to go to the county hospital. Once there, they'd waited hours in A & E, at which point she'd begged to go home and Bay had insisted she must be seen. When the over-cautious junior doctor had spotted the faintest of lines on the radius bone and put her in a plaster cast just in case, Pax had stayed quiet. She was almost certain it was an old injury – she'd smashed that wrist badly in a horse fall in her early teens – but if it meant her mother lived the dream, and it made Bay feel better, she wasn't going to argue the toss with a qualified medic.

'I'm just glad you're safe.' He put his arms around her and pulled her close, glancing up. 'Kes asleep?'

'With Mack tonight,' she reminded him, glancing up too.

'Oh yes.' He leant back so he could see her face, blue eyes playful. 'Which means we can...'

She felt the fireworks start in all the best, familiar places.

'... take it veeeeeery slowly,' he smiled. 'I love you, Pax.'

'Thinking aloud again.'

'Stop reading my mind.'

41

Chatsworth Horse Trials was held over three days in the thousand-acre stately seat of the Duke and Duchess of Devonshire. It was eventing at its historic, sportsmanlike, big-day-out best. The magnificent parkland with its jaw-dropping house were the theatre, the super-fit, sharp and talented horses at the top of their sport the players.

Backstage, it was slick, professional and workmanlike, the party atmosphere confined to rowdier corners of the lorry park. The Compton Magna team planted their flag at its quietest edge.

The temporary stabling was housed in airy rigid tents that were part hangar, part polytunnel. Having a stallion meant they were allotted a stall at the end of a row, fixing extra boards up so that Bay Horse wouldn't be distracted.

Their secluded corner nevertheless attracted intense interest, for their celebrity owner as much as the scandal of Blair and Ronnie being seen out together.

Kenny Kay would be bringing his first wife Tina on Sunday to see their horse showjump then go across country. The story of their extraordinary, rekindled romance had broken in the papers – Ronnie had heard village rumours that Janine had sold the story, but Lester assured her it was Pip Edwards – and everyone was agog to see them out in public together.

Meanwhile, Verity Verney's widower being seen back out with his mistress so soon after her death was quietly overlooked.

Ronnie was blown away to find that she and Blair were treated the same as always – as a couple of old friends, of lovers, of competitors, just a couple – and she was overwhelmed by the obvious delight that she was back in the saddle amongst the senior riders.

'About bloody time!' The pats rained on her back and shoulders as she set up camp, the hugs pulling her in, making her realize how much she'd missed her tribe. One day, after they had run away together, Ronnie hoped she and Blair might make this a regular thing again.

Devil's Bay seemed to relish the big occasion too. He had too much to look at to be grumpy, and the springy Chatsworth turf was a magic carpet beneath his small, hard hooves.

Their dressage was mercifully early on the Saturday, few spectators around to witness a workmanlike test that put them just out of the top ten. Ronnie liked the horse enormously, and while she didn't ride with her daughter's flair, she had the measure of him and the career mileage to make it work.

'I keep remembering how much I love all this,' she told Blair in the lorry that night after the camaraderie, course walks, horse talk and barbecues of a long evening in their temporary village of riders. It was an all-too familiar gypsy encampment that moved between these grand estates' parklands, and big, purpose-built equestrian centres through the season.

'Remember it tomorrow,' he said and started kissing her until she forgot her nerves and remembered something else she'd always loved about their shared life on four wheels and four legs...

Sunday was hot, crowded, and all about Kenny Kay and his coterie. He came with an entourage of staff whose names rhymed with their jobs. Tina refused to leave the car. Out of loyalty, Kenny stayed in it with her.

Pax and Bay had driven up from the Comptons first thing,

the stud left in the safe hands of Lester, Carly and the Austens' groom, their kids in the safe hands of co-parents.

'Leave it to us to make sure Kenny and Tina get a VIP day, Mummy,' Pax assured her. 'You focus on what you do best, which is something you will always do better than me, and we all love you for that. For being tough, positive, invincible you.'

Ronnie smiled to hide the fact she was feeling quite stupidly teary.

'Good luck.' Pax hugged her tightly. 'And thank you. We're so proud of you. I love you.'

Really quite stupidly teary. 'I love you too.'

Ronnie was relieved to get mounted. Being up in the saddle was her nirvana, like a scuba diver eighty metres underwater or a parachutist eight thousand feet above ground. She was in the zone at last.

Bay Horse loved the buzz of the crowd, tents and flags, his small, black-tipped ears constantly on the move, his small athletic body bouncing off the close-cropped sward like a ball on a racket when Ronnie warming him up for the showjumping.

Bay the man had spoken to the stewards and Kenny's car had been brought closer so that Tina could see more of the action and relay it excitedly to the man sitting beside her.

When Ronnie rode from the warm-up to the arena, the windows of an immaculately white Tesla were lowered amid cries of 'Good luck, bab!' They shot straight back up again when a few opportunists closed in with phone cameras.

But Ronnie was focussed on the job, keeping her ball bouncing on the racket. This was so her sort of horse. He was Dickon reincarnated, only with bigger springs and that touch of bloody-minded genius her beloved old friend had always been too kind to possess. He was just the sort of horse she wanted to breed.

They jumped clear, gaining another place to creep up to ninth.

The Tesla windows went down as she passed by on her way back to the stables, 'Well done, bab! Lovely!'

This time, Ronnie paused to bend down, wreathed in smiles. 'You have a super young horse here! Thank you for trusting this old-timer on him. So glad you could both be here.'

More camera phones jostled and the windows whizzed up.

Back at the tented stables, Blair debriefed her before the cross-country, talking her through the course again, their thirty-year shorthand at its most rapid fire. 'Time's super-tight. That's your key. He'll be strong. Use it, don't fight it. Watch out for the sunken hollow. Don't stop kicking. I bloody love you.'

'I bloody love you too.'

The cross-country for the four-star championship was run in reverse order after dressage and showjumping, from bottom to top of the leader board. In a class of almost eighty, being in the top ten made for an agonising, if gratifying, wait. Dressed in her familiar dark pink cross-country colours, wishing she could enjoy the chain-smoking competitor tent feedback of the old days, Ronnie lay low with Blair at the stallion end of the polytunnel stabling, scrolling the class's live results feed on her phone while Bay Horse rested in his stall, eyes half-closed, enviably zen.

Others went back to their lorries or to hospitality through long waits like this, but she preferred to stay close to the horse today, to conserve their energy. Blair understood; it was a given. They talked about where they'd like to go on walkabout: driving through Europe to cross the Alps into Italy maybe, or down through South America from charro to gaucho. Australia's New South Wales was mandatory, that deep, sweet treat of big sky and big family would welcome them both after a long, dusty road adventure. It was pie-in-the-sky fantasy, but it passed the time.

They were plotting their way between horse ranches along Route 66 with the aid of Google Maps when Pax and Bay hurried in to report that the Tesla had been relocated to an optimal cross-country viewing spot, then hurried away to get in position themselves.

'Am I seeing things or are those two holding hands?' Ronnie watched them go, surprised by how cheering this made her feel. She turned to Blair. 'Have we time to relax my nerves again?'

''Fraid not, Ron,' he said, glancing at his watch, then nodded at his groom who was helping them out. 'Time to get busy.'

'If I win this thing,' she joked five minutes later as Blair loped alongside while she rode down to the cross-country warm-up, 'I'll run away with you. Soon as you like.'

'Win this, Ron, and I'll bloody marry you.'

Talk around the cross-country warm-up buzzed with the latest gen from the course. Blair was right. The time limit was proving almost impossible to get, with just two combinations inside it when Ronnie entered the start box. She'd walked the course three times, memorising every minute marker, quick route and alternative, but she didn't know Devil's Bay well enough to be certain she trusted him to ask every second-saving question. As the starter counted her down, a tiny corner of her mind was still debating whether she should be doing this at all.

'Three, two, one, good luck!'

Six minutes and five seconds later, Ronnie was in no doubt how much she loved doing this. She also knew just how much she trusted the horse she couldn't stop patting. And the faith she'd just restored in herself was more than prize enough. But this wasn't about her glory.

She left Blair and his groom cooling Bay Horse and jogged to the Tesla. It had a small crowd around it. The window lowered a fraction. 'Congratulations, princess! He was bostin'! Tina described it jump by jump.'

'He did you both very proud, Kenny. I can't thank you enough. What a prospect to be standing at stud. He's something very special.'

'We're welling up here. Think we prefer the showjumping if I'm honest, but let's talk.' The window closed.

Accepting their third-place envelope and rosette at the prize-giving soon afterwards – still barely believing they'd climbed into the top three – Ronnie found the young, much-capped winner leaning closer. 'Bloody nice horse, that. Call me.' The second-placed rider congratulated her too, cornering her while their victor took her lap of honour. 'Heard half America's next Olympic hopefuls tried to buy him, but Blair got in there too quick. If you ever want to sell, let me know.'

'I'll keep you posted.' Ronnie loved getting ribbons, but nothing beat the buzz of horse-trading.

By the time the lorry ramp was back up and they were ready to drive home, she was keeping half a dozen riders posted whether Devil's Bay might be for sale.

'Kenny won't object to doubling his money,' she ran the idea past Blair in the horsebox's cab heading south, Bowie rocking on the stereo, 'and this isn't the right ride for Pax. She's always been better-suited to making youngsters into superstars, not reheating something ready-made.' Ronnie wasn't convinced that Kenny was a natural-born event-horse owner, she explained. 'Tina loves her showjumpers. Paul Fuchs has some super young stallions. I think we might even talk them into buying two.'

'What about running away?' Bay asked wearily as Bowie sang 'It Ain't Easy'.

'There's the rest of the breeding season to get through. I must make the stud profitable.'

He turned to look at her, gravelly voice full of smiles. 'Pack your bags, Ronnie. You've already bloody done it.'

'Team effort,' she dismissed, wondering if she dared to believe it. Not quite yet. 'We're going nowhere until I know Church Meadow is safe. We missed the *Ziggy* musical, but we can't miss *Mamma Mia!*'

42

It was the second May Bank Holiday. Chestnut candles blazed the way for the procession of villagers crossing the green to Church Meadow, now transformed into a Greek island, the stone witches sitting on the back row of a makeshift Cotswolds amphitheatre. Excited incomers trained their phones on a temporary decking stage ready to see a knighted National Treasure with a kalimavkion on his head.

Carly towed a protesting Ash and Janine to a roped-off front row where Nana was sitting with Kenny and the Stokes from Lower Bagot Farm. 'You all right, Nana Tina?'

Happy tears filled Tina's eyes as she ushered them in. 'Isn't this bostin', babs? I am *out* in the *open*! Kenny found me these amazing pills. Make all the difference.'

'What are you giving Mum?' Janine demanded.

'Smell that?' Kenny waved a hand in front of her nose.

'What is it?' she demanded, sniffing suspiciously. 'Hashish? Crack?'

'Country air!' Kenny shared the joke with Sid Stokes, his new drinking buddy at the Jug.

Jan Stokes gave them a wise look, stage-whispering, 'My money's on old-fashioned love.'

'How come you all get a VIP section?' Ash grumbled as

Brian Hicks hurried towards them to explain that they would have to sit elsewhere.

'It's disabled seating.' Jan smiled at him. 'But I'll take VIP.'

'Own it,' he told her.

Embarrassed, Carly towed him higher up the meadow's hill. 'That was *so* embarrassing.'

'What? Did I say something wrong?'

'Not you, Janine. Accusing Kenny of drugging Nana.'

'Love is the drug, so the song goes.'

'Then you're my dealer, bae.'

Ellis had clambered up ahead of them to share a straw bale with Kes and another boy, all three foreheads-together, gazing at a glowing screen.

Carly claimed a nearby bale for her and Ash. His hand found hers. The drug still worked.

Beyond them, she spotted Pax Forsyth perching with Monique Austen. They caught each other's eye and smiled.

Carly leant forwards to whisper across to the boys, 'Watch out for the donkey.'

The knighted national treasure Kit Donne had persuaded to play Father Alexandrios was universally agreed to be the bums-on-seats star turn of BOMB's *Mamma Mia!* outdoor fundraiser.

But was Coll the Shetland who stole the show.

The farts as he came on stage brought titters.

The fake ears earned huge love.

Eating the set won him more fans.

Breaking loose united his crowd.

Charging off back to the stud, bucking and squealing, raised a huge round of applause.

In the marquee bar after the show, where the audience picked holes in the cast, the singing, the staging and the direction, nobody questioned the obdurate, warlike method acting of the small pony playing the donkey.

★

'That was brilliant!' Pax tracked down Bay in the dressing rooms at the village school. He was wiping off a layer of fake orange tan make-up to reveal the rural tan burnish beneath.

'You were funny,' Kes told him, then charged off to hurl himself at his father two costume rails away. 'You were the bestest ever in the whole world ever, ever, Daddy!'

Pax couldn't bring herself to look in Mack's direction.

Catching her eye in the mirror, Bay's laughter lines doubled down. 'I love how partisan children are. Mine have not long been and gone.'

Having just seen Monique herding Tilly and Bram into a taxi, Pax stepped closer. 'It hurts though, doesn't it?

Bay's laughter lines changed angle. 'Like a blade in the heart.'

'You were outstanding tonight.'

'Almost as good as the Shetland.' He grinned. 'Have we made enough money to buy the meadow, do you think?'

'Maybe?' Pax couldn't tell him what she really thought.

'Completely agree. No chance in hell.'

She kept forgetting how often they both read each other's thoughts aloud.

Tonight's show had raised a decent chunk, fund-matched by several benevolent locals and businesses. Big cheques had certainly rolled in, but they both knew BOMB was well short of a competitive figure.

The land auction was two days away.

Kes charged back from his father. 'Wasn't Daddy brilliant? Mrs Bullock says he reminds her of Ewan McGregor so she's going to put on Mules are Rude next.'

'*Moulin Rouge...*' Pax caught Bay's eye in the mirror as she gave Kes a tight hug, wishing she didn't have to let him go. He was staying with his father tonight, Mack's dour parents and disapproving sister visiting too, all of them just beyond the second costume rail, pretending it was another dimension.

'So, Satine,' Bay eyed her reflection back, 'are you ready for seventies disco-dancing on the Meadow?'

The after-show party promised to be a legendary village event. The travellers – who had relocated to Plum Run to let tonight's performance happen – were going to join them, their musicians playing. There would be a *lot* of hooch.

Pax looked away, watching Kit Donne congratulating the opera singer who had played Donna. His open bottle of champagne was being used as a flirtatious prop. Much hand touching and eye contact ensued, she noted. Two grown-ups playing by the rules. She would never know how to do that.

'Do you mind terribly if I pass?'

Bay laughed. 'You were *so* like this at seventeen.'

'Is that a bad thing?'

'Tonight, it's a very good thing. Let's go home, shall we?'

'I'd like that.'

They didn't need to say which. Because both now felt like home.

43

The auction was being held at exclusive local hotel, Le Mill. Church Meadow was one of several land parcels, smallholdings and building plots to be going under the hammer that day. While a mini-heatwave had been feeding the fires of flaming June all week, anticipation in the Comptons had reached fever pitch, the BOMB campaigners appealing for donations up until the eleventh hour.

Mo got there early, overheating in her new business suit, an expensive gift from Kenny and Tina to 'look the part'. It was boxy and businesslike, in grey twill. She appreciated the kindness, even though she felt like a giant breeze block.

A big crowd had already gathered, many of them personally invested in the outcome: longstanding villagers like Brian and Chris Hicks, the Reverend Jolley and assorted ecclesiastic colleagues rubbing their hands together. Auriol and her theatricals were there too, along with Sandy and Viv Austen, the Saddle Bags and a tight-knit contingent of travellers with a large holdall that rumour had it was full of cash.

'Hello, Maureen!'

Mo found a small, solid figure planted in front of her striking a haka pose. It was Ronnie's oldest daughter, Alice, a Fosse and Wolds Pony Club despot.

'Are you working?' Alice gestured at the grey suit.

'Observing.' Mo reddened, not wanting to give too much away.

Mistakenly thinking this meant she was with the land agents, Alice stepped closer, her voice hushed. 'Is it true that Church Meadow has basically got Evian on tap? Got a small family nest-egg we might hatch if it's cheap enough.' She glanced round the room. 'You'll give me the heads-up who else is interested, won't you?'

'Everyone is interested, my love,' Mo told her kindly.

But Alice wasn't listening. 'Oh, there's my sister and Lester! Let's say hello.'

Wielding her bidding paddle like a pig board, Alice herded Mo to gather the others and push them into a prime spot.

'What on earth are you doing here?' Pax demanded, looking shocked to find herself at the front of the room.

'Just observing,' Mo repeated anxiously, equally alarmed to be up against the auctioneer's podium like a superfan at a pop concert.

'I meant Alice.'

'Couldn't bloody miss it.' Alice explained. 'I won my first bending race on that field. Now tell me what the hell Mummy's up to?' She dropped her voice to a whisper, the sisters soon muttering about trust finds, life interests and custodial accounts.

Finding herself close enough to the Bags to sidestep into their supportive orbit, Mo edged away until she was amongst them.

'What the feck is that outfit about, Mo?' Bridge reeled back in fright.

'It's a power suit.'

'I like it,' Gill said, drawing her closer to fill her in on the latest village news.

Mo learnt that the Buy Our Meadow Back campaign had raised a staggering eighty thousand pounds, much of it through anonymous donations. 'Fifty came from one just donor, can you believe? Is it Kenny? Everyone thinks so.'

Mo said she couldn't possibly say, although she was certain it wasn't.

It had been decided that Kit Donne should make the BOMB bid, Gill revealed with a wistful sigh, glancing sideways at the theatre director who was glowering by the bar with a large glass of red wine. 'He has *gravitas*.'

Petra took umbrage. 'He's a weekender! A Londoner.'

'You have a flat in London, Petra queen.' Bridge pointed out.

'That's rented out, it doesn't count. Plus, my gravitas is big. It gets heavier daily. I'm eighty per cent gravitas these days.'

'Is that some sort of muesli?' Mo asked.

'Shh!' Gill waved them down. 'It's starting.'

Pax was still crammed uncomfortably close to the front when the first lot was called, terrified to move in case she bought a dilapidated piggery in Earls Compton ripe for conversion.

Their auctioneers were two jolly, shiny-faced local surveyors, the Ant and Dec of land agents. One in tweed, the other suited with pinstripes as wide as motorway lanes, they were both miked up and armed with little remote controls to change the auction lot pictures on the large projection screen behind them.

Wedged in alongside sister Alice, Pax looked round to see where Lester had got to, spotting him at the end of her row standing close to one of the huge windows. Dressed in his best bib and tucker, he kept looking at his watch, then craning around to eye the doors.

She was worried he might be up to something. It was Lester who had insisted he needed to be here today and that she must bring him, fussing about what time they should set off, getting himself into quite a state about it.

Pax picked her way towards him as, hammer after hammer, the lots fell, all for far more than estimate. Alice followed her, still muttering about their mother.

Each time auctioneers Tweedy and Pinstripe asked the room for bids, the sisters froze like musical statues, waiting until danger passed before moving on again.

The place was packed tight with bodies now, a melting pot of anticipation, the pictures on the screen switching from a block of woodland to an old pub, then on to a courtyard of farm buildings. Phone and Internet bids cranked up the tension for those raising their paddles in the room. Church Meadow was coming up in a just few lots' time. The Reverend Jolley was pink with excitement. Another large holdall appeared beside the Turners.

Making it to the window, Pax watched, enthralled and anxious, as the farm buildings bidding went to three times the auction estimate.

'You're not going to bid on the meadow, are you?' she asked Lester after the hammer fell for an eye-watering amount.

'Your grandfather always said, buy land,' he muttered. 'And I have a tidy sum set by.'

'You mustn't, Lester. That's your retirement!'

'I'll go fifty-fifty with you, Lester, if it goes over a hundred,' Alice offered, cramming herself between them.

Lester didn't seem to be listening, still eyeing the doors at the back of the room, reaching up to pull off his flat cap and mop his brow. Then, as Tweedy and Pinstripe invited bids on a building site in Micklecote, his face lit up, spotting somebody coming in through them.

It was Bay, Pas realized with a familiar heart-skip. He looked troubled, his blue eyes hunting the room. Spotting her, he waved.

'Twenty thousand at the back!'

A flat cap was waved back.

'Thirty thousand I'm bid, thank you sir!' Tweedy pointed at Lester, who didn't seem to notice that either, his old eyes blinking worriedly as he watched Bay swimming his way through the crowd towards them.

'Forty thousand!' Tweedy pointed to someone on the other side of the room, and Pax breathed out with relief.

Bay reached them at last.

'I think we'll have to go over a hundred to get it, sir,' Lester muttered urgently.

'You're bidding?' Pax asked, shocked.

Bay shook his head, 'No – yes – I mean, I offered to help Lester out if he hasn't got enough but that's not why I'm here.'

'Is it not?' Lester looked put out.

'Can we speak outside?' he asked Pax.

'The meadow is about to come up!' Lester gulped.

'Can't it wait?' Pax checked her catalogue. It was just two lots away.

Bay put his hand on her arm, lowering his mouth to her ear. 'It's important.'

'One minute,' she said to Lester, who was looking highly agitated.

'How high can I bid, sir?' he asked Bay.

'I trust your judgement, Lester.' He put a protective arm round Pax and they squeezed their way to the exit, ignoring Lester's cries of protest and the waved flat cap.

'Seventy-five thousand by the window!'

Hurrying outside, Pax could sense Bay's tension beside her. He led her away from the noise to a shady spot between two topiary spirals where he put his hands on her shoulders,

'She's gone. Ronnie's gone.'

'What do you mean, *gone*?'

'She and Blair. She said to say they're on walkabouts and she doesn't believe in goodbyes.'

Pax took a moment to process this, not sure she'd heard it right. Bay was telling her that her mother had run away with Blair. 'And she asked *you* to tell me this this?'

'Only because I caught them coming down the drive in that sports car of hers. Talk about déjà vu.'

'How long's she gone for?'

'She didn't say.'

She knew she should be shocked. Angry. Furious, in fact. Now it made sense why Ronnie had been so busy with paperwork in recent days, making sure Pax had autonomy if she needed it, transferring various interests and signatory powers. She'd insisted this made running the stud simpler, omitting to mention that it would be without her there. Such flagrant, headstrong deception was outrageous.

Instead, Pax found she wanted to laugh. This was so infuriatingly, wilfully typical of her mother. The Bardswold Bolter had bolted again, leaving her daughter to close the stable door, all the stable doors, and run the stud without her. Which, when she thought about it, was something she wanted to do very much indeed.

'Ronnie asked me to keep an eye on you while she's gone.' Bay was watching her closely, a surprised smile breaking out as he sensed her amusement.

'I don't need keeping an eye on.' She smiled back excitedly, realizing just how much faith had been placed in her.

Bay tried to look serious again. 'I'm afraid I have to break it to you that I intend to eye you very frequently and lovingly and lustily because, as you know Patricia Claire Johanna Ledwell, I only have eyes for you.'

'You're not going to propose again, are you?' Pax glanced round.

Beyond the Le Mill entrance doors, they could hear a roar going up from the crowd in the conference rooms.

'Would you like me to propose?'

'One day, perhaps,' she turned to smile at him again, 'when we're not still married to other people, but before we're old and wizened and far too decrepit to make love.'

'So that's a provisional yes?'

'It's a cautious maybe.'

'I think it's traditional to kiss in these circumstances.'

'You're right.'

He cupped her face and drew her to his mouth.

'Unbe-fucking-lievable!' raged a voice nearby.

'Ignore them,' Bay, whispered into Pax lips, 'they're easily shocked round here.'

'Do you know about this, Bay? It's a fucking outrage!'

Kit Donne was stomping across the gravel towards them from the hotel entrance, pulling a packet of cigarette from his pocket. 'They've withdrawn Church Meadow from auction! Just now! The vicar went into a huddle with the surveyors and the lot was withdrawn. Sold prior to auction, they say.'

'You're kidding?' Bay fumed. 'Nobody's even getting a chance to bid for it?'

Other Compton villagers were spilling outside, complaining furiously.

Pax watched pink-faced Mo Dawkins hurrying past, court shoe heels wobbling on the gravel. Following more slowly, Alice helped Lester through the angry mob to join them.

'There's my bottled-water billions gone!' she huffed. 'Any idea who nabbed it?'

'Mummy's just gone walkabout,' Pax told them. 'Maybe it's her parting gift?'

'Mummy has no money,' Alice pointed out. 'What do you mean "walkabout"?'

While Pax explained the situation to Alice – who, to her surprise also laughed, albeit bitterly – and to Lester, whose reaction made her suspect he already knew, a large white Tesla pulled through the hotel's grand entrance gates.

Silent bar the crunch of gravel beneath Pirellis, it drew up to its front entrance where Mo Dawkins was waiting. Its window slid down. And a deafening shriek of joy came out. '*I BOUGHT IT, BAB!* You don't have to bid. I bought the meadow myself!'

Pax stopped talking. The crowd outside the lobby doors fell silent too.

It was a woman's voice coming from the car, broad Brummy and laced with jubilant giggles. 'I said to Kenny, I said, "You're not buying that meadow, my darling, cos I've got money of my own, as it turns out. You do look nice in the suit, Maureen, love. She does look nice in that suit, Kenny. I told you she would, didn't I?'

Now they all heard familiar dirty laugh from deeper inside the car. 'Spitting image of Kylie, am I right? Only with a flat head. Want a lift, Mo love?'

Mo bent down to the window. 'You're all right, thanks, Mr Kay. I might stay and have a drink. Half the village is here.'

'Tell you what, bab,' Kenny's trademark chuckle deepened. 'Why not buy everyone a drink on me? If I can't buy the village a meadow, I can stand it a pint for old time's sake! I'd do it myself, but my lady love wants to get back to look after the kiddies and watch—'

'No you won't, Kenny!' A shrill protest cut across him '*I'll* buy everyone that drink, Mo! Tell them it's on me.' The window slid back up and the car set off again.

Shaking her head and waving them away, Mo turned back to the hotel entrance, turning pinker when she found a crowd of faces staring at her expectantly.

'Who was that?' demanded Alice. '*Who* has bought the Church Meadow?'

'Tina Turner.' She beamed back at them all.

That evening, Pax and Bay walked their dogs up to the top woods, turning to watch the last golden slice of sun dropping behind the village. The standing stone witches were casting their long shadow fingers across the meadow, pointing towards the church spire and its yew tree companions.

Closer to, the stud's fields were criss-crossed with impossibly tall, leggy equine shadows, grazing and nursing, tail-swishing and ear-flicking, a herd of sunset giants.

All the foals were now out at foot, some mothers already

in foal again, the high-kicking, big-hearted, flight-instinct, matriarchal circle starting another year's rotation.

Horses! Pax shuddered with the thrill of them all, the joy of knowing she wasn't going to let them out of her life again. Not for a single day.

'We're going to make this place work,' she told Bay.

'We are.' He took her hand.

She turned and leant into him. 'I've found my way home.'

'Getting sentimental, now.'

'My heart's always been here.'

'Yup, seriously maudlin.'

'I love you.'

'Thinking aloud again.'

'Saying it. Shouting it. I LOVE YOU!'

'I love you too.' There was a long pause, then, 'Welcome home.'

About the Author

FIONA WALKER is the author of twenty-one novels, from tales of flat-shares and clubbing in nineties London to today's romping, rural romances set amid shires, spires and stiles. In a career spanning over two decades, she's grown up alongside her readers, never losing her wickedly well-observed take on life, lust and the British in love. She lives in Warwickshire, sharing a slice of Shakespeare Country with her partner, their two daughters and a menagerie of animals.

To find out more about Fiona visit:

fionawalker.com

@fionawalkeruk

facebook.com/fiona.walker.16568